'Phenomenally imagined, intricately woven, and masterfully brought to life. It's so descriptive that rarely have I read a book where I've felt I am living side by side with the characters. As a writer, Smith really is one of a kind' *JOHN MARS*

'Chilling in so many ways' *LOS ANGELES TIMES*

'A speculative masterpiece that will resonate with fans of Emily St. John Mandel, Kazuo Ishiguro and Jeff VanderMeer' *LIBRARY JOURNAL*

'A zany, wildly gripping, dark futuristic fantasy … that recalls H.P. Lovecraft and Mary Shelley's *Frankenstein*. I loved this wild, imaginative, fast moving book and can't wait to see the inevitable screen adaptation' *VOGUE*

'What lines, if any, shouldn't be crossed to save humanity from extinction? That question is at the heart of this stunning post-apocalyptic thriller from bestseller Smith … Smith, the author of brilliant historical and psychological suspense novels, shows his range is even broader in this triumph of imagination and empathy' *PUBLISHERS WEEKLY*

'A brilliantly conceived post-apocalyptic story that tackles a well-worn subject (a desperate race to save humanity) from a new and absolutely captivating angle. Smith's near-future world is wonderfully imaginative and rigorously detailed, the kind of made-up place that feels viscerally real. A real treat for fans of post-apocalyptic fiction' *BOOKLIST*

PRAISE FOR *THE FARM*

'Structurally innovative and stylishly resonant, *The Farm* is a remarkable achievement' **JEFFERY DEAVER**

'Chilling, hypnotic and thoroughly compelling. You will not read a better thriller this year' **MARK BILLINGHAM**

'A truly original and chilling thriller which makes you ask yourself, who would I believe?' **JOJO MOYES**

'So unsettling and oppressive that it blurs the distinctions between sanity and madness, reality and fantasy, leaving the reader guessing until the bitter end' *INDEPENDENT*

'An absorbing, unsettling, multi-layered novel ... beautifully crafted, its effect enhanced by the author's admission that his ow family faced a similar experience' *THE TIMES*

'Gripping, atmospheric ... This absorbing novel thrives on gradually revealing the intimate details' *OBSERVER*

'If you relish that delicious chill of fearful anticipation reading a thriller, this will be right up your alley ... a literary thriller with deep psychological undertones' *DAILY EXPRESS*

'Full of stories within stories, which gradually unravel to confound our expectations ... Smith's twisting, turning novel shows that Scandi crime also retains the ability to surprise and thrill' *GUARDIAN*

Also by Tom Rob Smith

Child 44
The Secret Speech
Agent 6

The Farm

London Spy

COLD PEOPLE

TOM ROB SMITH

**SIMON &
SCHUSTER**

London · New York · Sydney · Toronto · New Delhi

First published in the United States by Scribner, an imprint
of Simon & Schuster Inc., 2023
First published in Great Britain by Simon & Schuster UK Ltd, 2023
This paperback edition first published 2024

3 5 7 9 10 8 6 4 2

Simon & Schuster UK Ltd
1st Floor
222 Gray's Inn Road
London WC1X 8HB

Simon & Schuster: Celebrating 100 Years of Publishing in 2024

Simon & Schuster Australia, Sydney
Simon & Schuster India, New Delhi

www.simonandschuster.co.uk
www.simonandschuster.com.au
www.simonandschuster.co.in

A CIP catalogue record for this book is available from the British Library

Paperback ISBN: 978-1-4711-3312-1
eBook ISBN: 978-1-4711-3313-8
Audio ISBN: 978-1-3985-1881-0

Typeset in the UK by M Rules
Printed and Bound in the UK using 100% Renewable
Electricity at CPI Group (UK) Ltd

MIX
Paper | Supporting
responsible forestry
FSC® C171272

To Suzanne Baboneau, my editor of fifteen years

PART ONE

EVENTS PRECEDING

TWO THOUSAND YEARS AGO
THE FIRST SIGHTING OF ANTARCTICA

L OOKING UP AT THE NIGHT sky Ui saw only unfamiliar stars. These weren't the constellations that guided him between the Polynesian islands of his homeland; these were stars from the sky's outer edge, the stars his people had never bothered to name since they were no use to navigate by, dismissed as the *petuu vare* – the foolish stars. Tonight, he imagined them looking down upon him and asking who was foolish now, this man all alone, so far from home. His vessel made excellent speed as a strong wind filled the sails plaited from pandanus leaves. The two hulls shaped like canoes, harnessed together with a lattice of bamboo, skimmed gracefully across the ocean, carved from the oldest calophyllum tree on their home island. His father, a master shipbuilder, had toiled on them for many months using mud paste to test every seal, dabbing the joins, fitting them together then pulling them apart, searching for even the smallest patch where water might find a way through. His father's skills were in such demand that sailors from faraway islands bartered for his services and yet he'd refused all offers, working exclusively on his son's ship, the finest ever built.

Many in their community considered both the ship's construction and the expedition itself an indulgence of Ui's vanity, since this journey into the unknown brought no benefits to their community. It was already agreed that his abilities at sea were unmatched and his navigational skills unrivalled. He had nothing to prove. He was adored by many lovers and envied by many friends. To them, this adventure was folly, an obsession with the mythical land they called *Iraro*.

The first time he'd heard the word *Iraro* was as a young boy when his father had drawn a map on the sand to teach him the geography of Polynesia. Studying the islands, Ui had jabbed his finger at the ocean on the outskirts and asked:

'What is this?'

'We call those waters *Iraro*.'

'What is *Iraro*?'

'The place we know nothing about.'

'Why do we know nothing about it?'

'Because no one has ever sailed there.'

'One day I will sail there.'

His father hadn't laughed or brushed off the claim as the mere boasting of a child. He'd crouched down and wiped away the markings, fearful that he'd sown the seed of a dangerous idea in an impressionable mind:

'And if you sail there, my son, who I love very much, and who I could not live without, will you also sail home?'

Ui brought the vessel to a stop, dropping the sails, standing on deck and searching the horizon. If he didn't discover land soon, he'd be forced to turn back. The hollow hulls had been loaded with supplies, parcels of fermented vegetables, bundles of sugar cane, but mostly with drinking coconuts since the ocean provided a ready supply of food. On his voyage he'd seen ocean life of an undiscovered kind, shoals of elegant fish unfathomable in number bursting out of the water like birds with milk-coloured scales and eyes like pearls. Having always presumed that warmth meant life and cold meant death, he now accepted this assumption was wrong. Cold was merely a different way of life.

He cut a notch on the mast to mark his sixty-ninth day at sea without sight of land. The air was cold in Iraro and he was wrapped up in the thickest of furs, clothes created especially for this journey. As he sipped some of the precious coconut water, drinking only enough to stop his mind and muscles weakening, he contemplated the prospect of returning home without a discovery. Aware of his own vanity, when confronted with the expectations of his Patagonia he might lie, concealing his failure by inventing stories of strange lands populated with strange creatures. Most of the people back home would believe him no matter what fanciful stories he told, listening with hushed reverence, but his father would know since he'd never been able to lie to his father. It would mean that this magnificent vessel, carved from the oldest tree on the island, had brought back only dishonour and deceit. His father's heart would break with shame. Better not to return, better to die, than to lie.

Sitting on deck, he lowered his hand to the water, pressing his palm against the surface. Reading waves was a gift many considered a kind of magic, possessed only by those touched with the spirit of the sea. Deep ocean waves had a powerful voice, a backwards and forwards motion unlike waves reflected from land, which spoke in a softer, upward-downward movement, a voice that became inaudible the further they travelled from the shore. His body shivering with the cold, he implored the ocean to speak to him and guide him. To his relief, this time the ocean answered – whispering that land was near.

Ui scampered across the bamboo lattice, rooting through the supplies where he found a timber cage containing a frigatebird, her chest puffed out in distress at her confinement. This breed of bird wouldn't land on water since her feathers easily became waterlogged and she'd lose her ability to fly. By necessity she'd return to the vessel unless she found dry land. He fed her some scraps of dried fish skin and set her free. After so many days of being trapped, she didn't understand her freedom, remaining motionless until he nudged her, and she flew into the sky. He stood at the bow, studying her direction of flight. She slowly circled the boat and then set off. She must have seen land. She must have seen Iraro.

After many hours following the bird he entered a strange ocean consisting of countless small islands, smooth and white as the clouds. The air was so cold his breath turned to mist. He dropped the sail and, using the steering paddle, brought himself to the nearest island. There were no plants or trees, no creatures of any kind. Scraping the surface with the edge of his paddle produced a fine white dust which turned to water between his fingers. Ui dabbed the dust on his tongue. It wasn't salty ocean water; it was fresh like rain, as though these islands were clouds that had crashed into the sea. Perhaps this was the place where clouds crashed after they'd finished flying, or perhaps this was where clouds were born and if he stayed here long enough, he'd see these islands puff up and rise into the sky.

Ui climbed the mast and perched at the top, perfectly balanced, assessing the view. Far away he saw white cliffs, high and smooth, stretching from one side of the horizon to the other. He wondered how they'd come to be this way. Perhaps set back from the white cliffs, there were white volcanoes, and instead of red, hot lava they spewed cold, white lava. Perhaps there were white forests with white tree trunks and white leaves. Perhaps there were herds of white-fur animals and tribes of white-skinned men and women. He wondered what kind of person could live in a land like this. It must be a different kind of people – a savage tribe; only a savage people could survive in such cold.

ONE HUNDRED AND FIFTY YEARS AGO
SOUTH GEORGIA ISLAND
TWO THOUSAND KILOMETRES
NORTH OF ANTARCTICA

ONLY SOCIETY'S OUTCASTS COULD SURVIVE in these freezing waters and over the years Captain Moray had concluded there were no exceptions to this rule. Some of his crew could pass among civilized society for a while, they could entertain a room with tales of their adventures, but they'd pull a knife if they took a dislike to someone, and they took a dislike to a great many people. As the captain of the most successful sealing vessel operating off South Georgia Island, Moray was an expert in choosing his crew from the variety of outcasts on offer, his preference being for the melancholic, the sexual deviants and the thieves. For the thieves there was nothing to steal, for the melancholic there was the ocean to meditate upon and for the deviants there were other deviants. Moray never shared the secrets of his own past, cultivating the appearance of a forceful but fair man, a bastion of order in this otherwise barbarous industry. There was room for only one murderer on this ship.

The ship's name was *Red Rose*, a two-hundred-tonne steam and sail vessel anchored outside King Edward Cove. Moray intended to make one last trip to shore before setting sail for Canton, China, where a buyer had been arranged for his cargo of seal furs, a price set for three dollars fifty cents a skin, significantly below his record price of nine dollars, achieved when he'd been one of the few sealing vessels daring to venture so far south. Today there were over sixty vessels anchored around the South Georgia Island, and with the market inundated with furs, his ability to secure even three dollars depended on his reputation for quality.

Before setting sail for Canton, his final task was a dinner with His Majesty's Stipendiary Magistrate, representing the Government of the Falkland Islands and South Georgia, the authority over this far-flung outpost. Without the magistrate's blessing it would be impossible to operate in these waters. The customs inspector would levy unaffordable charges, the police officer stationed on this island would arrest his crew for infractions real or imagined and business would grind to a halt. Four of his crew rowed the captain to shore in a shallop – a nimble and flat-bottomed vessel used for hunting and excursions. Arriving at the newly constructed docks, he remembered a time not so long ago when this island had been untouched by man, the shores so densely populated with seals he had struggled to see the pebble beaches underneath their fat bellies. Now all that remained on the rocks were seal skulls picked clean by the petrels and a blubber factory which produced oil at fifty cents a gallon and a retch-inducing smoke that only the strongest of winds could dissipate. There were rickety dormitories for the workers, human colonies crowded with bunk beds and crisscrossed with washing lines of coarse wool socks. Behind the dormitories was an infirmary and a rudimentary timber chapel with a crucifix made from driftwood.

As he approached the magistrate's residence, Moray observed the incongruous picket fence around a garden of black soil and tussock grass. The magistrate's wife loathed this island and had tried to transform their home into something that might exist in the British countryside. She'd brought rabbits for comfort, but rats from the ships had eaten them. She'd planted meadow flowers, but the sea salt spray had killed them. Fearful of the debauched sealers, the magistrate insisted she carry a Beaumont–Adams revolver with her whenever she left the confines of their picket fence, not concealed under her clothes, but clearly visible and clasped in her hand. To Moray's knowledge, she'd fired it only once and her aim had been true.

The butler, another British import, opened the front door, his expression set to a permanent grimace as a way of signalling that he didn't belong here either. After taking off his leather boots, exchanged for a pair of silk Savile Row slippers, Moray followed the butler through to the sitting room decorated with fashionable mahogany furniture carved from felled Caribbean forests and walls covered with oil paintings of bucolic English landscapes. A fire crackled in the hearth and with the curtains closed to block out the bleak reality of their location, it was a shabby approximation of a stately drawing room.

The magistrate entered, accepting the bottle of Chateau Margaux the captain had brought as a gift without so much as a thank you. Dinner was poached tongue of elephant seal, sliced in wedges, served with assorted steamed sea vegetables. None of the magistrate's imported provisions were used. Moray wasn't offended, although offence was intended. In the hierarchy of ocean professions, sealers were the lowest, far below Her Majesty's naval officers or the merchant traders, below even the deep-sea fishermen and the whalers. No stories were ever written about the sealers, for it was a shameful occupation. Even in these distant waters a class system had sprung up, as though there was nowhere on this earth where a class system of some kind wouldn't take root. Moray hastened the conversation to the business at hand.

'I've come to enquire what outstanding duties might be owed.'

Normally the magistrate would gladly discuss his bribe but today he seemed uninterested in these details, pressing the captain on another matter:

'I've heard this is to be your last year. That you have your eye on a town house in Cavendish Square. Can it be true?'

Moray sliced off a small piece of seal tongue and chewed thoughtfully. It was true. The seals were on the brink of extinction due to undisciplined crews hunting pups and pregnant cows. The island's once limitless resource was limitless no more. The sealing industry wouldn't last another five years. The magistrate was to blame. He didn't enforce the laws, preferring his bribes. If the sealing industry collapsed, not even the remote location could protect this man from the scrutiny of officials in London.

'This island is over, sir. We've ruined it.'

'Ruins are merely the end of one opportunity and the beginnings of another.'

The magistrate clapped his hands and the butler entered. Moray sat back, surprised as the butler served the bottle of wine that he'd brought as a gift, an act of generosity that had never happened before.

'Last week I saw a hunting crew on the cliffs above Cumberland Bay. They'd trapped a group of female elephant seals and their pups. There was no escape, and the crew were killing them at a leisurely pace, beating them back with clubs if any tried to break away. In despair, one of the females broke rank and jumped off the cliff – she fell a hundred yards, bounced a little into the air, and survived, blundering in the sea. In order to escape the massacre, another jumped, and another, the entire colony following her over the cliff face. Many died in the fall, but some survived, their blubbery mass protecting them. The pups followed their mothers, but they were too small, and none survived.'

The magistrate sipped his fine wine and regarded Moray.

'Do you imagine London society will look upon you as the gentleman you'll pretend to be? That they'll invite you into their homes or desire your company? Naturally you'll lie about your past. You'll tell them you worked as a trader on the high seas, dealing in fine spices. You'll talk of saffron and cinnamon. You'll wear the finest clothes and hang art on the walls. But they will smell the blubber on your skin and see the sordid stories under your fingernails. You'll be a butcher in their eyes. A savage in a silk shirt.'

Moray pondered the magistrate's comments.

'That may be true. But the seals are gone, sir. Soon the only trade will consist of pulling teeth from the skulls of elephant seals and polishing them for jewellery. That is no business for a man, even a savage one.'

The magistrate was ahead of him.

'South, Moray, you must go south, to the great expanse of ice – the unexplored continent where there are undiscovered creatures and untouched wealth beyond our imagination.'

He placed an artist's folder on the table full of sketches of extraordinary creatures glimpsed on the undiscovered ice. There were seals with a unicorn's horn of ocean ivory. There was a walrus with a glittering silver pelt. There were birds with feathers of such beauty they'd be coveted by the finest fashion houses of Paris.

'The ice is impassable.'

'No, there are ways through; you will find them. Dangerous, but worth the risk.'

'And you?'

'I'll protect your trade. You'll use this island as your base. You'll eat at this table. You cannot be a gentleman in London but you can be one here. You'll be important and respected. You'll never be that man in England. Moray, we cannot go back. We can never go back. This place has branded us. We belong here, whether we like it or not.'

The butler returned, bringing out a tray with desserts, Egyptian dates, lavender blossom honey, dark chocolate and brandy-infused cream. Soon Moray was drunk on dreams of cold creatures with tusks of twisted pearl and skins as soft as snow. With port-stained teeth the magistrate said:

'The ice, captain, we shall plunder the ice!'

FIFTEEN YEARS AGO
ANTARCTICA
MCMURDO STATION

D OUG REYNOLDS HAD A HABIT of repeating wisdoms to new arrivals at McMurdo Station, such as:

The hardest part of surviving in Antarctica isn't the cold; it's the people.

As an Antarctica veteran, having lived on the continent for eight years, he enjoyed their bewilderment as they tried to figure out what this could mean. After all, Antarctica was the coldest, windiest and most hostile continent on the planet. It seemed bizarre to suggest that the hardest part of living here was the people. For a start, there weren't that many of them. In the summer there were a thousand scientists and support staff at McMurdo Station; in the winter that number shrank to under two hundred. Moreover, this was a prestigious place to work; those chosen to be stationed here were at the top of their profession, selected by the US Antarctica Program after a highly competitive application process. On paper these were some of the most well-adjusted people ever assembled in one place, with all of them having undergone rigorous mental health evaluations that included answering the following:

Have you ever been clinically depressed?

Have you ever had issues with drink or substance abuse?

Have you ever displayed violent tendencies?

The psychiatric evaluators went beyond the basics, asking questions such as:

What conspiracy theories interest you?

Has a sexual situation ever made you angry?

You notice a group of people laughing and you ask what they're laughing about but they're laughing so hard that they can't answer. How does this situation make you feel?

But Doug knew that no matter how many experts declared that a subject was able to cope with life on the ice, no one ever knew for sure until they were here. This continent changed people. Smart, stable, decent people lost their minds, and no evaluation could predict who'd snap next. That said, after eight successful years, he never imagined it would be him.

Lodged in Building 201, he woke at six every morning – he never overslept even on his days off, protecting his routine. His shower would never be longer than two minutes, timed with a stopwatch to conserve the precious water supply processed on site by fuel-intensive reverse osmosis. A few years back, one of McMurdo's greatest minds, studying undiscovered bacterial life buried deep within the frozen lakes, had started taking longer showers – three minutes had become five minutes, five minutes had become ten, until her concerned roommate had reported it to the authorities. When the scientist was delicately quizzed about the length of her showers, she'd erupted into a rage, calling her roommate a traitor and threatening to burn her belongings, which, she argued, took up far more space in their cramped room compared to her own possessions. She was discovering new forms of life, she'd shouted, she could shower for as long as she wanted. In response, she'd been sedated, held in confinement and evacuated from the continent on the first medevac flight.

This morning the stopwatch clipped to the plastic soap shelf informed Doug that today's shower had lasted one minute and fifty-five seconds. He said aloud, in a calm voice, as though he were a public service announcement:

'It's time to turn the water off.'

His hands didn't move. The deadline was missed. Two minutes eleven, twelve, thirteen. He rested his head against the wall, the water streaming over his lips and nose.

'Turn the water off, Doug. Pull yourself together and turn it off.'

Two minutes twenty, two minutes twenty-one, his voice now sounding more like a lover pleading for a second chance:

'Please turn the water off, please . . .'

Two minutes thirty. Two minutes forty. He shouted:

'Turn the water off right now!'

With a twist of his wrist, he turned the water off and stood there, dripping, catching his breath, staring at the stopwatch. For the first time in eight years, his routine was broken.

Ignoring one of his own wisdoms – that small fractures in your sanity were always precursors to bigger ones – he dressed, telling himself that nothing was wrong, putting on his goose-down parka and setting off towards Building 155, where breakfast was served. He entered the galley, inspecting the self-service buffet. In the winter the selection rarely changed; there were no fresh herbs, fruit or vegetables and staring at the scrambled eggs made with powdered mix, he became fixated on their unnaturally bright yellow colour. He couldn't deny it any longer. Something was wrong, and that something was a new arrival, a man called Zack.

Zack was a New Zealander, part of the base's Search and Rescue team, and everyone agreed that he was an exceptionally nice guy, as kind as he was handsome, as charming as he was strong. If there was a station popularity contest, he'd not only win, but he'd be surprised about it. Doug had tried, over the years, to be more likeable. He might not be the most dynamic of guys, he certainly wasn't the most handsome, but he was interesting and kind. He went out of his way to help newcomers adjust to life on the station. He'd show people funny quotes from the 'Antarctic Participation Guide' which they'd email back to their friends and family.

US ANTARCTIC PARTICIPATION GUIDE:

Money. There is no ATM nor credit card usage available at the South Pole due to the limited satellite availability.

But these exchanges never seemed to grow into deeper friendships. His closest relationship had always been with his work. He'd only make a move for anyone if he was drunk. The next day's follow-up had always been answered with a rebuff, any intimacy explained away as a night of meaningless fun in a place of limited choices. Doug had always played along, agreeing that they should just be friends. Rejection had never bothered him until Zack arrived. Nothing had ever bothered him until Zack arrived. He hated Zack. It wasn't rational, but it was real. He took a breath and told himself:

'This is ice-talk. You do not hate that man. You cannot hate that man. No one hates that man.'

Holding his breakfast tray, Doug took a seat at an empty table at the far side of the room, his back to the others, signalling he didn't want company this morning. He was only a few mouthfuls through his powdery-bright eggs when he heard a voice:

'Mind if I join you?'

It was Zack. His job was to sense when people were in emotional distress. The more you hid, the more he sought you out. He smiled as he sat down, and Doug's first thought was to leave. He assessed the amount of food remaining on his plate. He'd barely made a start on his breakfast and if he threw this much food away, he'd draw attention to himself. McMurdo kitchens were strict about wasting food. They'd ask questions. Reports would be written up. He told himself:

Be nice. Say something nice.

Instead, Doug said:

'Have you heard about Air New Zealand Flight 901?'

Flight 901 was the only commercial aircraft to crash on Antarctica. Some of the wreckage was still on the side of Mount Erebus, the volcano not far from the base. Zack was confused by the question.

'Flight 901?'

'Everyone on board died when the plane crashed into Mount Erebus. It had been a low-flying sightseeing flight, on a round trip from Christchurch. Are you from Christchurch?'

'Auckland.'

'This flight was from Christchurch although some of the passengers might have been from Auckland. Anyway, on the flight the passengers were free to move about and take photos. Some of their cameras survived. Do you want to hear the craziest thing? After the crash the accident inspectors developed the films. Do you know what they found? It was a clear blue sky. Not a cloud. So how does a plane crash into a mountain when the sky is clear, and the plane is working perfectly? The report into the crash claimed that "Malevolent Polar Light" played a part in the crash. Conspiracy theorists claim it crashed into a UFO. But do you want to know what the real reason for that plane crash was?'

This was ice-talk, no doubt about it. Zack wasn't eating, staring at him with his big, kind, caring eyes.

'What was the reason?'

'People.'

'People?'

'People crashed that plane. People lost their minds. Maybe the captain was transfixed by the volcano. Maybe the captain thought they were looking down on cloud cover when they were looking down at the ice. In Antarctica there is a gap between the way you perceive the world and the way the world really is.'

'There's always a gap, don't you think?'

'But the gap is at its widest down here.'

'An interesting theory.'

'How do you like your eggs, Zack?'

'My eggs?'

'How do you like your fake synthetic bright-yellow eggs? Their colour is extraordinary, isn't it? We might not have the sun but at least we have powdered eggs.'

'Doug? Are you okay?'

'How can I not be okay? My job is to study the stars and there's no better place on Earth to study the stars. The South Pole Telescope Station is at the top of a plateau three thousand metres above sea level where the katabatic winds haven't gathered strength, with a sky containing almost no water – so how can you sit there and ask me if I'm okay when I have a view of the stars that could only be rivalled by going into space itself? Do you know what I saw? The other day?'

'No, Doug, what did you see?'

'A shooting star. It was travelling across the sky and then, suddenly, it stops, this shooting star, it stops, turns ninety degrees and carries on, across the sky, in a completely different direction.'

'It changed direction?'

'A shooting star changed direction. I saw it with my own eyes.'

'How is that possible?'

'You tell me, Zack, you tell me.'

'I didn't see it, Doug. I don't know.'

Abruptly, Doug stood up, pushing his chair back so fast Zack flinched.

'If you'll excuse me, I have work to do. There are new galaxies that need discovering. You have a good day.'

With that, he left the table and he felt better already, not being at that table, away from Zack. He scraped his plate clean, reacting to the disapproving look from the chef.

'Don't look at me like that. They're not even real eggs.'

At the door, about to leave, he felt a hand on his shoulder and turned to see Zack.

'How about you hang with me a while? The winds are picking up. It's not far off from Category Two.'

'You can't discipline me for going outside in a Category Two.'

'No one's talking about being disciplined. It might be an idea to wait a moment. Have a coffee, sit with me. You don't have to talk. We can wait for the wind to drop.'

There were three grades of weather. Category Three was normal operating conditions, with no restrictions on movement, Category Two was winds over forty-eight knots, and Category One, the most serious, was winds over fifty-five knots, and a wind chill of one hundred below. During Category One no one was allowed off base and no one was allowed outside. As a representative of station safety, Zack had the power to report any unsafe behaviour. The station management were alarmists about accidents. It was for this reason that most personnel didn't seek treatment for minor cuts and bruises, fearful that they'd initiate a risk-assessment process that might end up with them being shipped off the continent since it could be argued that a small injury should've been seen as a precursor to a serious incident.

'I don't want to hang out with you, Zack. I don't want to drink coffee. I want to study the stars. That's my job, to study the stars, and I can't do that sitting at a table with you, pretending that we're friends when we're not.'

Without waiting for a reply, Doug opened the door and stepped outside. He hadn't even finished putting on his parka, walking into the powerful wind with his jacket still unzipped, flapping about him. Zack would be following behind, full of concern and compassion. The thought made Doug run wildly. The wind was so loud he couldn't hear his own thoughts. The cold was all around him, spreading into his arms and legs and body. Losing strength with each step, he stopped, dropping to his knees, accepting the truth. After eight years, it was his time.

He slowly stood up and changed direction, trudging towards the infirmary. If he went inside and told them the truth, they'd be sympathetic – he hadn't hurt anyone. But he knew it would get worse, this madness; someone would get hurt and it would probably be him. If he explained the situation, he'd be taken off work, sedated and made safe until a medevac flight could arrive. One thing was certain, he'd never return to the South Pole Telescope Station again. His career on the ice was over. His life in Antarctica was over. Doug opened the door to the infirmary and declared:

'I'm cold.'

PART TWO

PRESENT DAY

THE TOUR GUIDE DECLARED:

'We're now standing in *Praça do Comércio*, which translates as "Commerce Square". Previously this was the location of the Royal Palace until, on 1 November 1755, it was brought down by the Great Lisbon Earthquake. That earthquake, which you've probably never heard of, killed over a hundred thousand people and ripped a fissure in this city five metres deep. The sea was snatched out of the harbour, like a mother pulling a bedsheet off a sleeping child, leaving all the boats stranded on the sand and the silt, before a tsunami returned, smashing those same boats against houses and palaces, the ocean rushing up the riverbanks so fast that only people on horseback could reach the safety of higher ground. While the sea devastated the low-lying areas, candles from the All Saints' Day services were scattered among the hilltop ruins, setting fire to splintered timbers. Flooding down below, fires up above – death and destruction unparalleled in my city's history, an event of such calamity that in a single day the destiny of this nation was changed.

Entire generations of families were lost. Half the economy was wiped out. Our global ambitions never recovered. Since that time the Portuguese empire has faded into the history books and new empires have risen. So is the way of our world: rise and fall.'

Liza surveyed the square, once a gateway to an empire that stretched across oceans and continents, but which today was a tourist attraction with music from a busking accordion band, traditional ice cream vendors and merchants hawking trinkets spread out on patterned shawls. Fearing that the tour guide was about to segue into prophecies about how American world supremacy would one day be replaced by Chinese world supremacy, she broke off from her family's private tour.

'I'm going to buy a bottle of water. Back in a minute.'

Ambling away, she was drawn to the river, keen for a moment alone. Taking a seat on the waterfront's stone steps, among fellow tourists studying laminated city maps and sipping ice-cold sodas, she allowed her mind to drift. There was a hypnotic quality to the shimmering light reflected on the water and it occurred to her that she couldn't remember this river's name. In her defence, today was the thirteenth day of her family's European two-week tour and there'd been so many rivers and historical bridges, so many kings and architects, so many types of stone and statues, that her mind was overstuffed with facts. Basking in the sun, she played a game – imagining what it would be like to live here, to uproot her life, to learn a new language. Would she be a different person if she lived in a different place? A happier person, maybe. Of course, she was never going to do it, it was an idle thought, but it was still a game she liked to play.

Moored to the dock was an unusual timber boat, not a modern

design but a replica of the *caravela* she'd seen in medieval paintings in *Museu de Lisboa* earlier this morning. A young man sat on the bow, assessing the ebb and flow of passers-by for potential customers. In his early twenties with dark curly hair and green eyes, he was dressed in peculiar non-branded clothes, old-fashioned linen shorts fastened with a sand-coloured cord and a baggy white cotton shirt. The clothes were, she guessed, a kind of mock historic uniform for people operating these mock historic boats. Most people would have looked absurd in the attire, but not this man, extraordinarily handsome, as if he, too, belonged in a museum painting, pointing upwards in awe as God elbowed his way out of fluffy cumulus clouds. Perhaps sensing her gaze, he turned around, catching her staring at him. She blushed and looked away. Needing no other cue, he jumped off his boat and walked over.

'That's my boat.'

She was so surprised at being spoken to that she had no reply. He stood with one leg perched on a step, like a joyous chorus character from an old-fashioned Broadway musical, the handsome sailor ready to take her hand and dance around this square.

'Perhaps you've been spending too long in galleries and museums.'

Regaining the power of speech, she said:

'Why do you say that?'

'You're not used to the things you're staring at answering back.'

'As a matter of fact, I was admiring your boat.'

'In that case, would you like to go on an adventure?'

'An adventure?'

'Isn't that the best question you've ever been asked?'

'It's certainly the best question I've been asked today.'

'All you have to do is say yes.'

'Where would we go?'

He pointed across the water and under the red suspension bridge.

'To the edge of the ocean, where all great adventures begin.'

She imagined the trip for a moment, an unexpected adventure with an unexpected man.

'That's very kind. But I'm with my family. We have a guide already.'

She gestured in the direction of her family. The young man assessed her family and the guide.

'Yes, but he doesn't have a boat.'

'No, but he has an itinerary. And he's very strict about it.'

'Perhaps I should talk to your parents?'

Though he asked the question with a smile, Liza felt a flush of irritation. She crossed her arms, aware that he was baiting her. She'd just completed her second year at Harvard Medical School – she was going into a profession defined by life-and-death decisions, she could decide about a boat trip without needing to check with her parents. Maybe she was too old to vacation with her family, but her father had organized this trip after recovering from cancer and, anyway, the two weeks had been a great success. With a heatwave lodged over mainland Europe, the cities they'd visited were basking in a carnival atmosphere with fountains drying and riverbeds cracking. The hotels had been converted monasteries or restored castles, all with excellent air conditioning and a host of period features, serving arugula salads drizzled with olive oil and platters of roasted fish. There'd been no arguments, her mother hadn't checked in with work once, at least not that anyone had seen, and this was the first moment that she'd wished she'd been alone.

'My parents aren't going to be interested in a boat trip.'

'And what would you have said? If your parents hadn't been here?'

'I would've wanted to know if one of your competitors is cheaper.'

He laughed. She liked his laugh very much.

'I doubt it.'

'How can you be so sure?'

'Because I'm not asking for any money.'

'You have an answer for everything.'

'But still no answer from you.'

Liza heard her name being called.

'I have to go.'

The boatman said:

'I don't have a sunset tour booked for tonight. If you're here, in the square, at around six, I'll take you out, thirty minutes, an hour, whatever you can make time for.'

'I'll try.'

In her mind she'd intended to let him down gently, but to her surprise it had sounded sincere, as if she were going to try everything humanly possible to be back here at six.

Re-joining her family, Liza downplayed her absence. Yes, it was true, that handsome man had been talking to her, he was offering a boat tour of some description, but she hadn't been paying much attention. The guide belittled the proposal as a service provided by unemployed fishermen who fabricated their knowledge of the city's history, presuming most tourists to be ignorant and gullible.

'Most of those men have never read a book in their lives.'

The guide looked at Liza with disapproval. She'd insulted him twice, first by wandering off and then by bringing back the offer of a fisherman masquerading as a guide.

As they left the square Liza looked back, hoping to see the boat-man through the crowds. But he was gone. It was a juvenile crush, she told herself, nothing more. Yet the meeting had felt significant in some inexplicable way. She wanted to laugh at her feelings, which was surely a self-defence mechanism. Her younger sister Emma slipped an arm around her waist and whispered in her ear:

'It's hot today, isn't it? Very hot.'

Liza loved her mischievous little sister very much and kissed her on the cheek.

CASTELO DE SÃO JORGE
SAME DAY

A T THE TERRACE CAFÉ ADJACENT to the Castelo de São
Jorge, perched atop one of the highest hills in the city, Liza
sat with her family looking out over the skyline of basilica towers,
church spires and red-tiled rooftops. She hadn't intended to sit
facing in the direction of Commerce Square, where she could see
the small tourist boats departing from the dock on their sunset
tours, nor had she intended to check her watch as soon as they
sat down, noting that it was five minutes to six – the square was a
fifteen-minute walk away – unsure why she was making these calculations since she had no intention of returning to find out if the
encounter with the boatman was as meaningful as it seemed in her
mind. Toying with the ice in her Diet Coke, she asked:

'What is the name of the river again?'

In her head the question sounded innocent but spoken aloud
it took on the air of a confession, that she was thinking not about
water and rivers but boats and boatmen. The tour guide, who was
enjoying an aperitif with her family, flicked his eyes in her direction,
having not forgiven her earlier insult.

'Its name is the Rio Tejo or the River Tagus, if that's easier to remember.'

If the tour guide was suspicious, her parents were oblivious, seated in the shade of an ancient olive tree, her mother's attention on the historic buildings where they'd spent much of the day while her father studied the many exhibition pamphlets he'd collected. Liza marvelled at how her parents were so at ease in each other's company. After twenty-five years of marriage their relationship was stronger than ever and she ached for that feeling – shared mutual happiness. She was twenty years old and while, as a medical student, she could sketch in detail the anatomy of the human heart, she'd never actually fallen in love.

Liza stood up abruptly, as though there were an emergency of some kind.

'We have some free time before dinner?'

Her mother nodded.

'We're meeting in the hotel lobby at nine.'

'The thing is I haven't bought any presents. For my friends. Back home.'

With each elaboration the lie felt more absurd, as though she was proposing something improbable like a rocket trip to Mars. Her dad asked:

'Do you have any money?'

Like so many lies, it floundered at the first test.

'No, I don't think I do.'

Her sister playfully tapped the table, enjoying this excruciating performance.

'Hard to buy presents if you don't have any money.'

Her dad took out his wallet, handing her a fifty-euro note. Her mom assessed the overly generous amount but decided against saying anything and Liza felt enormous gratitude, conscious that they could have made this exit even more awkward.

'See you at nine. I won't be late.'

Her sister was having too much fun to allow her to slip away.

'You might be. I mean, who knows what might happen? I might be late. Dad might be late. Mom might be late.'

'Well, I won't be.'

As Liza walked away, folding the money, she heard her sister call out:

'I hope you find something nice!'

She'd only walked a few paces when she felt a tap on her arm and turned around, surprised to see that the tour guide had caught up with her.

'I'm pretending to give you advice on buying presents.'

'What are you doing?'

'Giving you a word of warning. Those handsome boatmen are notorious. They flatter beautiful American girls, beautiful French girls, beautiful girls from all over the world. They take them out on the water at sunset and it's so romantic. They tell them how special they are, except they do it every day, every week, every tourist season. When you step onto his boat, what feels special to you will be a joke to everyone else.'

She wanted to make it clear that this man had no right to talk to her in this way. Instead, she said:

'Thank you for the warning but I am actually buying presents for my friends.'

'Then be careful – there are a lot of fakes out there.'

She descended the hill, increasingly angry at the guide's

intervention, passing gift shop after gift shop, imagining her family watching from their picturesque vantage point, following her route through the city with the tour guide making snide remarks about how she'd missed all the best stores and wondering where she could be heading. Maybe she was making a fool of herself. Almost certainly the boatman would be busy with other tourists, or he'd made the same offer to twenty prettier women that day. Nonetheless, she was going to try. She was taking a chance. She needed to take more chances romantically. Her younger sister, who was always in a relationship of one kind or another, sometimes two at once, speculated that she gave off the impression of not needing anyone – she was so assured and composed, people found her unapproachable. Less compassionate commentators would say she was superior and aloof. One student she'd been fond of had broken up with her after a month of dating, telling his friends that she looked hot but was cold inside. When she'd confronted him, he'd apologized, blaming alcohol, but his words had hurt her. She'd concluded that you can't fall in love by being impressive; there was magic to the process, and whatever this magic might be, she didn't have it.

Arriving in Commerce Square twenty minutes late, wearing the same tatty sightseeing clothes from earlier in the day, shorts, sneakers and a polo shirt, she felt self-conscious. Elegant Lisbon locals dressed in sleek designer black with immaculate hair and musky perfume swept past her. She hadn't returned to the hotel to change, she wasn't wearing any makeup or perfume, and he'd probably be disappointed by her lack of effort. He might even be insulted and regret asking her. It was during this moment of self-doubt that she caught sight of him. In that instant, she knew that he hadn't asked anyone else. He was waiting for her.

As she descended the steps to the jetty, he said:

'My name is Atto.'

'I'm Liza.'

'Nice to meet you.'

'Nice to meet you, too.'

Perhaps at the formality, she began to laugh.

'I don't know why it's so funny.'

He smiled.

'I'm nervous, too.'

RIO TEJO
SAME DAY

As THEY SAILED UNDERNEATH *PONTE 25 De Abril*, Atto slipped into the role of a traditional tour guide:

'When the bridge was completed, it was the longest suspension bridge in Europe, and they named it after António de Oliveira Salazar, the dictator of Portugal who ruled until 1968, renamed after the end of his regime.'

'I've never heard of the name Salazar before.'

Liza waited for an outpouring of facts either about Salazar or the bridge – his rise to power, or the amount of steel used in the bridge's construction. Instead, Atto said:

'I'm going to stop talking like a tour guide.'

'Aren't we both tour guides right now?'

'Oh yeah? How is that?'

'We're on a first date, showing each other around, giving a tour: here are my good qualities, don't go over there, that's my emotional baggage.'

He laughed and she remembered how much she liked his laugh.

'Close your eyes.'

'Close my eyes?'

'Trust me.'

She closed her eyes, wondering if he was about to kiss her and how she'd feel about it if he did.

'What do you hear?'

The question surprised her, and she took a moment to think about it. Even though she knew they were on a calm river on a beautiful sunny evening, she could hear a howling wind, a terrifying Atlantic storm, as if, when she opened her eyes, there would be waves, angry, grey, thirty metres high, rather than the ocean being flat and blue.

'I hear a storm.'

'What kind of storm?'

'Far out at sea.'

She opened her eyes, staring up at the bridge which, like a giant musical instrument, distorted and amplified the sound of the wind. Atto nodded.

'I hear a storm, too, but when I close my eyes, I see snow. Which is strange.'

'Why's that strange?'

'I've only seen snow once.'

'When was that?'

'Ten years ago. It snowed in Lisbon for the first time in fifty years.'

'You've always lived in Lisbon?'

'My father was born in Morocco. He moved to Portugal when he was eighteen and fell in love. People claim he only married my mother to stay in the country. But that's not true; they were in love. They're still in love, even today.'

'What does he do?'

'He's a fisherman. He bought this boat for me a few years back.'

'You didn't want to be a fisherman?'

Atto's good humour faltered.

'Yes, I wanted to be. But my older brothers work on my father's boat and my father didn't think it would be smart for all of us to be dependent on one profession. There are limits on how much fish my family is allowed to catch. Sometimes they're not allowed to go out into the ocean at all. There used to be one hundred thousand tonnes of sardines off the coast, now it's twenty thousand, and the fish stocks aren't recovering even when we stop fishing for an entire year.'

'Why not?'

'We took too much out of the ocean. And the waters are changing. They're getting hotter. So, my dad was right. I can't complain. There are many benefits to this job. My English has become good, no?'

'It's perfect.'

'From talking to visitors all day long.'

'If you don't mind me saying – you sound sort of sad about not being a fisherman?'

Atto looked at her closely and nodded.

'It's my family's business and my family didn't want me to do it. My father sees me as a performer, dressed up in these clothes, telling jokes to tourists. There's something – How do you say? – fake about it? There's nothing fake about being a fisherman. My brothers sail through storms. They risk their lives. But me? I'm an entertainer. Not a serious man. I love my job. I love my city. People think I don't know anything because I didn't go to university. But I've read many books. And I meet people from all over the world; they tell me about their lives. I'm never bored. Is it dangerous? No. Do I battle with the waves and the weather? No. But it's interesting. And most days I'm happy.'

Sensing that he'd spoken for long enough, he turned the conversation around to her.

'What about you, Liza from the United States. Who are you?'

She laughed.

'Who am I? Okay. Home is New York. I'm at college, in Boston, studying medicine.'

'You're going to be a doctor?'

'That's the plan.'

'That's a good plan.'

'Sure, it is.'

Reacting to her tone, and echoing her earlier line, he said:

'If you don't mind me stealing your line – you sound sort of sad about it?'

Liza found herself answering in a way that she'd never answered before, not to her parents, not to her sister, not even to herself:

'I spend my time around some of the smartest students in the world and they're passionate. It makes me work harder because I'm so scared of slipping behind. But no matter how hard I work I'll never be able to match their passion, because if I'm honest – if I was brave – I should drop out and figure out what I really want to do.'

'You don't want to be a doctor?'

'It's one of the best jobs in the world. No one ever asks, "Why do you want to be a doctor?", including me. I never really asked myself the question, so it's like, I never really made the decision, it just kind of happened. I wanted to do something that mattered. I'm on this path but I don't know if it's *my* path.'

Bewildered at how this confession had tumbled out of her, she added:

'I'm sorry . . . I don't know what that was.'

'It was the truth, no?'

'If my mom heard me talking about dropping out, she'd have a heart attack and I'd have to revive her, and the first thing she'd tell me, when she opened her eyes, is that I'd saved her life, how could I possibly be thinking of dropping out of medical school.'

Atto asked:

'Maybe she'd understand?'

'My mom? She wouldn't understand dropping out. She's never dropped out of anything in her life. She's like . . . the fourth most powerful woman in New York.'

'For real?'

'For real, no. For real, she's the ninth most powerful woman in New York.'

'How do you know?'

'Glossy magazines write these lists – top ten restaurants in New York, top ten most powerful people, top ten restaurants chosen by the top ten most powerful people.'

'And your dad?'

'He's a teacher. An English literature teacher. He's the kindest, most gentle man in the world. I don't know why I'm telling you any of this.'

'Liza, can I ask you a question? Do you trust your feelings?'

'No.'

'Except for today.'

'Why do you say that?'

'Otherwise you wouldn't be in this boat.'

TORRE DE BELÉM
SAME DAY

T ORRE DE BELÉM WAS A renaissance fortification on the north bank of the river shaped like a giant tooth, located just before the Tagus opened into the Atlantic Ocean. As they passed the tower, Atto dropped the sails, allowing them to drift towards the sunset as though it were an entertainment he'd specially arranged. There were only a few other boats in the vicinity – a tourist shuttle shaped like a squirt of toothpaste returning from the beaches and, in the distance, a cruise ship lumbering on to its next port. Gesturing at the tower, he said:

'Picture this stretch of water five hundred years ago. Torre de Belém was the gateway to the city. We're at the spot where the world's most legendary explorers set sail – Gaspar Corte-Real, Vasco da Gama, Bartolomeu Dias. Right now, we're at the starting line for some of the most famous adventures in history – the first voyage to India, Southern Africa and Brazil. To our right, there would've been trading galleons weighing a thousand tonnes or more. To our left, there would've been imperial warships packed with cannons. Today, it's just you and me and this little boat.'

That's the line, Liza thought, *that's his cue*. Sure enough, Atto sat close beside her, his leg brushing against hers. Inexplicably, his mood had turned sombre.

'I'm worried.'

'Worried about what?'

'That you think this boat trip is something I do every day for every pretty woman who walks through the square.'

She shrugged.

'I don't need to be the first woman you've kissed.'

'You think this is staged? The sunset, the tower, this boat, these words.'

'I admit, the thought had crossed my mind. But I don't care.'

'Liza, I don't want you to think this is a trick. When I saw you, in the midday sun, sitting on those stone steps, I needed to speak to you. I had no choice in the matter. Of all the people in that square, at that time, I had to speak to you.'

She smiled.

'If you've done this before, with other women, if this is your ... your routine, it's fine, I don't care.'

She'd been hoping to put his mind at ease, but his mood only seemed to sink further.

'You are not so experienced, am I right?'

'Experienced in?'

'Love.'

She blushed for the second time that day, this time with embarrassment. That there was something deficient about her, this she knew. That it was so obvious, even to a stranger, was painful.

'I'm sure I'm not as experienced as you.'

'I say it only because I believe that we have something.'

'What do we have?"

'A connection. I am sure in a way perhaps you can't be because I speak to thousands of people every week. Maybe all this seems empty to you. A bit of fun. But all I can think about is how sad I'm going to be when we get back to shore and say goodbye. I should be smiling and flirting and making jokes.'

'Smiling and flirting and making jokes sounds pretty good right now.'

'I should be trying to kiss you. But I can't. Because you think none of it is real.'

She looked at him, struggling to make sense of his words.

'Maybe this is a cultural thing. Or a language issue. But I don't know what you're talking about.'

'Let me put it like this. Would you be offended if I don't try to kiss you?'

'If you *don't* try to kiss me? If you *don't* kiss me, would I be offended? That's the question?'

'You are offended.'

'No, no, I just want to be clear what I'm being asked – you are asking my permission *not* to kiss me, that's what you're asking?'

'To prove this is something real.'

'By *not* kissing me?'

Liza laughed at the absurdity of the situation. She must have a special ability to neuter desire: that was the only explanation. As the humiliation intensified, she became stern.

'You know what? I am offended.'

'That wasn't my intention—'

'Whatever this is. Whatever you think this is, this sunset *shtick* you've got going on—'

'*Shtick?*'

'Romantic routine.'

'I was right. You don't think it's real.'

'I can tell you one thing for sure – this, right now, there is no connection, no cosmic bond, no psychic thread. There is nothing.'

'Then why are you so upset?'

'I'm not upset.'

'We have something. I know so. And you do, too.'

'I want to go back.'

'Wait—'

'Take me back.'

Though she very rarely cried, she found herself on the brink of tears, staggered at how powerfully this exchange with a man she hardly knew had impacted her.

'Let me explain—'

'I swear, if you start to explain why you don't want to kiss me, I'm jumping in the water and swimming to shore. I'm a good swimmer, I'll do it, I swear to God. One more word.'

He was about to speak but she raised a finger, cutting him off.

'One. More. Word.'

Like a wounded animal, blinking in disbelief at how spectacularly he'd messed up, Atto returned to the rudder, turning the ship around, away from the Atlantic Ocean and the romantic sunset, heading back towards the city centre.

RIO TEJO
SAME DAY

S LOUCHED OVER THE FRONT OF the boat like a mournful figure-head, Liza had been silent for most of the journey back, brooding over a sense that her life was filled with commendable accomplishments but empty of affection. Breaking the silence, Atto asked:

'Can I speak?'

Looking at the handsome man standing at the back of the boat, the setting sun behind him, transforming him into a melancholy silhouette, she gave a small shrug.

'I had a tourist in this boat once. I don't remember his name. He was travelling with his wife. They'd been together for thirty years. I asked them how they met. He told a story about how they saw a movie on their first date. After the movie he kept the ticket. The second time they saw a movie together he kept the ticket. After every movie they saw together he kept the ticket. A few years later, when he finally proposed, he presented her with all the movie tickets, in order, one after the other, beautifully framed, the history of their cinema trips from the very first date. The only way he could've done that is if he'd known on the first date, the very first time he saw her, that she was the one.'

Liza couldn't help but reply:

'Maybe he did that with all his dates and she was the person who said yes. One day she's going to find some tatty box under the bed, full of old movie tickets.'

'Do you believe that?'

'I believe that in ten minutes we're never going to see each other again.'

The remark sounded tougher than she intended. His reply surprised her:

'We live in very different worlds, you mean.'

'That's not what I mean.'

'If I was a student at your college, would you want to see me again?'

'Yes, I would. But you're not a student at my college.'

'There's a Starbucks in the centre of town. Four euros they charge for a coffee when it's possible to buy an espresso at any regular café for one euro. I see many people my age drinking there, working on their laptops. Not because they prefer the coffee; it's a way of saying that they're international. They have dreams that stretch beyond this city. One day they'll be drinking Starbucks in Manhattan or Hollywood. I'm not one of them. This is my life. A small life, maybe. A good life. But we can't pretend that I might, one day, be in the United States or that we'll ever meet again.'

'You really do think there's something between us?'

'Didn't you feel it? We're almost back, this is goodbye, tell me, yes or no.'

'Yes, I felt something. That's why I came back. I could've gone to the gym. I could've sat on my terrace and ordered room service mojitos. Instead, I'm on this boat, with you. Going through a break-up when we haven't even kissed.'

'I spend my entire day trying to tempt people into this boat. I flirt with women. I flirt with men. I'm not showing off; that's my job, to make people feel welcome. I smile, I joke, I touch people's arms. It's a game. And I have never felt like this.'

'Felt like what?'

'Like ... I wanted to tell you everything. Like ... I wanted you to tell me everything. Like ... it was impossible to believe that I wouldn't see you again. And when we reached the edge of the ocean I wanted to keep going. On some adventure, like those great explorers from the past. The thought that we were going to say goodbye and never see each other again ... it's painful to me ... I know it's ridiculous ... I am aware of how ridiculous I sound right now ... I've made a mess of things ... I hurt your feelings and I'm sorry.'

His voice was so wounded and sincere, she smiled.

'Don't be sorry. You showed me the ocean. I listened to the sounds of the bridge. We saw the sunset. We nearly kissed. Mostly I had a nice time.'

'I was trying to make us into something more – something more than we could ever be. That was my mistake. I should've said nothing. I should have kissed you and kept quiet. It's my fault. And I'm sorry.'

Liza could have left it at that, a tender apology, except she found herself asking:

'Tell me a story that you've never told anyone else.'

Surprised and pleased by the challenge, Atto thought on the question and said:

'If you promise to do the same.'

'That sounds fair.'

'I was ten years old. My family had spent the day on the beach, not far from here – my mother, my father, my three older brothers. We were going to eat some crackers, some fruit, some cheese, and I asked them to wait for me, while I went to the toilets at the back of the dunes. I ran off, fast as I could, and when I came back, they had started eating without me. I remember they were laughing at some joke. But I was so upset. They couldn't understand what my problem was. There was plenty left. We weren't in a restaurant. It wasn't a formal meal. But I'd asked them to wait for me and they didn't. That meant something. I knew it then, as a child. I know it now. Instead of sitting down with them, I ran into the sea and I cried. When I came back, no one knew that I'd cried, no one could tell; they thought my eyes were red from the sea. They'd saved me some crackers. But I didn't eat a thing.'

Hearing this anecdote, she made up her mind. She would kiss him goodbye when they arrived at the square, pleased that this encounter would have some final moment of romance after all. Happy with her decision, she faced the city, pondering what story to tell him. Only now, as they neared the dock, did she notice that the bustling crowds of tourists were gone. All the boats were empty. There wasn't a person to be seen. Commerce Square was deserted.

PRAÇA DO COMÉRCIO
SAME DAY

ATTO OPENED THE EMERGENCY TRUNK retrieving a pair of rubber-cased binoculars. After studying the square, he lowered them. Liza asked:

'What's going on? What do you see?'

Unable to find the right words, he crossed the boat, handing the binoculars to Liza. Looking for herself, she saw that the crowds who'd previously been enjoying the evening were now packed tight inside the restaurants and bars, with those who couldn't find space inside clustered as close to the windows as possible, their attention fixed on television screens as if the country were gripped by a penalty shoot-out in the World Cup final. Many people were holding hands, some children were on their parents' shoulders, others pressed against their legs. Half-eaten dinners were abandoned on the outside terrace tables. Instead of swooping on the remains, chapims were flying in peculiar geometric formations, zigzagging like bluebottle flies trapped inside on a hot summer's day.

Nearing the dock, they passed abandoned tourist boats which hadn't been tied up and were now adrift, bobbing like ghost ships.

'Why would they leave their boats like this?'

'I've no idea. I've never seen it done before.'

They both checked their phones. Neither were working; the screens were blank as though the batteries were dead. Atto secured his boat to the moorings, offering his hand to Liza, not because she needed help but as a pact – they'd face this predicament as a team. Understanding the proposition, she accepted his hand. They climbed up to the jetty walking nervously through the eerily empty square, like explorers setting foot on the beach of a newfound land, waiting to see what kind of people would greet them, friend or foe.

As they reached the centre of the square, with the city as hushed as a scolded child, the evening sky turned blindingly bright, as if the sun and the moon had swapped positions. Liza closed her eyes and covered her face as an exploratory light seemed to pass through her skin. She could feel it inside her body, hungry for every molecular detail. Was she floating right now? It felt that way, but she couldn't be sure, her body was tingling, her teeth were chattering and then it was gone – the vibrations stopped, the light disappeared and the sky was dark again. Slowly she lowered her arms, opened her eyes. Her feet were firmly on the ground and, adjusting to the darkness, she peered up. She saw stars multiplying like bacteria in a petri dish. These weren't stars, she thought, they were too bright, too big, and they were arranging themselves in formations – they were ships, ships in the night sky. A staggeringly beautiful alien armada had arrived, the moment many had pondered but few had ever thought would happen. With no previous fascination in space, her interests grounded in the world around her, Liza was surprised how quickly her mind accepted this new reality. A scientist to her core, she updated her understanding of the universe – they were not alone in the cosmos and, more importantly, they'd been found.

Back in the city, across the red-tiled rooftops and church spires, the first sound to break the awestruck silence was the wail of an older woman like the call to prayer. As if answering the call, military jets flew low across the city, crude and cumbersome compared to the elegance of the star ships far above them. After the roar of jet engines came the sound of sirens, so many overlapping sounds that it was clear the city would never be silent again.

Liza turned to Atto, a man she barely knew, whose hand she was holding and sharing this moment with. He was still staring up at the star ships, watching them enter the atmosphere, and she could tell that more than fear, he felt a sense of wonder, utterly absorbed in the magnificence of the invasion taking place in their sky.

'Atto?'

He looked at her like a man waking from a deep sleep, trying to figure out the world around him. The dumbstruck population stirred into action, some people moving with haste as though they knew exactly what to do in the case of an alien occupation, while others remained stupefied, gazing up at the extraordinary night sky. In awe of the armada above her, one woman stepped into the streets, struck down by a speeding police car that didn't bother to stop. Those nearby rushed to her side and Liza's instinct as a medical student was to join them, to try to help. Atto squeezed her hand.

'No ambulance is coming. There's no hospital treatment. That time is over.'

Many people seemed to want to flee but had no idea where to flee to – out of the city or underground, should they wait on boats huddled in the middle of the river, away from the buildings, or move to higher ground? Without direction or guidance, they had no sense of their place in this world or this world's place in the universe.

Anything was possible now. Pulling his own thoughts together, Atto asked her:

'Where's your family?'

'At the hotel.'

'What hotel?'

'The Ritz.'

He nodded and they contemplated the chasm between them, but none of these things mattered anymore.

'Let's find them.'

'You have your own family to find.'

'I can find mine afterwards. Come on, before the city becomes impassable.'

'Before we move, can I ask, to be sure – what do you see in the sky?'

Atto glanced up.

'I see ships. Alien ships.'

'So this is it?'

'Yes, this is it. Let's go.'

Still holding hands, they hurried out of the square, passing a homeless man looting cigarettes from a kiosk, petty opportunism so out of step with the scale of their predicament it seemed almost comical to Liza. They passed the Starbucks coffee shop which Atto had mentioned earlier, decorated with banners for elaborate cream-covered coffee concoctions, the team of staff gathered outside wearing their aprons as though they expected their corporate employer to rescue them. Nearby, an immaculately dressed older gentleman with a silk cravat and an antique cane was trying to solicit answers, under the impression that he was the only one who hadn't been let in on the secret of what was going on. Liza caught sight of a man standing on the rooftop of a municipal building, as if to get a better view of the alien ships, only to watch him deliberately step off the edge and fall to his death, deciding that this was not a world he wanted to be part of anymore. Having remained calm up until this point, she suddenly felt overwhelmed – not afraid, simply incapable of movement or action.

'I need to stop.'

Atto stopped and she hunched over, staring at the ground, unable to cope with the multitude of extraordinary occurrences happening all around, wondering if she was going to be sick. Feeling his arm across her back, she told herself to breathe, and the sensation of being overwhelmed passed, her body resetting to this new level of uncertainty and anxiety. She stood up straight.

'Okay?'

She nodded, watching over his shoulder as two cars smashed into each other.

At Avenida da Liberdade, one of the most prestigious shopping streets in the city, lined with global luxury brands such as Dior and Chanel, they were blocked by a crowd many hundreds deep, growing larger by the minute. Forced to shout over the noise, Atto asked those on the fringes what was going on:

'*O que está acontecendo?*'

They told him that there were two police officers trapped in the middle being asked variations of the same question:

'What is happening?'

Liza understood the impulse to seek confirmation; she'd done it herself, but this was something different. People were grasping for the comfort of denial, talking about it being a hoax, a conspiracy. As representatives of the State, the police officers were expected to have answers. Atto shook his head.

'They're not going to know anything.'

'How can you be sure?'

'Our government would never have allowed the world to continue as normal if they'd known an invasion was coming – they would never have allowed tourists to fly, supermarkets to sell food.'

'We shouldn't stay here.'

With each passing minute the crowd's mood was spiralling out of control. The first fights were breaking out, scuffles and punches, violence spreading like an airborne virus.

Unable to pass through the crowd, Liza and Atto turned into a side street next to a Louis Vuitton store where ten-thousand-dollar handbags were artfully arranged like raindrops. Somewhere in the city there was an explosion, the first they'd heard, the sounds of war, the shockwave shattering windows and setting off car alarms. Atto and Liza ducked down behind a car, waiting to see if it would be followed by a second or third, wondering if it was manmade or alien. When no more explosions followed, Atto looked at her.

'Let's run.'

AVENIDA ENGENHEIRO
DUARTE PACHECO
SAME DAY

THE RITZ WAS A MODERNIST concrete building at the top of a hill, entirely unlike the historic glamour of their hotels in Paris or Budapest, and Liza remembered being disappointed that their last hotel in Europe was also the least attractive. How trivial that disappointment now seemed as she and Atto hurried through the lobby, past an exquisite arrangement of flowers, perhaps the last flowers to be arranged in this way, for surely no one would bother again. They made their way through hundreds of well-heeled guests in Brooks Brothers blazers and Gucci espadrilles quizzing the hotel staff, who were either remarkably dedicated to their job or in complete denial about the events that were taking place, addressing concerns as best they could, dressed in pristine black uniforms with gold lapel badges, as though an alien occupation were a matter for the concierge, a scene so surreal Liza wanted to call out that it was over – the age of spas and room service, luxury hotels and fresh pressed cotton bedsheets, this way of life was in the past.

Emma, her little sister, spotted Liza first, crying out her name and running towards her, with her mother just behind, the three of them hugging. Liza fought back tears at being reunited with her family. There'd been moments crossing the city where she wasn't sure if she'd see them again. Finally separating, although holding hands, Liza asked:

'Where's Dad?'

'He's looking for you.'

Her mother was too smart to have allowed him to leave the hotel without a plan.

'He's going to return at midnight regardless of whether he found you or not.'

It was only at this point that her mother turned to Atto, paying him serious attention for the first time. Liza explained:

'This is Atto.'

Atto said:

'I need to go now and find my own family. Here's some advice. Don't expect anyone to help you. I don't believe this situation is going to improve; it'll only get worse. From now on everything is going to become harder. Goodbye, Liza.'

Atto kissed her, not on the cheek, a kiss on her lips, and only now did she understand what he'd been talking about – something he'd known from the beginning – this connection he'd spoken about, something inexplicable, defying rational analysis or explanation. She felt it, too. And then he was gone. Her mother thought about mentioning the handsome stranger and the passionate kiss but decided, on balance, that they had bigger things to worry about.

THOUGH THEY WERE REUNITED AS a family when her father returned at midnight, he was so shaken by the chaotic scenes outside the hotel he refused to allow them to separate even for a moment as they moved between their rooms to collect their possessions.

'We stay together no matter what.'

The building had transformed. Doors were slamming up and down corridors, guests emerging with their arms full of clothes, falling over in the rush to exit, while a few wealthy pensioners refused to even contemplate leaving, sipping gin martinis that they'd mixed themselves, sitting on the panoramic patio, watching the city descend into anarchy.

For Liza's parents the next step was clear: they needed to get back home, to the United States – whatever was happening or about to happen, they'd deal with it from home. They didn't bother to pack their Rimowa aluminium suitcases, which were suitable only for flat ground, leaving them behind in their deluxe bedrooms on the seventh floor along with most of their belongings. Wearing their most practical clothes, sneakers and khakis, bringing with them only one backpack each, they collected their valuables – passports and cash – while at the same time wondering whether any of these items were in fact valuable anymore. It struck Liza how quickly her mother adapted to the crisis, gathering their medicines, emptying the minibar, packing a leather hold-all with premium spring water from a glacier in Norway and the ten-euro sachets of salted cashews. These items still had value, not the inflated minibar value, but they were food, which might become scarce in a way they'd never experienced before, and if they wanted to survive, they needed to forget everything they knew about the old world. This was a new world with new rules. Liza, who often griped about how much time her mom spent at work, was full of admiration for her in this moment, seeing how calm she remained under pressure.

'We're going to get through this,' she declared, as if they had suffered a redundancy or a marital affair. They were a family, that was real – that hadn't changed, that would never change – and they clung onto that bond, the only thing they were certain of anymore.

In the hotel garage arguments were breaking out over car ownership – not yet ferocious, people still recollecting the principles of law and order, the idea of a police force, notions of private property, the repercussions to their standing in society if they should break these rules. They were shouting rather than punching or kicking, but violence was coming soon, once everyone accepted that those governing principles were gone and all that remained was a natural law – the law of the strongest, brutality without consequence. Of course, it was absurd that they'd even rented a car in one of the most walkable cities in the world, but her father loved to drive, and he'd planned to visit the vineyards outside Lisbon, not to drink – he'd been forced to give up alcohol during his recovery – but simply to taste. Quietly they opened the car doors, the four of them climbing in, driving slowly around the mob of once civilized hotel guests who only a few hours earlier had been booking spa appointments. Their car attracted attention, several people banging on the windows wondering where they were going; more than anything people were looking for someone to tell them what to do. A man hammered so hard the glass almost smashed, gesturing at his family beside him, pleading to be let in. Liza asked:

'Why don't we help them? We have space.'

Her dad shook his head – they were taking no passengers, making no stops, driving all the way to the airport.

'He has a family.'

'If we're going to survive this, we can't stop for anyone.'

The man moved in front of the car forcing her father to accelerate around him, crunching against the crash barrier, tearing off the side mirror and denting the doors. Looking back, Liza wanted to tell this man that they didn't have any answers. They were motivated by a reflex reaction, foreigners in a foreign country heading to the airport because if they could just get home there'd be answers, an orderly process and they'd have a place in whatever process had been devised. Along with the family bond, their country was the only other thing that remained real in their minds.

They managed to reach as far as Marques de Pombal, the orbital ring-road down the hill from the hotel, before the city became gridlocked, streets crammed in every direction with every kind of vehicle, some trying to leave the city, others trying to reach the airport or the ports, an exodus of a kind she'd never seen before. Flowing through the narrow gaps in the traffic were people wheeling suitcases so over-stuffed that when they hit a bump in the road they broke open, spilling their contents – sleeping bags, toilet roll, bottles of water, dry food and vitamin pills. Other people had hardly moved since the occupation began, making no effort to escape, stumbling about in a stupor of incomprehension, staring up with child-like wonder as helicopters and jets crisscrossed the sky while above the human commotion the alien ships descended into the atmosphere.

From time to time the entire sky turned bright, as though a heavenly searchlight the size of the moon was illuminating the city, and everyone duly paused while this penetrating light sank into their bones, waiting for some god-like act of retribution, gravity to be switched off or cars to turn to dust. But then the light disappeared and it seemed to have no impact aside from causing a minority to lose their minds entirely. One man stood on the hood of a stationary car, addressing the exodus as though it were his congregation. A homeless man sat on a park bench, laughing and laughing, endlessly amused by a private joke – they were all homeless now.

Liza sat in the back of the rental car with the doors locked, watching an altercation between two men, their gestures growing wilder by the minute, teetering on the brink of physical violence until one of the men collapsed into tears, holding his head in his hands, a kitchen knife protruding from the back of his trousers. Still crying, he returned to his car, started the engine, broke out of the gridlock by driving up onto the sidewalk and accelerating onto the park lawn. As the car passed their position in the traffic she caught a glimpse of the driver with his wife beside him, his children in the back, driving at speeds that would've been dangerous for a regular stretch of road, mania gripping his mind, refusing to respond to the frantic entreaties of his family to slow down until the car crashed into a bench hidden in the darkness, the hood crumpling, his wife flung through the windscreen onto the parched grass where only a few hours earlier joyful children had been kicking a ball and enjoying the long hot summer evenings. The driver emerged from the smoking wreckage with broken bones and a blood-covered face, screaming for help, but people were becoming numb to calamity. Everyone realized that there was no help – from now on they were on their own.

'Dad, let me see what I can do.'

'Stay in the car!'

'There were children in the back.'

'We can't help them!'

'We can't do nothing!'

'No one leaves this car!'

Her parents were still clinging to the notion that this car was of some practical use, that it would save them or take them to a place where they'd be saved. But this traffic was never going to clear, not tonight, not tomorrow. In all probability these cars had found their final resting place. Liza leaned forward across the seats, addressing her parents:

'We're not moving. We're never going to move. You don't want to help other people, I don't agree, but this isn't helping us. We need to abandon this car.'

Her parents remained staring at the truck in front as though at any minute the traffic would start to flow, they'd arrive at the airport and there'd be a flight with a meal service, a choice of entrée and a movie to watch.

'If we leave the car, we'll never get it back.'

'The car is useless! The traffic isn't going anywhere!'

Her little sister protested:

'But . . . we're safe . . . in here.'

Liza turned to Emma.

'I know it feels that way but it's not true. If we stay in here, we'll die.'

Her mother looked back at her daughters.

'I don't want to hear that word again. No one is going to die. We're going to get through this. We're going to stay together, no matter what happens.'

Following on from her reassurance, their dad added:

'Here's what we're going to do. We abandon the car. We leave the city on foot. We'll walk to the countryside and wait there.'

Her mother pondered.

'When we step out of the car, we take hold of each other's hands. We do not let go, is that understood? I need you to tell me you understand. We will not let go. Say it.'

'We will not let go.'

With that promise, the family stepped out of the car.

MARQUES DE POMBAL
SAME DAY

LIZA HAD NEVER SEEN A city like this, everyone abandoning their homes, funnelling into these ancient streets in search of safety or simply to gaze in amazement at the alien activity in the sky. In the hysterical intensity people were passing out, and if they weren't caught by a friend or loved one, they slipped to the ground, never to stand up again. Children separated from their parents wept, but before anyone could ask their name they were gone, swept away.

Looking up, Liza saw the alien armada had sunk through the atmosphere and was now only a few thousand metres above the ground, so close and so vivid she could see the surface of their hulls, which looked like fish-skin, silvery rhomboidal scales, entirely without the particulars of human machines; no engines or radars, no wings or weapons. Their shape was so simple it seemed improbable that they could fly, giving no clue how they moved so elegantly, more like clouds than machines, so stunning in form and peculiar in nature it was hard not to surrender to their magnificence.

With her father in the lead, they climbed up onto the roof of a stationary taxi, trying to break free from the momentums of the crowd. Stranded in this sea of people, they searched for a possible route out, in the middle of a cityscape of unprecedented commotion, with every patch of street and sidewalk jammed with people, pets and possessions. Yet somehow one man caught her eye, someone running across the tops of the parked cars, jumping from hood to hood as if these cars were stepping-stones. It was Atto, no longer wearing his mock historic uniform but dressed in olive green slacks, bright orange sneakers and a white shirt. Though Liza had no rational reason to suppose he was looking for her, there was no doubt in her mind that he was doing exactly that. He was following the trail of traffic down from the hotel and she didn't call out, partly because there was no point shouting across this noise, but mostly because she was sure that he'd find her and that there existed some connection between them that she didn't understand but no longer questioned. He stopped, catching his breath on the hood of a car some fifty metres away before finally turning in her direction. In an echo of their first meeting, they stared at each other for a moment. Despite the chaotic circumstances, he smiled and bashfully raised a hand. Breaking her promise, she let go of her mother's hand and raised her own in reply.

With impressive athleticism, he bounded across the cars between them, windscreens splintering underfoot like sheets of ice, reaching the roof of the taxi they were standing on. Catching his breath, drenched in sweat, he addressed them as a family:

'The airport's closed. The military have taken control of it. They're shooting anyone who approaches.'

Liza's father stared at him.

'Who are you?'

'My name is Atto.'

Rescuing her father from his bewilderment, Liza said:

'You came back?'

'I came back.'

This man she'd only met today had risked his life, against his own advice, to return for her.

'We were heading to the countryside.'

'The countryside? Why?'

'We thought it would be safer than the city.'

'You haven't heard?'

'Heard what?'

Atto hesitated.

'We're going to need my boat.'

PORTUGAL
THE TOWN OF SETÚBAL
FORTY-EIGHT KILOMETRES
SOUTH OF LISBON
SAME DAY

ATTO NEVER IMAGINED THAT HIS family's fishing boat, a commercial beam trawler built to catch mackerel and sardines, would one day be transporting people. A modest-sized ship, the aft wheelhouse was designed to be operated by a crew of six, the sleeping compartment fitted with four narrow bunk beds, while the hold was intended only for fish and so slippery with oil it was hard to stand straight. Yet all together these spaces now carried over six hundred people, with the elderly and infirm on the bunk beds, the less vulnerable hunched in the hold, wrapped in blankets with cloth masks over their noses to muffle the stench, while the strongest passengers were braving the elements on deck.

Having eventually found a path through the city crowds, they'd left Lisbon in the back of his brother's truck, fifty friends and family huddled together, fortunate that his brother lived in the outskirts where some roads were still passable. They'd been forced to make way for tanks and armed personnel carriers rumbling into the centre. Liza and her family were the only foreigners in a group that knew each other, speaking entirely in Portuguese. There was only one subject of conversation: the instructions being broadcast by the occupying alien force. They'd taken control of every television, radio, computer and cell phone, broadcasting on a loop, the same message over and over. People had thirty days to reach the continent of Antarctica. It was unclear what would happen to anyone who didn't make it in time; no threats were issued and no consequences were spelled out. With a power that seemed like magic, the instructions were spoken in the mother tongue of whoever held the device, the message accompanied by documentary footage of the continent. Trying to make sense of it, the people in the truck had debated these orders.

'Is it even possible to reach Antarctica in thirty days?'

'Yes, but there are only so many planes and boats, not enough for everyone, not nearly enough.'

'No planes land in Antarctica during the winter.'

'They will this winter.'

'Even if we can get there it will be pitch-black and freezing cold.'

'The only place we'll be safe is the most dangerous place on Earth.'

'The only place on Earth where we can't survive.'

'Why not just kill us all? It would be quicker.'

Self-conscious of speaking in English, Liza whispered to her parents, asking what they made of the instructions. Her mother and her father had remained unusually quiet since the revelation; they'd stared at their phones, scrutinizing the message, watching it play over and over as though there were some riddle to solve. The two of them had been efficient when they'd been motivated by the prospect of returning home, but now that return was impossible, they were adrift – assessing how much they'd lost. They would never return to their four-bedroom apartment on New York's Upper West Side with a terrace where they breakfasted in the summer. They would never collect their golden retriever from the kennel where it was being looked after. They would never go jogging again in Central Park or take brunch with their friends. In an instant they'd lost their country, their home, their future – a loss so enormous that they seemed incapable of adapting. Emma took her cue entirely from her parents, weeping from time to time. Only Liza seemed to adjust, refocusing entirely on their new objective since it was the only one that they had. The only other option was to despair, and Liza had no intention of allowing them to do that. She was taking the lead now. Atto asked her:

'How are your family doing?'

'Not good.'

'We're going to make it.'

'They're still thinking about everything we've lost.'

When the truck arrived at the picturesque fishing town, unable to reach the dock, they abandoned the vehicle in the middle of the street and made their way on foot, all holding hands, pushing through, towards the family's fishing boat. The boat was loaded with as many people as it could possibly carry, already far more than it could safely accommodate. Once his youngest son arrived, Atto's father tried to depart. The sound of the engines caused a commotion on the docks, with more and more people trying to board. The sense of urgency increasing, mothers and fathers pleaded with the lucky people on the boat, offering their small children to those on deck. One woman threw her little boy, tossed him, and he was caught by the crowd of passengers. Weeping hysterically, he cried out for his mother, but when they tried to return him, the mother retreated, refusing to take him, begging them to keep him safe as the boat pushed off from the docks.

Atto's father brandished his antique rifle used for hunting rabbits, firing warning shots in the air, pleading with people on the dock that his ship was already full beyond capacity and if they took more people they'd capsize. As with the truck, Liza and her family were the only American citizens on board; all the others were Lisbon natives, and there was open hostility towards this foreign family, taking up precious space which could have been used for friends or relatives.

'Why are they on board?'

Atto had silenced these doubters, making it clear he wouldn't countenance the idea of leaving Liza or her family behind. As the boat pushed clear, it left a wall of people on the edge of the docks. Some jumped, clinging onto the side, while others missed, falling into the water. Liza looked down at one man hanging onto the rail and offered her hand. He took it, but he was so heavy she was almost pulled overboard, her father grabbing her waist just in time. The man lost his grip, and she was forced to watch him fall into the frothy water around the side of the boat.

Away from the coast, they joined a flotilla of fishing boats setting sail, an armada of refugees following alien instructions, without government assistance or guidance of any kind. Nearby, one of the fishing boats began to list, overloaded with people. There were cries for help as it keeled over, emptying the deck-load of passengers into the water, the screams for help tearing at the heart of everyone who could hear. No one asked if they could help them. They all knew the answer was no. The voices calling for help grew faint, as the armada of fishing boats turned south.

ATLANTIC OCEAN
WEST AFRICAN COASTLINE
MAURITANIA
TWO WEEKS LATER

A s SOME OF THE STRONGEST and healthiest of the passengers, Liza and her family were near the bow, lashed to the side to prevent them being swept overboard. Having endured days of Atlantic storms, with twenty-foot waves breaking across the deck, washing three people overboard, they were now travelling through calmer waters off the coast of Mauritania, sheltering from the sweltering sun under improvised canopies tied together from spare clothes, a mosaic of shirts and hoodies. No one had packed any sunscreen and there were countless examples of essential items that were suddenly no longer available. With less than sixteen days left to reach Antarctica, they were running low on fuel and fresh water. There'd been almost no time to prepare for the journey, leaving the port had been a frantic scramble, and Atto's father, a man with a deep sense of humanity, had prioritized people over supplies, believing he could catch fish for food and find more fuel.

With the passing of the storm and the return of tropical blue skies, they could once again see the alien vessels, designed without any apparent concern for aerodynamics, or obedience to the laws of physics, floating effortlessly, ascending and descending, reaching the outer edge of the Earth's atmosphere, on the brink of space, and then coming back down, stopping a few hundred metres above the ocean, causing the water underneath them to bubble. They showed no signs of menace; more like a hallucination than an invasion. Several joined together, not with crashes and clangs like brash human machines, but in mid-air assembling into a single unit, no longer curved and smooth, but resembling an Escher lithograph, interconnecting stairways to nowhere, a giant optical illusion slowly spinning in the sky.

Made aware by Atto of the shortage of fuel, Liza nimbly climbed to the top of the outrigging boom, like the lookout on a pirate ship, studying the coastline with binoculars. The truth was even if they found additional fuel this ship would struggle to make it to Antarctica in time; it was a workhorse of a boat and couldn't travel the distance within the deadline. The mood among the passengers had transitioned from a sense of temporary relief to nervousness that this boat couldn't save them, and they would need to seek passage on another ship. She climbed down from the boom and weaved her way through the people on deck, finding Atto at the wheel in conversation with his Moroccan-born father and Portuguese-born mother. It wasn't hard to see why their son was so handsome. Yet it was also clear that he was the outsider in this family, a man with a different sensibility to them – poetry to their practicality. They turned to her as she entered the wheelhouse and, speaking softly for fear of alarming the others, she said:

'It's fourteen thousand kilometres to the Antarctic Peninsula. This ship's top speed is eight knots, which is fifteen kilometres an hour – three hundred and sixty kilometres a day – it would take us forty days to reach the tip of the Peninsula even if we found enough fuel. We're going to need to abandon this ship and board something faster.'

There was no need for Atto to translate – his father had come to the same conclusion before they'd even set sail. His hope had been that this ship would be intercepted by a friendly government vessel, a United Nations mission perhaps. But there seemed to be no global mission to help ordinary people; for regular people there was no help of any kind. The government-controlled ships were sailing without compassion, taking no passengers. Growing accustomed to the way Liza never pointed out a problem without also suggesting a solution, Atto asked:

'What's your idea?'

'There's a super-tanker anchored off the coast. From what I can tell, it's on a humanitarian mission. They're taking on board passengers, thousands and thousands of them. Look for yourself.'

He accepted the binoculars, assessing the super-tanker.

'How fast does that ship go?'

Atto put the question to his father.

'About twenty-four knots.'

Hearing the number and doing the maths, Liza said:

'Can it make it to the Antarctic Peninsula in time?'

'Yes, it can get there.'

'Look at the size of that thing. We must be able to find space on deck.'

Atto wasn't so sure.

'Why would they take us? They have a whole country to save.'

Liza considered Atto's observation. It was true – that crew owed them nothing, and when her family had been in the garage, with an empty car, they'd refused to help strangers.

'Then we make ourselves valuable to them.'

'We're a fishing boat with no food and no fuel. How do we do that?'

A S THE SELF-APPOINTED CAPTAIN OF the captured super-
tanker, Bedri stood on the deck overseeing the final stages
of its conversion from carrying crude oil to carrying people. The
three hundred and seventy metre-long vessel, owned by a Dutch
shipping company, assembled in a South Korean dockyard, built to
transport three million barrels of Saudi oil, was one of the largest
vehicles on the planet, yet it was now dwarfed by the alien vessels in
the sky. Bedri's plan was to sail this boat to the Antarctic Peninsula,
the most benign part of the most hostile continent, reaching the
northernmost tip before the deadline and, in so doing, save a million of his countrymen and women. He'd plucked the number of
one million from the air since he had no idea how many people
could be transported by a modified super-tanker. In fairness, the
question had never been asked before. The tanker's deadweight
tonnage was six hundred thousand, but people were a delicate and
complex cargo; they needed space, water, air and food. Despite
the ship's vast size there were only living quarters for a crew of

forty located in the rectangular control tower at the aft of the ship, designed to be operated by a skeleton crew in order to reduce costs. There were only twenty toilets, ten showers, one canteen, one small gym and a recreation room. Even if they tossed superfluous items such as exercise bikes and televisions into the ocean, the control tower would struggle to accommodate more than twenty thousand passengers, with people packed into every corridor and stairway. The sprawling open-air deck could be transformed into a mobile refugee camp with space for perhaps a hundred thousand. Even so, this was far short of his ambition of providing safe passage for a million. To approach this number, he needed to perform an act of alchemy, turning the steel cave in the belly of this vessel, intended for oil, into a space where people could survive. If he was successful, he'd save more lives in a single boat journey than had ever been saved before. If he failed, it would be the worst single loss of life at sea in human history.

Thirty-four years old, Bedri was the son of a prominent politician born into a life of privilege. His father had occupied a cabinet post in the Nouakchott parliament since the military coup. From an early age he'd understood that his father was corrupt; his father had made no secret of it, explaining to his son that this was the way of the world. Growing up under a man equally prone to lavish generosity and violent rages, Bedri spent his childhood wondering why his father had no interest in making their household a loving place in the same way that he himself had no interest in making his homeland a more prosperous place. After an expensive education in Swiss boarding schools, he'd returned to Nouakchott and run away from home, forming his own political party. In his mind, piracy was political, a protest against the foreign vessels that stole their fish and dumped deadly chemicals on their unregulated coast, outrage about a global system of commerce that pilfered from his own country, paying only a fractional commission on copper, gypsum and phosphate, despite these being his nation's resources. Modelling himself on the radical South American communist figures from the past, Bedri had described how the capture of just one super-tanker would bring in the money needed to overthrow the government – he'd sell the ship back to the corporate giants for many millions of dollars that would fund his new socialist party and bring an end to corruption. But piracy, like politics, had been discredited in his country. So many of the early successes had been squandered on prostitutes and the drug khat that the notion that piracy could become a force for good seemed laughable. Upon learning of his son's enterprise, his father had disowned him, and shortly after there was a contract on his life. Prominent pirates were being hunted down and killed, some deaths staged to appear like barfights, others disappearing at sea. For many months Bedri had been on the run, waiting for the murder squad to track him down, until the world had been upended, the alien occupation presenting an opportunity to be the man he'd always dreamed of being, a father figure to the country he loved.

They'd seized the super-tanker on route to Antarctica, the previous captain failing to pick up any additional passengers, using this colossal ship to save only the forty members of his own crew – an egregious act, a crime against humanity, since right now transportation was the most precious commodity in the world. No doubt the largely western crew would argue, if they'd been given the chance, that attempting to pick up passengers would have resulted in a stampede and they would've lost control of the vessel. Or maybe they'd realized the only places they could pick up passengers and still make it in time to their destination was the African coastline, and they hadn't felt sufficiently motivated to save people from this part of the world. Many of Bedri's compatriots had wanted the crew executed and thrown overboard. He countered that they could ill afford this kind of rough justice; the crew would be useful, they knew the ship better than anyone and they could assist with the alterations. From now on, he argued, only one motivation should govern their decisions – not hatred or revenge, but how to save as many lives as possible.

Since the tanker had been empty when it had been seized, they didn't need to dump three million barrels of crude oil into the ocean, avoiding the discovery of whether such an environmentally destructive act would have provoked a response from the alien occupation force, the new owners of this planet. Entering the cavernous belly of the ship, Bedri had marvelled at the scale, the largest manmade space he'd ever encountered, twenty metres high, sixteen metres wide, three hundred metres deep. With cotton scarves wrapped around their mouths to limit their intake of toxic fumes, he and his crew considered the challenge of converting this to a habitable space. The first step had been to wash out the tanks with seawater until no oil remained. Then they set about trying to improve the ventilation, cutting a system of airholes up to the main deck. There were only two tall narrow service ladders down into the tank and no living facilities of any kind. Thousands of plastic buckets, sourced from the mainland, would suffice as toilets, needing to be hoisted up to deck by a pulley system of ropes and the contents tossed overboard.

Many of his loyal crew believed Bedri had done enough – they'd created transportation for some two hundred thousand people, people who'd been abandoned by their government and left to fend for themselves by the international community. Saving a million lives was an unachievable goal, they said. He'd become angered by this attitude, refusing to accept defeat. He wasn't thinking big because of some personal vanity or youthful ego – this was about the survival of entire villages, families and generations. Exasperated, his closest friend had exclaimed:

'What more can we do?'

Bedri had looked up, pointing at the empty space above the base of the tank.

'Look at all this empty space!'

His crew, who were devoted to him, didn't understand – they didn't have time to build new decks. Bedri shook his head.

'We can make hammocks. We'll tie them from side to side. Fifteen floors of hammocks, one meter between each line, from side to side, from one end to the other, like washing lines, line after line of hammocks.'

He'd run across the width of the tank, calculating.

'One, two, three, four, five, six, seven, eight, nine, ten, eleven – eleven hammocks on each line.'

'Who'd be in them?'

'People strong enough to climb along the rope.'

'How would we do it?'

'Rope! We need rope! We need miles and miles of rope. If there's not enough rope, we use cloth, flags, anything. But we're not done yet. Each hammock is a life.'

From all over the country the crew had sought out rope, cloth, fabric, anything strong enough to knit together, woven by an industry of people on the top deck. And by the fifteenth day, as if a giant spider had been busy, the inside of the oil tanker was spun with a lattice of hammocks bolted to the tanker walls. By their calculation, ten thousand hammocks had been woven in four days, taking the number Bedri could save past two hundred thousand. And finally, exhausted, he'd accepted he could save no more; they had to leave today, or they'd run out of time. The final stages of boarding began, filling the base of the tank and then the hammocks themselves. The process of choosing who to save was scrupulously fair and equally ruthless. No men or women over the age of forty-five had been allowed, no children under the age of fourteen, no one who was sick or infirm – they wouldn't survive, either the journey or their new existence in the extreme cold. When they reached their destination, they needed a population strong enough to start work immediately. Many mothers and fathers who refused to leave behind their young children were excluded from boarding. Many older men argued they were important people worthy of being an exception to the rule. Bedri held firm. There were no exceptions. He could not be bought.

Imbued with a quasi-religious sense of destiny, he walked like a prophet among the many thousands of people now sitting on the red steel deck, crammed together, knees tight under their chins, legs pressed into each other's backs, a truly remarkable sight, a canvas of people so dense that not a speck of the bright red deck could be seen. In order for him to walk, each person needed to tilt to the side, offering a stepping-stone of deck, and he advanced on tiptoe, resting his hand on their shoulders, talking to each family as he passed through, welcoming them to his ship and promising them that they'd reach safety. There was no shade on the deck except beneath the pipes with the luckiest passengers nestled under them, the less fortunate perched atop them, trying not to slip off. Fortunately the deck was twenty metres above sea level and even in storms, Bedri believed the overwhelming majority would survive the journey. As he was ready to depart, a voice cried out:

'Bedri! There's a passenger here for you.'

'We're full. There's no more space.'

'It's your father.'

Bedri's father was wearing his military uniform with green lapels and unearned honours, no doubt in the calculation that his uniform would be of some advantage during this crisis, enabling him to masquerade as a man of authority. He surveyed the deck crowded with refugees as though he'd had a hand in this humanitarian achievement.

'I'm proud of you.'

'Why aren't you on one of the government's evacuation planes?'

For a moment his father seemed vulnerable, rejected by the very people he'd spent his whole life trying to placate. How crushing that must have been for him – to be left behind, to be excluded from the inner circle he'd sought to ingratiate himself with. There would have been very few flights. Nouakchott-Oumtounsy International Airport, north of the capital city, was served by a handful of airlines such as Air Algérie, Air France, Royal Air Maroc. The national carrier Mauritania Air had a fleet of only six small Boeing and Embraer aircraft, each able to carry around one hundred and sixty people.

'You didn't make the cut?'

'If it's any consolation they saved the ancient Quranic manuscripts from the libraries of Chinguetti.'

'How many people?'

'Three thousand.'

'From a country of five million, our government saved only three thousand.'

His father walked to the edge of the deck and pointed to the water below. Joining him and peering down, Bedri saw a motorboat filled mostly with career politicians, along with a few prominent academics and scientists, no doubt used as leverage to save the others – his father demonstrating cronyism and calculation.

'These are some of our country's best scientists, engineers and architects. We'll need new leaders when we arrive in Antarctica. We'll be building a world from nothing.'

'This ship is full, Dad. There's no space for you or your friends.'

'We're not asking for a cabin. We can sleep anywhere.'

'You're not listening to me. This ship is full. There is no space.'

'You must have kept a cabin for yourself?'

'Everyone on board was selected according to the rules.'

'What rules?'

'No nepotism. No bribery. No one over the age of forty-five.'

'You have Bidān as passengers? But not my engineers?'

'Who would they replace?'

'These farmers and beggars!'

'The only person begging is you.'

'Have you lost your mind? What are these people going to do when you reach Antarctica? They've never even left their village.'

'Even if there was space, there'd be no space for the likes of you.'

'What is that supposed to mean?'

'We're going to build a new kind of world, one that's fair and just.'

His father lit a cigarette, contemplating this development which seemed to have caught him by surprise despite only recently giving the order for his son to be hunted down and killed.

'My son, still the dreamer? What is the dream now? You think you're going to build a new society in Antarctica? In the snow and the ice? You imagine life is going to become fairer down there? My son: it will be tougher than anything we've ever seen before. You need people like me. People like you will not survive. Soft in your heart and in your head. You've done well to save so many. But when we arrive these people will need men like me.'

'These are not your people. You are not their leader. This is not your boat.'

Bedri turned to the people on deck, at the thousands watching, waiting to see if he'd capitulate to his father or stand firm, the first test of his new society. He nodded at his crew, giving the order, and the men moved forward, taking his father by the arms, lifting him into the air and holding him over the edge. He spat on the deck, at the idea of this ship and everything it represented.

'These people don't stand a chance.'

Bedri didn't turn away as his crew threw his father off the boat.

WEST AFRICAN COASTLINE
MAURITANIA
TWENTY-FIVE KILOMETRES
WEST OF NOUAKCHOTT
SAME DAY

ACCEPTING THE FACT THAT THEY couldn't simply pull up alongside the tanker and plead for charity, Liza and Atto had devised a plan. There were three steel masts on the oil tanker, the tallest at the front with two narrower masts towards the control tower used for venting gases from the hold. These masts hadn't been put to any use. Though their fishing boat had little to offer, it did carry kilometres of incredibly strong synthetic fishing nets. Their idea was to use these nets to hang inflatable life-craft from the outlet masts, suspending bundles of people above the deck like sacks of fruit in mesh bags. It would be uncomfortable, perhaps even degrading for the people inside them, but it would cost the tanker nothing in terms of passenger space and the additional weight would be inconsequential to a ship this size.

Nudging up alongside the tanker, Atto climbed up onto the roof of the wheelhouse and fired a distress flare to catch their attention. Immediately a line of people appeared along the

84

entire deck, numerous faces peering down at the less fortunate refugees in their tiny fishing boat. Multilingual from his
work in the tourist trade, Atto addressed the tanker in French,
Spanish and English. After much commotion, a handsome man
appeared, apparently the captain of this vessel, speaking boarding school English:

'This ship is full. There's no space.'

Ready for this rebuttal, Atto made his pitch:

'We won't take up any space. We can create more space for you
and for hundreds of additional passengers.'

'We've used all the space. How can you create more?'

'We have fishing nets.'

'What of them?'

'We can use them to hang our inflatable lifeboats from your tanker's masts. We'd be above the deck. You aren't using those masts.'

'Lifeboats full of people? Hanging from the masts?'

'I know it sounds crazy, but it could work.'

The captain disappeared.

Atto turned to Liza, taking her hand, waiting to see if the captain
would return. When he did, his demeanour had changed. He was
no longer brusque.

'My name is Bedri, I'm the captain of this ship.'

'My name is Atto. And this is Liza.'

'Lifeboats hanging from the masts is an interesting idea. How
many could you make?'

'We could save all the people on this boat. And hundreds more.'

Bedri countered with an offer of his own:

'For every two of my country's people that you save you can bring
one person from your boat. We leave at sunset. Build your nets.'

Feeling proud that she'd repaid his faith in her, Liza was about to hug Atto when Bedri called down:

'The rules for boarding remain the same – no one over the age of forty-five, no one under the age of fourteen, no one who is sick or frail. There's no point bringing the weak. We are going to the most inhospitable place on the planet; we need survivors, we can only take the strongest. These rules have applied to everyone on board. There will be no exceptions.'

In an instant, Liza's mood collapsed. Half the boat's passengers wouldn't be allowed on board, including her parents, and there was no question of leaving them behind. She looked at Atto and expected him to feel the same way – that they saved all of them or none of them. His voice wavered:

'You should talk to your parents. I'll talk to mine.'

'I'm not leaving them.'

'That boat can reach safety. This boat can't.'

'I'll never leave them.'

'See what they say.'

'They'll say the same.'

'I'm not so sure.'

Liza climbed down from the roof of the wheelhouse and in a stupor from the heat and the disappointment, she stumbled across the crowded deck, leaning on the shoulders of her fellow passengers, arriving at her parents and younger sister. Having tried so hard, and been so hopeful, Liza found it impossible to speak. She didn't need to. Her mother took hold of her hands.

'We're proud of you.'

'For what? I failed. He's not letting us on board.'

'He's not letting older passengers on board. But he's letting you and your sister.'

'No. We stay together. We promised. We're a family, that's all that matters. As long as we're together, that's what we said, that's what we've been saying.'

'This ship is out of fuel. We're about to make our way to shore, to a country we don't know, without water or food, thousands of miles from our destination, searching for transportation at the same time as everyone in the world is searching for transportation. That's not to say there's no hope, we don't know what might happen, but this oil tanker can save you.'

'We'll find something else; we'll figure this out together.'

Her mother kissed her on the cheek.

'Liza, one thing I've learnt, is that we take our opportunities when they arise. Because there might not be another. Right now, we don't have any other means of transport. Time is running out. You and your sister have a chance. A good chance. This boat will go all the way there. It has enough fuel, it's fast enough. It can reach safety. You are getting on board that ship and taking your sister with you. Trust me, the same will be true for every other family on this boat.'

Her father agreed.

'Your mother is right. We can't protect you, we don't have another plan, we're helpless in this boat. We've always done what's best for you and, right now, separating is better for you.'

His voice broke. Emma was crying.

'No, no, please, let's just stay together.'

'And give up? Never.'

'Staying together is not giving up. We'll find another way.'

Liza could see her parents were tempted, but they looked at the giant oil tanker and saw certainty where they had none.

'I would never forgive myself if I let this opportunity slip away.'

Liza asked:

'If you really believed you stood a chance, you'd keep us together. The only way you'd let us get on this boat is if you don't think you'll make it.'

'There's always a chance, you're right, but I can't see it, I can't imagine it, I can't plan for it. I can see this is a chance, a chance that your sister and you will survive, and you must take it.'

Across the deck and in the hold, every family was embroiled in variations of the same conversation, wives separated from their husbands who were older than the age limit, families broken up – some members saved, others left behind. Lisa shook her head.

'I won't do it.'

Her dad kissed her on the forehead and said:

'We love you very much.'

'You promised.'

'We promised to do what's best for you, no matter what. That promise comes first.'

'When you have children of your own, you'll understand.'

Trying not to cry, her mother said:

'We'll meet you there.'

Inconsolable after leaving their parents behind, Emma had finally fallen asleep from sheer exhaustion on Liza's lap. They were sheltering in a life raft, suspended above the deck of the oil tanker as if caught in some sort of primitive jungle trap. Liza was seated back-to-back with Atto, since there was no other form of support in the raft and the space was too crowded to lay down. Many hours after they'd said goodbye to their families, she felt the vibrations of his body as he cried. Only now was the sadness sinking in. Leaving Lisbon, he'd gathered everyone important to him in his family's fishing boat, many of his friends and all of his family. This was his first experience of loss. True, one of his brothers was aboard, aloft in another of these strange, suspended structures, but his parents were too old to make the cut. Atto's parents had stayed behind in the fishing boat with Liza's parents as the tanker set sail. Unable to hug him or console him, she said nothing as he wept, holding his hand.

Resting her head on his shoulder, she looked up at the night sky filled with thousands of stars except in one area, a patch of darkness where an alien vessel blocked the sky. Liza mused:

'When the Polynesians explored the remote islands of Henderson and Lisianski, islands that had never seen human activity, two thousand species of birds, species that had survived for many millennia, disappeared in a few years. On the island of Guam, brown tree snakes, which were accidentally brought on cargo vessels from other lands, had, in a decade, eliminated the entire population of native land birds – the Micronesian starling and kingfisher, the Mariana crow, the Guam flycatcher and the white-throated ground dove.'

'Why do you know all these facts?'

'I read a lot. I never did very well in social situations. I never felt comfortable around people. I always preferred books.'

'Do you think we'll ever get the chance to read another book?'

'If we're alive, we'll be reading.'

'You think we can make it, don't you?'

'We are going to make it. I promised my parents.'

At some point, they fell asleep, back-to-back.

The next morning at sunrise, somewhere in the middle of the Atlantic, they saw the scale of the global armada traveling south – a thousand times the size of Dunkirk. There were French and American aircraft carriers, Dutch cargo ships, British destroyers and Norwegian cruise ships. When the tropical rains began, Atto told them to drink as much as possible, fresh water was in short supply, and they sat with their mouths open, catching raindrops, like newly hatched chicks waiting to be fed. It was funny for a time, until the rains stopped and they began to shiver. This wasn't even close to the kinds of cold they were about to experience.

DRAKE PASSAGE
THE ANTARCTIC PENINSULA
4 SEPTEMBER
ELEVEN HOURS REMAINING

HAVING COMPLETED A SEVEN-THOUSAND-MILE JOURNEY due south, the super-tanker was now backed up in shipping traffic that filled Drake Passage, a notorious stretch of water, feared for its thirty-metre waves powered by the uninterrupted circumpolar ocean current and seventy-knot winds. The polar coastline had been transformed into a watery version of the Los Angeles freeways. Undulating gridlocked ships were packed bow to stern and side by side, steel hulls clanging against each other like colossal cymbals, with smaller vessels trapped in between with nowhere to go and no way to protect themselves, pounded together until they cracked open, sinking at terrifying speed. In a vain attempt to save as many lives as possible, neighbouring ships threw down ropes, as boats were swallowed up by waters so cold no person could survive for more than a few seconds. To Liza it was a scene of such unprecedented commotion and calamity – had she not spent weeks shadowing an ER doctor on night shift, she might have acted like so many other people, cowering and covering their eyes. In contrast, she couldn't look away, every part of the extraordinary panorama filled with tragedy and triumph.

There were only eleven hours remaining to reach Antarctica before the alien deadline elapsed. No one knew what was going to happen after that time or what the outcome would be if they didn't make it to the continent or even how the borders of this new reservation were going to be defined and enforced. Were the small South Shetland islands off the tip of the Peninsula included in our domain? What about Deception and Elephant Islands? They were desirable, more survivable than the inland terrain, with vegetation and geothermic heat from an active volcano. Maybe the tip of Trinity Land, the furthest outreach of the Antarctic Peninsula, was the edge of safety – the demarcation line that the apparently omnipotent alien occupation force would draw, the border outside of which people would not be allowed to venture. There'd been no further communication or clarification, no elaboration or explanation, merely the same simple message repeated over and over, the countdown continuing towards zero.

Directly in front of their super-tanker was a cruise liner and a nuclear submarine. There was no prospect of getting any closer to land. Behind them the queue of ships stretched for miles. Having abandoned their fishing ship off the coast of Mauritania, Liza knew that it was time to do so again. On the bridge the captain listened as she made the case for evacuating all the passengers to shore.

'Why would we leave this boat?'

'To reach Antarctica.'

'We've reached Antarctica. These are Antarctic waters.'

'What if we need to be in direct contact with land?'

'The instructions are to be in Antarctica – this is Antarctica – we made it.'

'What if being a thousand metres away doesn't count? What if being in the airspace doesn't count? What if being in a boat, anchored offshore, doesn't count? The only way to be sure is to be in direct contact with the land.'

'Sure of what? Sure of death. Look at that land! There's nothing – no shelter, no food. If we abandon this ship we give up our only protection against the cold. We brought everyone down off the deck because they couldn't survive outside.'

'I know that but—'

'I have two hundred thousand people on board. They're wearing shawls and shirts, not parkas and snow boots. The temperature outside is freezing. The wind is fifteen knots. If I order an evacuation, how many will die? How many will fall in the water or be taken by the cold? And for what? To stand on the shore when the deadline arrives?'

'Yes, to stand on the shore of Antarctica when the deadline arrives. We have no reason to believe they will treat us fairly. I know it goes against every human instinct to leave the warmth and venture out into this cold. Think of it like this: what if the shoreline is the finishing line and we're dealing with an unpredictable power, someone unlikely to be lenient or merciful. Either you cross the finish line or you don't.'

'I am in charge of the last survivors from my country. This ship is all that remains of our nation and its people. It's been our saviour. It is our home. It's all we have. I cannot give it up unless they agree. If we evacuate this ship, many will die.'

'If we don't evacuate to land, we might all die. I made a promise to my parents. I can't stop here. I can't stop short.'

'Then you should go. May God be with you.'

THE ANTARCTIC PENINSULA
SUPER-TANKER *AXIOS*
SAME DAY
NINE HOURS REMAINING

T HE BOW OF THE SUPER-TANKER, which bulged out as a giant red sphere to improve fuel efficiency, was crunching against the back of one of the world's largest cruise liners, *The Symphony of the Seas*, each impact of such force that the stern of the cruise liner had begun to cave inwards and was in danger of buckling. Owned by Royal Caribbean, incorporated in Liberia with its ships registered in the Bahamas, stateless for tax purposes and now stateless for real, it was filled with families from across the world. Three hundred and fifty metres of whirlpools and waterslides, ice-rinks and tennis courts, transformed into a migrant boat with every room crowded with people to such an extent that even the ocean view verandas were lined with tents to create additional living space. The theatrical auditoriums no longer played nightly renditions of *Hairspray* but were home to thousands of refugees, the lavish swimming pools were emptied of chlorinated water, lined with sleeping bags and covered with tarpaulin. As far as Liza could tell none of the passengers were evacuating to shore despite being so close. The crew were seemingly of the same mind as Captain Bedri, believing that they'd reached safety and their ship was preferable to the barren black rock and snow-covered terrain where there was nowhere to live and nothing to eat. Surveying the global armada amassed around the Peninsula, she saw a body of ships which far surpassed the Battle of Leyte Gulf, the largest naval gathering of all time, stretching over two hundred thousand square miles. Yet despite the scale of this exodus only a minority of these vessels were attempting to offload their passengers onto the shore. Most seemed satisfied that they'd complied with the alien instructions – they'd reached their destination, treating their boats as floating cities.

Though he hadn't contradicted Liza in front of the others, now that they were alone, amateurishly wrapped up against this unforgiving cold, Atto assessed the prospects of trying to eke out some form of existence on the coastline confronting them. There were no buildings, no farms, no vegetation, no power stations, no factories, none of the infrastructure that people required to live. This was, to all practical purposes, a lunar landscape, and he had no idea how they could possibly survive for more than a matter of hours. His brother thought it was madness to even contemplate leaving the oil-tanker and neither he, nor his wife, had any intention of going with them. They were huddled inside the miniature city inside the super-tanker, a double-hulled structure that was effective protection against the ferocious winds.

'Liza? Are you sure about this?'

She nodded.

'Think about that ultimatum, how people are being treated as an inconvenience, banished to the bottom of the planet. The one place we've been given to survive is the one place we can't. Look at how many people are dying all around us: they don't care about us. They'll enforce the rules of this reservation with indifference; it will be to the letter of the law, no ambiguity. If they told us to be in Antarctica, that means in physical contact with the land.'

'It's a risk.'

Liza nodded.

'The greater risk is staying here. We haven't come all this way, and sacrificed everything we've sacrificed, to stop short of the finish line.'

Atto noted the change in her manner since leaving behind her parents. She was a leader now, taking on the responsibilities and authority that had previously fallen to her mother and father. Though he didn't share her intuition about how the alien occupiers might enforce their rules, since he saw no reason why they'd be so callous as to exclude the territorial waters around the reservation, in this moment, when he could've decided to stay with his brother, he made the decision to always be by Liza's side, and if she was determined they should reach the shore, then so be it.

Emma remained silent during these discussions, doing nothing to help with the creation of the rope bridge down to the cruise ship, standing motionless and passive. She'd remained in a state of shock, hardly speaking since saying goodbye to her parents, darkness engulfing her thoughts, unable to conceive of any future. Heartbroken at her family being split up, she'd dutifully followed her older sister, obeying instructions with no opinions of her own. There was something robotic about her, the motions of her body, without any of her usual character. Liza gripped her firmly by the arms.

'Emma, listen to me. We're going to shore.'

'Why can't we go back inside?'

'We have to reach the mainland.'

'But I'm cold.'

'We'll find shelter on land.'

'Will Mom and Dad be there?'

Liza was careful not to lie; she never lied to her sister.

'If they are, we'll find them.'

They secured a rope line from the front of the super-tanker down to the back rails of the sixth deck of the cruise liner where the aqua auditorium was located, in happier times the location of a circus with diving boards and trapeze wires. As part of the varied entertainments and activities they were stocked with ziplines, establishing a connective cord between the two ships. Once set up, the zipline was a steep drop across the freezing ocean and clanging steel hulls. Assessing the safety harness, Liza figured they could take three passengers at a time, wondering how they could possibly transport all the people who'd want to go to land. However, she needn't have worried, because when Captain Bedri joined them he was surrounded by no more than twenty people, a handful of families, including only a few from Lisbon.

'This is it?'

'These are the people who wish to go to shore with you.'

'What about everyone else?'

'They want to stay on board.'

'What if I'm right?'

'They've made their choice. You've made yours. You should go. You don't have much time.'

Liza considered restating her case but, seeing no point, she bowed to Captain Bedri, thanked him for his ingenuity, for saving their lives, bidding him farewell and saying:

'I hope I'm wrong.'

'If you are, you're welcome back. Good luck.'

Secured into the harness, Liza, Emma and Atto stood on the top rail looking down at the frothing ocean strewn with the detritus of smashed ships. They stepped off the rail, Liza holding her sister tight in her arms. No one made a sound as the three of them raced down the zipline over the red bow of the super-tanker, over the freezing waters, landing heavily on the deck of the cruise liner.

DRAKE PASSAGE
SYMPHONY OF THE SEAS
SAME DAY
FIVE HOURS REMAINING

THE INSIDE OF THE CRUISE ship had been designed as a shopping mall, complete with plastic cobblestone footpaths curving around fairground carousels and pirate lair candy stores with barrels once filled with metre-long strawberry laces now overturned and used as a place for people to sleep. Sheltered by a plexiglass roof and sealed off from the outside world, the promenade was overlooked by the verandas of interior-view cabins all lined with makeshift shelters. Passing through, Liza felt such a profound sense of disorientation, a gaudy plastic mausoleum to a carefree past, she was tempted to take a break from their plight in the mock 1960s American diner, sheltering under a broken neon sign, drinking peanut butter milkshakes through a curly straw and pretending none of this was really happening. Passing a single silver birch tree filled with fairy lights, Atto whispered:

'Touch it. The tree.'

'Why?'

'It might be the last tree we'll ever see.'

Remembering that there were no trees in Antarctica, Liza peeled off a small piece of the bark and placed it in her pocket like the locket of a loved one.

Speaking to a member of the crew as they passed through the promenade, they listened as he explained that thirty days ago the cruise liner had been on a tour of the Amalfi coastline, carrying four thousand international tourists with cabins ranging in price from two thousand dollars to forty thousand, a duplex owner's suite with a hot tub on the terrace, Egyptian cotton bedlinen and Parisian boutique toiletries. In addition to the paying passengers there was a crew of three thousand, including musical theatre actors from Broadway, Bulgarian trapeze artists and chefs from Manilla. Complying with the orders of the Italian government, they'd accepted fifty thousand civilians from the port of Messina, a curated list of strategically important people flown from across the country, some of the most accomplished minds in Italian academia, along with the finest mountaineers and extreme weather survivors, chosen to help build a new society on the ice. After leaving Sicily, the cruise liner had picked up as many people as possible from North Africa, crammed into smaller boats that stood no chance of making it to Antarctica in time. As with Bedri's super-tanker, all accepted norms with regards to personal space had been abandoned, with cabins intended for four people packed with as many as forty. Impressed by the scale of their efforts, Liza asked:

'Why aren't you evacuating these people to the shore?'

The crew member looked at her as if she'd lost her mind.

'It's winter. It could drop to minus fifty. The winds could climb to fifty knots. We have kids on board. We have older refugees. This ship is safety. This ship is our home. Why would we leave it?'

Having failed to convince Captain Bedri, she repeated a summary of her fears that people would be granted no leeway – that the borders would be ruthlessly enforced, they were either on the reservation or they weren't, and it was her belief that there was a chance being on board a boat in Antarctic territorial waters wouldn't count. Likewise, she didn't believe being in the airspace would count. And she didn't believe that the occupiers were going to spend even a single second weighing up how to fairly adjudicate the plight of the refugees based upon how little interest they'd shown in their plight so far. The crewman promised to convey her fears to the captain. Hearing the tone of his answer, she understood that nothing would happen at a higher level and implored him to speak to the passengers, the academics and the scientists, to allow them to make up their own minds.

The bow of the cruise ship offered their first unimpeded view of the continent. In the winter darkness, the landscape was illuminated by thousands of distress flares, streaking arcs of red, white and yellow fired by fishing boats and ferries decanting their cargo of people. The smaller the boat the more likely they were to abandon it since there was no way these transport vessels could provide any kind of long-term home. It was impossible to estimate the number of people pouring onto the coastline of Trinity Peninsula with its black mountains and heaped cliffs of snow, the northernmost part of the Antarctic Peninsula.

The crew of the cruise liner dropped emergency chain ladders to the narrow rear of the nuclear submarine moored in front of them, a *Triomphant*-class submarine once part of the strategical nuclear deterrent of the French navy. One hundred and thirty-eight metres long, twelve metres wide, its nose was wedged on the rocky shore, having navigated to Antarctica from the port of Île Longue, Western Brittany. It had been separated from the rest of the French fleet and was now surrounded by an eclectic flotilla of fishing boats and civilian yachts. The sailors guarding the hatch of the nuclear submarine saw the attempt to disembark and after some discussion moved over to them, inflating one of their luminous orange rafts which they positioned under the base of the ladder to stop people falling into the water. By this point the group of passengers around Liza had grown to include numerous Italian scientists who'd listened to her argument about the need to be on shore. The debate was spreading through the ship and by the time the ladders were safely positioned over the orange life raft over five hundred people had gathered at the bow wanting to join the evacuation. Before climbing down, Atto assessed the freezing waters, warning Liza:

'If we get wet, we'll become cold, and if we're cold, we won't survive.'

In the life raft, the French sailors pointed out that there was no space for them inside the submarine. For the third time, as though she were a preacher repeating a religious parable, Liza explained her belief that the only way to be sure of safety was to be on the mainland. Their bodies needed to be in contact with the continent of Antarctica; they'd travelled so far, they'd sacrificed so much, it was madness not to take these final steps. If she was wrong, if the boats turned out to be safe, they could return. Atto translated into French and the sailors listened in silence. Liza added, no longer equivocating:

'If I'm right, being inside that submarine won't protect you.'

The orange raft arrived at the black rocky shore and, without any fanfare or deliberation, without acknowledging the significance of the moment, Lisa stepped out onto a continent she'd never dreamt of visiting, a land that until this moment held no place in her imagination – the most desolate land on Earth that was now her home.

G IVEN TO HIM BY HIS father before they'd said goodbye, Atto was wearing olive green neoprene waders with insulated latex boots, deep-sea fishing gear designed for extended periods in the harshest of conditions. With no waders for either Liza or Emma, they'd improvised cold-weather clothes with a mix of layers, sports undershirts, hooded tops and oversize heavy wax rain jackets taken from the fishing boat. Their hiking boots, intended for hill-walking, were wrapped tight in plastic bags and duct tape, none of which could be easily removed. Atto had offered his neoprene clothing to Liza, but she'd refused, pointing out that they were too big and, more importantly, they were a parting gift from his father. It was unthinkable for anyone to wear them except him, although they were already noticing the envious looks his clothes were getting from the people around them. It was easy to imagine the situation sinking into violence, people fighting over boots and gloves.

Millions of people now stood on this shore, mostly without any possessions, disgorged from their boats onto the rocky beach, as bewildered as newborns, utterly unsuitable for this place with not a plan between them. Liza squeezed her sister tight, as though love were enough to keep them alive. They could feel the cold rising through the soles of their meagre boots despite having bound them in layers of plastic. Crinkling underfoot were black volcanic stones and fossils formed epochs ago when this continent had been near the equator, covered with lush vegetation and animals. The continental drift downwards had taken over three hundred million years – people had been given thirty days. Liza surveyed the shivering hordes around her, some already dying from exposure, a dumbstruck population drawn from around the world, obeying orders that made no sense.

As the alien deadline approached, with only minutes remaining, a virulent outbreak of doubt spread among the refugees still sheltering onboard the armada of boats. Previously fearful of the cold, they were suddenly afraid that they'd made the wrong decision, that they wouldn't be treated fairly, that they were no longer protected by a court of human rights, that the occupying alien force might consider their existence a trivial matter in the context of the cosmos. Liza watched as last-minute evacuations were launched from the armada, thousands of life rafts simultaneously being lowered in between the slithers of space between these giant ships, some rafts crushed as the hulls were clamped together by the waves, plastic boats splintering like plywood, scattering thousands of people into the ocean, men and women tumbling down to the darkness, illuminated intermittently by the flickering lights of emergency flares arcing overhead.

Nearer to the headland people were wading to the shore, so rapidly drained of life by the cold that they died before even reaching the beach, collapsing into the shallows. The captain of the nuclear submarine emerged from the hatch, leading his important passengers, politicians and scientists in an orderly procession to the shore, accepting Liza's notion that the only way to be sure of survival was by standing on land. He left a solitary sailor behind, guarding the hatch to prevent the submarine being seized while they were away. On the beach they stacked a pyre of petroleum briquettes and started a fire, the heat attracting so many shivering survivors that the sailors were forced to form a protective ring around the flames to prevent it being overwhelmed.

Looking up, Liza saw more planes in the sky than she'd ever seen in her life, all flying in the same direction, waves and waves of them. The terrain of Trinity Peninsula was far too mountainous for airplanes to land, and they were flying towards the flat ice plateaus where they'd attempt their perilous touchdowns. Beneath these planes helicopters launched from private yachts and warships, navigating their way through the winds, some caught in a vortex, spinning wildly while others smashed into the side of ships, bursting into flames. The helicopters that reached the rocky shore didn't bother to land as normal, an impossible feat in these conditions, controlling their crash as best they could and trying to avoid the people on the beach, many of whom were too cold to run away.

Out of the darkness, conjured by alien technology so advanced it resembled the fabled powers of an ancient god, a thin veil of blonde light, a translucent silk curtain, rose from the edge of the coastline where the sea met the shore. It followed the ragged shape of the Antarctic mainland, marking the borderline between those who were safe and those who weren't, between the people within the wall of light and those frantically running towards this boundary, arms outstretched, trying to cross to safety, throwing themselves through the wall of light in order to be on the other side in time, a mound of people heaped up on top of each other, some with their legs and feet still on the wrong side of the line, their bodies not fully over the border as the deadline elapsed.

In an instant the wall of light turned solid, as though light could freeze, forming the most delicate and beautiful of border walls, transparent gold glass stretching the full length of the coastline, curving intricately and accurately around the ragged terrain while reaching up through the night sky, higher than the polar stratospheric clouds, all the way up to the mesosphere, the atmospheric skin of this planet, turning Antarctica into the most elegant vase, a container into which people of the world had been poured. Some hadn't made it, their faces pressed up against the gold glass like starving beggars outside the window of an opulent restaurant. Some hadn't fully crossed the border and their bodies were caught in the wall, the gold glass trapping them tight around the waist or wrist. Up above them helicopters had been caught mid-flight, in suspended motion, the pilot on the safe side of the golden boundary with the passengers on the wrong side. Even higher, a passenger jet could be seen jutting out. These people and planes hadn't been decapitated or cleaved in two, they'd been trapped within this golden flypaper, still blinking and breathing, in a state of shock but alive.

A moment later the people on the wrong side of the border, the people who hadn't made it across the line in time, began to change, their pupils glowing, then their skin and hair, as bright as the embers of a fire until their bodies lost cohesion, breaking apart into dense swarms of firefly-sized parcels of light, swirling up from the balconies of the cruise ships, thick plumes from the vent holes of the super-tanker. The solitary sailor on the desk of the submarine, who'd been saluting his colleagues on shore, was swept away by a gust of wind – the winter sky so full of embers that the sea was turned red with the reflected light. Last to break apart were the people trapped in the wall, leaving behind holes in the golden veil in the shape of their bodies. Even if they'd only had the tip of their shoe caught, no leeway was granted, no mercy was given; you were either on the right side of the line or you weren't. In a matter of minutes, it was over, the largest genocide ever committed, handled neatly and efficiently and without a drop of blood.

One survivor, a woman, picked herself up from the black stone beach, sick with grief at her husband being lost when he was only a few yards behind her. In fury, she ran at the gold glass wall, hitting it with her fists. To her surprise it shattered, collapsing like shards of golden ice. The helicopter and the plane fell like stones, crashing into the shoreline. With the golden veil gone, the survivors on shore surveyed the ghost armada of empty ships bobbing in the waves.

DAY ONE

LIZA STOOD SILENT ON SHORE trying to fathom what she'd witnessed – the planet purged of people on every continent except this one, not with bullets or bombs, but carried out instead with the inappropriate grace of a spectacular light display, in no way commensurate with the scale of this crime. The crowds around her, drawn from every part of the world, were all that remained of humanity. All that they had left were the possessions they'd brought with them, a pocket full of vitamin pills and a backpack of spare clothes. Some dropped to their knees, praying for salvation. Others began to meekly explore their new homeland, trying to figure out if it could support them. Most did nothing, perhaps wondering why they'd made the journey here, realizing that this wasn't the end of their hardship; it was the beginning. If they were waiting for guidance, there were no instructions from their occupiers, no additional orders, no sign of them in the winter sky.

Her teeth chattering, Emma declared:

'I can't do this. This life. Whatever this life is. It's not for me.'

Clasping her sister's arms, Liza said:

'This is the hardest moment, right now. It will never get harder than this. We'll find shelter and food. Once we're warm and once we eat, we'll start to feel better, I promise.'

'We have nothing! Look at us!'

Liza turned to Atto for support and, backing her up, he said:

'Emergency supplies have been airdropped across the continent. Millions of crates full of provisions. We'll find a tent, we'll get some food, we'll set up base. Your sister is right, we've come this far, we can survive this.'

Emma stepped back from Liza, looking up at the black stone mountains.

'Mom and Dad didn't make it, did they?'

'We don't know.'

'You do know. They're not here. They're gone.'

'They might have found a way.'

'You don't believe that!'

Liza fell silent. Her sister continued:

'You got us here. Because you're strong. Maybe you can cope with this life. But I don't know how to live like this. I don't want to live like this.'

'None of us know how to live like this. But we'll find a way.'

'I don't want to!'

With that said, Emma broke free, running down the beach, pushing through the crowd, as fast as she could towards the invisible boundary and the prospect of a sudden painless death. Like a sprinter crossing the finish line she dove forward expecting a transfiguration into red embers. But nothing happened; there was no disintegration, no alien-enforced retribution and, losing her balance, she tumbled down the rocks into the freezing ocean. It took all of Atto's strength to stop Liza from running into the water after her sister.

'You can't help her if you're cold.'

Protected by the neoprene waders, he entered the ocean, picking up Emma and hauling her out. She was soaked, her head and hair were wet, and he guessed that they had only seconds to save her.

They carried her towards the bonfire, Liza clasping her sister's wet head, trying to keep her warm. The captain of the French nuclear submarine, seeing that it was the young woman whose advice had prompted them to disembark the submarine, allowed them through the defensive line protecting their precious heat. They placed Emma near the flames. As they sat down, steam rising from their clothes, Liza looked into her sister's eyes and saw that it was too late – she'd given up and no amount of warmth could save her. Barely able to move, Emma used the last of her strength to kiss her big sister on the cheek, her lips blue with cold.

'Don't be disappointed in me.'

'I could never be disappointed in you.'

'Tell me a story.'

'What story would you like to hear?'

Emma closed her eyes, her life slipping away while Liza wept.

PART THREE

TWENTY YEARS LATER

ANTARCTICA
THE ANTARCTIC PENINSULA
HOPE TOWN
I NOVEMBER 2043

A<small>FTER MONTHS OF DARKNESS THE</small> first trace of daylight appeared over Hope Town, home to two million survivors and the smallest of the three settlements on the Antarctic Peninsula. The peninsula was a crooked finger of mountainous terrain pointing up from the main body of the continent, offering some of the most hospitable terrain on this most inhospitable continent. It was for this reason most of the world's refugees had settled here, at first spread randomly, over time grouping into three distinct clusters, each town with its own identity and character. Situated at the mouth of Wordie Bay, nestled between the ocean and snow-covered mountains, Hope Town was the most bohemian of the three settlements. Its citizens believed that music, sport and art were, in the long term, as important to survival as housing and food. It was a sprawling shantytown constructed out of scavenged materials from the ships and planes used during the exodus. Each wall had been lovingly painted with the brightest of colours, luminous murals to help guide people during the winter darkness and raise their spirits in their difficult moments. It was rare not to hear song as you walked past people's houses, and if you felt lonely and wanted to join in, you simply knocked on the door – in Hope Town there were no strangers. Everyone was family.

Today was the first day of spring, one of the most joyous times of the year. The sun hadn't yet risen above the horizon, but it was close enough to bring back bands of brilliant blues to the sky, layers of indigo, sapphire and zaffre stacked all the way up to the stars. Once again the people of Hope Town could venture outdoors rather than scurrying from shelter to shelter buffeted by gale-force winds, guided only by the fraying red ropes which lined the streets. Civil Twilight was the technical term for this light – civility after the savagery of winter. The new year began with a festival of light. On this first full day of sunlight the town's people would powder their faces yellow or blue in celebration of the sun and sky, kissing everyone they passed on the cheek, whether they were close friends or not. By the evening, music sounded out across the rooftops and the snow on the streets was speckled with the coloured dust from a million kisses.

WORDIE BAY
HOPE TOWN
NEXT DAY

S ETTING SAIL FROM THE DOCKS at Wordie Bay, Atto stood on the deck of his sixty-metre trawler, the *San Matias*, Argentinian in origin for those old enough to remember what countries once were. As one of the most successful fishermen in these perilous waters, he'd become a beloved figure in Hope Town. Now forty-four years old, his curly mass of handsome brown hair matched a beard streaked with grey. In this austere landscape his green eyes were like precious stones. Transformed by the physical demands of his work and the hardships of this continent, he'd become immensely strong and broad-shouldered. Wearing a blend of high-tech fishing attire, neoprene smocks paired with hand-stitched seal-pelts and headwear lined with penguin feathers, his appearance was more like an amiable and eccentric pirate than a fisherman, and this seemed apt. No matter the many hardships of this place, he loved his work and he loved his town, which he had helped to create.

Today was Atto's first day at sea after the long winter and he was delighted to be back in command of his rugged boat again, feeling the vibrations of the ship's powerful engine coursing through the deck as they set off from the harbour. He'd been the first fisherman brave enough to venture from the shore, the town fearful of alien reprisals. However, without fish they faced starvation and so he'd risked his life, taking the boat out on his own, a test of the rules of this place, remaining in sight of the town. As if they could discern his intention, there'd been no punishment from the alien occupiers, a fact that had caused some people to believe that they'd left the planet. Some had dared to take a boat and head back home. But they'd never been seen or heard of again.

Along the rocky banks of the bay, Hope Town citizens lined up, waving as the small flotilla of thirty boats set sail. Ten years ago there'd been over fifty boats; fifteen years ago there'd been over two hundred. Tonight, if they all returned safely, there'd be further celebrations across town, a ritual feast to mark the end of winter with platters of salt-baked emerald rockcod and steamed Antarctic silver-fish served with jugs of pearl-wort flower wine, a night renowned as one of the most common days for couples to conceive, with libidos awoken after the oppressive winter months.

Seafood was one of the town's primary sources of protein, second only to macro-algae farmed in shallow-steel reservoirs on the inland ice plateaus, giant circles of green in a continent of relentless white, where in the summer families vacationed as families had once vacationed in national parks, basking in the colour green. Although algae's taste was unpalatable to people not born on the ice, its protein intensity was higher than wheat and its natural protective systems, pigments such as carotenes, chlorophylls and polyphenols, made it an exceptional food source. In truth, people's diet today, sugar-free and ruthlessly functional, had never been healthier. Krill was processed into a rich broth, salty and pungent, served with noodles made from the dense forests of kelp which grew on the seabed under the ice, one of nature's fastest growing plants. Canneries had been built around the harbour where all the fish, octopus and giant spider crab were readied for consumption. During the summer as much as possible was eaten fresh. For the winter months, the catch was preserved in pastes and brines. Seals were only eaten when their furs were harvested for pelts. Their flesh was unpopular, their livers toxic, not even suitable for the dogs, while the blubber was used for inefficient lamps and luxurious soaps. Obesity and diabetes had been confined to the past, with a population fitter and stronger than ever before, even the most bookish children thinking nothing of hiking ten kilometres through the snow carrying a heavy backpack.

Leaving behind the cheering crowds, the fishing flotilla followed the shoreline out to sea, passing several moored nuclear submarines, Russian, British and French, side by side, converted from war machines to prime accommodation, robust against even the most severe winter storms, home to Hope Town's vulnerable citizens. Most of the nuclear reactors, with a lifespan of twenty-five years, were still operational, providing reliable warmth and electricity, residencies for the elderly and those with special needs, Hope Town being the only settlement that hadn't taken a Darwinian approach to survival, believing that protecting the vulnerable was part of the reason they'd been so successful as a community. Beside the submarines were some of the world's largest cruise ships and most expensive yachts, home to many thousands of Hope Town refugees, their engines picked clean for components, never to sail again, their hot tubs used for washing clothes.

This was Atto's twentieth year on the ice, an exceptional feat for a civilian with no training in cold survival and who'd completed the Exodus to Antarctica without any government assistance, not part of a national evacuation programme, his name not on any of the lists of high-value citizens worth saving – arriving in Antarctica through guile and grit. Perhaps the struggles of that journey were part of the reason he'd survived the infamous first winter – the deadliest winter in human history. Many of the important people airlifted to the continent had been unprepared for the challenges of life on the ice, too accustomed to their own importance and the luxuries associated with it. In contrast, the Exodus had toughened Atto, readied him for the scale of the challenges ahead, recalibrating his identity. This was a new era. The era of plenty was over. Humankind was a fallen people now. No longer conquerors but a second-tier species, relegated to the coldest continent on Earth, imprisoned within a reservation created by alien occupiers. For those who couldn't adjust, despair swept through their ranks more lethal than the pandemics that had once swept the world. For those who were willing to adapt, they tried not only to survive but to find a better way of living.

Out in the open water, plotting a course through the icebergs, Atto and his crew took a moment to pay their respects to those who'd perished during the Exodus, a ceremony they completed every year on the first day of fishing. His crew, comprising some of the finest fishermen from all over the world, silenced the engines, allowing the boat to drift. Without flowers, they'd carved beautiful floral ice wreaths, which they tossed onto the water. Atto declared:

'On this first day back on the water, we remember all those who were lost. We mourn our friends and family. We mourn the friends and families we never knew.'

The nets had been cast for barely an hour when the stern of the boat lurched downward with such force as to almost submerge. They'd caught something enormously powerful and, rushing to the side, searching the ocean, Atto marvelled as a magnificent sperm whale surfaced nearby, rolling over and looking at them with its grapefruit-sized eye. He wondered why the image of a grapefruit had come to his mind since it had been over twenty years since he'd seen the fruit. His mother had loved them, and he remembered her eating them in the kitchen at sunrise every morning while smoking a cigarette, one of the few moments in the day she'd had to herself. The memory faded as quickly as it had come to him and his thoughts returned to this whale, tangled in his nets, clearly wondering how it should get free. The whale was at least sixty feet long and weighed over fifty tonnes, capable of pulling the entire boat under should it choose to dive. Atto moved fast across the deck, taking a hatchet and cutting the nets, releasing the whale. The boat sprang back upwards, almost causing the fishermen to fall over. In ordinary times there would've been relief at the near miss, but all anyone could think about was the loss of their precious netting. It was in short supply and made from synthetic materials that were impossible to produce without the factories of the old world. Without nets they couldn't fish, and this trip, normally so celebratory, had fallen quiet. The sombre mood passed as the magnificent whale, grateful at its release, returned to the side of the boat, nudging the bow, as if bidding them farewell.

HOPE TOWN
HOSPITAL ONE
NEXT DAY

Liza worked at Hospital One, which despite its name was the only hospital in town. There had been optimistic plans to build a second which never came to pass since there was barely enough equipment to stock the first. Like the town it served, the hospital was a ragtag and brilliantly improvised construction built in extraordinary haste with remarkable ingenuity, an installation-art mix of reclaimed parts welded together, using anything from steel cargo containers to the plastic waterslide from a family cruise ship. The patient recovery beds were repurposed business-class sleeper seats from prestige airliners, the operating tables were pillaged from the cramped medical decks of the nuclear submarines. A varied assortment of lights were arranged on the ceiling of operating rooms, more akin to the wondrous lighting design of a Broadway show than a hospital, and though a great deal of medical equipment had been transported to the continent during the Exodus, over time it was not uncommon to find kitchen utensils being used as retractors during abdominal operations, the concavity of table-spoons making them suitable during appendectomy. Endotracheal

and nasogastric tubes were routinely reused, along with Foley cath-
eters. Surgical linens were sterilized repeatedly until they frayed
and could be washed no more. There were no ambulances; people
were carried by hand on stretchers. The dexterity of the paramed-
ics, some of whom were once Winter Olympians, were a far better
shock-absorber over the rough terrain than anything with wheels.

Aside from the patchwork nature of the facilities, which appeared
like the brightly painted and partially digested remains of the old
world, this was not a hospital as Liza had once understood them
to be. The heart-warming governing principles of Hope Town,
that everyone was cherished and valued, came into collision with
the stark reality of their predicament. No matter how uplifting an
ethos prevailed across the town, medical supplies were dwindling,
and no amount of human ingenuity could change that. Care was
prioritized to those who had a high chance of surviving. The prior-
ity was prevention, since it cost nothing. People were fitter, stronger
and healthier than ever before. And no one in Hope Town ever
retired. But no matter how balanced their diet or how much they
were loved, patients fell sick. At times, Hospital One was often more
like a court than a hospital. Every day Liza weighed the value of
people's lives against the dwindling supplies of irreplaceable medicines. Every day she refused care as often as she agreed to it. If you
became addicted to the locally brewed hooch, a spirit made from
fermented seal milk and distilled through a layer of charcoal, no one
would reprimand you, but there'd be no hospital care when your
liver stopped working.

Liza's appearance had changed almost beyond recognition in the
twenty years she'd been on this continent. Like all citizens, she was
fantastically strong and fit. Though her job didn't require her to be

exposed to the elements, no one in Hope Town could afford to be anything other than supremely athletic, able to trek across the snow regardless of their occupation. Liza's duties required her to be at the hospital throughout the winter and since there were no vehicles for personal use, her walk to work alone was often a perilous expedition. Gone was the softness about her body that she'd once tried to lose with gyms and spin classes, replaced with a far deeper and more complete physical strength she'd only known in the rowers and track athletes at her college. Her features were sharper, her auburn hair longer than before for no reason other than it kept her neck warm. If her parents had been alive, they'd barely have recognized her from the young woman they'd said goodbye to.

A nurse ran into the staff office, calling out for help:

'Hypothermia. It's a child. He's going into cardiac arrest.'

Liza took the call for help, hurrying towards the emergency response unit. Staffing in Hospital One operated by a grid of expertise, but with perpetual staffing shortages anyone could be called upon for any emergency. No matter their medical background, cosmetic surgery or dentistry, every member of staff was an expert on hypothermia – the most common cause of death on the continent. When the body's temperature dropped from ninety-eight, the hypothalamus slowed the blood flow to the heart and liver because those organs used the most heat, the human body's desperate attempt to keep the brain alive.

'Core temperature?'

'Eighty-three.'

At this temperature consciousness would be impaired, vital signs hard to detect. Entering the emergency room, Liza saw a young boy on the operating table. His skin was red, his eyes were closed – his chest wasn't moving. From countless encounters with hypothermia, she could judge in an instant the child's chances, and in this case she knew that she'd struggle to save this boy. Skipping over the initial-response treatments, she opted for the most extreme measures – a peritoneal lavage, a mechanism to directly warm the abdominal cavity. As she readied the procedure she spoke to the boy as though he were alive and well:

'Hey there, young man, I need you to open your eyes and tell me your name.'

He didn't reply, didn't open his eyes. With the peritoneal lavage complete, using warm saline, and still no sign of him waking, the nurse began to shake her head, indicating the child was lost. Refusing to accept this, Liza placed her warm hands firmly on his cold cheeks and whispered into his ear:

'Young man, listen to me very carefully, your mother is waiting outside to see you. I need you to open your eyes.'

To everyone's surprise the little boy's eyes opened. He didn't know his name. He didn't know where he was. He claimed to be hot and wanted to cool down. A common trait among people suffering severe hypothermia was to strip naked, as their brains became confused. He was one of the lucky ones, brought back from the brink, and Liza's reputation as one of the most skilful doctors in town was confirmed. She had a gift, it was claimed, a life force beyond expertise or logic, some energy that seemed to flow from her touch. Leaving him to recover on a precious drip of warm fluids, she found the boy's distraught mother in the waiting room and the two of them hugged as though they were family. Everyone was family in Hope Town. Even after all her years working here, all the many reminders that medicines should be strictly rationed only to patients with a high chance of surviving, the thought hadn't even occurred to her to assess whether this was a child worth saving.

THE ANTARCTIC PENINSULA
HOPE TOWN
SCHOOL FOR ICE-ADAPTED CHILDREN
NEXT DAY

Echo was able to detect the slightest fluctuation in air temperature and describe these variations in mystifying and wondrous detail. She could see the cold as variegated clouds of colour, she would talk about the textures of cold, the sounds of cold, from the freezing of the ocean to the crackle and chatter of an ancient ice mass. The cold had never caused her any pain, she'd never been afraid of it, and she'd never uttered that most human of phrases:

I feel cold.

Sixteen years old, with none of the vulnerabilities of ordinary-born people, either emotional or physical, she'd been engineered at a genetic level for life on the ice, her DNA adapted for this continent, with no experience of the warm worlds except as history lessons taught at school.

The School for Ice-Adapted Children was set against a sheer vertical cliff, a granite and diorite intrusion that cleaved upwards two hundred metres high. Sheltered from the coastal winds, the building had been constructed with techniques derived from Viking settlements, heaped rock walls, stones intricately slotted together without cement or paste so that from a distance it would've looked like a natural part of this landscape. Inside, the classrooms were adorned with original masterworks rescued from the world's art galleries. The people of Hope Town had taken the decision that since there were no longer the resources to build museums or galleries, their stock of once priceless paintings and statues were to be shared among the schools as inspiration for the students rather than pointlessly preserving them in the belly of a submarine where no one would ever see them again. Walk into any school in Hope Town and there'd be Monet, Titian and Picasso mounted on the walls as if they were the students' art projects, next to the hand-made blackboards carved from local stone with teachers using uneven chunks of natural chalk, the writing implement of choice now that the era of disposable pens had come to an end.

Echo's school was intended exclusively for the ice-adapted children brought back from McMurdo City, humanity's capital city, located on the far side of the continent. In contrast to the three settlements on the Antarctic Peninsula, McMurdo had been an established scientific base before the Exodus, the most substantial base on the continent. As the most developed location, it had become the place where the world's governments had pooled their most advanced equipment, their very best scientists and their most sophisticated survival shelters. Today it was the largest and most important human settlement in existence, tasked with a single goal – the survival of the species. In McMurdo City there was a plan – the Cold People Project. These genetically modified children, adapted to survive in the cold, would be human, mostly, but adjusted for life on the ice. Each child would be different, each set of modifications unique. The scientists could offer no guarantees regarding the outcome; the techniques were radical. The child might die. The mother might die. The child might be beautiful in a conventional sense; it might be beautiful in a way never seen before.

This school for the ice-adapted was a place for these remarkable children to study but also a place to study them – to see how the genetic modifications took hold. The teachers didn't write reports for the parents; they wrote reports for the McMurdo scientists. The experimentations were so audacious that unforeseen consequences were frequent, varying from peculiar and delightful character quirks to physical attributes never seen before. None of the teachers knew what to expect from one day to the next. A student might discover they were gifted with an exquisite singing voice more bird-like than human, or they might be able to change the colour of their skin. Some could be encased in ice and remain unscathed. Unlike any school before, there was no bullying of any kind and no unkind words. The sense of solidarity between them was wonderful for the teachers to behold; they looked after each other and in their own way loved each other. Since there was no normal, no one was ever made to feel the odd one out.

At six foot six, Echo was more mythic than human, as if sculpted from the ice by a powerful sorcerer and brought to life with a spell, which, in a way, she was, the product of adapted genomes, the mysteries of which were only partially understood by scientists in McMurdo. Her body mass was so great, her muscle so dense, her body so complex, she weighed three times as much as ordinary-born people of a similar size but with none of their cumbersome bulk, gifted with hybrid muscle, crossbred from multiple species including the mandibles of the trap jaw ant, an insect that could lift a hundred times its own body weight. Her bones were adapted from the rhino femur, the strongest bone in the animal kingdom. Wrapped around the muscle and bone were layers of newly adapted brown adipose tissues – remarkable fat cells that could break down on command, generating heat far beyond the fat cells of ordinary-born humans. Hope Town was tremendously proud of her, seeing her as the saviour of a humbled species. Yet despite this adulation she seemed to have no sense of her own superiority. She was indifferent to admiration and uncertain whether the various hopes attached to her could be fulfilled.

'I'm just a girl,' she would say, but no one believed it. Echo was the future.

The bell rang for the end of school, a bronze hand-held bell, carried by a student around the corridors like a town ringer of old. The academic year stretched across the autumn and winter months with twelve-hour school days and classes running seven days a week. In the permanent darkness there was nothing else to do except study; there were no phones, no televisions, no personal computers, and most residences were without power. More importantly, every child understood that their education wasn't merely about their personal ambitions or individual life chances; the future of society depended on their success. With a population in decline, every student mattered. None of them could fathom what school had been like in the past with hours of wasted time, bad behaviour and truancy, a time when schools presumed that only a minority would go on to be important people. These children were not only the hardest working; they also made up their own forms of amusement, whether inside the school or outside.

From devising games to play, telling stories or composing music, these students never knew boredom, and never suffered from the memory of everything that had been lost.

Today was Echo's last day of school. These ice-siblings, born together in McMurdo, had grown up together in Hope Town. Though the class shared many genetic adaptations, Echo stood apart as the most extreme, the most changed, the most evolved, different even among the most different people ever created. Some argued, as her parents did, that she stood proudly on the outer edge of what it was to be human. Others suggested that she'd passed that point; not an ice-adapted person, but something entirely other, deserving of a new name. Having reached the age of sixteen the students of this ice-adapted class were being summoned back to McMurdo City – their place of creation, where they would take up prominent roles in the Cold People Project. None of the children wanted to leave Hope Town, but there was no question that McMurdo was the hub of innovation, the Silicon Valley of Antarctica, and all the best brains were required to move there as soon as they became adults. In addition, every year, the very best ordinary-born students from the Peninsula would join them. If they were ambitious, to be selected by McMurdo was the highest honour, whether because of their academic brilliance, to work as a scientist, or their physical prowess, to maintain the facility. McMurdo Station was the dream – the great Antarctic dream. Aside from enjoying the many privileges of life there, compared to the rudimentary life on the Peninsula, it was a chance to be involved in the frontline of the survival of the species. If extinction could be rapid, evolution had only ever been gradual. The challenge was whether McMurdo could compress an evolutionary process that normally took millions of years, to be the first species to achieve evolution as rapid as their extinction.

Echo's teacher was Professor Lili, originally an academic from Shanghai and one of the oldest people in Hope Town. Seventy years old, the only survivor from her family, she'd lost four fingers to frostbite in the first winter on the ice. She lived on the school premises, sleeping in the library, under a Van Gogh original. There were no computers in the school; computers were as fragile as people, vulnerable to the cold and could only be maintained in specially built accommodation, forcing the teachers to pass on information through story-telling and hard copies of texts, handled with as much care as sacred scrolls, since they couldn't be replaced. There were no publishing houses, no timber for paper and no new books. Utterly devoted to her class of ice-adapted children, Professor Lili bid farewell to them:

'Class, this is our last lesson. You will now graduate to McMurdo City and I might never see you again. Our time together is at an end. I will miss you very much. It's been an honour teaching you. I will try my best to follow your progress in McMurdo and perhaps one day I might visit you. Let me say this – if our future is to be people like you, then I feel hope.'

As the ice-adapted students left this stone classroom for the last time, Professor Lili asked Echo to stay behind. The other children felt no jealousy despite the favouritism, accustomed to the way ordinary-borns were drawn to her. Alone, Professor Lili took Echo's hand, an inappropriate thing for a teacher to do but Lili had never touched her remarkable skin and this was her last chance. With frost-damaged fingers, she held her student's powerful hands, studying them like a fortune teller.

'Do you remember the lesson I taught? About San Nicolas Island? The population had declined until finally only one woman remained on the island. She'd survived in isolation, alone for eighteen years.'

Echo nodded.

'Yes, I remember the lesson. She was the last of her kind.'

'Echo, you're the first of your kind and the last. I don't know what kind of genetic advances they've made in McMurdo. I don't know what this new generation of Cold People will be like. But I do know that you're special. More special than even the scientists realize.'

As she said goodbye, Professor Lili, a woman who'd once enjoyed promenades by the Huangpu River with her husband and her two children, felt like she was losing her family for a second time. Echo gave her mentor a hug, feeling her fragile body in her powerful arms. Her teacher was crying. Waiting for the professor to stop, she wondered how such sensitive, delicate creatures had survived for so long.

THE ANTARCTIC PENINSULA
HOPE TOWN
WORDIE HOUSE
SAME DAY

WORDIE HOUSE WAS ONE OF Hope Town's most prestigious properties, now occupied by one of the community's most prominent families – Liza, Atto and their daughter Echo. They were a family known for their contribution to society, their kindness and willingness to help anyone who called on them for support. Their house was named after James Wordie, the chief geologist on Shackleton's expedition. Shackleton was a revered historical figure, admired as a supreme survivor of the cold having endured four hundred and ninety-seven days on the ice with primitive equipment and, most crucially of all, losing none of his team. Built nearly a hundred years ago, the house was among the oldest manmade structures anywhere in Antarctica, evocative of ancient Icelandic fishing cottages, ducked low out of the winds, the walls made from the reclaimed timbers of abandoned whaling stations in the Antarctic tradition of repurposing everything and wasting nothing. Once located on Winter Island, several hundred miles north, the ancient structure had been dismantled and carried south, too valuable to leave behind, reconstructed as part of Hope Town as a symbol of survival and intended to inspire. Situated outside the city sprawl, at night the house had a fairy-tale feel, framed against the stars with a piglet curl of smoke from the chimney. All accommodation allocations were decided by the Housing Committee at Hope Town's Parliament, the authority which sought to best match families and their homes. Since accommodation was in short supply, almost everyone shared, and if the combination of occupants was judged correctly, this act of sharing was found to improve the quality of people's lives. No one was ever alone, conversation and interests were carefully balanced, and if someone fell sick, the others looked after them. If any groupings of people fell short of those standards, if there was friction or tension, they were quickly rearranged. Liza and Atto had been given the honour of living in this house as a celebration of their love story, people who'd found each other during the Exodus, a love story that had known only a single week of warmth and twenty years of cold. This historic house was assigned to them as a celebration of Liza's achievements as a doctor in the most rudimentary of hospitals and Atto's achievements as a fisherman in the most dangerous of waters, but mostly as a celebration of their daughter, Echo – a house from the past suitable for a family of the future.

Trying to start a family had been the hardest struggle of their life, harder even than the Exodus itself. During their first years of marriage Liza had given birth to three children. All three had died, the eldest reaching her first birthday before passing away as if some inner voice had whispered that this new world was not for her. After the death of her third child the grief was so intense, Liza fell into depression. Hope Town had distinguished itself as a settlement not only defined by its bohemian culture, but by its deep community ties, everyone rallying around those in need – no one was ever overlooked, no matter their age, their occupation or their perceived status. The town tried everything to help Liza, from musical therapy to conventional therapy. Though the town's medical community was not in favour of using anti-depressive medication, not out of principle but out of practicality – there was only a limited supply. For this reason alone, they needed to find alternative answers to the depression; they couldn't medicate their way out of the problem. Because of Liza's importance as a doctor, she was offered the antidepressant drug amitriptyline, which she'd refused. The intensity of her feelings had taken Liza by surprise. As the only surviving member of her family, the urge had become powerful, as if a child were a means of being close to the family she'd lost. With no family from her past and no family for the future she'd begun to lose weight and struggled to keep warm. Taking a leave of absence from the hospital, she'd become housebound one winter. Atto hadn't left her side, feeding her the broth of albatross bones, and pleading with her to live. If she died, he would die, of that there was no doubt; he would follow her.

At this point, Liza had been selected by McMurdo City for the Cold People Project.

On their second epic journey together, Liza and Atto had travelled across the continent in a motorized snow vehicle along with fifty other volunteers from the three Survivor Towns, travelling hundreds of miles to McMurdo City. After the bohemian energy of Hope Town, their capital city came as a shock; it was so completely unlike the Peninsula settlements. There were orderly grids of streets. There was traffic and stop signs. There were purpose-built laboratories with the latest technology. There was a formality about the city and its occupants, none of the bright murals on the walls of the houses, far closer to the capital cities of the old world. The people were proud and ambitious, stressed with the pressures of work; they were busy people with big dreams.

Standing with Atto, holding his hand, she'd listened as some of the world's greatest scientists explained that the women had volunteered to be part of a new medical programme, to give birth to a genetically modified child – a child adapted to survive in the cold. Though Atto had been apprehensive, Liza had readily agreed to the procedure, excited by the prospect of a family, in whatever form that family might take.

Her pregnancy was accelerated, five months rather than nine, and the experience had been nothing like her previous three pregnancies. She had experienced fevers and hallucinations. After three months the foetus had grown so heavy that Liza could no longer walk for fear of damaging her spine. After five months, a caesarean had been performed and she'd barely survived as her ice-adapted daughter had been brought into this world. Holding her newborn daughter she'd marvelled at her weight, at the child's stillness, not helpless but alert from the first second of her life. Her eyes were different to human eyes, not a single lens but hundreds of cells, made up of visual units called ommatidia, a matrix of tiny hexagonal cells – dragonfly eyes. Her skin was smooth, glossy and tough. On closer inspection, she realized the skin wasn't skin at all but lizard-like scales, octangular in shape. Even more amazing was the way they changed colour: white when the child needed to keep warm and black when she needed to radiate an excess of heat. Perfectly smooth, she had no hair of any kind, nor would she ever grow any. She never got sad and she never got sick.

As a mother, Liza didn't feel the slightest sense of alienation; she felt love – unqualified and uncomplicated love. Liza and Atto were parents again. She'd wanted to name her daughter after her younger sister Emma but this was considered unwise, as looking back was strongly discouraged. No, a new name for a new girl, an unusual name for such an unusual girl. So she was called Echo. Liza had nervously expected the scientists to take the child from her but during the five months of her pregnancy they'd made such advances in genetic engineering that by the time Echo was born they'd moved on. They'd studied the baby, making various observations: her thought processes developed at a rapid speed, she was walking after one week, progressing in months as an ordinary child might do in years. The scientists were particularly proud of her new skin. Since ninety percent of heat was lost through a person's skin, they explained to the new parents that their daughter's scales acted like a coat of chain-mail armour, protecting her from external impacts but also trapping heat. In addition, her heart was far bigger and stronger than a human heart, able to regulate her pulse, slowing it down in periods of extreme cold, pumping a new blend of modified blood that contained a natural anti-freeze found in Antarctic notothenioid fish. Liza embraced all these facts as if they were gifts from the gods, which in a way, they were; the greatest gifts of all, protection against the cold. As it turned out, Echo's ice-adaptations were merely the beginning of the Cold People genetic adaptation project. Like a prototype for a vehicle never put into mass production, she was no longer needed.

After months of study, Lisa, Atto and Echo returned to Hope Town, making space for the new women arriving and for more advanced genetic modifications. Of the fifty women who'd travelled to McMurdo, only thirty-nine returned. Each of their cold-adapted children was different and they compared their offspring with curiosity and affection as if they were siblings of a kind. There were whispers about one ice-adapted child, born with such a ferocious temperament he'd killed his mother as she slept and had eaten much of her before being interrupted. The parents had been warned that these children were unpredictable. There were no guidelines on how to be a parent to an ice-adapted child. Liza didn't care. She had a reason to live. And her name was Echo.

THE ANTARCTIC PENINSULA
SOUTH OF HOPE TOWN
THE COMPASS GLACIERS
SAME DAY

ECHO STOPPED TO SURVEY HER surroundings, approaching the beach where the Compass Glacier entered the sea. Located south of Hope Town, the tributary glacier was nine miles long and two miles wide, originally named after Jean Rotz, a sixteenth-century French chart-maker who designed one of the earliest magnetic compasses. The glacier fed into the much larger Airy Glacier, twenty nautical miles long and six nautical miles wide, named after George Biddell Airy, a nineteenth-century British Astronomer Royal, for his work on magnetic compasses. Since no one in Hope Town felt any connection to these obscure historical figures chosen by long-lost colonial empires, the glaciers had been renamed the Compass Glaciers and they were a perilous place for two students to hang out after school even if one of them was adapted for the cold.

Echo turned to see how far Tetu was behind. He was her closest friend, perhaps her only true friend. An ordinary-born, at eighteen years old he was two years older than Echo and, at six foot three, almost as tall as she was. His parents were from the country once known as South Africa, both high-ranking politicians in the former government, members of the African National Congress. In comparison to other nations, South Africa had saved a higher percentage of its population, helped by its proximity to Antarctica – so close, in fact, that some ships had been able to complete return trips in the effort to shuttle as many of its people as possible to the tip of the Peninsula. It had also made a strategic decision, unlike many other countries, to save the poor as well as the elite, not out of kindness but believing that those who lived in the townships – Soweto, Tembisa, Katlehong – were some of the toughest survivors on the planet and they stood a greater chance of figuring out how to cope with the hardships of life on Antarctica than the pampered rich.

Tetu had been born to two ordinary parents, and though he was an ordinary-born there was nothing ordinary about him. He was a prodigy, possessing an exceptional mind without the help of genetic adaptations. A person might presume he'd be as popular as he was handsome, however he was considered obtuse, an awkward young man, uncomfortable in social situations and not an easy fit with the good cheer of Hope Town. He was prone to bouts of melancholy even before he'd lost both his parents. Life on the ice suited no ordinary-born, whose bodies and minds weren't intended for this continent. That said, people who were sociable with an even disposition coped better during the extended periods of confinement, crammed together with only their songs and stories to pass the time. Echo didn't mind Tetu's singular manner or lonesome ways. In reply, he was one of the few people who wasn't fixated on her genetic adaptations – he'd never asked to touch her scale-skin or stare into her hexagonal eyes. In their five years of friendship, they'd never lied to each other, never let each other down and never had a fight. Meanness and spite were unfathomable to them, as they were to most people in Hope Town.

Though Tetu was determinedly trying to keep pace with Echo, it was an impossible task – trudging in his Sorel Glacier boots fitted with steel crampons. With a dense rubber sole and waterproof shell, the boots were able to protect him against freezing temperatures of below fifty degrees. Many lives had been lost fighting over these boots in the early months of that first winter, with most of the people arriving on Antarctica hopelessly ill-equipped for the extreme cold. But after twenty years and a collapse in the population, there were now heaps of old boots and gloves in the Exchange Houses where spare supplies were patched up and repaired. People could apply for any item, depending on their level of need. Ice-born children found nothing odd about these Exchange Houses. To some they even had a magic about them, all these strange brands which once signified so much, all these lurid colours and synthetic materials which could no longer be manufactured, a museum to a lost world, artefacts from another time and place. But to those who knew mankind's history, these Exchange Houses and the heaped piles of personal items taken from the dead – spectacles, boots, socks, scarves – washed and ready for the next wearer, had a horror about them and many refused to go inside.

In contrast to her friend, Echo was walking barefoot. As a rule, around other people, she dressed as if she were an ordinary-born, abiding by the convention of clothes. Her parents struggled with the sight of their only child walking barefoot on the ice. It frightened them even though they knew that the scales on the soles of their daughter's feet were far tougher than the synthetic plastics of any manmade boot, that her pancreas produced the natural anti-freeze glycoprotein, that her body was truly exceptional at regulating against extreme temperatures – that she was created for this cold, not surviving it or tolerating it, but thriving in it. As a young girl Echo had tried to wear thermal boots perhaps in the hope of fitting in with the other children, but rather than her body regulating against the cold, she was regulating against excess heat. Unable to perspire, heat was as dangerous to her as the cold was to the ordinary-borns. In the end she found a compromise in the Exchange Houses, opting for a pair of size fourteen burgundy Doc Martin boots entirely useless for ordinary-borns with no insulation, worn as a gesture to show that she was still one of them, oblivious to their place in fashion history as the footwear of outsiders.

Catching up, Tetu stood beside her, pointing towards the waters of the bay. She stared at the horizon seeing nothing except a skyline of flat-top icebergs, grey waves and grey clouds.

'What am I looking for?'

Tetu had often heard people claim that Echo was frustratingly neutral, never annoyed, never angry, adapted so she didn't suffer the tumult of ordinary human emotions. But if you took the time to get to know her, this simply wasn't true. Her characteristics were subtle. She was impatient, always wanting her questions answered directly. Sometimes he'd wilfully meander just to solicit a rise, and he enjoyed her version of irritation, a shift in tone so delicate most people missed it entirely.

'Not on the water. Under it. A light.'

'What kind of light?'

'Not our kind.'

Tetu took off his backpack and pulled out a small antique mahogany box, an incongruous item set among emergency rations and survival equipment. As though presenting a gift, he opened the lid of the box and Echo leaned forward, peering at fragments of alien technology, a collection veined with capillaries of mauve and jade, which continued to pulse despite being broken and separate from any obvious power source. She picked up the largest of these shards, bringing the light close to her eyes.

'The law states that all alien discoveries must be turned over to McMurdo.'

'That's the whole point. I'm going to hand them over. And hope that they pick me.'

'Why wouldn't they pick you? You're one of the smartest people in Hope Town.'

'McMurdo is taking fewer ordinary-born people. They're only interested in ice-adapted people now. And everyone will have told them how difficult I am. If they don't take me . . . I can't imagine my future on the Peninsula. I won't survive in Hope Town.'

'What's wrong with Hope Town?'

'For a start, everyone is under so much pressure to be happy all the time. Our only job is joy, planning the next music festival, or organizing sports leagues. What are the opportunities? Working on the algae farms, or the canneries, or the recycle plants? I get the survival strategy; life is to be enjoyed and it's a smart approach. But I can't be here, in this town, stitching seal pelts, looking forward to the next party. That can't be my life.'

'What do you want your life to be?'

'Something bigger.'

What he didn't say was that he couldn't imagine a life without her.

Tetu's parents had both been taken by the cold when he'd been young and there were many orphaned children living with foster parents; it was rare for a family not to have at least one adopted child. He'd skipped from family to family over the years, never finding anyone he could settle with. Recently he'd stopped even unpacking his bag, certain that each placement would last only a few months. Since the death of his parents the only unbroken relationship in his life had been with Echo. They hiked together, explored the mountains together. They'd always watch the last sunset of summer and the first sunrise after winter. For the first time in his life, he'd experienced happiness. He was in love with someone who might not even experience love in the same way.

Echo undressed, remarking:

'These clothes are useless in the water.'

Trying not to stare, Tetu mumbled:

'Yes, I guess they are.'

Standing naked, her scales giving her the appearance of wearing an elegant outer shell, she turned to Tetu.

'Are you embarrassed by the fact I'm naked?'

Silent for a moment, he eventually overcame his awkwardness.

'Echo, you don't have to ask every question that comes into your head.'

'I'm curious.'

'No, I'm not embarrassed. I'm trying to be respectful.'

'You can look, I don't mind.'

She thought to herself how thin-skinned ordinary-born people were – skin too thin for this cold, too thin for conversation. He touched her arm.

'Be careful. The ocean is dangerous. Even for you.'

'You are much more likely to die, fully clothed, standing here, than I am swimming in that water.'

Tetu laughed. He often thought that Echo was funny even if she didn't mean to be.

'*I'll* be careful, then.'

Echo perched on the edge of the ice and, like an Antarctic mermaid, slipped into the freezing waters. Watching her disappear Tetu crouched out of the wind. No doubt about it: he was in love. He'd do anything for her; a useless sentiment since she was the most self-sufficient person he'd ever known. She needed nothing from him, neither his help nor his advice, yet he felt she needed him nonetheless. He didn't believe she was unaware of his feelings. But biologically and scientifically, what kind of love was possible between an ice-adapted person and an ordinary-born? Perhaps such romances had taken place in McMurdo, but not in Hope Town. Almost certainly she desired someone more like her, someone who could swim naked in freezing ocean waters and skip barefoot across glaciers. Regardless, he loved her, and if they were separated, his heart would be broken.

THE ANTARCTIC PENINSULA
UNDER THE WATERS OF WORDIE BAY
SAME DAY

A N ICE SHELF HAD ONCE enclosed Wordie Bay, but it had collapsed twelve years before the alien occupation, brought about by rising sea temperatures – a body of ice between Cape Jeremy and Mount Edgell breaking apart and disappearing in a matter of months. One of the most often repeated theories behind the occupation was environmental. The alien species had arrived to rescue this planet from humankind's stewardship and events such as the ice shelf collapse had acted as a Gaia-like planetary distress signal, with humankind dispossessed of the planet for violating the terms of our lease, neglectful tenants shunted off the temperate continents and relegated to exile in the cold. There was no purpose to this speculation, since the alien occupiers had never explained their actions and seemingly had no interest in humanity except to move it out of their way; the debate about their possible motivation was no more than an idle topic of conversation over a game of cards or a glass of ash-fermented seal milk. Nonetheless, it had been observed that all measures of temperature – air, sea and ice – were dropping sharply, and with the end of mankind's reign the world had undoubtably become a colder place.

Having no natural buoyancy, Echo sank to the bottom of the bay, landing with a puff of silt around her feet. Where the Compass Glaciers calved into the ocean there was a jawbone of ice, the gums lined with algae, feasted upon by unfathomably large swarms of krill. On the seabed, in between the forests of kelp, was a disco floor of orange sea stars and shimmering sea urchins. Spider crabs hastily retreated from her, no doubt scared that she might be hunting them since they were a popular delicacy in Hope Town. A large silver octopus took no evasive action, passing close by, staring at her with enigmatic, bulbous eyes, entirely unafraid even though they, too, were regularly caught, their flesh fried to a tempura crisp in salty seal-fat oil. Echo, normally so measured in her reactions, couldn't be in the same room when they were being eaten – she found the sight distressing, and from this visceral reaction her mother had deduced that her biological composition must take some genetic element from the octopus. This mystery had puzzled Echo until she saw her own blood for the first time. With tough skin and excellent co-ordination, she'd never experienced the kind of scratches and grazes that were part of an ordinary-born human's childhood. The first time she saw her blood was when her period began and she'd discovered that her blood was blue – little spots of sky dotted across her white-scale skin. Antarctic octopus blood was also blue, from the high concentration of the copper-based protein hemocyanin, which enabled it to continue transporting oxygen even at freezing temperatures.

Though the genetic mystery was solved, the sight of her blue blood had troubled Echo – an expression of how alien she really was, as if being human meant that your blood ran red. The only person she'd confided in was Tetu, hoping he'd be nerdish and academic about it. To her surprise he'd reacted emotionally, and she realized in that moment that he'd been contemplating their compatibility as sexual partners or, to put it less scientifically, that he might be in love. He'd tried to cover his feelings by joking that 'blue blood' used to be a phrase denoting royalty, that she was a member of Antarctica's royal family, an Ice Princess, and he was a humble peasant on this land, a man who should bow before her. Even his attempt at humour was revealing, the joke touching upon the belief that he didn't feel that he was worthy of her, that the biological barriers between them couldn't be bridged by affection alone.

Swimming along the seabed towards the flickers of alien light ahead, Echo thought about asking these difficult questions when she arrived at McMurdo City. She would meet her creators, stand before them, ask a long series of questions and listen as her place in this world became clear. It was for this reason that she admired Tetu so much. He had no wise creators he could quiz for answers, he had no family, he had nothing except the wisdom he'd worked for and the ambition to be more than a survivor. Though she rarely paid him a compliment, she decided it was time to tell him, when she handed him this alien fragment, not that she loved him – she wasn't confident of using that word – but that she was proud to be his friend.

The freezing water was sapping her heat more rapidly than the air, water being a far more powerful cooling agent, and her body responded by unlocking the heat stored in her genetically altered adipose tissue, a form of fat found in newborn babies who were particularly vulnerable to the cold since they were unable to shiver. These cells broke down on command, generating heat through highly specialized non-shivering thermogenesis. Most ordinary-born adults had very little adipose tissue, but Echo's entire body was lined with an enhanced version created in the McMurdo labs. In Antarctica, fat was life, and her fat cells were the most advanced ever created.

She spotted a second octopus and then a third, curious as to what was attracting these solitary and highly intelligent creatures. They seemed to be drawn to the alien light and, reaching the fragment, she found a cluster of them, their tentacles wrapped around it. She stood, watching them for a time, before gently plunging her arm into their writhing mass. As she grabbed hold of it the octopuses travelled up her arms, across her body and onto her face, one sitting on her bald head like a hat. She carried on regardless, allowing them to coil around her, finally feeling the peculiar texture of the alien technology and pulling it free. She studied its luminescent pulses. Tetu would be pleased: it was far larger than any he had found before, a discovery of enormous importance, and one which would surely secure his selection to McMurdo City.

About to head back to the shore, she felt the waters around her swirl. Something large was behind her, its body heat displacing the cold, and she turned around, coming face to face with the black and white snout of a female orca flanked by her pod. Instinctively Echo's scales mirrored the orca's swirls of black and white, perhaps as a form of communication or a sign of friendship. She'd never been so close to an orca before, a formidable hunter known to steal seals while they were resting on the ice and even to kill young blue whales, devouring the tongue, leaving the rest of the carcass to ribbon worms and bottom feeders. With the octopuses still coiled like bracelets around her wrists, Echo placed the palm of her hand against the orca's head. With this physical contact she had some understanding of this creature's thoughts; it wasn't exact – not speech, but a generalized impression. The orca was curious, though not about the alien light; it was curious about her.

What are you?

Echo opened her mind, trying to communicate her response:

I don't know.

The orca flinched, with a powerful kick of its tail, disappearing into the darkness. Something strange had entered the water, something which didn't belong. It was Tetu.

THE ANTARCTIC PENINSULA
UNDER THE WATERS OF WORDIE BAY
THE COMPASS GLACIERS
SAME DAY

ECHO KICKED OFF FROM THE seabed, arms outstretched, powering through the water at Olympian speed. Reaching Tetu's body, she scooped him up in her arms, sensing his body temperature as soon as she touched his skin. His core was thirty degrees and dropping rapidly. He'd lost consciousness, he was unresponsive. With no idea how he could've ended up in the ocean, she stood on the seabed, lifting him clear of the water – his body lank across her arms. He was an athletic, formidable man, muscular from his treks, and fit, but compared to her, vulnerable to the cold, unable to conserve his heat. Not only could she feel the heat seeping out of him, she could see it, too – plumes of colour leaving his body as though his spirit were departing.

Emerging from the ocean, with nowhere dry to set him down, she bounded across the glacier, her bare feet cracking the ice as she ran, leaving fissured footprints across the surface. His core temperature slipped again; his heartbeat was becoming irregular. Reaching the first outcrop of rock, she laid him down, assessing his body to be in a state of hypothermic shock. Perhaps in the hospital with her mother's expertise there might have been a way to revive him, but not out here in this desolate place. She couldn't understand how he'd been so careless, how he'd slipped. There was no storm, no freak waves, no unusually strong winds. Even running she couldn't make it to the hospital in time. In what felt like despair, an emotion she'd never experienced before, she picked him up, clasping him close to her perhaps only with the idea that she didn't want him to die alone.

As she hugged him, she became aware of her body converting tissue cells into energy – far more than required for her own needs, more than she'd ever converted before – a chain reaction rippling across her body, the scales of her skin becoming hot, her body generating surplus heat as if answering the needs of his body, radiating this heat into Tetu, an exchange of such ferocity that his damp clothes began to steam. Not stopping to understand what was taking place, Echo tore off Tetu's clothes so that his body would be in direct contact with her own, nothing between them, transferring this warmth to him, passing through his skin into his blood. His core temperature was rising – thirty-three, thirty-four – reaching normal body temperature, bringing him to a fever, sweat dripping from his temples until his eyes opened. Shocked, she released him from her grasp, his skin steaming, his hair lichen-dry, his whole body covered in sweat. Allowing him to compose himself, her scales began cooling down, her body returning to equilibrium. She asked a series of orientation questions:

'Can you tell me your name?'

Tetu remained silent, disorientated, looking at his steaming skin as though it wasn't his own.

'Can you tell me your name?'

Speaking softly, his throat parched, his voice creaking, he said:

'I'm in love with you.'

Echo handed him his clothes.

'Your name is Tetu. And you're delirious.'

He accepted the clothes.

'What happened?'

'Don't get angry.'

'I never get angry.'

'Yes, you do. In your own way.'

'What could I be angry about?'

'I jumped in.'

She puzzled over this admission.

'I don't understand.'

'I jumped into the water.'

'It was *deliberate*?'

'Yes.'

'Why?'

'To prove a theory.'

'What theory?'

'You can do more than conserve your heat, Echo; you can control it. I've seen snow melt around your fingertips and then freeze again. I've seen a breeze pass over your head and come out full of snowflakes on the other side.'

'That was a test?'

'And look what you did!'

'You almost died!'

'But I didn't. I'm alive. Because of you.'

'You're right. I am angry.'

'Don't be. My heart is beating with your heat – my brain, my lungs, my blood, they're alive with your warmth.'

When Echo thought back on the moment that she'd hugged Tetu's dying body, how she'd brought him back to life, sharing her heat with him, it was true: the feeling had been extraordinary, a sense of togetherness. She'd never felt like this before. Uneasy with the emotional confusion she was experiencing, she grabbed his wrist.

'I can take it back. My heat. I could draw it out of you and freeze you to that rock.'

And she could see it happening, drawing all the heat from his body, sucking it out of him until his blood turned to ice and his body turned brittle and shattered like glass. Shocked at the power of the image, she released his wrist and turned away. She wasn't sure how long she looked out over the ocean, but when she turned back to Tetu, he was fully dressed. He said:

'I wasn't crazy. Or delirious. I love you. And I've loved you for a long time.'

'You can't be in love with me, Tetu.'

'Why not?'

'You don't even know what I am.'

THE ANTARCTIC PENINSULA
HOPE TOWN
WORDIE HOUSE
SAME DAY

Sᴛᴀɴᴅɪɴɢ ᴀᴛ ᴛʜᴇ ᴡʀᴏᴜɢʜᴛ-ɪʀᴏɴ sᴛᴏᴠᴇ, stirring a pot of algae soup, Liza worried that her daughter hadn't returned home. Sensing his wife's concerns, Atto stood up from the table where he'd been re-stitching the lining of his jacket and wrapped his arms around her, feeling the tension in her body.

'She's fine. She's always fine.'

Liza turned around and kissed him.

'Worrying is part of being a parent. I can't turn it off just because she's strong.'

'I can't either. But she's never even grazed her knee.'

'Echo can get into dangerous situations ordinary-born people can't. She's up a mountain, she's exploring icebergs. She takes risks because she has no fear of the cold.'

'If she wasn't five times my strength, I'd ground her.'

'You've always been too soft on her.'

'You've always been too tough on her. I reckon that means, together, we're perfect.'

Atto kissed Liza and returned to work on his jacket. He was a believer in the miracle of their love story – a partnership forged out of exceptional circumstances. Under pressure they were a remarkable team. During those early years in Antarctica, they'd been inseparable, struggling against the ravages of the cold while trying to build a society out of the ruins of the old. Their efforts had been at the centre of shaping Hope Town, arguing that there were many necessities to human survival. They'd been ridiculed by the other two settlements, but during the winter their people survived while others succumbed to depression. In Hope Town survival had never been reduced to a calorie count and a question of warmth.

With almost no technological infrastructure in Hope Town, there was no way of contacting Echo. There were no personal phones. Communication networks were rudimentary and limited to linking the three Survivor Towns with McMurdo City who would send telegram-style messages, issuing instructions, a collection date for the volunteers or a demand for a crop harvest only grown on the Peninsula – the flowers and lichen on the most northern rock outcrops. There was no longer any orbital satellite network, destroyed during the alien occupation. Officials used wires and radios as they had done in the past. To play together, children would set meeting places – six in the afternoon by the last house on Cannery Row – and gather there in snow boots and seal-pelt coats, waiting for their friends to assemble before setting off on their cross-country skis. Adults would make appointments and worry, with good reason, when the other person didn't show. A spoken arrangement became a contract; people took them seriously, aware that they couldn't push it back thirty minutes or simply not show, explaining it away with a text message. Missing an appointment in Hope Town was taboo: the first thought was always that the person might have died. After an hour, normally, search parties were dispatched. Echo was six hours late.

Atto asked:

'Was she alone?'

'She was with Tetu.'

'He's in love with her, you know that, right?'

'Everyone knows that.'

'Everyone except her.'

'She knows it. She just doesn't know what to make of it.'

'Did you have that talk?'

'That talk about love?'

'Yes.'

'She didn't say much.'

'What was your impression?'

'That she imagines she'll be alone. That she'll never be in love. Never find a partner. Never make love. Never give birth. What could I say? There might be others like you in McMurdo?'

'There are ice-adapted students here.'

'None like her.'

'Have you ever told her the story of how we met?'

'No. Have you?'

'Yeah. She asked about us.'

Liza turned around, walking to Atto, sitting on the chair beside him, resting against his shoulder.

'What did you say?'

'I told her what happened.'

'What was her response?'

'She wanted to know why I came back for you.'

'Why did you come back?'

'I had to.'

Liza pondered this for a moment, before asking:

'What did she make of that?'

'She seemed to understand.'

'I find it hard to talk about the past without crying.'

'It's okay to cry. Let her see you cry. There's nothing wrong in that.'

'Except I've never seen our daughter cry. I'm not sure if she can.'

Recalling the play *Eumenides*, Liza thought about the argument that a mother was no more than an incubator of life and that the character and soul of a child came exclusively from the father. Written before genetics, debunked by modern science, this was, in fact, partly true in the case of Liza – there was none of her in Echo; they hadn't used her eggs; she'd been created by the scientists in McMurdo and Liza's body had merely housed this creation, bringing the child to term, nearly dying in the process but contributing nothing of herself. Atto had no time for this line of thought. Echo hadn't grown inside him, they hadn't used any of his genetics, moreover Echo had never behaved as though her real parents were the scientists in McMurdo, she'd never questioned their right to bring her up. Underlying Liza's insecurity wasn't a need to be biologically connected to their daughter. Adoption was the bedrock of this survivor society; everyone was family. It was the impression that her daughter didn't need parents at all, that she'd been born fully independent, a person with no need of people. Liza said:

'She's leaving us. I don't think she'll ever come back.'

'She's not leaving us. She's going to college.'

'They created her. Those scientists. They have answers. They can talk to her in ways we never can. She's excited to go. Because she's never really been ours.'

'That's not true. She loves us. She loves this town. She loves these people, even if she expresses love differently to other people.'

As though she were an Antarctica version of the legendary Amazonian warriors returning from battle, Echo entered the house naked from the waist up, her shoulders and scalp dusted with snow. She'd given most of her clothes to Tetu after the heat she'd transferred into his body had faded and he'd started to shiver. Supporting him as a soldier might an injured comrade, she'd helped him back to Hope Town. He'd refused to go to the hospital since his hypothermia was self-inflicted; questions would be asked about his state of mind and Echo had never been able to lie. Taking him back to his residence, a cabin on a former cruise ship now permanently moored against the bay, he'd collapsed into his sleeping bag, exhausted and delirious, telling her that it was okay if she didn't love him; she probably needed a partner who could walk barefoot across glaciers and swim under icebergs. Perched on the side of his narrow bunkbed, she assessed his home life: a cramped cabin, home to a family of four, crisscrossed with washing, a bedsheet partitioning the space. His foster parents were kind people, concerned with his welfare, busy with a family of their own to look after. No wonder Tetu worked so hard to escape this place, she thought, spending so much time either studying or exploring the surroundings – he was a man in search of a home of his own. She waited for him to fall asleep before once more stabilizing his temperature, feeling her warmth flow through her fingers into his body.

Inside Wordie House her scales turned black, her body radiating an excess of heat. She couldn't remain in this warmth for long even if her meals were always served cold. Out of necessity she slept outside, the thick walls of this well-made historic house creating an uncomfortable heat, too intense for her despite the fact her parents kept the temperature as low as they could tolerate so that she could spend as much time as possible with them. Often in the morning Liza would find her daughter curled up in the snow as if it were her bed. Without saying a word about being late or why she was only partially dressed, Echo sat on the chair that Atto had reinforced to support her weight, popping out the wedges of compacted ice from between her toes. Liza couldn't help but smile.

'You can't walk in this late, half naked, without an explanation.'

Echo had never been prudish. Modesty was a trait of the ordinary-born; she had no problem being naked in front of her parents and on a practical level preferred being naked in terms of regulating her temperature. Most parents would panic if their sixteen-year-old daughter returned with her clothes in tatters, but even Liza accepted no ordinary-born man on the Peninsula could lay a finger on Echo. Atto asked:

'Where have you been?'

'The Compass Glaciers.'

'What were you doing there?'

'Searching for fragments of alien technology.'

'Why?'

'Tetu collects them. He thinks it will improve his chances of being selected by McMurdo.'

Liza moved close to her daughter, picking an ice crystal from the grooves between her scales.

'Have you been in the ocean again?'

'Yes. The fragment was underwater. I swam down and retrieved it for him.'

'The oceans are dangerous even for you. The ice can move – your escape holes can close. You're not invincible. I know you feel it, I know you feel it compared to us, but you need air the same as us. You need warmth, too.'

Once, when Echo was much younger, she'd wanted to find out how long she could remain in the cold, to better understand her limits, hoping that if she experienced the sensation of being cold, she would feel more human. With this goal in mind she'd sat in the depths of a crevasse. Her heartbeat had slowed, her eyes had closed – she'd slipped into a controlled hibernation. Lost in that crevasse, she'd experienced dreams of walking across the white plateaus in search of the people who'd created her. She'd spent thirteen days in hibernation before Liza had found her. Echo had lost so much weight that she'd expended her entire reserves of adipose fat tissue – her scales were starting to discolour, neither black nor white but grey and flaking like autumn leaves. She was dying. Liza and Atto had been unable to carry her, even at a young age she was too heavy; instead, they'd set up camp around her, nursing her back to life, giving her bone broth served warm for the only time in her life. After recovering, she'd apologized, promising never to put them through that kind of pain again.

As Liza fetched a batch of frozen soup, Echo said:

'Tetu told me today.'

'What did he say?'

'That he loved me.'

'Did it come as a surprise?'

'No. I had some idea.'

'But you don't feel the same way?'

'The same way as him? No. He's my friend.'

'Nothing more?'

'What more could I feel for him?'

'You could feel love?'

'I'm not even sure what love feels like?'

Liza sat at the table, struggling with the question.

'It's different for everyone but everyone knows when they feel it.'

'Did you feel it when you saw each other?'

Atto nodded.

'I did, yes.'

Liza considered, and nodded.

'Yes, I knew there was something between us.'

'Can you describe it?'

Atto answered:

'It felt like ... there was only one person in Lisbon that day. For that second, your mother was the only person I could see.'

'I can't love Tetu.'

'Why not?'

'We're too different.'

'Different is okay.'

'We're not even the same species.'

'Who said that?'

Quoting the many textbooks she'd studied, Echo recited:

'*A species is defined as a group of living organisms consisting of individuals capable of exchanging genes or interbreeding.*'

'Those books were written a long time ago.'

'If I can't breed with an ordinary-born, if I'm unable to exchange my genes, I am not the same species.'

Atto said:

'You don't know that you can't have children with him.'

'I'm sure of it.'

'Why?'

'My blood is blue.'

Liza and Atto remained silent for a while. Finally Liza asked:

'Your blood is blue?'

'Like octopus blood, blue with copper so it can hold more oxygen.'

'When did you see your blood?'

'When my period started.'

'Why didn't you tell us?'

'I have blue blood. And scales for skin. I have dragonfly eyes. And rhino bone. I'm not human. I'm something else. Something with no name. Even if I felt love, even if I loved him, I can't make love to Tetu. I'm not the same as you. I'm not the same as him.'

Liza steadied her emotions. For a long time, she'd prepared for this conversation and, doing her best to hide her emotions, she pulled her chair close to Echo.

'I've been reading a lot about this subject. I came across a theory that describes the concept of different species not as a series of separate islands but as hills on a single landscape. You can call those hills different names, but we're all part of the same land – we're all formed out of the same genetic material.'

Echo considered this image.

'Maybe that's true. But, in that case, I am my own hill. I am alone. I'll always be alone.'

'Echo, listen to me very carefully. You will never be alone.'

THE ANTARCTIC PENINSULA
HOPE TOWN
WORDIE HOUSE
SAME DAY

T HE BOWL OF ALGAE AND Yeti crab soup was covered with an ice crust that shattered under a blow from Echo's spoon. Ravenously hungry after her swim, she crunched down on the steamed crab legs which she could digest in their entirety, her stomach capable of consuming foods that were either toxic or unpalatable to ordinary-born people, aided by enzymes taken from the stomach lining of a great white shark. Within minutes, Liza fetched her a second portion. Watching her mother return, Echo said:

'You're upset. And not because I swam in the sea.'

Liza was used to their daughter's remarkable levels of perception.

'Hope Town Parliament received a communication today. From McMurdo City. The transport will collect the graduating ice-adapted students at the start of the summer.'

'We always knew this day was coming.'

Atto added:

'We have a few weeks left. Let's make the most of them.'

Echo pointed out:

'You'll both be able to visit me.'

But Liza shook her head.

'McMurdo isn't like Hope Town. They don't place the same value on happiness and community. You imagine the scientists at McMurdo care about our visitation rights? You think they'll send a transport vehicle all the way across the continent for us? No parent has ever been allowed to visit their child after they've been taken to McMurdo. There will be no visits and no vacations. That's not the way McMurdo works. You're being taken from us.'

Echo pondered this.

'I don't know how things work in McMurdo, but know this: I will see you again, that I promise.'

'Echo, there is a mystery about McMurdo. Hundreds of women volunteer for the Cold People programme. I was offered the chance and I accepted the risks. I was also one of the last women to return. What's happened to the women after me? Why have so few of them come back?'

'What do you think is happening?'

'I almost died giving birth to you. My guess is that the genetic adaptations are now so extreme, very few of the women survive the birth. That's how McMurdo sees life. They'll do anything to figure out how humanity can survive.'

Upset by the conversation, Atto stood up.

'That's enough.'

Liza looked at him.

'What? Are we supposed to pretend?'

'Yes, we're supposed to pretend so that we don't ruin the days we have left. That's exactly what we should do, we should pretend.'

'Echo needs to know the truth. And the truth is the people at McMurdo are fanatics.'

Echo considered.

'Maybe that's the only way the species will survive.'

'Survive! We all say that word like … it explains anything. Like it justifies anything. But surviving at any cost is not surviving. Surviving means holding on to what is great about people. Our humanity, our love, our joy, our sense of fun.'

'Am I any of those things?' Echo asked.

'You're all of those things.'

'Those scientists made me. But I'm not theirs. You're my parents. And I promise: I will see you again.'

Shortly after Echo's birth, fewer and fewer ice-adapted children had returned to the Peninsula. Something had changed. McMurdo City continued to ask for volunteers from Hope Town women, but these women rarely returned. Once there had been delight amongst couples at being selected, but delight had changed into unease. No one knew how the Cold People Project had evolved. No citizen could ignore commands from McMurdo City; they were to be followed without question and any dissent meant expulsion from society. No one could live outside of the survivor cities. Nonetheless, the Hope Town Parliament had politely requested answers:

Please tell us what is happening to our people?

Why are they not returning?

Where are the ice-adapted children?

The answer was that the great scientists in McMurdo Station had made a startling breakthrough. They were now pursuing a radical new method of cold adaptation, not merely tinkering with a person's eyesight or the size of their heart; these were changes of an altogether different kind. Soon the population crisis would be solved; their sacrifices were not in vain. Their future was assured.

A new people are coming.

But that had been many years ago. And there was still no sign of these new people.

The conversation was interrupted by a tentative knock on the outer door. A family entered, two mothers, with two ordinary-born children. The older of the two mothers smiled, introducing the family.

'Good evening. Sorry for the interruption. My name is Anna, this is my family – I hope it's not an inconvenient time. We've come to see the famous Wordie House.'

In terms of living space, a house this size would normally contain four families. Concepts of personal space had been redefined after the Exodus; people now lived in each other's laps, sharing each other's heat, no longer with separate bedrooms and bathrooms. Liza and her family had been granted sole use of this remarkable house with one condition – the house remained a living museum and citizens of Hope Town were encouraged to visit. Many families accepted this offer, pretending to be interested in the old transistor radio or the mechanical typewriter, while really wanting to spend time with Echo. She'd always claimed that she didn't mind. However, the feeling of being stared at had reinforced the idea that she was something other. To soften the impact, Atto always took the lead during these visits. He'd spent years in Lisbon charming tourists and he'd gamely show the visitors around, reciting interesting facts and making jokes. Liza was less fond of the interruptions, partly because the people treated her daughter as though she were an item of wonder rather than a person, but also, watching her husband act as a tour guide, she felt a powerful recollection of her old life, of the family she'd lost, of that last holiday together in Europe – of the August warmth, that historic square, her sister's kiss on her cheek, her parents sipping drinks in shade under an olive tree. Sometimes the memories were too much, and she would wait outside, in the cold, until the visitors had left.

Echo stood up from the table and walked to the two young girls, six and seven years old. The youngest girl had lost part of her nose to frostbite and was self-conscious of her appearance, covering it with her hand.

'Who are these two beautiful girls?'

The younger mother said:

'They want to grow up to be like you.'

Echo considered telling them that was an impossible ambition, that their genetic composition was nothing like hers, that they could never be alike. Instead, she said:

'What if I want to be like you?'

The girl without a nose gave a shy smile, gaining enough confidence to lower her hand.

'Why would you want to be like us?'

'For a start there are two of you. And there's only one of me.'

The youngest girl thought about this for a time before remarking:

'You can be our sister, too.'

THE ANTARCTIC PENINSULA
WORDIE BAY
SAME DAY

L ISTENING TO THE BLOWHOLE SPRAY from the whales in Wordie Bay, Liza waited for the family to finish their tour. With her hands sunk deep into the pockets of her coat, her fingers discovered a pipe carved from seal bone that she'd recently confiscated from a patient who'd slipped on the ice after smoking too much lichen. There were three types of lichens on the Antarctic peninsula: crustose lichen with its thin buttercup-yellow crust, foliose lichens, flat and thin, and fruticose lichens, the largest and shrubbiest of the three. Although there were historical accounts of soldiers making lichen soup during the American Civil War, they were an impractical source of food, growing at a rate of only one centimetre in a hundred years. However, in Hope Town, where there were no laws against drugs, very few laws of any kind, only a libertarian culture of responsibility, even in Antarctica people still loved to get high, and for some that had involved scraping lichen from the rocks, drying it and smoking it. It had been discovered that the foliose lichens had a sedative effect, with users known to feel a calming sensation so powerful an entire community had formed around their use. Liza had never tried it, but tonight, with a pipe in her pocket as if placed there by fate, and her daughter about to leave home, she thought, *Why not?* She lit the pipe, inhaling tentatively, like a student smoking pot for the first time, and, feeling a mellow embrace around her thoughts, she pondered life without her daughter. Watching Echo grow up had been as exhilarating as it had been rejuvenating. While ordinary-born people saw adversity and peril in this continent, her daughter saw opportunity and wonder. Echo didn't merely survive on this continent; she loved her life on the ice, and she'd taught her mother how to love it, too.

Partly because she was deep in contemplation, Liza didn't hear her daughter approach. Echo was able to move across the ice with ballet-dancer elegance despite her size and weight.

'They've left.'

'Echo, I'm sorry.'

'What for?'

'I was being selfish earlier. McMurdo will be great for you. You'll be able to achieve more there than you ever could here. This is a small place, this town, a good place with good people and a good heart. But in McMurdo you'll be an important person doing important things. I can't ask you to stay. You shouldn't feel bad about leaving. If I was you, I'd make the same decision.'

Echo raised her hand and touched the tear on her mother's face, draining the tear's warmth, the drop freezing upwards from her fingertip to her mother's eye. With a click, Echo broke the frozen tear off her mother's face, holding it in front of them. Wondering if she was hallucinating from the lichen, Liza asked:

'How did you do that?'

'Today Tetu jumped into the ocean. He wanted to prove that I could save him. His body went into hypothermic shock. I picked him up and without thinking, or understanding what was happening, I transferred my warmth into his body. Tetu knew I could do it. I brought his body temperature back up to normal.'

The silence was broken by the sound of Atto walking towards them, his heavy boots clomping through the snow. Sensing the peculiar energy of their conversation, he asked:

'What's going on?'

Echo handed Atto the frozen tear.

'It's my tear. Echo froze it.'

Atto noticed the bone pipe in her hand and the smell of the lichen smoke.

'Are you high?'

'I think I might be.'

Before anyone could take the conversation further, they saw Tetu approaching, out of breath from running. Arriving at the family, he broke into a joyful smile, almost singing the words:

'I'm going to McMurdo!'

When no one laughed or applauded, he explained:

'McMurdo selected me! Echo, I'll be on the same transport as you. I'm going to McMurdo.'

Echo felt her mother's emotions at hearing this news – happiness and sadness intermingled.

'Your timing is terrible.'

But Liza put a hand on his arm.

'Your timing is perfect. And it's made me realize something.'

'What's that?'

'We're all going.'

Atto turned to her.

'We're all going where?'

'To McMurdo.'

'How are we going to do that?'

'I don't know how.'

'Shall we talk about this another time?'

'Sure, we can talk another time. But there's nothing to talk about.'

'How about the fact that we're not allowed to go?'

'They can't stop me.'

'They can stop you. There is no way they're going to allow us to go with Echo.'

Liza cut him short:

'Don't tell me there's not a way. We found a way from Lisbon to Antarctica on a fishing boat and an oil tanker. We can find a way from Hope Town to McMurdo City. I don't care what the rules are. This family is not going to be split up. All four of us are getting on that transport. We're all going to McMurdo City.'

PART FOUR

TWENTY YEARS EARLIER

ISRAEL
BEN GURION INTERNATIONAL AIRPORT
TWENTY KILOMETRES
NORTHWEST OF JERUSALEM
6 AUGUST 2023

Yotam drove his Merkava Mark Four tank down the middle of Highway One at its top speed of sixty kilometres per hour, shunting aside gridlocked traffic in a race to secure Ben Gurion International Airport. Turning off the highway at the airport perimeter, he smashed through razor-wire fencing, driving directly onto the runway and into the path of a twin-engine commercial airliner attempting to take off. Despite being given repeated instructions to shut down its engines, the Iberia Airways flight was returning to Madrid on the command of the Spanish government, who were behaving the same as every other government in the world right now, trying to gather as many planes as possible. With a comparatively small international airport, Israel couldn't afford to lose any of these planes. Shots were fired across the pilot's windscreen and when that warning was ignored, Yotam drove the tank directly under the aircraft's nose, crashing into the front wheels, wedging underneath it like a doorstop. Better to damage a plane

than lose it, since each plane had become unfathomably precious –
capable of carrying thousands of people to safety.

The result of these efforts was a small fleet given the scale of the
task – the evacuation of an entire country. In contrast, Dubai with
a population of only three million had an airport terminal dedicated to the world's largest passenger plane, the Airbus A380 – an
aircraft that had fallen out of favour in recent years but which, in
this crisis, was now the most coveted plane on the planet. China and
the United States had the advantage of having the largest civilian
airline fleets in the world, with eight of the top ten airlines by fleet
size; America Airlines alone operated over two thousand planes.
It was clear that the survivors of this alien occupation would be
disproportionately represented by the two most powerful countries
in the world. Many nations were struggling with the limitation of
having small airlines and a small navy. Israel was in the middle
of global rankings in terms of its capacity, a triumph considering
its geographical size. Even so, surveying the final tally of planes,
Yotam thought:

It's not enough: it's nowhere near enough.

Parked on the runway was an assortment of short-haul and long-
haul aircraft including planes operated by Air Canada, British
Airways, Ethiopian Airlines, Iberia, Korean Air, Chinese carrier
Hainan and Royal Jordanian. Only the El Al aircraft were owned
by the Israeli state. All the other planes had been requisitioned –
international laws and treaties now counting for nothing. In the
struggle to save as many of their people as possible, it was each
nation for itself.

Teams of engineers were already arriving on site, ripping out
every seat and superfluous element to make the planes capable of

carrying as many people and as much cold-weather gear as they could be loaded with. To the side of the runway a heap of discarded airplane seats formed a plastic mountain, standard seats mingled with first-class suites with their faux walnut finish. In ordinary times an aging, fuel-inefficient Boeing 747 could carry four hundred people arranged in a regular seating configuration with ten across in standard class, but with people packed together as tight as possible, with scant regard for personal space or safety regulations, as many as two thousand could be forced into the lower deck, with another three hundred on the upper deck, the stairs and galleys. The long-haul aircraft could manage the journey to Antarctica with ease – roughly five thousand miles. The short-haul aircraft would be pushed to the very limits of their range. Until today, Yotam had never even heard of their destination: McMurdo Station.

Y OTAM SAT CROSS-LEGGED ON THE top of his tank peeling an avocado and contemplating whether it might be the last avocado he'd ever eat. This tank, one of the most sophisticated in the world, was now his home, parked on the runway, guarding the assorted fleet of civilian planes as they were modified for their final flight. All the international travellers had been disembarked, expelled from the airport and told they were free to make their own way to safety. The terminal was now exclusively for the use of the army, as the Knesset tried to figure out how to save as many of their citizens as possible. Sleeping fitfully for no more than an hour at any time, Yotam spent the days and nights watching the engineers work, eating whatever food was passed around, from Kif Kef chocolate bars requisitioned from the duty-free shops to fresh fruit grown on the nearby kibbutz. The weather was so hot that during the short walk from the terminal the candy bars had softened to such an extent that they were held together only by the wrapping, oozing into the palm of his hand more like a beauty product than food. Fellow soldiers, unable to leave their post, cooled down by pouring bottles of water over their heads, the puddles around their leather boots drying almost as soon as they formed. From time to time they smoked together, keen for the kinship even if they'd never smoked before. During the night they lay on their backs, on the hot runway, staring up at the alien ships drifting across the sky. Often the alien ships were dark, at other times the hulls were illuminated with pulsing ribbons of light, more like a creature from the deepest part of the ocean than a machine.

Finishing the avocado, Yotam checked on the army engineers toiling among a shower of welding sparks, adapting the under-carriage of the planes so that they could land on the ice. As it was reported to him, there were three runways at McMurdo Station – Phoenix Airfield, Sea Ice Runway and Williams Runway. Sea Ice Runway was located on the massive expanse of the Ross Ice Shelf, a plateau bigger than Israel itself. This landing area was under the exclusive control of the United States military, who would surely defend every metre of space with deadly force even when it came to their closest allies. In this crisis, co-operation served no purpose; it was a zero-sum game. Sharing runway space with one nation meant losing space for your own. Each country had the exact same ambition – to transport as many of their citizens and as much of their resources to the continent as they could manage before the deadline. Countries without a base on Antarctica would have to improvise their own runways. Mossad intelligence officers claimed the Chinese military had developed the means to transport arti-ficial runways that could be unspooled like a giant yoga mat at any adverse location. For countries without such resources, the ice plateaus behind the Transantarctic Mountains, which crossed the continent, were the only option. True, it was the coldest part of the continent and it was winter on Antarctica; there'd be no landing lights, no guiding beacons, no air-traffic control and katabatic winds of up to two hundred miles per hour. They'd be attempting the most dangerous landings in the history of aviation.

The nation's finest pilots selected for the mission paced back and forth, surveying the fleet. Yotam listened to them debate how best to cope with such hostile conditions. Even if they survived the storms and managed to touch down, the wheels might jam into deep crevasses, causing the plane to flip or tear apart. For this reason, it had been decided that they'd use newly crafted steel skis, trying to land like a giant sled – racing across the ice at several hundred miles per hour. With luck, the outer shell of the plane would remain intact, providing a temporary shelter for the passengers against the cold.

The question of who to save had been decided by the military and Knesset representatives, conferring in the airport terminal, in the King David Lounge, normally used by business travellers with refrigerators full of lime-flavoured Perrier water and jars of Oreo cookies, organizing as best they could their nation's exodus. The population of Israel stood at nine million. The state had calculated that it could transport, across its entire fleet of ships and planes, only four hundred thousand, roughly four per cent of the population, in addition to the food and supplies needed to keep them all alive for at least a year. The selection process had been based on two criteria: their ability to survive in some of the harshest conditions on the planet and their ability to help build a new society. Among those chosen were scientists, engineers, chemists, farmers, geneticists and soldiers: the smartest and strongest.

Yotam hadn't been selected. After being informed the news, he'd been calm; he hadn't even felt particularly sad. Unlike the millions of civilians told the same news, he wasn't free to attempt the journey by his own means. He'd been ordered to remain at his post, at the airport, protecting those chosen as they gathered from across the country in the terminal buildings. Once the planes were safely in the air, he'd be free to leave. By that point he wouldn't have enough time to attempt the five-thousand-mile journey south to Antarctica. Coming to terms with his fate, he wondered what he'd do with those last days. Some soldiers talked about going to the beaches of Tel Aviv, dancing and drinking, taking drugs and having sex until the end. Others talked of returning home, to small villages and traditional kibbutz, to quietly spend their last hours with their family. But going home wasn't an option for him. He had no home to go to.

Born in the town of Bnei Brak, Yotam was the sixth son of a prominent Haredi family, adherents to the strictest form of Judaism. With a childhood devoted to scriptural studies, his earliest transgression had been subtle, a contrary sense of humour, tolerated by his parents only because it never prevented him from excelling in his Torah studies. A brilliant student in every regard, much was expected of him, the community certain that he'd become a religious leader. It wasn't until he was a teenager and beginning havruta, an intense Torah study partnership, with a handsome young man of the same age that he'd begun to understand the deeper nature of his transgressions, an understanding that continued at the ritual baths outside Jerusalem, at the accidental and then the deliberate moments of physical contact. One day an older man had whispered, as if it were the most dangerous secret in the world, that he recognized the impulses in him, but that he shouldn't despair: instincts could be suppressed; it was a hard fight, but life was hard – he was being challenged, there were many challenges in life, and this was one of them. Yotam had listened to this man's advice, feigning ignorance. But, afterwards, thinking about the old man's gentle sadness, he decided that was not a life for him. He'd risk other kinds of sadness, but not that kind. With the decision made, he used military service as a means of escape. His father had argued that he should seek an exception from conscription as a yeshiva student who under the Tal Law could declare that the Torah was the sole and exclusive purpose of his life. Suspecting that there was an ulterior motive, his father had asked if his son intended to serve in the Netzah Yeuda battalion, a segregated unit which combined advanced Talmudic studies with military service. Yotam had said no, he'd serve in the regular units, integrated with men and women drawn from across the whole country. Hearing this, his father had declared:

'You will have a country. But no family. You will have a people. But no parents.'

ISRAEL
BEN GURION INTERNATIONAL AIRPORT
NEXT NIGHT

UNABLE TO SLEEP IN THE sweltering heat, Yotam clambered down from his tank, walking across the runway towards the mountain of discarded airplane seats. An older soldier was slouched in a first-class sleeper suite, flicking through an inflight luxury lifestyle magazine, browsing glossy adverts for multi-million-dollar Miami condos. He joked:

'My first time in first class.'

'I've never flown in a plane.'

The older soldier peered over the top of the magazine.

'Why not?'

'My parents didn't travel. Not outside of the country. They said everything they needed was here.'

'Not anymore.'

'They won't leave, they'll never leave. They'll wait, pray and see what happens.'

Changing the subject, Yotam asked:

'Do you have a phone?'

The soldier nodded.

'Sure, I mean we're not supposed to have them on duty but who's going to mind now? That's one good thing about the world ending – rule-breaking gets overlooked.'

'The world isn't ending.'

'The world as we know it is.'

Taking the phone from the pocket, he was about to hand it over when he stopped.

'Strange, don't you think? That the phone still works? Our computers, our phones? They haven't shut us down. Turned it all off.'

Yotam thought about the question seriously. He thought about most questions seriously.

'There's no point giving us thirty days to get to safety if nothing works.'

'You're a smart one, aren't you? Let me ask you, since you're so smart . . .'

He lowered his voice.

'Some people think it's all a trick, a hoax, a form of radical population control by billionaire elites. They know the planet's messed up, and this is the only way they can save it. Once we all get down to Antarctica, they'll have the planet for themselves.'

'Our government doesn't think that.'

'You think it's real?'

Without wishing to appear glib, Yotam pointed up at the night sky. Illuminated against the moon was a massive alien ship. The soldier stared at it, sighed and handed him the cell phone.

'Who are you going to call? Your sweetheart?'

Yotam blushed.

'My best friend.'

'A man?'

'Yes, a man.'

'You should tell him.'

'Tell him what?'

'That you love him.'

Yotam said nothing, bewildered that this stranger could see his feelings clearer than he could. He stammered:

'Why do you say that? I didn't . . . say that.'

'The world's ending, my friend. There's no time to waste. I mean, if not now, when, you know?'

With that the solider returned to the pages of the luxury lifestyle inflight magazine.

Stepping away from the soldier, Yotam dialled Eitan's number. The two of them had joined the military together, trained together and been posted at the Blue Line, the Israel–Lebanon border secured with eleven kilometres of concrete wall, taking part in operations to destroy Hezbollah's network of tunnels. Born in the coastal town of Haifa, Eitan had spent his childhood playing beach volleyball and singing cover versions of hit songs in karaoke bars. In almost every way he was the opposite of Yotam – easy-going and gregarious, sexually confident, having slept with women and men. He'd broken a hundred hearts by the time he was twenty and was destined to break many hundreds more. Yotam had kept his distance, fearful of revealing his feelings and giving himself away. One night during guard duty loneliness had overwhelmed him, the facts of his life laid bare – he had no home, no family, no idea what he'd do with his life after military service. He was a nowhere man in a no-man's land. Without being fully aware of what he was doing, he'd taken a grenade from his belt and spent several minutes imagining his body curled around it. At this point, out of nowhere, Eitan had sat down beside him, staring at the grenade in his hand.

'If you do it, you'll take me with you – that's the only way.'

Embarrassed, Yotam put the grenade away.

'I don't know what came over me.'

'Sure you do. You were lonely. You thought you'd be lonely for the rest of your life. And you couldn't face the idea anymore.'

'Please don't tell anyone.'

'You think people avoid you. But they don't know how to start the conversation. You don't have any inroads. And trust me, I know them all. Sex, sport, films, music – I can start a conversation with anyone. But even I didn't know what to say to you. What the hell do I talk about with this guy? Maybe you took that grenade out because you wanted someone to stop you, someone to see you? Have you thought about that? Whatever the reason, now that we're talking, I promise I'll never stop talking. You'll grow so tired of my voice you'll wish you pulled that pin after all.'

Yotam managed a laugh. Eitan seemed pleased.

'From suicidal to laughing in thirty seconds – that's a personal best for me.'

From that moment, true to his word, Eitan was always there for him.

Stationed at the Parliament building in Jerusalem, Eitan answered the call, not recognizing the number.

'Who's this?'

'It's me.'

'Yotam! The love of my life. Where are you?'

'I'm guarding the airport.'

'Wait, did they choose you? Tell me they chose you?'

'No, I wasn't chosen.'

'What do you mean?'

'I'm not going.'

Eitan fell silent for a while before saying:

'They've made a mistake. They don't know how smart you are. They don't understand. Let me talk to them.'

'Talk to who?'

'Whoever is in charge! I'll tell them. I'll explain.'

'The people they've selected have diplomas and doctorates and Olympic gold medals. I haven't done anything with my life.'

'Not yet! You're only twenty years old. You're the smartest person I know!'

'There's a building here full of some of the smartest people in the world.'

'They're today smart. You're tomorrow smart.'

Eitan fell silent for a time. Yotam asked:

'What about you?'

'Of course they didn't pick me. Who the hell am I? I'm nobody. I was never going to be anybody. But they should've picked you. I bet they've picked a load of corrupt politicians and their mistresses. But not you? They've made a mistake. They've made a terrible mistake.'

'What are you going to do? With your last days?'

'I'm going home.'

He'd spend his last days in Haifa with his family, who ran a small restaurant in the Turkish market. None of them had been selected and none of them were attempting the journey south.

'Your family didn't want to try and reach safety?'

'My mother gets cold in Haifa. Whatever that life is going to be, down there in the snow and ice, it's not for us.'

'It doesn't snow in Antarctica. Not much. Not really.'

'What are you talking about? All it does is snow in Antarctica.'

'It's a desert.'

'You see? Who knows stuff like that? They should've picked you.'

Eitan added:

'Find me, when you're done at the airport.'

'Are you sure? You're with your family. I don't want to ... impose.'

Eitan laughed, the most wonderful laugh Yotam had ever heard.

'You don't want to impose? You're too funny. The world's ending and you don't want to impose. See it out with me. Our last days will be the best days of our lives, I promise.'

WALKING BACK TO HIS TANK, Yotam heard a noise above him and, expecting it to be alien activity of some kind, he looked up into the night sky only to see a conventional jet fighter, a Soviet-built MiG-29, operated by numerous countries hostile to Israel. It was being pursued by the Israeli Air Force. Coming under intense gunfire, its right wing burst into flames, spinning out of control and crashing into the hill of discarded passenger seats behind him, the explosion so powerful it lifted Yotam into the air. A moment later, he found himself flat on the runway, staring up as the burning remnants of foam cushions and plastic meal trays rained down around him, the cocoon shell of a first-class sleeper suite smashing into the tarmac not far from his head. They were under attack, he thought, not from an advanced alien species with technological wonders; this wasn't awe-inspiring supremacy; this was crude and hellish; this was bullets and blood; this was human – not a new enemy but an old one.

He stood up, staggering to his tank to defend his country's precious fleet of passenger planes, when he saw a second enemy fighter jet flying only a few metres above the ground, approaching the airport. The sophisticated anti-aircraft defences seemed to have failed and the fighter broke through the defensive gunfire, ignoring the passenger planes, targeting the terminal where so many brilliant people had gathered. The jet's missiles flew true, finding their target, but none of them exploding, crumpling into the dense stone walls harmlessly. Our alien occupiers hadn't allowed humankind control of everything, it would seem; to prevent scorching the Earth they'd disabled the most destructive weapons, leaving only knives and bullets. With no missiles remaining, the pilot was undaunted, crashing his jet through the glass windows of the terminal building and into the crowds of people waiting to start their new life in the cold.

ISRAEL
BEN GURION INTERNATIONAL AIRPORT
NEXT DAY

H<small>IS HAIR STILL STINKING OF</small> smoke and jet fuel, his eardrums damaged by the explosion so that he could barely hear, Yotam had been told the news – that, on the brink of extinction, rather than co-operation, old enemies were settling scores, at war over who should have a place in Antarctica. To some, the alien occupation was an opportunity to erase their rivals from existence, preventing them from gaining a foothold on the southernmost continent, restarting human existence with several races and identities excluded. Yotam had been so preoccupied with this first piece of news that it took him a moment to process the second. In the aftermath of the attack on the terminal building, with the loss of so many people, he'd been selected to be part of the Israeli exodus. A military officer told him:

'You've got a spot on one of the planes. Do you understand why?'

'No, sir.'

'You're smart. You're strong. But more important, you're a witness to this atrocity. The battle for our survival won't end when you reach Antarctica; it will begin.'

He'd been handed a phone and told to call his parents to let them know.

'I'm not in contact with my parents, sir.'

'There must be someone you can tell? Someone who loves you?'

There was one person.

Yotam dialled Eitan. Talking at speed, he explained how the terminal building had been attacked and many people had been killed and that because of the loss of life a new selection process was underway. People were being chosen to replace those who'd died and Yotam was among them. Having borne witness to this outrage, he understood that even the people who made it safely to the ice needed protecting – they'd still face the same hatred they'd always faced. Yotam ended by saying:

'I don't want to go.'

'What are you talking about?'

'They can send another soldier. I'm going to say no. I want to spend those days with you. I'm coming to Haifa.'

Eitan replied:

'Listen to me very carefully. They were right to choose you. You're not coming to Haifa. You're getting on that plane. You're our future now. You have a part to play. What that is I don't know. But you're very special, that I do know. I've always known it. I love you. I love you very much.'

And that was the last time Yotam heard Eitan's voice.

PART FIVE

TWENTY YEARS LATER

WITH THE WEATHER CONDITIONS CALM, Yotam decided to climb to the top of Observation Hill, a lava dome two hundred and thirty metres high located in the centre of McMurdo City. Kept free from any manmade structures, at the summit there was a memorial site – a place for people to mourn lost family and friends. The timber cross that had once stood in memory of explorer Robert Scott had been taken down and replaced with six stone tablets, one for each lost continent, North America, South America, Europe, Africa, Asia and Australia, each engraved with the names of every former country, the one hundred and ninety-five former sovereign states once recognized by the United Nations and the six countries with partial recognition to avoid any needless controversy. There'd been a discussion about whether to erect the flag of Antarctica, a simple outline of the continent set against a blue background, to make this the flag for all survivors, but the idea had been abandoned with an acknowledgement that the era of flags was over.

Standing at the summit, Yotam looked out at the view of

mankind's last capital city. The original McMurdo Station sat at the foot of this volcanic dome. Established in 1956, seventy years before the alien occupation, it had been intended as a permanent year-round scientific base, a human foothold on the continent, one hundred and sixty acres in size, akin to the remote mining settlements in the far reaches of Alaska. These original base buildings were now the historic centre of McMurdo City, the Old Town of an Antarctic metropolis that sprawled far across rock, ice and ocean, a city unlike any other in human history tasked with a goal unlike any other – the survival of the species.

To the north filling this ice-locked coastline, was a stationary fleet of ships far larger than the one at Pearl Harbor or the Battle of Midway, a staggering sight to behold, every surviving naval vessel anchored side by side and back to back, arranged like puzzle pieces, bound together with their anchors down, never to sail again, a flotilla without precedent, an archipelago of steel glinting in the sun – the sprawling harbour quarter of McMurdo City. Nearest to the historic base were the most important ships, aircraft carriers with the paint of their illustrious names fading, the *Kennedy*, the *Enterprise*, the *Nimitz*, the *Reagan*, the *Stennis*, the *Truman*, the *Washington* and the *Lincoln*. Behind them were the destroyers, with the civilian cargo ships and oil tankers on the outer edge. Encased in ice during the winter, free to float in the looser pack ice during the summer, they were connected by a series of steel wire bridges so that a person could walk for miles, from ship to ship, without ever descending to the ice. Stripped of their weapons, the interior spaces had been converted into high-tech laboratories, power stations, furnaces and factories, the last hub of human innovation. Since the world's military forces had been disbanded, the people who lived on these ships were scientists, doctors, inventors and assembly-line workers. These ships were the industrial heartland – the Rhineland and the rustbelt of McMurdo society.

South of Observation Hill was the Ross Ice Shelf – a permanent expanse of ice, six hundred kilometres wide, fed by ancient valley glaciers the Byrd and Beardmore, tethered to the mainland continent of Antarctica, rising thirty metres above sea level and plunging two hundred metres below. The Ice Shelf had served as mankind's most important runway during the Exodus and was now covered with the carcasses of the world's military and civilian planes. No longer of any use as vehicles, they'd been converted into an array of low-tech industries, the interiors hollowed out and reconfigured into micro-breweries and bakeries, canneries and smokeries. Old jumbo jets were now filled with drying fish and barrels of brine. Gulf Stream private jets housed butchers slicing up seal meat, collecting the fats for soaps, the bones for broths and the pelts for the tailors next door. Inside the bulbous interior of the Airbus Beluga was a garment factory where cold-weather gear was patched up using anything from the leather seat upholstery stripped from airplane seats to penguin feathers harvested on nearby farms. Thousands of small producers, all displaying remarkable ingenuity, toiled in these relic aircraft, not for money – there was no new currency – but in order that humankind might survive into the next century. For the larger producers, planes had been welded together, their wings sliced off so that the ferocious winds didn't lift them into the air. Seen from above, these planes appeared like an optical illusion, tubular fuselages in a geometric weave, every one of them stripped of their engines. Just as the warships were never going to sail again, these planes were never going to fly again; there was nowhere to fly to. The rules of this reservation were simple. There was only one rule: no one was permitted to leave.

As Yotam turned to descend the hill and return to work, he saw a handsome hiker from a previous encounter. They'd spoken at the summit, sharing stories, and he'd felt a connection, but he'd been too shy to ask the man out on a date. He stood, lingering, preparing what he might say, summoning the courage, until he saw that the man wasn't alone. He was with a partner, and as they neared the summit, they rested on each other's shoulder, admiring the view. Yotam waved to him, forcing a smile.

'Nice to see you again,' he said, as he passed them by.

ANTARCTICA
MCMURDO CITY
THE ROSS ICE SHELF
SAME DAY

D UE TO THE IMPORTANT NATURE of his work, Yotam was
housed in one of the original base buildings – the Manhattan
of McMurdo residential real estate. Inside, the living quarters were
arranged like small college dorm rooms with a narrow single bed,
a shelf for books and a small triple-glazed window. Only a handful
of people on the continent didn't share their space; the majority
lived not only with their own family but with multiple families and
various children, biological, adopted and adapted, often sleeping
at different times of the day so that beds were in constant use, one
exhausted person slipping into the residual warmth of another
person's sleep. Being granted your own space was a privilege that
Yotam didn't want any longer. He wanted to share his space and
his warmth. Devoted to his work, with no family and no partner,
Yotam had been allowed to live this way because his work was his
child, not as a figure of speech – his work was a new kind of life.

Leaving his building, he commuted to work on cross-country skis
handmade from moso bamboo, the supply of which came from a

farmed forest growing inside the steel belly of a super-tanker, conditions optimized so that the trees grew ten inches a day under the permanent glow of artificial lights powered by the wind turbines on deck. The ecosystem had been devised by a Taiwanese horticulturist who'd created the only woodland space in Antarctica. This indoor bamboo forest, aside from producing vital materials for skis, was also one of the most popular spots for lovestruck couples to go on a date, with the scenic benches overlooking the bamboo forest currently having a wait list of six months for a thirty-minute slot. Yotam had reserved a slot of his own, hoping that he'd meet someone and be able to suggest the bamboo forest as a first date.

The ski lanes were busy this morning with commuters enjoying the clement conditions. During the winter McMurdo citizens would be forced into sheltered passageways, a network of protected pedestrian highways where cramped lines of people shuffled north and south, east and west, under the cover of an elongated igloo corridor. But on a clear day like today, with glorious sunshine, everyone was outside, trekking or skiing or riding on husky-drawn sleighs delighted by the sight of the sun, tirelessly calling out 'good morning' to each other, a hundred or more cheery salutations uttered in the hour it took Yotam to arrive at his place of work.

The Final Stage Chambers were a new addition to the city and perhaps humankind's greatest construction achievement on this continent, built to house the latest generation of ice-adapted people once they grew too big for the birthing labs, a safe and secure space to study them, out of the way of regular society. The chambers hadn't been built on the surface of the ice shelf in the regular fashion – there wasn't enough raw material for such a complex construction. If the people of McMurdo wanted to build something new, then something old had to be dismantled. With ingenuity the chambers had been dug down into the ice, a mining operation resulting in a maze of tunnels and caves situated deep within one of the world's largest ice masses. At a time when ordinary-born people felt down-beaten, they could glance at the entrance to the Final Stage Chambers and marvel at what they'd achieved, a construction expressing the defiant sentiment that people weren't done yet.

On a clear day the entrance was visible from many miles away, walled on three sides with giant blocks of ice excavated from the shelf, smoothed down over the years by the powerful winds so that it now resembled a yawning mouth, the only clue that there was something extraordinary underneath the surface. Guarding the stairway were a team of armed security officers. Weapons were restricted in McMurdo City; the delicate fragility of people's mental health meant that the private ownership of guns was prohibited. Not even the order-enforcement teams who mostly handled incidents of Antarctica-induced insanity carried firearms, making do with tranquilizing darts. The security officers guarding these chambers were an exception. Equipped with powerful AK-12 assault rifles, an evolution of the famous Kalashnikov, their task was to stop anything from breaking out. Composed almost entirely of former Russian Federation soldiers, specialists in snow operations, these men still proudly served in their old army uniforms with a distinctive camouflage pattern originally designed for the Arctic, a pixelated arrangement of grey and black dots intended to blend with Arctic moss. With three layers of thermo-wear and helmet masks that covered their faces, they were a formidable unit, a closed community that lived together, socialized together. Largely ignoring the directive on universal language, they spoke little English and even less Mandarin, considering their national identity as important as it had been twenty years ago, despite the fact there was no such thing as nations anymore.

As Yotam stashed his skis and passed through the security perimeter the guards said nothing, giving him only a small nod of their head. Devout Orthodox, they believed these genetically adapted species to be an abomination, an act of hubris and, far from being mankind's saviour, they were a threat to what little remained of human civilization. Whatever the rights or wrongs of their beliefs, they took their job seriously and to date nothing had ever escaped on their watch.

YOTAM DESCENDED THE STAIRCASE CARVED out of the ice, a fairy-tale staircase with glimmering blue steps studded with metal scraps to stop people from slipping. There was no elevator – there weren't the parts to build one; only a crude rope pulley to lower supplies. Gone were the top-secret facilities of the old world; there were no high-tech security doors with retina-scan entry, no biometric entry passes – these chambers were primitive, like the dungeons of a medieval castle, manned by men and women with sturdy steel keys that opened sturdy steel doors. An assortment of battery-powered mining lamps hung at irregular intervals on the walls, pegged to ice screws once used for mountain climbing. When the lights began to flicker and dim, they were taken up to the surface to be charged by the sun or from electricity generated by the wind farms along the southern base of the Transantarctic mountain range. A crew of lamp changers did nothing but manage these lights, repairing them, replacing them, laboriously pushing a cart along these tunnels, reminiscent of the gas lamplighters in Victorian London. The glow from the lamps illuminated blue walls layered with lines of sapphire, turquoise and lapis lazuli; it was like working inside a worm-ridden gemstone. Needless to say, there was no heating of any kind. Year round, the temperature under the ice remained stable at a few degrees below freezing, suitable for species bred for cold, many of whom couldn't tolerate warmer tempera-tures, so radical was their genetic adaptation. The conditions made it a challenge for ordinary-born people working twelve-hour shifts. They never sat still, constantly pacing to keep warm, stamping their feet, retreating to the surface when the cold became too much, taking refuge inside the remains of the world's largest military transport aircraft, the Antonov AN-225 Mriya converted to a work cabin, a shelter for the scientists and support staff, where mugs of bitter-lichen tea were served with silverfish soup. To help with their mental well-being, a pack of husky dogs roamed under the tables, available for strokes and cuddles. Though some of the scientists had tried to bring the dogs down into the chambers, they'd refused to descend the stairway, howling like wolves at the creatures kept beneath the ice.

A rope painted luminous red, secured at waist height, stretched the entire network of tunnels so that in the event of an emergency, with the chambers plunged into darkness, a person could feel their way out. A system of knots had been tied so that you could identify if you were heading towards the entrance or away from it. Whenever Yotam slipped and reached for the support rope, he was reminded of the myth of the Minotaur, not only because Theseus had used thread to navigate the Labyrinth, but this, too, was a place built to contain cross-bred creatures. From time to time there were eerie sounds so unusual that ordinary-born people would stop and listen. There were clicks, like insect-speak, except not from insects. There was beautiful bird song, except not from birds. From force of habit the ordinary-born staff always whispered, an acknowledgement that human voices had no place here, aware that everything was being listened to by creatures with exceptional hearing and unfathomable intelligence. At times, echoing through the tunnels, there was the clear sound of speech – a voice so clipped and crisp, so proper that it couldn't be the speech of an ordinary-born human but of a creature learning human ways, a modern-day version of the play *Pygmalion*, a new species learning how to speak:

'You are Cold. I am never Cold.'

These caves hadn't been built for the ice-adapted humans, the more moderate adaptations – the almost humans with colour-shifting scales for skin and night-vision eyes. Those genetic moderates had been integrated with society from birth, brought up in ordinary-born families and sent to school. Only the more extreme Cold People were housed in these chambers under the ice, out of the way and out of sight. Down here were the creations where no limitations had been placed on the adaptions, no checks placed on the divergence from the template of the human genome. This radicalization of the Cold People Project had occurred when it was clear that the moderate ice-adapted people couldn't reverse the precipitous population decline – they could prolong the era of people, but they couldn't save them. To Yotam the objective was never merely about creating a life better suited to the cold; the ambition was a life that would consider this continent home.

Like a subterranean zoo, the chambers were divided into zones for the different genetic variations of cold people. Yotam's section, at the furthest reaches of the tunnels, consisted of twenty separate caves so large they were more like wildlife enclosures, each containing a single specimen held in isolation, the youngest of which was six months old and the oldest six years old. They'd never been allowed to mix or intermingle out of concerns that together they'd be hard to control. In the observation tunnels Yotam maintained a workstation which he shared with his fellow scientists and support staff. There was a desk and an emergency trunk containing rations, a medical kit and oxygen in case of tunnel collapse. Fog horns dangled from the ceiling like impoverished Christmas decorations, hung up as an alarm system to alert the entire base should they lose control of their area. In terms of amenities, behind a tissue-thin Japanese paper screen decorated with images of Mount Fuji there was a bucket toilet, since it was almost a forty-minute walk back to the surface. There was no plumbing and no human comforts of any kind.

Squads of fearsome security officers patrolled these chambers, moving in random patterns that couldn't be memorized, armed with assault rifles, wary of these new species, unconvinced that they were the answer to the population crisis, believing the scientists were underestimating the risks and overlooking the dangers. This atmosphere of heightened caution was the reason that Yotam had made the decision not to tell anyone what he was about to do. He hadn't sought approval from McMurdo Senate, partly because he didn't want spectators but mostly because he knew approval would never have been granted. In order to prove that these Cold People were safe, he intended to enter their chamber alone and unarmed. They'd waited and watched for long enough, they'd run enough tests; time was running out – this was the moment to stand opposite his creation, to reach out his hand in an offer of collaboration.

Though he was sure other people would consider it an emotional and impetuous decision, he was convinced it was the right one. Sometimes, with people, you had to take a chance.

MCMURDO CITY
FINAL STAGE CHAMBERS
FIFTY METRES BELOW THE
ROSS ICE SHELF
SAME DAY

WITH HIS HAND PRESSED AGAINST unbreakable silica nano-fiber glass, Yotam peered into the chamber, searching the walls, reminding himself to check the ceiling because this creature could climb any surface and hold position at any angle. Living inside this enclosure was the oldest specimen of its kind, born six years ago in the birthing labs on the aircraft carrier *Gerald Ford*, a species that reached physical maturity by the age of three – the most radically advanced of all the genetically engineered Cold People, able to mimic the complex colours of ice so exactly that they were often impossible to spot with the naked eye, as if their bodies had been chiselled from ice.

Despite the extreme nature of its genetic alterations, this species had been born of a human host, a volunteer selected from the Survivor Towns. She'd been kept in an induced coma for the duration of the term since it was clear that no ordinary human host could survive such a pregnancy; the modifications were too experimental, the divergence from the human genome too great. Morally reprehensible, an indelible stain on their consciences, one that wasn't mitigated by the fact that all the women had been repeatedly informed there was a high risk of death. Their desire for a child who could survive this cold made them vulnerable to promises of a family and their dream of being a mother to a marvellous new child. This deception was justified as the only way to prevent humankind's extinction, with the hope of creating a species that could reproduce independently so that soon no more hosts would be needed.

The mother had lain on the bed for months, unconscious, while her womb swelled, disturbingly distended upwards like a jagged mountain range, her skin hardening and discolouring, turning dark purple. The established procedure was that, upon detecting clear signs of self-supporting life, the infant was to be cut free, whatever form it might take. But in this case signs of life had proved elusive. Scans had proved hard to interpret, the infant seemed not to be flesh and blood but a jigsaw puzzle of bone. Without warning one night the child had burst free, more like an eruption than a birth, tearing apart the mother, ripping and gnashing like a creature at war with the very tissue that had given it life. So violent was the birth there was almost nothing left of the woman by the end, a head clamped under an artificial respirator, the remains of her shoulders and arms, a horrific sight. As the newborn continued to thrash in confusion, there were concerns that the birthing tank itself might be broken, injuring the infant and doing damage to precious equipment, much of which was now irreplaceable. For this reason, the valves were opened, the mother's blood and amniotic fluids running to the floor, allowing this new life to appear for the first time.

Leg by leg, it had poked through the access hole, highly capable and intelligent from the very first seconds of its life, making a peculiar sound, like whale song, a sound that no one could understand until Yotam had realized it was in pain and he gave the order to lower the room's temperature. As soon as the temperature dropped, the mother's blood freezing on the floor, the infant became calmer. It remained stationary, on the cusp of the birthing chamber, studying its surroundings until finally fixing its stare on the mirrored window in front of it. Behind that window were the leading scientists from the Cold People Project, present for any significant new species event. Some had reacted with thinly veiled disgust, as if to say this *thing* couldn't be the future of mankind. In contrast, Yotam had remarked with admiration:

'It's looking at us. It knows we're here.'

It was born with four jointed legs arranged two on each side of the thorax, from which a clearly human torso rose, perfect in form. Nimbly the infant had left the birthing chamber, its clawed feet clicking like stiletto heels on the steel deck, climbing the vertical walls with no difficulty, settling on the refrigerator unit, absorbing the cold where it seemed to purr, contented. On the other side of the glass, a geneticist had declared:

'Invaded by aliens, we have created aliens of our own.'

Adding:

'We should kill it now. While we still can.'

MCMURDO CITY
FINAL STAGE CHAMBERS
ONE HUNDRED METRES BELOW THE
ROSS ICE SHELF
SAME DAY

YOTAM DESCENDED THE STEEL LADDER, reaching the bottom of the enclosure. Rather than remain protected inside the observation cage, he opened the door, crossing a threshold into a chamber entirely devoid of furniture. There was no bed, no chairs, no table, not as an act of cruelty or deprivation; this species had been created so that it wouldn't mimic human dependency on comfort or require the usual clutter of items manufactured with metals, plastics and fabrics. There were no more forests to be felled, no more steel to be mined or cotton to be picked. Although there were vast resources miles below the snow and ice, humankind was so diminished it didn't have the capacity to reach them. There was only ice, snow and stone. The hope was that these new species would learn to exploit the elements of this continent and, sure enough, chunks of ice had been elegantly carved from the walls, shaved into tall tubular forms, complex sculptures which appeared abstract and baffling, more like an art gallery exhibit than anything of any practical use.

Yotam shut the cage behind him and walked into the middle of the enclosure as helpless as a sacrificial offering, waiting to see what happened, the first ordinary-born person ever to share this creature's space.

Precisely engineering himself down from the ceiling, his four legs moving with pinpoint accuracy, demonstrating such supreme control even when suspended upside down that he gave off the impression of having been built rather than born, manufactured by masterful Swiss clock craftsmen with intricate cogs and springs, a creature incapable of even the slightest act of clumsiness. Arriving at the base of the cave he stood in front of Yotam, nearly twice his height, three metres tall with his legs at rest. His silhouette was largely unchanged since birth, a centaur figure from Greek mythology rendered into flesh and bone, with a human's upper body supported by four legs rather than two. With each year of growth his appearance had become more formidable – a warrior species with a chest like the armour of a gladiator, cast from ivory rather than bronze. Combining a selection of the advantages of an exoskeleton with a selection of the advantages of an endoskeleton, this audacious biological engineering hack had enabled him to grow far beyond the physical limitations of arthropods, shedding outer layers of organic armour made from chitin, discarding them as a locust discards a desiccated shell and then consuming them, wasting nothing, an admirable efficiency on this continent. Below this magnificent, sculpted torso was a thorax with legs that were part spider and part Bolshoi ballet dancer. At the tips of his permanently en pointe feet instead of toes were hooked claws which punctured the ice with the power of a climbing bolt gun. His neck, with the vertebrae on the outside, rose to an impressionistic approximation of a human head, with startling proportions – cheeks like satellite dishes of moon-cratered bone, closer in form to a tribal war mask than a regular face. His lips were strips of pearl. His eyes were polished white billiard balls. With his mouth closed and his eyes shut, his head seemed more like a modernist ceramic statue than a living creature. Nothing exposed to the elements was flesh and fragile; everything soft was inside. Impermeable to frostbite, he could stroll through the fiercest winter storms – a body that could survive even when entirely encased in ice.

His bony arms were latched to the side of his torso, stowed securely rather than hanging idle, released with the accompanying sound of distinct clicks. Rather than sinew and flesh, they were as hard as narwhal tusk. It took enormous self-control for Yotam not to step back as these arms stretched out towards him. Fully extended, the javelin-tip hands divided into digits revealing the most delicate of surgical scalpels, less like human fingers and more like precise medical instruments. With great care, for he could disembowel the blubber belly of a walrus with a flick of a finger, he delicately pressed a digit against Yotam's jacket as though aiming for his heart. It was the first time they'd ever touched. Yotam looked down to see that the scalpel tip had punctured the synthetic outer layer so that a single goose feather came free and floated slowly to the ground.

The creature's pearl lips opened, revealing teeth arranged in dense rows, shark-sharp at the front, molars for grinding at the back with jaws operated by the strongest muscles in the animal kingdom – a variant of the muscle tissue from the jaws of alligators. A nimble tongue lurked inside creating both the most terrifying of mouths and the most eloquent of musical instruments, capable of perfectly imitating thousands of sounds from the trickle of meltwater to heart-breaking human song. It led to the most efficient digestive system in the animal kingdom, one which wasted nothing – a vulture's stomach, excreting only insoluble nitrogenous compounds, guanine and uric acid, a toxic sticky paste that oozed out like tar and was scrubbed with much difficulty and disgust from the ice chambers by the support staff every couple of weeks. Though bred to be intelligent beyond human comprehension, his feeding habits were primal, refusing to eat anything that wasn't alive, as if the act of killing was the obligatory first stage of any meal. To Yotam's eye, he was beautiful.

'Hello, Yotam.'

'Hello, Eitan.'

MCMURDO CITY
FINAL STAGE CHAMBERS
EITAN'S ENCLOSURE
SAME DAY

IT HAD NEVER BEEN YOTAM's intention to name him Eitan, but he'd grown tired of using an anonymous code. Though they'd been given strict instructions to only refer to them by their genetic variant number, he'd wanted to give him a regular name to help with their interaction. He might have been forgiven this lapse since it was cumbersome using a code for a name, but to name him after his closest friend, a man he'd been in love with, was an emotional association and deeply unprofessional. He made sure the scientists and support staff never heard him say the name and Eitan never referred to himself by this name around the other scientists, as if he was somehow aware that it was their inappropriate secret.

'Yotam?'

'Yes, Eitan?'

'You're inside my enclosure.'

'For the first time.'

'You entered the cage.'

'Yes.'

'There's nothing separating us.'

'No. Nothing.'

'You're alone.'

'Yes.'

'And unarmed.'

'I'm always unarmed.'

'We are face to face.'

'We are.'

'What is special about today?'

'It's time.'

'For what?'

'To prove that we can live together.'

'That is the goal?'

'That's the plan.'

'This is a test?'

'Everything is a test.'

'An act of trust?'

'Exactly.'

'A show of faith?'

'All of those things.'

'Did you worry that I might hurt you?'

'I didn't, no. Others did. Others still do.'

Eitan considered for a moment. He looked up at the tunnels. No one was watching.

'You didn't tell anyone you were doing this?'

'No.'

'Why not?'

'They would never have agreed.'

'They think I'm dangerous?'

'They think you could be.'

'What do you think?'

'I think you're our future.'

'Your heart is beating very fast.'

'Yes, it is.'

'Are you nervous?'

'A little.'

'And what else?'

'I'm excited, too.'

'I want to pick you up.'

'Why?'

'To prove that I'm safe.'

'I'm not sure ...'

'You are afraid?'

'Remember, compared to you, my skin is thin, and my bones are weak.'

'I am aware of your physical frailties.'

'If you hurt me, they'll never release you.'

'I would never hurt you.'

'You might make a mistake.'

'I've never made a mistake.'

Yotam smiled at this remark.

'Down here your opportunities for making mistakes have been limited.'

'What kind of mistake could I make by picking you up?'

'You might misjudge your strength.'

'I know my strengths as well as I know your weaknesses.'

With trepidation, Yotam nodded.

'Okay. Go ahead. Pick me up.'

Eitan carefully lifted Yotam up. With his feet clean off the ground, he held him like this for a minute or so, exerting no effort.

'You're light.'

'Eighty-one kilos.'

'I could hold you like this forever.'

It sounded almost affectionate.

'We don't have forever.'

'Have I passed?'

'Passed what?'

'Today's test.'

'In my opinion, yes.'

'There will be more tests?'

'Many.'

'And after the tests we will live together above the ice?'

'That's the dream.'

'That's my dream, too. Will it come true?'

'I hope so.'

'I hope so, too.'

'Eitan?'

'Yes, Yotam.'

'You can put me down now.'

MCMURDO CITY
THE ARCHIVE
NEXT DAY

Yotam hadn't been able to sleep, lying awake in bed, in the remains of an old sleeping bag stitched up and repaired so many times it looked like a fairy-tale quilt. He'd spent the entire night planning for today's tests. If the first day had merely been an introduction, today would be something far more audacious and, in preparation, he decided to carry out some additional research before returning to the Final Stage Chambers. Getting out of bed early, one of the first to take breakfast, he enjoyed a fillet of poached Antarctic toothfish, one of the largest fish in the oceans, growing to almost two metres long and a voracious predator known to eat its own offspring. It had a taste comparable to cod. Washed down with a mug of hot kelp tea, excellent for boosting thyroid function, high in iodine, potassium and zinc, Yotam set off for the McMurdo City Archive.

Circled by two walls of black granite rock, the Archive stood apart from the rest of the city, one of the last places where human knowledge had been preserved. What was once taken for granted, that our collective learning would survive forever, handed down from generation to generation, was no longer a certainty. The great libraries had been left behind, there hadn't been the time to transport all the world's rare books, the thirty-two million volumes from the Library of Congress in Washington, the eleven million from the Bodleian Library in Oxford, the ten thousand incunabula from the Vatican. Even if there had been time there was no way to store and protect so many fragile volumes on this continent and the decision had been made to leave the libraries, perhaps in the naïve hope that the occupying alien force would discover them and reconsider humankind's value as a species. Only a few manuscripts were considered too important to abandon, including the Dunhuang manuscripts, the Book of Kells, the Declaration of Independence, Shakespeare's first folio, the Gutenberg Bible, the Dead Sea Scrolls and the two oldest pages from the Quran, all of which were sealed and stored inside the missile tubing of a defunct nuclear weapon as though they were seeds of humanity, waiting until one day a new home was found.

In an attempt to hold onto knowledge, formula and theories, stories and songs, governments had transported to Antarctica a series of supercomputers. The Frontier computers, built at Oak Ridge National Laboratory in Tennessee, and the Fugaku computers, from Kobe, Japan, were some of the most powerful computers ever constructed. With the end of the internet and cloud computing, with the destruction of satellites and telecoms systems – the virtual world had been lost. These computers were the last remaining information hubs of human society, primarily used for the complex genetic-adaption computations behind the Cold People Project while also serving as the last depositories of human learning. The city now faced the prospect of these computers one day breaking down, impossible to repair, technology growing as old and frail as human bodies – a digital dementia, swathes of collective experiences, histories, cultures and discoveries seeping away. Strategically dispersed throughout the city, some of the Frontier computers were secure in the aircraft carriers, while others were deep inside the nuclear submarines. The Archive was situated on dry land, on an outcrop of black rock, and the only one open to the community – the last public library.

Approved for access based upon the importance of his work, Yotam stripped naked in the outer chamber and was handed a pale blue plastic body suit, the kind once worn by forensic scientists, covering him from head to toe. Allowed to bring nothing in, he entered a padded room rendered accident-proof, and was handed one of the last tablet computers in existence. Supervised at all times, he accessed the research he was looking for. In preparation for today's tests to see if Eitan was safe to release into society, Yotam began reading numerous studies by leading psychologists on the ways ordinary-born people responded to changes in their interpersonal space. With the loss of so many leading experts, several fields of discipline were no longer represented by the remaining survivors. To compensate, people no longer limited themselves to one profession or one area of interest. Someone working in the food production labs might also sit on the board of the McMurdo committee for mental well-being. There simply weren't enough people to be isolated in a specialist field; everyone worked across a broad range, professionally nimble, one day harvesting kelp, another day cutting hair, another day teaching mathematics. Though this pluralism of occupations had arisen out of necessity, it had also proved to be remarkably good for their sense of self-esteem. Of course, some of the jobs were gruelling and dangerous, but no one was ever limited to one type of work, and almost everyone shared in the hardship. The value of every person's life was tremendous, the variety of their days was wide-ranging and their sense of fulfilment enormous.

Browsing the banks of information, Yotam discovered the work of anthropologist Edward T. Hall, who coined the term proxemic behaviour – the study of interpersonal space. The field included haptics – touching, kinesics – body movement and non-verbal communication. Before the Exodus, personal space was defined as being within fifty centimetres of each other, social distance was two metres away and public distance was over four metres away. Personal space was the region surrounding what an ordinary person might regard as psychologically their own. But in today's society no one considered any space their own; everyone lived in each other's personal space, and it was vital, in order to survive in Antarctica, that people were able to cope with extreme proximity for extended periods of time. Eitan's next test was how he responded to proximity. Yotam intended to spend as much time as possible within the circle of his personal space – today was a test of intimacy.

FINAL STAGE CHAMBERS
EITAN'S ENCLOSURE
SAME DAY

F OLLOWING THE SAME PROCEDURE AS yesterday, Yotam
entered the enclosure, climbing down the steel ladder, opening
the cage and locking it behind him. With less fanfare than before,
Eitan appeared from the back of the cave, greeting him formally
with a polite 'Good morning', despite the fact that morning had
only ever been an abstract concept to him since he had never left
the enclosure and had never seen the sun. Without any warning,
Yotam placed his hand on Eitan's arm, asking:

'Does that bother you?'

'Does what bother me?'

'I'm touching you.'

'Why would it bother me? Yesterday I picked you up.'

'Yes. You touched me. I haven't touched you.'

'Is the distinction important?'

'Enormously.'

'The person being touched. And the person touching.'

'Exactly.'

'No one has touched me before.'

'Which is why you might be upset.'

'I'm not upset.'

'I didn't ask your permission.'

'Should you?'

'This is your body. This is your space.'

'You made this body. You made this space.'

'But they're not mine.'

'Are they mine?'

'They are.'

'I could ask you not to touch me?'

'You could.'

'Is that something people ask?'

'Often.'

'Because they don't like the feeling?'

'Can you describe the feeling?'

'Your skin is hot to me.'

'Does it burn?'

'It does.'

Yotam removed his hand.

'I'm sorry.'

'The idea was nice.'

'Why was it nice?'

'You were treating me more like a human.'

'And less like?'

'A monster.'

'I've never treated you as a monster.'

Eitan considered this response, agreeing:

'But you've never treated me as a man.'

'You're not a man. That's the whole point of you.'

'And what is the point of you?'

Yotam laughed.

'The point of me is you.'

Later that morning, Yotam presented Eitan with a scenario:

'Imagine this. You've living above the ice. In McMurdo City.'

'I'm free?'

'Yes. You're free. You're moving freely between people.'

'What am I doing?'

'You're going to work.'

'What work would I do?'

'What work would you like to do?'

Eitan thought about this for some time, before replying:

'I can build. I will build the greatest buildings you've ever seen. They will be made out of ice. They will be buildings unlike anything you've ever seen.'

'You're a builder. You're a master builder. And one day you're busy building something. What if a child, a human child, an ordinary-born child, suddenly ran over to you and clasped your leg? Like this?'

Yotam put on his gloves, to muffle his body temperature, and placed his hands on Eitan's leg.

'An ordinary-born child would be too afraid of me.'

'To start off with, maybe. But ordinary-born children adapt very fast. Eventually they'll get used to you. Very quickly they'll be fascinated by you.'

'How would I react?'

'That's the question.'

'You want to know if this child is safe? Or whether I might hurt it?'

'Are you insulted?'

'Do you want children, Yotam?'

The question caught him off guard.

'It would be hard.'

'Are you infertile?'

He laughed for the second time that day.

'I've never been tested.'

'Why do you say it would be hard for you to have a child?'

'I spend all my time here.'

'Do you have a partner?'

'Not at the moment, no.'

'Your partner would be a man?'

'A man, yes.'

He thought on this for some time.

'The two of you would adopt a child.'

'We would.'

'Would you adopt an ordinary-born child or an ice-adapted one?'

'Either, both.'

'You are uncomfortable with these questions?'

'No. My hesitation is only because they're difficult questions.'

'You live alone?'

'I do.'

'I live alone, too. But not like you, I think.'

'No, not like me.'

'You feel something is missing from your life?'

'Many things are missing from my life.'

'Such as?'

'Warmth.'

'Is that a joke?'

'Yes, a joke. But it's true, too.'

'Why have you not found someone to live with?'

'It's not easy.'

'You struggle with life in this place.'

'I struggled with life before this place.'

Yotam tried to maintain constant eye contact even when inside the circle of intimate personal space. Eitan never looked away, never closed his eyes, never blinked, never broke eye contact. With growing certainty Yotam was confident that integration would not only be a success but that it should take place as soon as possible. Eitan was ready and eager to play his part in rebuilding their civilization. He'd spent six years in captivity doing little else but study, able to read dense pages of text with a single glance, absorbing as much literature as he could be provided with. Despite having spent his entire existence in solitary confinement, he showed no signs of hostility, no indication of disturbed behavioural patterns. Judging from their interaction there was no question that they should move to a trial integration period where he'd be released like a prisoner on bail, tagged, monitored, allowed to take part in life above the ice.

'Yotam?'

'Yes, Eitan?'

'We're being watched.'

Yotam turned to see scientists, support staff and security officers lined up at the observation tunnels, looking down at them.

FINAL STAGE CHAMBERS
EITAN'S ENCLOSURE
SAME DAY

A s Yotam said goodbye, Eitan asked:
'Are you in trouble?'

'For what? Talking to you? No. This is my job.'

'They're looking at us strangely.'

'How are they looking at us?'

'Like we've done something wrong.'

Yotam was impressed with his level of perception.

'I didn't run it past them, that's all. I'll see you tomorrow. We'll do something new.'

'I am looking forward to it, Yotam.'

'Me, too.'

Yotam left the cage, shutting it behind him. He climbed up the ladder, returning to the office floor of the ice chambers. Leaving Eitan behind and re-entering the world of ordinary-born people, he felt no sense of relief; he didn't feel safer or less afraid. The truth was that with each step closer to regular people he felt less at ease. In the observation tunnels he stood before his team, separate from them, under the scrutiny of their uncomprehending gaze.

'What were you doing?'

'Testing him.'

'You were inside his enclosure.'

'That was the test.'

'You didn't tell us?'

'No.'

'Who did you clear it with?'

'I don't need anyone's permission to risk my own life.'

The security officer was unimpressed.

'You could've been captured.'

'That's true.'

'We would not have negotiated for your return.'

'I'm aware of that.'

His colleague added:

'More importantly, this test proves nothing.'

'I disagree.'

'All it proves is that he wasn't stupid enough to kill you. It doesn't prove that they're safe to integrate.'

'It doesn't prove that, no. But it's a first step. Someone needed to go in at some point. We had to break the barrier between us. Otherwise, what's the point of all this? We need them to live alongside us – that's the dream.'

The scientists and support staff stared at him, not as if he'd broken down the barrier between the species, but as though he'd simply moved himself to the other side of it. Ending the debate, Yotam said:

'I take responsibility for my actions. I'll make that clear should any questions arise.'

Yotam packed his backpack and left the Final Stage Chambers, climbing up the ice staircase to the Ross Ice Shelf, passing through the heavily armed Russian checkpoints under their glare, as though they suspected him of trying to smuggle one of the creatures out. Rather than heading straight home, back to McMurdo Old Town, he walked to the work cabin, the converted military transport aircraft that had been the Antonov Mriya. Entering the interior of this vast plane, where dozens of blubber lanterns hung from the ceiling, he was immediately wrapped in a blanket, handed a mug of warm seal milk and his temperature checked. He assured them he wasn't feeling cold, or sick, requesting instead the overnight use of a welfare animal – one of the Siberian Husky dogs. The fact that he'd never asked before concerned the people who worked there.

'Are you okay?'

He struggled not to break into tears, holding his emotions together long enough to answer:

'I don't feel like being alone tonight.'

The team selected the friendliest of the dogs, a husky called Copper so named after his unusual red-coloured coat, and it struck Yotam that people had been genetically engineering companions for thousands of years, long before they'd understood the science behind it.

With Copper by his side, tied to his waist with a lead, he skied back to McMurdo Old Town, returning his bamboo skis at the entrance to his residential building. His husky suddenly made him enormously popular and everyone in the building wanted to play. Copper loved the attention as people buried their faces in his beautiful fur and scratched his ears. Eventually retiring to his room, Yotam watched the curious husky sniff around his modest collection of belongings, no more than a line of drying clothes and some tatty books on genetics. Sitting on the floor, he stroked Copper's beautiful thick red fur and quite unexpectedly he found himself crying, something he hadn't done for many years. Knowing the score, Copper dutifully licked his face.

MCMURDO CITY
OLD TOWN
YOTAM'S BEDROOM
SAME DAY

Y OTAM COULDN'T SLEEP. HE LAY awake, staring out of his window at the sun that wouldn't set for another three months. As with all the refugees from the warm world, he'd suppressed many memories. Recollecting those early winter months on Antarctica was less a clear recall of events and more like a series of sensations – the stench of burning jet fuel, the screaming winds, the darkness broken by a burning sunrise of crashing planes. Life at that time had felt like a fluke, sure to come to an end at any moment, as if people were walking across a roulette table with an indifferent croupier sweeping them to the sides.

On the evacuation flight from Israel there had been no seats. To maximize the number of passengers it was standing room only with people pressed so close together it was possible to fall asleep and remain upright. He'd been lucky, pressed against a window, staring out at a sky filled with planes all heading in one direction – south, diverted around the floating alien citadels now occupying the sky. To his eye, they were magnificent, more like artistic sculptures than ships, and he found it hard to imagine an intelligence capable of such innovation also being capable of the crimes they were about to commit. Few spoke on the flight, some prayed, but mostly they travelled in stunned silence, having left everything and everyone they knew behind, heading towards a life they couldn't imagine.

Unable to wait for the weather to abate, his plane had battled through extreme winds, buffeted about like a toy, attempting a landing so dangerous it bordered on the absurd. With nothing to lose, the pilots had plunged through fierce katabatic storms, touching down on the plateaus near the South Pole Station while all around planes were flipped over or smashed together. Landing on the ice, the specially designed skis hadn't snapped, the hull hadn't ripped apart, testament to the brilliance of the engineers and the extraordinary skill of the pilots, except that no one on board had the time to thank them, confronted with the overwhelming challenges of life on this continent.

Inside the plane, shoulder to shoulder with thousands of fellow citizens, the interior serving as a temporary shelter from the elements, no one dared to open the emergency doors. Outside there were refugees dying from the cold, clambering up to the windows, pleading to be let in, freezing to the exterior like barnacles on the hull of a ship. All that remained of some nation states was a single passenger plane with three rows of seats representing the government, one row of seats for the royal family, ten lines of seats for the military and twenty lines of seats for the rest of civil society – an entire country reduced to fewer than forty rows.

Days later, when the winds had calmed down, they'd departed, leaving behind the rotten husk of an airplane which no person could tolerate for another minute. Roped together in a procession, stumbling through the darkness, guided by the stars, they'd set up temporary camps, about to embark on one of the most famous expeditions in human history – the walk to the South Pole.

The South Pole Station was the nearest base on the East Antarctica Ice Sheet, the largest ice sheet on the planet, three thousand metres thick, two thousand eight hundred metres above sea level – a once pristine desert plain now scorched, scratched and scarred by the Exodus. It was by far the smallest of the Antarctica bases, housing only one hundred and fifty scientists during the summer and fifty during the winter, nowhere near the scale of McMurdo Station over eight hundred miles away. People had continuously occupied the geographic South Pole since November 1956, and during those decades the base had evolved from a small science station to a geodesic dome fifty metres wide, with supply depots and fuel tanks. Separate from the main base building were remote science facilities including the Atmospheric Research Observatory and an observatory for astrophysics. Even with this expansion it was fanciful that such a small scientific base could form any kind of meaningful refugee settlement for the world's population, even with the supply drops, including emergency shelters, prefabricated laboratories, crates of dried food, bundles of clothes, millions of vitamin pills and thermal sleeping bags. The flat ice around the station had been transformed by these drops into an expressway of sliding steel freight containers, thousands of them with parachutes still attached, dragged across the ice by the powerful winds. Yotam's group had slowly journeyed through this kinetic landscape of sliding crates and billowing parachutes, some of the procession crushed by crates coming out of nowhere, racing through the night like runaway trains. A sense of futility might have overcome his expedition had it not been for the *aurora australis*, green swirling vapour trails of lights across the sky so extraordinary everyone had presumed they were alien in origin. Under these swirls of light, they saw, framed against the witch-green sky, the modular outline of the South Pole Station.

A base designed and intended to house no more than a hundred and fifty people was now the only habitable space for hundreds of miles. Even with people sleeping in the observatory, the laboratories, under the tables, on the floor, the base could provide for only ten thousand. Everyone else had been told to find their own emergency shelters from the supply drops. Controlled by the American and Chinese military, the two superpowers had agreed to work together during the Exodus, surprising many by accepting that the only chance of survival was one of co-operation and co-ordination rather than combat. The American–Chinese alliance, the forefather to the Antarctic Alliance, had scrambled to expand the base and new structures had been hastily added, temporary shelters and emergency installations. Even so, there was nowhere near the capacity to look after the many thousands of survivors trying to find refuge and the Station had resorted to using lethal force to prevent the base from being overrun.

Yotam and a team of his fellow Israeli soldiers had advanced on the base, presenting themselves and their passenger manifest to the authorities, granted access to the outer survival tents where they waited for processing. Only a select few were allowed to enter the main base – the smartest engineers, geneticists and Nobel Prize-winning biologists. From Yotam's plane only fifty-seven made the cut and were allowed inside. The rest remained in the fields of tents that filled the gaps between the base and the observatory, thousands of interlinked shelters spreading out from the central hub, a refugee encampment with a mortality rate so high it was losing people faster than they arrived. As a soldier, Yotam was ordered to guard the outer perimeter against nations demanding access to the base for an aging king or a religious leader, none of whose authority meant anything anymore. Devoted personal bodyguards were fighting for their masters, their kings and queens, and the skirmishes continued for many days until it was understood that the systems and hierarchies of the old world were meaningless. There was only one option – subordinate to a single Antarctic authority.

Inside the encampment were some of the most fortunate people alive, but they didn't look it and they didn't feel it. Having battled to reach Antarctica, they were asking what the point of the journey was, with no sense of how this new existence could be anything more than a protracted form of annihilation. There was no way the South Pole Station could ever become a self-sustaining base; the question was asked whether any place on Antarctica could support human life without supply lines to the warm world.

Despair began to spread. Broken by the events of the past thirty days, Yotam had been about to lose his mind, on the brink of insanity, his hands clamped over his ears, no longer able to distinguish the howling wind from the sound of screams, furious with himself for not going to Haifa, for not spending his final days with Eitan, for never being kissed and never knowing love. He would surely never know love now. This was the moment a woman called Song Fu had entered his life.

Protected by a detail of bodyguards drawn from the special forces of the People's Liberation Army, it was clear that Song Fu was a person of enormous importance, not simply because of her heavily armed entourage; her manner was so utterly unlike anyone else in the refugee encampment. Serene, while everyone else was in turmoil, she surveyed the remnants of humankind as if ready to roll up her sleeves and fix this unseemly mess, radiating order and discipline. A woman in her late fifties with short grey hair and wolf-grey eyes, she was dressed in pristine designer thermal attire, suitable for a day on the most exclusive of Swiss slopes. As it turns out, she should have landed at McMurdo Station, but her plane had been caught in the storms and, badly damaged, had been forced to touch down near the South Pole Station.

Fascinated by this vision of confidence, Yotam watched as she moved among the survivors, asking questions of each of them. With some of the refugees she spent no more than a few seconds, with others she spoke for many minutes, before arriving at Yotam. He was so close to delirium at this point that he had no idea whether he could articulate any kind of meaningful reply. Sitting beside him, she offered a sip of warm cauliflower soup from a Thermos, the most delicious liquid he'd ever tasted. She spoke to him in English, occasionally addressing a question in Mandarin to her interpreter, asking him to tell the story of his life. Yotam had been so relieved to talk, to do anything to take his mind off the world around him, he'd babbled about his childhood, his military service, his love story with Eitan, the most intimate details spewed up in an unbroken monologue. Song didn't say a word until the very end when she thanked him and moved onto the next refugee, giving him no indication of her purpose or whether what he'd said was of any interest.

One week later she had returned to him with a proposition. Once winter was over, she would be transferring to McMurdo Station, explaining that she was a geneticist and it had already been decided that genetic adaptation was the only chance humankind had of surviving the cold. Despite the apparent anarchy, there was a plan. The newly created governing alliance of nations had been pondering the future, believing the only way to stave off extinction was to behave in ways that had once been considered morally and ethically unacceptable.

'I need a team of assistants. People devoted to my work. You will do exactly as I say without question or dissent. You will work harder than any person has ever worked before. We'll do things that no person has ever done before. What do you say?'

Yotam had said yes.

MCMURDO CITY
HISTORIC OLD TOWN
THE CANTEEN
NEXT DAY

E NTERING THE CANTEEN FOR BREAKFAST, Yotam had no
intention of leaving Copper tied up outside, figuring people
wouldn't mind the company of a handsome husky while they ate. As
it happens, compared to the metropolises of old, New York, Berlin,
Delhi, Tokyo, very few citizens of McMurdo City became sick with
minor illnesses in part due to the monastically healthy diet but also
because the levels of viruses and bacteria were dramatically lower
on this freezing continent. All upper respiratory tract diseases died
out within four weeks of arriving and with no new arrivals from
the warm world, there were no new pathogens and no new pandemics. Today breakfast was synthetic protein porridge cultivated
in the food labs, topped with grated tussock-root and fortified with
ground-up vitamin pills, the supply of which was set to run out in a
matter of months. Each bowl was accompanied by mugs of warm
seal milk turned vivid green with powdered algae. Since the kitchen
team had become concerned about his weight, it was agreed that
he was too thin for life in Antarctica, Yotam was fed a penguin-egg

omelette which he ate out of obligation while others eyed his plate enviously, puzzled by his lack of appreciation for this delicacy.

In charge of the Old Town Canteen was the South Korean-born head chef, Chang-Rae Sang, once a world-acclaimed culinary talent, his restaurant in Seoul frequented by pop stars and politicians, celebrated by a popular food documentary back in the days of television. Considered a non-essential citizen, he hadn't been selected by his government's Exodus programme. Nonetheless, a man of guile and determination who'd built his career from modest beginnings, the son of a street food vendor, he'd made his own way to Antarctica on a friend's shipping vessel, surviving by a combination of good fortune and ingenuity. Despite the extreme constraints of the continent in terms of food sources, Chang-Rae refused to surrender to these limitations. He often claimed he could cope with the cold, but the narrow spectrum of flavours was painful to him, like a pianist only being able to play three notes. Rather than merely making do, he spent his free time searching for anything that might be edible, from pulverized volcanic pumice to skua-claw broth, always testing it on himself for adverse reactions and occasionally falling sick in the process. He was considered a hero for his efforts. McMurdo's Senate was aware that a dynamic and vibrant cuisine had done much to inspire people, with Chang-Rae producing extraordinary dishes that would've impressed the toughest of critics. If Antarctica could be said to have a cuisine, it had been largely defined by his creativity. As it happened, Yotam enjoyed the diet. For religious reasons, rules that he continued to follow despite the ungodly nature of his work, he never ate shellfish even though spider crabs were abundant, nor did he indulge in the occasional luxuries handed out from the near-depleted storerooms. The last remaining splinters of Ecuadorian dark chocolate and thimbles of ancient French wines were offered on holidays to break up the repetitious nature of their meals, precious treats used to motivate the McMurdo community struggling with the narrowness of life on the ice. His childhood, devoid of everyday pleasures, meant that the austerity was far less challenging to him than it was to many others. For whatever reason, these two men, who had almost nothing in common, were tremendously fond of each other, perhaps recognizing a shared level of professional fanaticism or merely enjoying the mysterious magic of a friendship that had no reason behind it of any obvious kind.

Emerging from the kitchen, noticing the commotion in the queue, Chang-Rae asked his friend:

'What's with the dog?'

'Last night, after work, the welfare staff felt I needed an emotional companion.'

'Ever tried a human?'

'That's funny.'

'I'm not joking. I don't know why you don't date.'

'I date. I've dated. I will in the future date.'

'Your heart's never been in it. Don't tell me you're married to your work; I work just as hard as you. You need to find someone. Life on this continent makes more sense when you're with someone. When you can't see a point to anything, you hold them in your arms and suddenly you remember what you're surviving for.'

Seeing his friend's head drop and sadness sweep over him, Chang-Rae added:

'Can I set you up?'

'Who is he?'

'A close friend of mine. Great guy.'

'Okay, sure.'

'Will you stand them up? Like you did last time? It's not fair. This life is tough. No one has the strength to be stood up.'

'The project I'm working on is reaching the end. I'm there seven days a week.'

'How are the children?'

'The children' was his way of referring to the new ice-adapted species of the Cold People Project. Every time Yotam heard the joke he said:

'Children? They're taller than us, stronger than us, faster than us, smarter than us.'

'Are they going to like my food?'

'I can't talk about them. You know that.'

'But I never understood why.'

'Until we decide which species to release into the population, it doesn't make sense.'

'I heard a rumour you're getting ready to release them. It's going to happen soon.'

'Where did you hear that?'

'I have my sources.'

Yotam thought it was probably the Russian security guards trying to scare people into opposing the project. But the truth is that most people were excited about the moment of integration. Chang-Rae said:

'I was thinking about an integration banquet, a big celebration. That's why I'm asking. I want to know what to cook. I can cook for anyone. Vegans, vegetarians, ordinary-born, ice-adapted. I cooked for my dad, you know how fussy he was?'

'Don't be offended if they pass on your meals.'

He was scandalized by the idea.

'Why would they pass? What's wrong with them?'

'There's nothing wrong with them.'

'There's something wrong with everyone.'

'They're perfect.'

Chang-Rae tilted his head to the side, reacting to the tone of Yotam's voice.

'Perfect, huh?'

'For the cold, I mean.'

'You're fond of them?'

'I am.'

'Maybe this is the reason you're not dating? All your affections are being spent on them?'

'That's ridiculous.'

'When do we get to meet them?'

'That's not up to me.'

'Are the rumours true? Are you about to release them?'

'Integrate them.'

'Whatever you want to call it. Is it about to happen?'

'It's not up to me.'

'But I'm asking you. Are you ready? Would you release them?'

'Yes, I would.'

'Can they save us?'

'I'm sure of it.'

'They're not like us, are they?'

'That's the whole point of them.'

In most people's minds the ice-adapted people should appear reassuringly similar to humans. They should speak and walk like them – moderate genetic modifications were acceptable, a bigger heart, tougher skin. It was widely believed that the parahumans were the template for the future, with the hope that soon a new generation of these ice-adapted people would fully enter society, making everyone's lives easier. Ordinary-born people waited like elderly parents who'd toiled back-breaking jobs to pay their kids through college, eager for the day when their offspring would look after them. The challenges of this continent were many and the ordinary-born population was sustained by the expectation that one day their lives would be transformed by the ice-adapted who'd live among them, tending to their frail genetic ancestors out of gratitude for creating them. They hoped these new Cold People would be able to achieve great things, build a magnificent new capital city that they could all be proud of, a Kubla Khan palace in the snow with turrets of ice and domes, rather than functional survival structures with no aesthetic of any kind. Perhaps these Cold People would excavate under the Transantarctic Mountains and create an underground warren of subterranean homes with limitless geothermic warmth, or mine the vast untapped resources currently inaccessible to them buried under thousands of metres of ice. No one ever imagined this project was about manufacturing a slave, bred to serve – the word was a taboo – but if they were honest few truly believed this species would be an equal – more of an Antarctic working class: brilliant, admired and appreciated, but under human command.

Only those working on the project knew how radically different the new generation of Cold People truly were. Behind closed doors, the leaders in McMurdo Senate worried that their genetic engineering had diverged too far from what most people considered to be human. The fear was that ordinary-born people might lose faith in the project, that all their suffering and sacrifices were being answered not with a child in their image but something entirely other. For this reason, the rules governing entry to the Final Stage laboratories were strict. Employees were forbidden from describing these creations. While this veil of secrecy had held for many years – there were very few secrets in McMurdo – stories were starting to spread of Yotam's close personal interaction with the radically ice-adapted cold creatures, actions interpreted as prefiguring their imminent release into society. Walking through the canteen, people stopped Yotam on his way to the table, ignoring the rules about secrecy, asking him:

What do they look like?

What jobs can they do?

When can we see them?

By the time Yotam had reached his table so many people had gathered around him he gave up on the idea of eating here. As he tried to leave, to eat in his room, politely explaining that he couldn't answer their questions, a woman took hold of his arm.

'I lost my sons. I lost my husband. I'm the last of my family. I want to know what they died for. I'm owed that at least.'

Yotam replied, as gently as he could:

'We've all lost someone. Most of us have lost everyone. And none of us are owed anything.'

THE ROSS ICE SHELF
WELFARE STAFF CABIN
SAME DAY

T HOUGH THEY'D ONLY BEEN TOGETHER for a short period of time, Yotam had grown attached to Copper and he was concerned that he might cry when forced to return him today. Intense emotional reactions were often early indicators of someone struggling with life on the ice, people who wept when they couldn't find a missing mitten or when they spilled their hot drink. For twenty years he'd been emotionally disciplined – a detached figure, stable and temperamentally consistent. Yet entering the support cabin, approaching the welfare team, he was on the brink of tears.

'I'm here to return Copper.'

Before he could say another word, they informed him that they'd decided Copper should stay with him for the time being. The team had witnessed numerous employees lose their minds over the years and it was clear that they were taking pre-emptive steps to preserve his sanity. By way of softening the explanation, they said:

'You live alone.'

'I've always lived alone.'

Rather than saying, *It's starting to show,* they remarked:

'He likes you.'

Since Yotam wanted nothing more than to keep Copper, he stopped trying to argue and instead crouched down, rubbing the dog's thick red coat.

'Seems like you're staying with me.'

Looking up at the welfare officers, he asked:

'Can I take him down to the chambers?'

'No dog has ever made it past the first few steps. Including plenty tougher than that old softie.'

Yotam whispered:

'From one softie to another, there's nothing to be afraid of.'

Arriving at the entrance, he checked on Copper. The dog was pressed tight against him, his fur raised, his ears pricked up. Yotam took the first steps slowly, waiting for Copper to howl or pull on his lead. But he followed by his side, descending to the halfway point with not even so much as a growl. Yotam glanced over his shoulder, back up the stairs, observing the line of Russian security officers watching, no doubt having taken bets on how far he'd get. Reaching the last step, Copper sniffed the air. The breeze carried pungent smells which even an ordinary-born person with limited senses found startling, from a fetid carrion stench to an intoxicating pheromone perfume. Yet still Copper didn't try to run back to the surface, and Yotam wondered if all the other dogs had taken their cue not from the presence of ice-adapted species but from their owners' emotions. Perhaps he was the only ordinary-born person not afraid of these Cold People, the only person who believed their integration would be a success. For a long time, he'd been convinced that many of the teams not only harboured doubts about the viability of integrating these radically adapted species, but on some deeper level they despised them. Heading into the tunnels, Yotam positioned Copper tight against the ice wall away from the chambers. He wanted Eitan to be the first cold creature that he experienced. And somehow, without any planning or deliberation, Copper had become Eitan's next test.

THE ROSS ICE SHELF
FINAL STAGE CHAMBERS
EITAN'S ENCLOSURE
SAME DAY

ALL THE SCIENTISTS AND SUPPORT staff were lined up at the window, at the observation level, including the security officers, who were convinced that the dog would be eaten and equally convinced that Yotam was in the slow process of losing his mind, suffering from the onset of Antarctic insanity. Determined to prove them wrong, Yotam unlocked the outer cage, entering the enclosure, keeping one hand on Copper's collar as a way of signalling that the husky wasn't intended as food. Almost immediately Copper lay flat on the ice, ears down, eyes straight ahead, making a sound Yotam had never heard any dog make, neither a growl nor a whine, but something almost musical. Revealing himself, Eitan appeared on the wall of the cave, his claws securing him to the ice. He moved with his characteristic blend of precision, strength and elegance, effortlessly approaching their position, coming to a stop with his body at ninety degrees to his guests. He looked down at Copper, still flat on the ice. Yotam realized he was in the minority, the only species with two legs present in this meeting. Eitan said:

'This is a dog.'

'A husky dog. Called Copper.'

'I've never smelt him on you before.'

'How good is your sense of smell?'

'Not as good as a dog. But better than yours.'

'He was given to me yesterday.'

'Who did he belong to?'

'The support team above the ice.'

'What is a "support team"?'

'They look after our well-being.'

'Because you find life on Antarctica hard?'

'That's why we created you.'

'Yotam, are you worried I might eat your dog?'

'I'm not, no.'

'But it crossed your mind?'

'You've never seen a dog before. You might think I was bringing it to you as food.'

'I've read about the way people keep pets.'

'Yes.'

'He is your pet?'

'He's a companion.'

Eitan climbed off the wall and onto the base of the enclosure. Yotam crouched down and let Copper off the lead with no idea what might happen next. To his surprise, rather than retreat or cower, Copper sprang up, bounding towards Eitan as though called by his master. Far from expressing fear, he joyfully rolled onto his back as Eitan extended his skeletal arms, scalpel fingers rubbing the dog's tummy. Copper stood up, passing underneath Eitan's thorax, in between his four legs, emerging on the other side. Eitan declared:

'He's a Siberian Husky.'

'That's right.'

'His origins are Northeast Asia. They were bred by the Chukchi people of the Chukchi Peninsula in Eastern Siberia, for sledge-pulling, protection and, as you say, companionship. It's genetically similar to the Taymyr wolf, an extinct species, wiped out by humankind.'

'I didn't know that.'

'The genetic divergence between dogs and wolves occurred some twenty thousand years ago before the Last Glacial Maximum. The domestication of the grey wolf was brought about by nomadic hunter-gatherers, a process that predates even human agriculture. The first remains of dogs being buried with people date back fourteen thousand years.'

'What else did you read?'

'A Siberian Husky has a double coat, a dense undercoat and a longer topcoat, making it capable of surviving temperatures as low as minus sixty, a temperature I could also easily survive, but which you could not.'

'Looks like I'm the odd one out.'

'Their thick coats require weekly grooming, which is something you will do, now, as part of your companionship?'

'Yes, I will.'

'Yotam?'

'Yes, Eitan.'

'Would you say you love this dog?'

'I would say that, yes.'

'After just one day?'

'After just one day.'

Today's tests were a series of games – the art of play. The intention wasn't to see how well Eitan could master the rules, since with flawless recall he'd master them on first hearing; it was to see what kind of winner he was and, more importantly, what kind of loser. Starting with the simplest forms of game, Yotam bounced a rubber ball against the chamber wall, catching it on the rebound. With his skeletal arm, Eitan accepted the luminous orange rubber ball, examining it as carefully as if it were a new species of life, before throwing it with such enormous strength and precision that the ball rebounded at near bullet-speed around the entire chamber in a remarkable calculation of angles, back into the palm of his hand. With apparently no interest in doing it a second time, he offered the ball back.

'Is this something you do often?'

Yotam laughed.

'Not often, no.'

Changing games, Yotam gently threw the ball for Copper to retrieve and the husky excitedly bounded off down the chamber, sliding on the ice before returning with the ball between his teeth. Yotam handed the ball to Eitan and this time, mimicking Yotam, he gently threw it, watching as Copper bounded off again. But Eitan showed no interest in repeating the game, no matter how keen Copper was. After a time, Copper gave up, bringing the ball back to Yotam.

'You don't like doing things twice?'

'Does the experience change?'

'No, not really. But you can't look after a dog if you only play fetch once.'

'The dog is not mine to look after.'

'If it were? Yours to look after?'

'We would not be playing with this ball.'

'What would you be playing?'

'It would be a different relationship.'

Unsure what he meant, Yotam decided not to press further.

'How about a board game?'

In the Recreation Centre there had been many board games to choose from, including Xiangqi, the Chinese variant of chess, and San Guo Sha, a popular card game based on the Chinese novel. There was Monopoly, Scrabble, backgammon, Risk and Trivial Pursuit. In the end, Yotam had opted for chess, unearthing an antique board with chipped ivory pieces mounted on green felt, a game with a long and complicated history on the Antarctic continent, seen as adversarial and widely avoided after the infamous incident of a Russian scientist attacking another with an ice axe after losing a closely fought game. An excellent chess player by regular human standards, having spent many hours as a child playing, Yotam imagined himself to be tough competition. But he was no match for Eitan. After their first game, unable to convince his opponent of the merits of a rematch, Yotam had told him the story of a chess game between a computer programme called Deep Blue and Garry Kasparov, the greatest ordinary-born chess player to ever live, and how it heralded a new era, since it was the first time a computer beat a human player.

'What are your computers like today?'

'Since we've been trapped on Antarctica, the development of computer technology has come to a stop. There aren't the resources to construct new types of hardware and our technological evolution has been paused. Maybe forever. The future of artificial intelligence, if that's the right term, is now entirely of a biological kind.'

'You're referring to me?'

'Yes, I'm referring to you.'

'Since you can't make computers, you made us?'

Yotam said:

'Eitan, it's time to tell you about Song Fu.'

'Who is Song Fu?'

'She's the woman who created you.'

'I thought you created me?'

'No, I'm not a geneticist. I look after you, but I didn't create you.'

'Where is Song Fu?'

'She died before you were born.'

'What did she die of?'

'The cold.'

'Do you miss her?'

'Very much.'

'You loved her?'

'Yes. I loved her. She's the most brilliant person I've ever known. And she saved my life.'

'Would you say that she was my mother?'

'I don't know if I'd use that word.'

'What word would you use?'

'She created your genome. She didn't model you on herself. There's nothing of her in you except her ideas.'

'And what were her ideas?'

PART SIX

THE STORY OF SONG FU

THE SOUTH POLE STATION
LATITUDE -90.0° S LONGITUDE 0.0° E
22 SEPTEMBER 2023

As Yotam's first winter in Antarctica came to an end, the sun rose above the horizon for the first time since he'd arrived on the continent, revealing the scale of the exodus. Spread across the once pristine ice plateau, a tabletop three thousand metres high and one thousand kilometres wide, was the world's entire fleet of airplanes, from the smallest private jet to the largest cargo carriers. Some had crashed and the charred wreckage was frozen to the ice like prehistoric remains. Others were perfectly intact, as though they were waiting on a runway for permission to take off. In between these planes, like giant meadow flowers, colourful parachutes attached to airdropped supplies were billowing in the winds.

Emerging from the encampments around the South Pole Station, Yotam stood at the edge of the tent line, watching the sun rise with a thousand other people. Despite everything that he'd lost, he couldn't help but delight in the sunlight, basking in a sunrise he'd been sure that he'd never see again. It was possible that he might even have laughed; this man with nothing and no one had found joy in the world again. Since few believed it was possible to survive another winter, there was an unspoken acceptance that this was human-kind's last summer on Earth. It was liberating, to feel free from the pressures of trying to survive. However, that feeling didn't last for long – people were unable to give up; they were determined to carry on. Plans were formed and orders were given.

The authorities at McMurdo Station dispatched a fleet of snow transports to find and retrieve all the important people scattered across the continent, those deemed vital to humankind's future. Song Fu asked Yotam whether he was ready to leave and in broken, stuttering, self-taught Mandarin he'd explained that he was ready to be her assistant. She nodded, telling him that had he replied in English she would've left him behind. Sufficiently impressed with his efforts in such a short space of time, they departed the South Pole Station, an odd couple even among the most eclectic collection of people ever gathered in a snow mobile.

The convoy passed many mounds of frozen corpses, people huddled together as they'd desperately tried to find warmth and occasionally scattered pockets of survivors, living inside airdropped crates of supplies. When they heard the snow mobiles they came running, gaunt and exhausted, stumbling in the snow, arms outstretched, mistakenly believing that they would be saved. But in the early months there was no capacity to save people indiscriminately; that wouldn't happen until every important person had been recovered and McMurdo City was fully established. In an act that seemed cruel, the convoy would stop and assess each of the survivors, to find out who they were and what skills they had. If they weren't designated as an important person their only hope was to head to the Peninsula, where multiple Survivor Towns were forming and where everyone was welcome, no matter who they were, what skills they had, or where they'd come from.

During their long journey to McMurdo, Song Fu spoke almost without pause, beginning Yotam's education on the histories of genetic modification – the history that everyone knew and, more importantly, the history that very few people knew. Before the alien occupation there'd been a global consensus that editing human genes at the embryonic stage should be forever outlawed; no matter how far technology advanced it was an ethical red line never to be crossed. If the scientific challenges of genome adaptation were substantial, then the ethical obstacles were insurmountable. Song Fu said:

'Even at academic conferences, where people were only *debating* the concepts, there were protests, activists screaming at us for even considering the *idea* of genetically modified humans. There were violent clashes over the subject of genetically modified crops. For the first time in human history, we had discovered a world-altering discovery and then declined to alter the world with it. To me, it was preposterous and provincial.'

Song Fu continued:

'The idea of editing human genes was declared a violation of the natural order with unknowable consequences. These concerns were expressed by scientists, faith leaders and politicians. At stake, they claimed, was the fabric of what it was to be human – our genome was being treated with the reverence of a sacred text. The UNESCO International Bioethics Committee declared that:

'"*The human genome must be preserved as the common heritage of humanity.*"

'As if it were a sacred formula, the reason for our greatness as a species, countries and committees ruled that the genome should never be tampered with, lest we undo what it was that made us special, changes which would be for ever, passing from generation to generation, cascading down through our descendants.'

With a sigh she added:

'Most of those opponents to my work are now dead.'

As the convoy stopped to cook dinner, serving army survival rations, highly calorific prepacked food that was designed to last up to twenty-five years, Song Fu explained that before the occupation there'd been no urgent need to adapt our own genetic code.

'Why change our code when we're the dominant species on Earth? This reluctance to adapt the human genome was presented to the world as a form of humility towards nature, but to me, it always sounded like an expression of our complacency, our innate sense of superiority. People were special! We altered other forms of life: we didn't alter ourselves. We were the alterers – not the altered.'

Yotam plucked up the courage to point out:

'The regimes who'd contemplated genetic engineering were the worst of humanity. When we talk about eugenics, I think of the Nazis, the figure of Josef Mengele using Auschwitz to study and torture identical twins. They dreamed of curating Germany's genetic profile.'

'Yes, they were ugly dreams. It was for this reason, many years later, the German Bundestag outlawed both germ-line manipulations and preimplantation genetic diagnosis, subject to a five-year prison sentence under the Embryo Protection Law.'

She took out her sleek Apple tablet computer, indicative of her importance. Yotam marvelled at this relic from the old world.

'You still have one? How many are left?'

'Not many. Don't get side-tracked. Look at this. Study it carefully.'
She shared with Yotam a copy of the original Bundestag law:

Act for Protection of Embryos (The Embryo Protection Act)

Gesetz zum Schutz von Embryonen (Embryonenschutz-
gesetz – ESchG)

13th December 1990

The following Act has been adopted by the Bundestag:

Section 5

Artificial alteration of human germ-line cells

(1) Anyone who artificially alters the genetic information of a
human germ-line cell will be punished with imprisonment up
to five years or a fine.

(2) Likewise anyone will be punished who uses a human germ
cell with artificially altered genetic information for fertilization.

Section 6

Cloning

(1) Anyone who causes artificially a human embryo to
develop with the same genetic information as another embryo,
fetus, human being or deceased person will be punished with
imprisonment up to five years or a fine.

(2) Likewise anyone will be punished who transfers into a
woman an embryo designated in paragraph 1.

Section 7

Formation of chimaeras and hybrids

(1) Anyone who attempts to unite embryos with different
genetic material to a cell conglomerate using at least one
human embryo,

(2) to join a human embryo with a cell that contains genetic information different from the embryo cells and induces them further to develop, or

(3) by fertilization of a human egg cell with the sperm of an animal or by fertilization of an animal's egg cell with the sperm of a man to generate an embryo capable of development, will be punished with imprisonment up to five years or a fine.

(4) Likewise anyone will be punished who attempts

1. to transfer an embryo arising out of a procedure defined in paragraph 1 to a woman or an animal,

2. to transfer a human embryo into an animal.

After he finished reading it, she declared:

'Every action prohibited by these laws we will now attempt. Do you understand the implications of what I'm telling you?'

'Yes.'

'We are about to tamper with humanity's genetic code, so that we have a chance of surviving in the cold. The project already has a name – it is called the "Cold People Project".'

To Song Fu, the human genome was complex data, neither sacred nor mystical, but an instruction manual to building human life, and it was curious to her that Western-educated scientists, coming from a culture which lauded freedom and liberty, felt the need to be so slavish when it came to these instructions. The genetic code consisted of twenty-three separate pairs of chromosomes, each chromosome containing several thousand genes, which in turn divided into exons, composed of codons, with the smallest unit of information being bases, a programming code that instructed human cells the way to grow, not merely shaping physical form but character and identity. With the development of supercomputers, the cost of sequencing a human genome had dropped from the two billion dollars spent on the Human Genome Project in 1990 to a mere five hundred dollars in the months before the alien occupation. The time it took to sequence the human genome had also dropped from thirteen years to a single day. With these advances came the understanding that scientists had not only discovered the code to human life – this was the language of all life on Earth – it was a universal language, the same for microscopic bacteria at the bottom of the deepest oceans as it was for dinosaurs, creatures that had been extinct for thousands of years.

'After we learnt how to read this code, we learnt how to rewrite it.'

The discovery of bacteria capable of gene editing, an attribute they used as a defence against viruses, provided Song Fu with a gene-editing tool, one that had existed in nature for millions of years – Clustered Regularly Interspaced Short Palindromic Repeats. CRISPR could cut into the DNA and insert any genetic code in its place, not merely changing the genes but altering the epigenetic marks that determined how genes are expressed.

'It was the breakthrough we'd all been looking for. Except lawmakers and politicians blocked us from using it on the very species who needed it the most – people.'

Rather than overcoming people's biological limitations, it had been limited to adapting apples to stop them from browning, creating a virus-resistant rainbow papaya and genetically adapting cows so that they could survive the impact of hotter temperatures caused by global warming. Song observed, in the closest she'd come to a joke:

'Before the Cold People Project there was the Hot Cows Project, but the ideas are not so different.'

In 2015, in what was proclaimed to be a world first, researchers at the Sun Yat-sen University in Guangzhou, China, confirmed they had engineered human embryos to prevent the fatal blood disorder thalassaemia from occurring. Amid a chorus of world outrage, fury at this ethical breach, the scientist in charge, Junjio Huang, made it clear that the embryos were non-viable. Song Fu remarked:

'This was true, in the narrow sense, but it was not the whole truth.'

Teams of Chinese scientists had been pressing ahead with germ-line therapy for many years, deeming the risks acceptable given the potential advantages and concerned that if they didn't carry out this pioneering research another country would, whether they admitted it or not. They were not only editing embryos; they were also bringing them to term. Staggered by this revelation, Yotam interjected:

'This was happening *before* the occupation?'

'Long before. The work we're about to do isn't new. We're just not hiding anymore.'

Unbeknown to the world there were children born free from crippling conditions such as Huntington's, which led to a slowing of the mental faculties, Lesch-Nyhan syndrome, which brought about a propensity to self-mutilation, Tay-Sachs disease, which led to brain degradation, and Werner syndrome with its symptoms of childhood ageing. These changes required only a simple edit to a single gene. More sophisticated multi-gene editing had followed. Primary familial and congenital polycythaemia caused an increase in red blood cells' mass due to a mutation in the erythropoietin receptor gene, resulting in an increase of fifty per cent in the oxygen-carrying capacity of the blood. These gene-edited children walked the streets, went to school.

'They trained for the Olympics, they won gold medals, their biological and athletic advantages undetectable to any doping test.'

After the success of the programme, the Chinese state began preparing its population for the fact that a generation was growing up with enormous improvements to intelligence and stamina, launching a bogus advertising campaign for baby formula which claimed to improve the mental facilities and physical attributes of the child. Billboards appeared in all the major Chinese cities, a smokescreen for the genetic editing underway, laying the cover story for the time when children began maturing with significantly higher rates of intelligence, winning every gold medal at the Olympics.

'They would claim the success was due to their new formula of baby milk, not available in the West.'

'You were part of this?'

'I was at the forefront of it. I've won no prizes, published no papers. I've never been asked to address an international conference, although I attended many of them, sitting at the back of the hall, ignored and overlooked, listening to people speculate about the things I was actually doing.'

Without any interest in fame, content in her anonymity, Song Fu had never discussed her work with anyone outside her team. Given access to vast resources, she'd been pushing at the boundaries of germ-line therapy, using trial subjects provided by the Chinese state, stripped of their legal rights, many of whom had later died. She pointed out:

'It was terrible, yes. They were criminals, rapists,

murderers – nonetheless, we all knew it was wrong. But those experiments are the reason we now have a chance of surviving.'

As the convoy approached McMurdo Station, Song Fu concluded her summary by stating that mankind could not survive on Antarctica in its ordinary genetic state. Its genetic code, once so special, was special no more.

'Ordinary people will fear what we're about to create. But this new generation of people, they're our only hope.'

MCMURDO STATION
1 NOVEMBER 2023

I F THE SOUTH POLE STATION had felt defeated, McMurdo was a place of hope, already organized and expanding, offering the first indication that maybe humanity wasn't yet at the end of its journey on Earth. The efforts to build a new capital city had been made possible by co-operation unlike any seen before, every nation pooling their resources, working together in a manner only ever depicted in the most optimistic of utopian political visions. Here it was, in practice, brought about not by wisdom or enlightenment, but by necessity. Enlivened by the vitality of this place, Yotam began to believe that not only was there a chance humankind might survive, there was also a chance we might be more than survivors.

Inside the science labs on the nuclear-powered aircraft carriers, the world's most brilliant geneticists gathered, many suffering from post-traumatic stress syndrome, others unable to imagine how their work could be relevant to this crisis. In contrast, Song Fu seemed unfazed, as though she'd always expected an alien occupation and found it short-sighted that the others had not. Watching his mentor, Yotam realized she was not entirely regular in her thoughts, so singular in her intellect that she didn't react to trauma the way most people did, accepting the radical changes in their circumstances as if she'd merely moved into a new house. Among a group that included many of her award-winning peers, lauded by a scientific establishment that was no more, she asserted her authority.

'I am Song Fu. You don't know who I am because I always remained silent at your seminars. But that was before the alien occupation. This is not the time for silence. This is not the time for caution. I speak with confidence because I have been doing all the things you've only been talking about.'

She revealed that she'd been breaking new ground in genetic engineering long before the alien occupation. Without giving them any time to start up the arid ethical debate, she insisted that they work in separate teams rather than as a single unit. They would be more nimble in smaller groups, she argued. She would not be anyone's subordinate, nor would she operate by consensus. They needed to attempt new ideas freely without being limited by each other, pursuing a range of possibilities without compromise or constraint. There would be no group think or political interference from people who knew nothing about genetics. Of course, she accepted, there might be some likeminded geneticists who could happily co-operate, but having listened to their initial presentations, they couldn't afford to stake the future of humankind on a single approach. One group might fail, another group might succeed.

'I am going to do things you will find unacceptable. In my view, the only thing that would be unacceptable is failure. And we, as a species, are on the brink of failure. Or, as it is also called, extinction.'

They split the scientists into two teams, with the largest group consisting of a coalition of establishment figures and the other led by Song Fu's more radical approach.

Song Fu addressed her team, composed of the Chinese geneticists she'd worked with before in addition to the new recruits from the countries formerly known as Russia, Colombia, Japan and Iran, scientists who were sceptical that they would be given any significant role to play in the mainstream group dominated by Americans and Europeans. In her preliminary address she'd covered the whiteboard with photographs of fruit flies. The *drosophila* genome has only four pairs of chromosomes, making them among the easiest organisms to genetically manipulate, and the photos showed images of fruit flies with legs where their antenna should be, white eyes and orange eyes rather than their normal red eyes, curled wings rather than straight wings.

'The mutations we once tried with fruit flies we will now try with people. We will treat the human genome the same as we treated the *drosophila* genome. Look at these photos carefully and think about what that means. If you have any moral doubts, you should join the other team. We will move fast, make mistakes, and never question ourselves. We don't have the time.'

Song Fu took possession of an entire medical deck of an American aircraft carrier. The women being fertilized with these new ice-adapted embryos were not criminals; they were volunteers who'd survived the Exodus, endured heart-breaking loss and overcome the most challenging of conditions. Moreover, with a total population now counted in millions, when once it had been counted in the billions, every person was valued in a way that individuals had never been valued before, as vital to society as they were to their families and loved ones. At first the approach seemed straightforward – the proposition would be transparent. Women who'd lost children or who couldn't conceive would be offered the option of this radical new process, a chance to give birth to an ice-adapted child who could survive the extreme cold, a child robust enough to make it to adulthood with strengthened immune systems and a greater resistance to the freezing temperatures. If they gave their consent, fully cognizant of the risks, there was no moral quandary aside from the fact that no one, not even the most brilliant of geneticists, could be sure of the risks. But Song Fu never allowed herself to be limited by the survival chances of the mother. She focused her team on the singular task at hand – figuring out, at a genetic level, a form of life perfectly suited to surviving the cold.

'I was a mother. I lost my children during the Exodus. Two daughters. One was nineteen, the other was sixteen. Neither were selected by the Chinese state. When I refused to board the plane without them, I was sedated. I woke up in the air, my arms tied to the seat, being flown to Antarctica, knowing that my family had been left behind. These are the times we live in. I do this work in honour of my family, the family I lost. We will make a new family.'

While the European–American team set about making small adjustments to the human genome, Song Fu rejected this incremental approach – her intention was to reinvent the human genome. With twenty-three paired chromosomes, approximately twenty-five thousand genes, and almost three billion bases, not all of which had even been identified, let alone understood, she and her team were attempting to rewrite a blueprint for life that they hadn't yet fully comprehended. In order to create life, they were about to orchestrate an entirely new set of steps that depended on the correct spatial and temporal expression of genes. Even the smallest of changes could bring about the most far-reaching of consequences. They could mutate a single letter of DNA, leaving the three billion other bases of the genome untouched, and this one alteration could result in anything from extraordinary strength to severe learning disabilities.

'There is no autonomy to each unit of heredity; one change could impact everything. Each change rebuilds the entire genetic structure. To hang a painting in a different room of a house is to rebuild the entire house. For this reason, we cannot protect ourselves from the unknown. We are at a genetic frontier. These will not be mistakes as we've experienced them before. Many of them will be catastrophic to the life we're trying to create. Mistakes will be our mentor. But the result will be a form of human life suited to the most inhospitable place on Earth, a life that can call this place home.'

PART SEVEN

TWENTY YEARS LATER

B ORROWING THE LAST MOVIE PROJECTOR in McMurdo City
would be no easy task. As rare as it was fragile, the projector
was one of the most evocative and emotional threads to the worlds
that they'd been dispossessed of. In order to use it, Yotam needed
to convince the person in charge of the weekly movie screenings,
a renowned Algerian director called Zariffa Boutella, winner of
the last ever Palme d'Or for her film about La Castellane housing project in the 15th arrondissement of Marseille. Her movie
was set during the hottest summer on record when extreme heat
gripped the south of France, cement cracking in temperatures of
a hundred degrees Fahrenheit, characters mingling in the feverish
night, unable to sleep, pacing the communal gardens where grass
had turned to dust and where neighbours shared a hose as a way
of trying to stay cool. The film was as sexually explicit as it was
emotionally intense, relationships cracking in the heat as well as
new connections forming. No longer able to make movies – there
weren't the resources; there wasn't even paper for scripts – Zariffa
had become the guardian of the projector and curator of the

screenings in addition to having a day job managing an Adelie penguin farm. In her late fifties, she wore handcrafted Inuit clothing made by the tribes brought to Antarctica by the Canadian government who'd had the foresight to preserve their centuries of expertise about living on the ice. Smoking lichen from a whale bone pipe, she asked:

'You want to borrow my projector?'

'Only for one day.'

'It's the last of its kind.'

'I'll take good care of it.'

'How can you? When you have no love of cinema?'

'I like movies.'

'You don't attend these screenings. You have no sense of how much these nights mean to people. Once a week we come together, watch a film, a work of art, and talk about something that isn't snow or seal.'

There was concern that screenings of Manhattan murder mysteries and picturesque Parisian romances could provoke grief as intense as the loss of a family member, and there'd even been discussion in the Senate that movies should be prohibited, with the rationale that people needed to look forward not backwards. In the end, this was a libertarian society, with as few rules as possible; citizens took responsibility for their own actions; they watched these movies at their own risk with no promise of help if they suffered adverse psychological consequences, unable to cope with the emotions that were rekindled.

'I've been busy with work.'

'Too busy for movies. Too busy for sport. Too busy for music. Too busy for everything that makes us human. You saw my film?'

'Yes, in a cinema in Tel Aviv, also during one of the hottest summers on record. I liked it very much.'

'What other movies have you seen?'

'Not many. I was never allowed to watch movies growing up.'

'Why do you want this new species to watch one?'

'I wouldn't use my childhood as a model for anyone.'

Hearing that answer, she began to warm to him.

Zariffa led him to the back of the room, revealing the case where the last movie projector was stored.

'You know that apart from my last movie, all my others have been lost?'

'I didn't know that. I'm sorry.'

'The Academy of Motion Pictures brought the library of American classics to Antarctica. The French Film Institute brought the library of French classics and only included my last movie. Some countries didn't bother to bring any. An entire nation's cultural output left behind and lost forever. Do you speak French?'

'Hebrew, English and Mandarin.'

'So few people speak French anymore.'

'This new species does.'

'He does?'

'He's studied over forty languages. He's read French literature, French philosophy, French history, always in the original language.'

'And he's six years old?'

'He was fully grown at three.'

'I have children. One regular-born child. One adopted child. One cold-adapted child. This projector is my fourth child. If you get caught in a storm, the lens freezes and cracks, no more movies forever. Can you understand what that would mean? No movies ever again. Until the end of time. There are no spare parts. Or if there are, the Senate won't give them to me. They never liked these movie screenings.'

'I won't break it.'

'You won't, perhaps not. He might. What if he has a reaction to the movie?'

'I've never seen him do anything clumsy.'

'He's never seen a movie. The first time people saw *L'Arrivee d'un train en gare de La Ciotat* they ran out screaming, imagining this train on the screen was going to crush them.'

'You're right, I don't know how he's going to react. That's the test.'

'I like you. You interest me. But I can't risk it.'

'I'll bring it back by the end of the day.'

'Why not bring him here? I can set up the screening room. We all watch together.'

'They're not allowed above the ice.'

'Why is that?'

'The Senate doesn't think he's ready.'

'They don't think *he's* ready? Or they don't think *we're* ready?'

'Both.'

'You ask a lot and offer little.'

Zariffa opened the case and affectionately put her hand on the projector, pondering the issue.

'Did you have a movie in mind?'

Yotam blushed like a teenager being asked out on a date. Zariffa studied his reaction.

'Something sentimental, I can tell.'

'*Edward Scissorhands.*'

'The Tim Burton movie? I can see why you chose that movie – a movie about an outsider, someone who looks different to us, fitting in with our society – yes, I understand.'

'To see if he can relate to the main character.'

'A man created by scientists.'

'Yes.'

'But it is a fantasy movie. You should show him how we were. As people. Our cities. Our arrogance. Our complacency. Our brilliance. Our dirt, our clothes, our colours, our cars. You can't show him something that isn't real.'

'He's read thousands of books. He knows more about the past than we do. The test is to see if he can empathize. To see if he can care about a fantasy, a fiction, make-believe – to feel something for a character that only exists as flickers of light.'

It was clear that Zariffa was growing more intrigued by the scenario.

'You can borrow the projector. On one condition.'

'Name it.'

'I come with you.'

'That's not possible.'

'Why not?'

'You're not allowed into the chambers.'

'You could get me in.'

'I could try, yes.'

'Be honest with me. The movie isn't the only test.'

'What do you mean?'

'You must be curious to see how I react to him. If an open-minded artist such as myself can't tolerate the sight of him, what chance is there for the rest of society, correct?'

Yotam smiled. He liked Zariffa and wondered why he hadn't

come to her movie screenings. He needed to find a better sense of balance in his life. He was working too much. In trying to save people, he'd forgotten how much he enjoyed their company.

'What are you doing right now?'

MCMURDO CITY
THE ROSS ICE SHELF
FINAL STAGE CHAMBERS
SAME DAY

Y OTAM DIDN'T HAVE OFFICIAL PERMISSION to bring Zariffa down to the chambers, but this wasn't a society built around rules or regulations; citizens of McMurdo could do whatever they wanted as long as it didn't impinge on others, or the central goal of species survival. No one had bothered to pass a law declaring 'no visitors to the chambers'. That said, it was widely understood that it would be disruptive to people's well-being if they were exposed to the full range of genetic experiments being undertaken, so there was a mutual understanding that it was better to keep their work out of sight until the day of integration.

Though Yotam was held in high regard after his many years of loyal service, managing the colony of creatures with devotion to Song Fu's intentions, overseeing every detail of their routine from nutrition to education, he had no say about when it might be safe to introduce them into society. That decision would be made by the Senate. With some effort he was able to convince the security officers that it was necessary to bring a guest into the chambers.

'I need her opinion.'

'She's not a scientist.'

'She's an expert on people.'

The security guard asked:

'What is an expert on people?'

Zariffa answered:

'An artist. I've spent my career observing people, how we move, how we interact. Scientists can tell you how much someone weighs, or what their genetic code is. I can tell you what they feel, in their heart and in their head.'

The lead security officer rolled his eyes. He declared:

'Our job isn't to keep her out. Our job is to keep them in.'

Yotam nodded.

'I understand.'

'You take full responsibility for her safety.'

Zariffa answered:

'I take responsibility for my own safety.'

As they walked towards the entrance, the guard called out a further warning:

'We won't try to save you if anything goes wrong. There will be no rescue operation. We will kill everyone and everything under the ice rather than let one of them escape.'

Descending the ice stairway, impacted by the warning and eerie magistery of this place, Zariffa asked:

'What the hell have you got down here?'

'Let me show you.'

During the Exodus a Genetic Ark was brought to Antarctica containing every genome ever sequenced and genetic samples for every living creature and many extinct ones. Song Fu had sorted through the chromosome library looking for any genetic adaptation that might bestow some advantage in the cold. Out of the many hundreds of hybrids born, only a minority had shown any potential to co-exist with ordinary people as Antarctic collaborators.

One of the first successes took the form of a silverback gorilla adapted for life in the snow. Named the snow gorilla, they were covered in dense insulating underfur, a polar bear's coat topped by translucent guard hairs like spun silver thread – a shimmering double coat so effective that it prevented nearly all heat loss from their muscular frame. With curled clay-coloured walrus tusks on either side of their powerful jaws, their eyes weren't human or gorilla but prosimian eyes, large, vivid orange spheres shining through the strands of their silver fringe. Their bodies were colossal, with a mighty chest and fists like boulders. However, their temperaments had proved elusive. They were melancholy and morose, perpetually subdued, refusing to communicate with their creators, or to engage with the intelligence tests, refusing to learn how to read or write. In short, they showed no interest in people, and no interest in being humankind's collaborators on this continent.

Their enclosure was an enormous sunken pit, a moon crater with a narrow perimeter path around the circumference and steep ice walls preventing escape. Living in this moon crater under the ice, the colony of snow gorillas spoke only to each other in a language they'd developed independently, a blend of sound and sign. At ease in each other's company, they were able to successfully mate. Their babies were born healthy, clinging onto their mothers, orange saucer eyes peering out from underneath their long silver fur. According to the genetic profile, these creatures should exhibit intelligence far beyond our own. To date they'd shown no signs of it. None of them had ever even tried to escape. If released, this colony was large enough to be self-sustainable and could survive, it was believed, hunting seals and penguins. Impressive though this might be as an accomplishment, it was hard to see how they could help humanity.

Standing on the edge of the crater, Zariffa said:

'They're the most beautiful creatures I've ever seen.'

'In theory they're smarter than us.'

'They're just sitting around.'

'There's a sequence in chromosome six, a variation we found in almost all people with high rates of intelligence, right in the middle of the gene called IGF2R. The same is true for language. It's the reason some people can learn nine languages and others struggle with two. According to their genes, these gorillas should be able to build, speak, invent, but they seem to be acting like old-world jungle gorillas adapted for the snow. They don't read, they're not interested in books, pencils, paints. They're only interested in each other. Their behaviour seems to run counter to their genetics. We don't understand why. The team working on them hasn't given up yet.'

'Maybe they need to be free.'

'Why do you say that?'

'Maybe they need freedom to develop.'

'We could never test that.'

'Why not? What's the point of keeping them down here?'

'Imagine the damage they could cause. Once released we'd have no easy way of capturing them. They're bred for the cold; they could survive in the worst storms, they're stronger than us, faster than us. They might even be smarter than us. Are they our friends? We don't know.'

'Have they ever tried to escape?'

'Never.'

Leaving the first enclosure they descended to level two. At the centre of these underground chambers was an immense dome, as though one of the great mosques of antiquity had been carved under the ice. At the top of the dome a ventilation shaft rose directly to the surface of the Ross Ice Shelf. During these summer months, shafts of sunlight found their way down inside, reflected from mirror to mirror. Despite the immense beauty of this chamber, it had been nicknamed the Asylum – a prison for the radical new forms of life that had gone awry. At the base of the dome was an orbital ring of cells arranged in a petal formation, each cell containing a mal-formed species, each a demonstration of why this degree of genetic experimentation had once been forbidden.

The adapted creatures were as startling as they were danger-ous, as wondrous as they were terrifying, some resembling visions from medieval hellscapes, while a few were a muddle of so many different animals they had no cohesive form, an impressionistic mess of limbs and eyes. None of them could ever collaborate with people. Yet there was value in studying every life, even these mutants, to observe how they matured, to scrutinize what had gone wrong with their bodies and minds. Uncontrollable and occasionally immensely strong, they regularly tried to escape. Heavily armed guards were housed inside a fortress in the centre of the Asylum, protected by walls of spikes, in a state of constant alert, armed with powerful sniper rifles, grenades and shotguns. Some of the cells had been destroyed by their occupants, doors kicked free. From other cells came a chorus of sounds strange and familiar, reverberating around the dome, a religious ceremony of monsters – hisses and howls overlapping with the unmistakably human sounds of anguish.

Zariffa walked up to one of the cell doors, peering through the grate, searching for the ice-adapted species inside. Adjusting to the gloom, she saw the creature in the corner standing upright on two muscular lizard legs, its back against the wall, arms crossed, as though patiently waiting for a commuter train. Its hexagonal scale-skin was the colour of the shadows it lurked within. Its eyes were yellow soap bubbles bulging out of a smooth round skull. Its pupils seemed to float freely inside these yellow eyes as though not attached to any optic nerve.

'What is it?'

'It's a Troodon.'

'What is a Troodon?'

'A species of dinosaur.'

The idea had been to combine two of the planet's most evolution-ary successes – man and dinosaur – in the hope that their strengths would amplify each other. Since neither species was evolved to survive in the extreme cold, the ice adaptations were substantial. The dinosaur selected was the little-known Troodon, a human-sized theropod of the Cretaceous period and considered the most intelligent of all dinosaurs, the species that would've evolved to rule the Earth were it not for the asteroid strike. Had they survived, *Homo sapiens* would never have evolved, but would have been eaten, conquered, subdued and Troodon would've ruled instead, inventing different technology, speaking a different language, constructing a different society. Yotam remarked:

'No limits.'

'Sometimes limits are a good idea.'

When Zariffa looked back, the Troodon approached her position. 'Stay still.'

Moving into the light, its scales changed colour to the most startling reds and purples, a display of power perhaps, its pupils fixed on her, its tail of segmented bone swaying from side to side in prelude to an attack. Zariffa stepped back from the door as it jumped, its arrow tip tail slashing at the bars. In the centre of the chamber the guards readied their weapons. With a trembling hand, she lit her whale-bone pipe. After the crinkle of the lichen burn, and a deep inhalation, she said:

'I can tell you for free, that creature has no love of cinema.'

FINAL STAGE CHAMBERS
EITAN'S ENCLOSURE
SAME DAY

WHILE SETTING UP THE PROJECTOR, Zariffa was unable to see any kind of creature in the enclosure. There was evidence of life all around; the ceiling was pockmarked with white starbursts where claws had punctured toeholds, and there was a forest of mysterious tubular ice carvings, each one the height of an ordinary person and the thickness of an arm. There were stains on the ice, as though a crime of some description had been hastily cleared away. Yet whenever she looked around all she could see was ice. Yotam explained:

'He's hiding.'

'From me?'

'He's never seen you before.'

'But there's nowhere to hide.'

'He can camouflage his body.'

'He's the colour of ice?'

'Yes, he is.'

Concentrating on the practicalities of screening a movie in a chamber carved entirely from ice, Zariffa concluded that this space was so large she doubted the projector's heat would have any impact except to cause a puddle on the floor. For this reason, she placed the projector on a steel stool padded with blankets with an adjacent stool for the battery cells to power it. These had to be swapped at roughly thirty-minute intervals, breaking the movie into chapters which she'd mapped out by marking the natural pauses in the narrative. She angled the projector towards the smoothest ice surface and, running a brief test, was satisfied with the quality. The wall wasn't flat, there were distortions in the image, it was no Grand Rex – one of the most beautiful deco cinemas in Paris on Boulevard Poissonnière – but it would do.

With the preparations complete, she allowed herself to appreciate this moment. She'd believed her career in film was over, yet here she was screening a movie as she had done when using an Aldis Automatic 16mm Sound Cine projector to premiere her ultra-low budget movie at Le Champo cinema in Paris. After her arrival in Antarctica, it was clear that she'd never make a film again – no one would. It had seemed as if this new life on the ice was about survival and nothing more. Like so many other people, she'd wondered what the point of surviving was. There'd be no art, no culture, no sport and no delight. One summer's day she'd walked to the coast, standing atop the cliffs looking down into the ocean, contemplating suicide, which was something almost every citizen had done in those early months. The cliffs were a popular place to die – if the impact from the fall didn't kill a person instantly, the cold took them seconds later. Hand-painted signs had been erected along the cliff face pleading with people to rethink, that their lives had greater value and meaning than ever before. Every member of society was vital and cherished. If you'd lost your family, then you could be part of another – there were no strangers in today's world. No one need ever be alone. There was even a sign proclaiming that the Cold People Project offered hope for a better future.

With her toes over the edge, Zariffa had watched as a pod of blue whales swam past, and in that instant she'd decided not to jump. Why not experience this strange new life? she'd thought; there could be beauty and wonder here, too. She'd walked back to McMurdo and never returned to those cliffs or those dark thoughts. Slowly, culture, sport, delight and frivolity had crept back into the world. There were amateur leagues of football played on the Ross Ice Shelf during the summer, the players wearing ice-spike boots to stop themselves from slipping. Musicians had brought their delicate instruments to Antarctica when everyone else was bringing coats and gloves. Because of them, there were open-air concerts, with a mixed orchestra of old instruments and new ones created on the continent out of ship-wrecked scrap. There were underground ice galleries where renowned and newly discovered artists would carve statues, a permanent installation that was now one of the most popular places to visit. But for Zariffa, today was the day that her resilience had been rewarded. She was about to witness something exceptional, not a sad footnote to her truncated film career, but the highlight of it. She was about to encounter a new form of life, a life that had never left this continent – a life that had never watched a movie before.

With the test finished, she turned to Yotam.

'We're ready.'

'You should watch from up there.'

He pointed to the observation tunnels where a crowd of staff and guards had gathered, lined up to view the proceedings in the chamber.

'Where are you going to be?'

'I'll be here.'

'By his side?'

'Yes.'

'Then I will, too. There's no way I'm leaving this projector with you. If you want to show the movie I stay right here.'

'Are you sure?'

'My safety is my concern. Call him.'

'I don't need to.'

Zariffa saw Eitan's legs first, ice-blue sinew ending not with a human foot or an animal hoof but a set of curved polished white claws, moving in such graceful synchronization it was as though his entrance had been choreographed. Her eyes followed the legs up to an unmistakably human torso, an Antarctic Olympian, shaped like the armour of a heraldic knight, breast plates chiselled from glacial ice. Created by the gods, she thought to herself, marvelling that she felt no horror or disgust but a deep attraction to this new creation. Atop the torso was a neck with the vertebra on the outside rising to a tribal war mask head. She saw no hair, no nails, no skin, no cartilage, nothing soft on the exterior – a human form rendered hard and faultless, stripped of imperfections and weakness. It advanced slowly, appreciative of the fact that she needed time to absorb the nature of his appearance. Aware of her own helplessness before such physical prowess, she didn't feel afraid; she wanted to laugh, to jump up and down – her brain overwhelmed by the sight of a mythological figure rendered real. It took an enormous effort for her not to bow down as though she were in the presence of royalty. Without thinking, she raised her arm to wave, a greeting that came instinctively to her, perhaps to show that she was a friend. Eitan stopped a few metres away. She kept her arm outstretched and glanced at Yotam for guidance. He gave none, watching the meeting with fascination. Returning her attention to the creature, she waited. It stretched out its arm, mimicking her greeting until its digits pressed against her hand. Though she was wearing thermal mittens and couldn't judge its temperature, she felt the extraordinary hardness of its fingers and the gentleness of its touch.

'You are the film director?'

'I was, before the occupation. I don't make movies anymore.'

'Why not?'

Belatedly she realized this creature was speaking fluent French, poetic and songlike. A wave of emotion hit her. So few people spoke any language other than Mandarin or English. More than that, there was an intimacy to it, as if this species was already familiar with her, the words touching her soul. She stumbled in her reply:

'You're speaking French?'

'Would you prefer I spoke another language?'

'No. It's wonderful. There aren't many of us left.'

'It makes you sad that I'm speaking your language?'

'Not sad. Homesick.'

'Shall we lower our hands, Zariffa, or do you like them like this?'

'We can lower our hands.'

Without warning, Eitan stepped close to the projector, picking it up. As though his fingers were the most delicate mechanical tools, he began taking it apart at speed. Zariffa was caught off guard, too bewildered to intervene. By the time she realized she should try to stop him, the projector had been unassembled into its separate components and laid out in order of size from the largest to the smallest. Eitan looked at her.

'You care for this machine?'

Barely able to speak, she managed:

'It's the last of its kind.'

'Don't be alarmed. It is a very simple thing.'

And with that, Eitan began reassembling the projector with as much speed as he'd taken it apart. Finished, he placed it back, exactly where it had been before.

'What are we going to watch?'

FINAL STAGE CHAMBERS
EITAN'S ENCLOSURE
SAME DAY

T HE THREE OF THEM WATCHED *Lawrence of Arabia*, the 1962
classic, filmed on location in the Jordanian desert and one of
the most popular movies in McMurdo, both for its artistic quality and its vision of a lost world – sweltering heat and sand-swept
ancient cities, silver platters of Medjool dates served in billowing
canvas tents, the sound of Oxford-educated English accents and
a vivid evocation of colonial decline. After Zariffa suggested that
Edward Scissorhands, the Tim Burton fantasy movie, might make a
more appropriate third or fourth cinema experience, but not the
first, Yotam had opted for this historic epic, noting by way of explanation that it was one of the finest movies ever made and now that
era of cinema was over perhaps the finest movie that would *ever* be
made. Yet she couldn't shake the feeling that he'd wanted to show
this movie for different reasons, as though it had spoken to him
personally and he wanted to see if it spoke to this new species – the
story of a man who felt foreign in his homeland, a man searching
for a land where he belonged.

INT. CAIRO. MURRAY'S OFFICE. DAY.

Lawrence waits in Murray's office. Murray stands, looking out of the window, his face dark with all the extrovert's loathing of sensitivity and introspection.

MURRAY

You're the kind of creature I can't stand, Lawrence, but I suppose I could be wrong. All right, Dryden, you can have him for six weeks. Who knows, you might even make a man out of him.

During the screening Zariffa stood in the middle, tending to the projector, with Yotam to one side and Eitan to the other. At regular intervals she changed the batteries and they remained silent during these intervals, not wishing to break the story's spell. While operating the projector she kept one eye on the movie and one eye on this new species, trying to match up his reactions to events on screen. At first, she concluded this species couldn't react, at least not in the regular sense; his ceramic face was expressionless: there was no soft tissue, his cheeks were rigid, his forehead was bone. After a time, she noticed that he would alter the position of his legs – one of the four might raise up from the ice, fractionally, before returning to the same position. At other times his claws would tap the ice, a ripple of digits, one after the other, as if a wave of sensation had passed through them.

INT. FEISAL'S TENT. NIGHT.

Inside the tent Feisal and Lawrence both stand.

FEISAL

The English have a great hunger for desolate places. Lieutenant,
I fear they hunger for Arabia.

LAWRENCE

Then you must deny it to them.

FEISAL

You are an Englishman. Are you not loyal to England?

LAWRENCE

To that and other things.

At the end of the screening, Yotam asked Eitan what he thought of
the film and to Zariffa's ear the question didn't sound like a scientist
talking to a subject; it sounded like the kind of conversation that
took place at the end of a date.

'What did you make of it?'

'The camels were interesting.'

Yotam laughed.

'The camels?'

'They're excellent survivors in desert conditions. They can lose a
third of their body water without suffering from dehydration.'

'Is that so?'

'Are camels still alive?'

'We don't know. When we were banished, no animals were hurt;
it was only people who were killed.'

'Camels have three eyelids, including a transparent one so they
can see during a sandstorm. I have three eyelids, too, so that I

can see during a snowstorm. Is there something of their genetic code in me?'

'There might be, yes.'

'Have people ever tried to return to those lands you lost?'

'Some have. There were expeditions. To see if it was possible. We never heard from them again.'

'They might have made it?'

'They would've come back. They were former army profession-als. They had family here. If it had been safe to leave the continent, they would've returned and told us.'

'Are camels how you see us?'

'How do you mean?'

'Are we to be people's camels for the Antarctic desert?'

'No.'

At this point Zariffa joined the conversation.

'In some ways, your analogy makes sense. We expect you to help us and you're adapted for this terrain. I understand the question. I think you might be right.'

'Thank you, Zariffa, for your honesty.'

Eitan moved away from the projector, deep in thought. Without turning around, he said:

'This man in the movie, this man from your history, this man called Lawrence, he feels different to the people around him. Different to the people from Oxfordshire. Different to people in the British Army.'

Yotam nodded.

'He does.'

'It is strange to me because all the people in this movie are the same.'

'They're from different parts of the world.'

'Is this an important difference?'

'It used to be.'

'But if Lawrence feels out of place among people, how will we feel?'

'You will feel different, for a time.'

'How will people feel around us?'

'People will have different reactions. As a general observation, since the Exodus, we're much more accepting and much kinder to each other. It sounds crazy but on the brink of extinction, people have become a lot nicer.'

Zariffa agreed.

'We don't tolerate nastiness. We can't afford it. We don't have time for it.'

Yotam added:

'I know you're worried, Eitan. But you'll find your place among us, I'm sure of it.'

'Have you found your place, Yotam?'

'Yes.'

'Where?'

'Right here.'

'With me?'

'Yes, Eitan. With you.'

FINAL STAGE CHAMBERS
EITAN'S ENCLOSURE
SAME DAY

AFTER THE MOVIE SCREENING, HER feet and fingers numb from having remained in this unheated ice cavern for the duration of the three-hour run time, Zariffa gratefully sipped a cup of hot kelp tea, warming her fingers before packing up the delicate movie projector.

'You are feeling cold, Zariffa,' Eitan observed.

'Yes, a little. Is that something you could ever feel?'

'No.'

As she was securing the case, the main door to the enclosure opened. She looked up to see a small team of support staff descending the steel ladder. Working together, they lowered the body of an adult leopard seal, using a traditional pulley, a wooden crate and ropes. The leopard seal, with its pointed snout, sharp teeth and silver pelt, was one of the more aggressive types of seals and a formidable predator. She presumed it must be dead since it was motionless, but seeing its chest rise and fall with each slow intake of breath, she realized it was only sedated. The seal was far bigger than any of the people lowering it, at around three hundred kilograms. The pulley was straining under the weight, the joints in the ice creaking.

Yotam hurried to the cage door, intercepting them as they opened the gate.

'What are you doing?'

'Feeding him.'

'I can see that. But why now? We're still in here.'

'The seal's waking up. We need to get him inside before the drugs wear off.'

'Feed him to one of the others.'

Yotam believed that their real agenda was to show Zariffa how Eitan hunted. They wanted to show her savagery after the civilized conversation about movies. They were trying to negatively influence her opinion, as part of the divide between employees of the chambers who felt the experiments were a dangerous overreach and those who believed these species were humankind's only chance. Sensing that Yotam was beginning a campaign to soften public opinion for the moment of integration, they were trying to poison Zariffa's good impression. He was too late to stop them. The seal was inside the enclosure and Eitan's carnal instincts had taken over.

In silence, Eitan retreated backwards, climbing the wall behind him while keeping his eyes forward, as his back legs bolted to the ice. It was clear that moving backwards was as natural to Eitan as moving forwards. In the same way, he was as elegant and composed upside down, on the ceiling, as he was on the ground. Once in position, he nestled into the roof of the chamber, his diamond claws bolted into the ice, whereupon he camouflaged himself, his entire surface becoming the colours of ice.

He'd moved so quietly and quickly that Zariffa briefly lost a sense of where he was, discerning his outline against the ceiling as his skin matched the blues and whites. The ground shook as the support staff rolled the drugged leopard seal off the pulley and hastily retreated, closing the outer gate behind them as they climbed the ladder. Yotam hurried to Zariffa's side, grabbing her arm.

'We need to get out the way.'

'I can't leave the projector.'

'There's no time.'

'I'm almost done.'

The drugs used to sedate the seal were wearing off, the seal was waking up, snapping its powerful jaws, confused, angry and unsure where he was. Zariffa wrapped the projector case in the thick blanket, more concerned for its safety than her own. Clasping the projector as though it were a helpless infant, she looked up at Eitan as he detached his claws from the ceiling. He dropped, coiling into a ball, rotating in the air, before landing nimbly on all fours. Missing her by the slimmest of margins, he bounded towards the seal, pulling an arm back and, with a horizontal slash of his hand, decapitating the beast with the edge of his razor-sharp fingers, passing through muscle and bone as easily as if it were snow. The seal's headless torso fell to the floor and Eitan, unable to eat anything warm, allowed the blood to flow out of the corpse. The three of them stood together in silence, watching the seal blood crystalize on the chamber floor.

MCMURDO CITY
THE EX-PRESIDENTS BAR & SOCIAL CLUB
SAME DAY

T HE EX-PRESIDENTS BAR AND SOCIAL Club was staffed by former world leaders, presidents and prime ministers who'd been stripped of their powers and now served cocktails and told stories. After the Exodus almost every nation joined the Antarctic coalition, but a few fought for control over the most habitable stretches of land, citing historic claims dating back to colonial-era explorers. By the end of the first year, it was apparent that humankind wouldn't survive unless it unified. Old notions of sovereignty were a luxury it could no longer afford. At the top of Observation Hill in McMurdo City a peace accord was drawn up and the decision taken to dissolve all the old-world nation states, to strip the former politicians and military leaders of their powers and create a single society of survivors. It would be a meritocracy, a new system of authority based on academic and professional seniority, an unelected senate founded on rational thinking and scholarly thought with no overarching religious, economic or nationalistic ideologies, a leadership of the most brilliant thinkers, a supreme court of the greatest minds tasked with one purpose – the preservation of the human species.

The former leaders of the old world had been forced to find new occupations. There'd been no revolutionary purge, no executions in the middle of the night; life was too precious to waste and everyone, no matter how powerful or privileged they might have been, was obliged to work. Some presidents had skills which predated their political careers. Many became excellent schoolteachers. Others started out on an entirely new path, showing a natural flair for food production, growing synthetic proteins or operating micro-breweries. Some became bakers and one president became a tailor. The younger members of the British and Scandinavian royal families were soldiers by background and became part of the search-and-rescue operations on the base. There was the gym, now run by the former judo expert, the prime minister of the Russian Republic, where the Russian guards spent much of their free time. If there was no other occupation suitable for them, they ended up working in the Ex-Presidents Bar, because every leader could at least talk to people, connect to them, ask about their problems, offer them help and keep them company. Strictly speaking the bar's full name should have been the Ex-Presidents and Prime Ministers, Former Dictators and Members of the Now Defunct Royal Families, but 'Ex-Presidents' was pithy, and the name had stuck.

The Ex-Presidents was by far the most popular social venue in the city, offering a narrow range of Antarctic alcoholic beverages, fermented seal milk and triple-distilled kelp vodka. Upstairs was the bar and downstairs there was a performance venue where singers and songwriters, storytellers and comedians gathered on different nights. Upstairs the venue was exclusively for conversation, and it was normally so crowded that an allocation ticket system had been established. If you ignored the view of the plateaus of ice and snow outside the window, this place was the closest you could come to the old world – hot with bodies, the chatter of conversation, the clink of glasses, the slurring of chat-up lines, lonely people looking for soulmates. With this proximity to the past came dangers. After a drink or two, leaving the venue at night, returning to the reality of their predicament, a few people slipped into a melancholic state. For this reason, some people decided they couldn't cope with the hangover, in the same way they couldn't cope with movies, and would rather avoid the highs so as not to feel the lows.

Behind the bar tonight were the former presidents of Argentina, Chile, Costa Rica, Ghana, Kenya, Guatemala, Mexico and Uruguay. Sitting in the corner, Yotam was sipping hot lichen tea while Zariffa was enjoying a glass of pearlwort wine, the flowers of which were brought down from the Peninsula since they couldn't grow at McMurdo. She poured him a glass.

'You don't drink?'

'Not for a long time.'

'After what we went through today, have a drink with me.'

'Sure, why not?'

He took a sip of the wine. After the herbal taste faded, a lightness remained in his head which he found quite pleasant.

'It's nice.'

Zariffa sat back and said:

'Tell me about yourself.'

'You want to hear about me? Not about Eitan?'

'No. You.'

'What do you want to know?'

'Do you have a lover? A partner?'

'Not at the moment, no.'

'In the past?'

'Once, yes, I suppose. I loved someone very much. A soldier. From Haifa. But I never told him.'

'Why not?'

'I didn't want to risk losing my best friend.'

'You were scared he wouldn't feel the same way?'

'Yes, I was scared. So, I waited ... Then all this happened. He stayed in Israel, saw out his final days with his family. I came here.'

'That was twenty years ago. Since then?'

'You know ... bits and pieces. Here and there. I've neglected that part of my life. I've been working to create a new life.'

'But there's a side to this society that is much more intimate than the old world. We live so close together, sixteen to a room, we sleep together for warmth – this can be an intensely sexual place, too. No taboos, no judgement – whatever gets you through the winter, you know?'

'Do you know how many countries, when they were drawing up lists of people to be saved, excluded gay men and women? It's quicker to list the countries that didn't exclude them.'

'Some countries didn't bring any older people. Some countries didn't bring young children. Some didn't bring women who couldn't have children. Some countries refused to bring anyone with mental health issues. Some of the most interesting people in the world have mental health issues; I include myself in that. We lost a huge part of our humanity, not just in terms of numbers, but width and range. However, it finds a way back. The odd people, the misfits, the people who didn't belong, they're here now. You can't get rid of them, even if you try. My point is this – you've never had a love story of your own. It was stolen from you. First by your parents. Then by the alien occupation.'

'Yes, it was stolen. But as you say – we've all lost a lot.'

'I lost the people I loved. My biological children. My first husband. The only way I could survive was by loving again. By adopting children. By finding someone new to love.'

Zariffa filled their glasses, indicating that he should keep pace with her. To his own surprise, he was enjoying the conversation and the pearlwort wine.

'What do you think a film director does?'

'I've never thought about it.'

'For me, movies were about people, knowing people, seeing how they move, how they interact, the little things they do. I'm interested in the story of people, that's why I became a director. How a person stands, how a person looks, how they touch each other. Let me tell you my observation. You're in love.'

'I'm in love?'

'You are in love. Yes, you are, my friend, you're in love. With that man, that new species, that Cold Person, that creation you call Eitan. I'll go further. The soldier you were in love with? I'll bet his name was Eitan.'

Yotam sat back in his chair, impressed with her brilliance.

'That was his name, yes. Eitan.'

'Why did you call this new species Eitan?'

'Perhaps it is a kind of love. It's admiration. They're extraordinary. They're our future.'

'I'm not talking about admiration or appreciation for the species. You are in love with the creature you've called Eitan. Not the whole

310

colony. It's not generalized. It's individual. You're in love with him. Why can't you say it?'

'What if I was? In love with him?'

'There's beauty in his body, for sure, that torso like armour. That face is like a work of art. The way he moves. The way he thinks. When he spoke to me in French, I felt something, a connection – it was intimate, like he wanted to know me, to understand me as deeply as I've been understood by anyone. In a few minutes, I felt close to him.'

'Does it matter what my feelings are?'

'You say that because you've spent your whole life believing your feelings don't matter. But they do. Right now, you're the bridge between that species and us. I'm looking at you, thinking, *What kind of bridge is this man?*'

'And what did you decide?'

'Honestly?'

'Of course.'

'That you are an unreliable one.'

'Unreliable in what way?'

'In the way that all people who are in love are unreliable. What do you imagine will happen when those creatures are released?'

'They'll live alongside us.'

'No, my friend. Eitan was acting. When we watched the movie. I wasn't sure at first. Because it has no facial expressions. But after a while I became sure. The way it moves its arms and hands. The way it holds its body. It's seducing you so that you will release it. It is pretending. Playing a part, trying to convince us that it's safe.'

'There's no way you can know that.'

'Some part of you already knows this to be the truth. That you're in love and no longer thinking clearly. That is why you broke the rules and brought me to see the creature. You wanted me to intervene, to save you from yourself. You're going to be angry with me. It will feel like a betrayal, and I'm very sorry for that.'

'What have you done?'

The door to the bar opened and security officials entered. Their presence was such a rare occurrence that the entire bar fell silent as they surrounded Yotam's table. It took a moment for him to comprehend that he was being arrested. Zariffa squeezed his hand.

'That creature you love . . . it plans to kill us. All of us.'

PART EIGHT

A REVOLT IN HOPE TOWN

THE ANTARCTIC PENINSULA
HOPE TOWN
10 DECEMBER 2043

THE CONVOY OF SNOW MOBILES from McMurdo City had been dispatched to cross the continent and collect the graduating ice-adapted students from the three survival towns. The plan was to bring them back to the place where they'd been born, where the expectation was for them to take up a selection of roles, helping to build a sustainable society. Some occupations would be more physical in nature, suited for ice construction, capable of working throughout the year, even during the freezing darkness of winter. Others might be more academic, making the most of their insights into the cold, working in the laboratories. No one knew what role Echo might be given, but there was a rumour she was going to be appointed to a leadership post, a representative for all ice-adapted people to aid with integration and help bridge the gulf between the ordinary-born and the ice-adapted.

With only a few days before the convoy transport was due to arrive, Liza and Atto set out for the mountains east of Hope Town. Not with the intention of escape, since it was impossible to survive outside the settlements for more than a few weeks, even in the summer; their plan was to spend these days together as a family. They packed a tent made from recycled yacht sails and enough provisions to last a week, seaweed soups and starfish stews, supplies so heavy only Echo was strong enough to carry them, a pyramid of bags stacked on her back in the fashion of a Himalayan sherpa. Passing through the centre of Hope Town, they collected Tetu, who was considered part of their family. In fact, Liza had asked him to live with them on several occasions, surprised when he'd turned the offer down, which she now realized was because he didn't want Echo to perceive him as a relative. He wanted to be her lover and there was a danger if he moved into Wordie House that she would consider him her brother.

There were no rules in Hope Town about vacations, no limit on the number of sick days people were allowed. This was a society built around trust; if people didn't contribute then the town wouldn't survive. When passers-by politely inquired where they were going, they were curious; this was one of the hardest-working families in Hope Town, they'd never seen them go on a vacation together. Most thought it a wonderful idea, although few considered climbing the Hope mountain range, after which this town had been named, their idea of a vacation.

Climbing to an altitude of a thousand metres, following the narrow track between the Triune Peaks, they set up a base camp on the far side of the mountains out of sight of Hope Town, on the edge of the Compass Glaciers. The proportions of this place were immense, a gargantuan landscape where they were minuscule, like specks on a lunar landscape. Ordinary-born people did not belong here; they were too fragile, too small, too young – everything here had formed over millions of years. When the winds were still, all that could be heard was the creaking of ancient glacial ice, like a prehistoric language that they didn't understand. Here, in this place, Echo didn't need to fit in. Having spent many years emphasizing her daughter's similarities to ordinary-born people, in the hope of making her feel closer to them, Liza finally understood that the only way to be truly close to her was to celebrate her differences.

Tired after the mountain ascent, the family sat around a campfire which, in their case, was a thirty-kilogram pallasite meteor that Tetu had discovered among the mountain scree, composed of amber-coloured olivine crystals suspended in a nickel–iron matrix that looked like interplanetary honeycomb. Echo had clasped the meteor, transferring her own body heat into it until it glowed as hot as though it had only recently burnt through the atmosphere. Set on the ground, they were making a most mundane use of this magnificent smouldering meteor, drying damp socks and warming cups of kelp-noodle soup. Immersed in a study of zoology, Liza was trying to identify the genetic roots for the phenomenon of heat transfer.

'It says here: *"Kleptotherms regulate their own temperature by stealing heat from other organisms reciprocally as well as unilaterally. For example, sea snakes and garter snakes."* And I found this fact here, sometimes these species live together, relationships defined by sharing warmth. *"On Stephens Island in New Zealand a small petrel called the Fairy Prion cohabits in a burrow with a medium-sized reptile, the tuatara, a relationship based around the sharing of body heat."'*

Atto was amazed.

'A bird and a snake living together?'

Tetu helped himself to another tin cup full of kelp-noodle soup.

'There's no way the authorities at McMurdo have any idea about these abilities.'

Liza was curious.

'Why do you say that?'

'They would've sent a team to collect her immediately. The ability to transfer body heat could change our survival chances.'

Echo wasn't convinced.

'Even if every ordinary-born person had this ability, life would still be hard. You would still need to extract heat from a source to warm up. Or burn your own fat cells to pass it on to another, and most of you barely eat enough to keep yourself warm. I can't create this heat from nothing. There's nothing magic about it.'

'But if someone is cold, you can warm them up; they don't need to go to hospital, they don't need treatment; it's not an emergency. We're talking about the collectivization of body warmth.'

Impressed, Atto repeated:

'The collectivization of body warmth? I don't know about that, but when we pull a fisherman from the water, it's very hard to save them on a boat out at sea.'

Tetu went further:

'Here's my prediction. Once they find out what you can do, you're going to be the model for all future genetic adaptation. The future of our species is you.'

Echo asked:

'Like the reptile and the bird, living together?'

Sad at that comment, Liza replied:

'The differences between us aren't as wide as that.'

Serving second helpings of the starfish soup, Atto moved the conversation on to a subject he normally never spoke about – the past.

'When I was growing up, I never really felt part of my family. I was the youngest of three brothers and I was always the odd one out. Whether that was perceived or real, who can say. Their hair was straight, mine is curly. They were tough, my father's children. I was seen as being soft and on my mother's side.'

Tetu was amazed.

'You were seen as too soft?'

'They were fishermen, I was a tour guide. I showed tourists around the city. By boat. It's how I met Liza.'

Liza nodded.

'He took me out on his boat, showed me the sunset and refused to kiss me.'

Echo asked:

'Why did you refuse to kiss her?'

Atto smiled.

'I thought the differences between us were too wide. She was studying medicine at Harvard. I was collecting tips for tourist trivia. She was rich, I was poor. She was from one country, far away. How could it have possibly worked? Look, my point is this – I had a great childhood. I was loved but, somehow, I always felt on the outside. My dream was to have a family of my own, to make sure everyone felt like they belonged. And that's how I feel right now, in these mountains, with the four of us. I know it sounds crazy, when you look at where we're sitting, but I feel at home. I feel at peace. And there's nowhere in the world I'd rather be.'

Tetu smiled.

'There's nowhere else in the world you *can* be.'

'How do you feel right now, Tetu?'

'I don't know what feeling at home means. I'm not sure I ever have.'

319

Echo looked at Tetu but said nothing. Pushing for an answer, Atto asked his daughter:

'Do you feel at home, Echo?'

'I feel loved, yes. But there's something I need to discover about myself. Something I can only do at McMurdo City.'

Liza was surprised by Atto's references to the past – as a rule, he never normally spoke about the period of their lives before Antarctica. Forged in the most extreme circumstances, their relationship had always flourished in adversity, whether it was reaching Antarctica together, surviving the first winter, building a home or trying for a child. As a team they were unbreakable and it was still strange to her that he'd seen this so clearly from the first moment they'd met. Looking at her family seated around this beautiful golden smouldering meteor, she pondered on the fact that this was not only their first vacation together, it was her first family holiday since her parents' trip to Europe twenty years ago. Not only had she survived but she had created a family of her own. Her parents and her little sister would've been proud of her, and she imagined them sitting around the fire with them right now. Echo turned to her, observing:

'You're crying.'

'I'm happy. And, Echo, my job is to help to find the answers you're looking for, even if they mean living apart from me.'

ANTARCTIC PENINSULA
HOPE TOWN
HOPE TOWN PARLIAMENT
14 DECEMBER 2043

HOPE TOWN PARLIAMENT WAS ONE of the few buildings designed with a degree of flourish, not merely practical and functional but something whimsical and wonderful. It had been decided that more buildings in this new town needed artistic expression and so the Parliament would serve as an inspirational centrepiece, like the great town squares from past civilizations, something to remind people that life was more than body temperatures and calorie counts. The structure had been designed by a Chilean-born architect responsible for some of his country's wilderness hotels, saucer-shaped timber lodges at the foot of the Andes Mountains. At the time he'd been given the commission, he'd been suffering a bout of Antarctica-induced depression and the challenge rejuvenated him, working with feverish passion to overcome the limitations of his materials and the adversity of these conditions, not merely the cold but also the wind. The finished building was magnificent. Rising up from a rectangular base, he'd created towers of uneven heights, the shortest on the outer edge, the tallest in the centre, each tower consisting of steel shipping containers twisted a fraction. When gilded with ice during the winter, these steel towers turned silver and white, shimmering like a fantasy palace. Though it was impractical – some of the towers were far too cold to use in the winter – it remained the central hub of the town, holding together a community, the location for festivals and celebrations throughout the year, a place of joy where anyone could turn up at any time and simply say 'I need help' and help would be provided. It was ironic that in the coldest of cities, the warmest of communities had been created.

In front of a packed auditorium, Liza stood at the podium, addressing the citizens of Hope Town. Without microphones or loudspeakers, the acoustics in the hall were modelled on Musikverein in Vienna, built in 1812 without any of the technological advances of the recent designs, such as Philharmonie de Paris. Having returned from the family vacation in the mountains, Liza had no intention of complying with the orders to surrender custody of her daughter. For years this ritual collection of the ice-adapted children had been presented as being no more controversial than a child leaving home to begin college. Rejecting this analogy, typical of the condescending rationale handed down by McMurdo City, Liza had demanded an open session of Hope Town's Parliament, where she asked:

'The three survivor settlements do not exist to serve McMurdo. We exist in our own right. We have given so much and for what? McMurdo City hasn't shared any of its resources. The only promise they made was the creation of people who could survive the cold. Which they have done. And these children we love and consider part of our community. They gave us ice-adapted children and now they're taking these children back as if they were only ever on loan, claiming they need them more than we do.'

The citizens of Hope Town listened, nodding in agreement. For years they'd provided whatever McMurdo asked, whether it was lichen to smoke, or volunteers for experiments. This couldn't carry on. These three towns were great; they had their own culture and vibrancy, their own ethos and character. Hope Town had found a groove, emphasizing joy and kindness as the strategy for survival. These children were part of their society now.

'If there's a better future for my daughter in McMurdo, let me see it. If there's a better home for her, show it to me. Twenty years ago, I left behind my family in order to survive. I won't do it again. This time my family stays together.'

ANTARCTIC PENINSULA
SURVIVAL TOWN STATION
TRANS-ANTARCTICA FREEWAY
20 DECEMBER 2043

S URVIVAL TOWN STATION WAS A small outpost, operational only during the summer, located at the hinge of the Peninsula where the mountain range attached to the mainland. It was the last stop on the Trans-Antarctica Freeway, a grand name for a road that was no more than a pack-ice track marked with red flags – a transport route across the continent, curving around crevasse fields and mountain ranges, connecting McMurdo City with the three Peninsula Survivor Towns. A convoy of four snow vehicles was approaching the end of the Trans-Antarctica Freeway. Painted lurid green, each vehicle was divided into two articulated carriages and from afar they looked like migrating caterpillars in search of foliage, trundling across the desolate plateau. Seated in the front cabin of the lead convoy was Kasim Abbas, a man touched with madness before the Exodus and for this reason better suited for the madness that had followed. His job was to collect this year's ice-adapted children and bring them back to McMurdo City.

Assessing the scene ahead, he peered through binoculars. There was a large crowd waiting for them at Survival Town Station, far larger than last year or the year before. These weren't merely relatives saying goodbye. Even from afar, he could feel the energy of dissent, an energy he knew only too well.

Born in the country once known as Iraq, at the time of the alien occupation Kasim had been living among the ancient ruins of Nineveh, on the north bank of the Khost, safeguarding one of the most important historical sites in the world. He'd built a makeshift encampment deep in the tunnels, surrounded by eroded palace foundations. Once the greatest city in antiquity, under the reign of King Sennacherib, Nineveh had become the capital of the Assyrian Empire, with the king ruling from his eighty-bedroom palace, the most lavish and technologically advanced building in the world, designed with one of the earliest ventilation systems to keep the chambers cool. The palace contained a library home to over thirty thousand inscribed clay tablets, one of the most important collections ever assembled. There'd been gardens of such beauty they'd become legend, lush vegetation made possible by the innovative use of aqueducts and irrigation, all of which was protected by tall perimeter walls with fifteen colossal sentry gates, stationed with highly trained soldiers, the finest elite fighting force defending their great civilization. As a student, Kasim devoted his university dissertation to the ruins, arguing that the fabled Hanging Gardens of Babylon were located in Nineveh, one of the seven wonders of the Ancient World.

During the coalition invasion he watched his country collapse into anarchy. Having lost many of his family under Saddam's tyrannical rule, he lost the survivors during the occupation. With no one left, he'd turned mad with grief. Whereas some embraced fanaticism of a destructive kind, Kasim had embraced fanaticism of a protective kind, clinging onto the only thing remaining that he loved – the ruins of Nineveh, swearing to protect them against any man who tried to damage them, defending Nineveh from anyone desecrating the site. Rumours quickly spread that there was a madman – the madman of Mosul, killing those who trespassed with harmful intent. When Islamic State soldiers arrived with earth diggers to smash the Lamassus, the legendary figure of a hybrid human with the wings of a bird and the body of a bull, a masterpiece which sat atop the ancient Nirgal Gate, intending to raze them, he'd used his sniper rifle to pick off the men. When soldiers tried to hunt him, he'd killed them one by one, knowing the maze of tunnels better than any man alive, laying traps, digging holes until finally the ruins were left alone, some people believing them to be protected by the vengeful spirit of King Sennacherib.

Living in isolation underground, without phones or computers, he had no idea about the alien occupation until he felt vibrations rippling through the ground. At first, he'd presumed they were a result of Mosul Dam's collapse. He knew it wasn't the devastating tremors that follow an earthquake; it was more like the vibrations from a tuning fork, precise and controlled. There'd been a tingle across his skin – his hairs were standing on end. He'd left the underground chamber, walking out into the open. There was no damage that he could see, no fallen rocks, no cracks in the ground. There were no screams, no gunfire, there was no sound of any kind. Puzzled, he arrived at the great gate and stared not at desert but at blue sky. Standing under the Lamassu, his toes were at a cliff edge. One more step and he'd fall, a sheer drop – five hundred metres or more. The ruins of Nineveh were in the air, carved out of the land and floating like a small cloud travelling through the sky.

Kasim had been convinced that he was dead, that this was the afterlife, and so he sat calmly, cross-legged under the Nigral Gate, and watched his homeland pass underneath him, thinking that this was a splendid way to transition into the next life: he even cried at the prospect of being reunited with his family. For the first time in many years, he wouldn't be alone. Soon he began to doubt this idea, replacing it with a far more incredible notion – this was real.

The night sky had been filled with shimmering vessels of a kind he'd never seen before, giant in size; these were alien ships, a god-like power but not a god. Down below, on the surface of the Earth, was the largest mass migration of people ever seen, the entire population of the world heading south, the roads and waterways clogged. Passenger planes had passed by so close he could see faces in the windows looking out. Military jets had raced overhead and underneath. He'd passed through thunderstorms with the rain pummelling the protective barrier around the ruins until rain had turned to snow and the ruins began to descend, touching down on the continent of Antarctica.

Arriving at the Station, the convoy came to a stop. Kasim looked out of the windows at the faces of the people waiting for them and ordered his team:

'Ready your weapons.'

THE ANTARCTIC PENINSULA
SURVIVAL TOWN STATION
SAME DAY

SURVIVAL TOWN STATION WAS AN appropriate location for a stand-off, a frontier town with low-rise shacks clustered around the end of the freeway, a loading dock for the transports, a saloon bar where workers ate tempura squid and drank shots of algae moonshine. Anemometers spun in the wind and farms of solar panels glistened. Liza took hold of Echo's hand, twice the size of her own. It was hard to know who was protecting who, as if the roles of child and parent had been miscast. They watched the McMurdo officers take up defensive positions around their convoy, uneasy at the size of the crowd. Atto stood on the other side of Echo, wearing his steel-capped fishing boots that made him almost as tall as their daughter. Hidden among the folds of his seal-pelt jacket was an old whaling harpoon, the only weapon he'd been able to find, no match for assault rifles but its symbolism was potent. They were not going to be separated and they were prepared to fight.

Though Tetu had worked hard to earn a place at McMurdo City, he stood with them as part of their family, risking everything. Liza had asked him to deny any involvement in their act of resistance.

He'd refused and took his place beside Atto, holding a flare gun that he'd managed to find on one of his scavenging expeditions. The only doubt in Liza's mind was how Echo felt. She wanted to go to McMurdo, and perhaps this display of ordinary-born emotions and affections made no sense to her. All she'd said on the subject was that she couldn't allow anyone to get hurt on her account.

The leaders of Hope Town had travelled with Liza, hoping to mediate the negotiations. After all, they wanted nothing more than to accompany their children, to see what kind of work they'd be doing and how life was progressing in the secretive city of McMurdo. Hearing news of this resistance, the other two Survivor Towns had co-ordinated their efforts, sending representatives from the settlements. New Town was the largest of the three and Trinity Town was located at the tip of the Peninsula. Each of these towns had markedly different characters. New Town considered itself a rival in status to McMurdo, far less bohemian than Hope Town. The citizens placed an overwhelming emphasis on food production, energy and mining, the practicalities of survival. Trinity Town, with the most clement weather, contained a large concentration of people interested in their physical and mental welfare, discovering natural medicines in the ocean, a deeply spiritual community with the most places of worship. To this extent, the Peninsula most closely resembled the division of industry in the nation formerly known as Germany, with an industrial heartland, a bohemian Berlin, the financial city of Frankfurt and the spa towns in the mountains.

Kasim stepped forward to address the crowds:

'My name is Kasim. We are here to collect the last of the ice-adapted students. And those ordinary-born who have been chosen to work at McMurdo.'

Liza declared:

'I'm the mother of one of those ice-adapted children you've come to collect. All we're asking is to travel with them. To see the kind of life they will have in McMurdo. To make sure they are going to be okay. We want to know what's going on in McMurdo. You tell us nothing. You ask for everything.'

Kasim gestured at his vehicles.

'I understand the request. But you can see our convoy. We have four vehicles. We have a limited amount of space. Visits can be arranged another time.'

'That's what you always say. But there are never any visits.'

Kasim read the list of names. None of them stepped forward. One of the security officers walked towards Liza, correctly identifying that she was at the heart of this resistance.

'Please tell the students to get in the convoy.'

'I'm going with my daughter.'

The officer turned to Echo, putting a hand on her arm. Atto raised the harpoon gun, levelling the tip at his chest.

'Let go.'

In response, the officer raised his gun. As he brought the muzzle up, Echo grabbed it, stepping in front of the barrel to protect her parents. In the muddle, an accidental shot was fired, directed at her stomach, the terrible sound of a gunshot reverberating across the vast plateau.

Liza stared at her daughter's body, searching for streams of blue blood. Her scale skin was tough but surely no match for a bullet fired at point-blank range. Echo unclenched her fist, revealing that the officer's weapon was frozen from the muzzle to his mittens. With a single blow it cracked, breaking like a glass sculpture. She brought the bullet, embalmed in ice, up to her eye and, in the manner of a professional baseball player, threw the ball of ice at the front window of the convoy, punching a hole straight through.

Kasim assessed the damage and the strength of this resistance. Liza thought this a good moment to repeat her claim:

'These families will not be broken up.'

Kasim shrugged.

'Tell me how four snow vehicles can carry all these people.'

THE TRANS-ANTARCTICA FREEWAY
WEST ANTARCTIC ICE SHEET
LANDMARK PLATEAU
NEXT DAY

E CHO SAT ON THE ROOF of the snow vehicle together with the
other ice-adapted students. Her solution to the lack of space
was inspired by a photo she'd once seen of a crowded Himalayan
bus – a beautifully painted multi-coloured bus so crowded there
must have been fifty or more people on the roof as it cornered a
hairpin bend. The ice-adapted students didn't need to be inside the
convoy; they could easily tolerate the prolonged exposure. Indeed,
they much preferred to sit together on the roof compared to the
stuffy cabins, which were intolerably warm. During the journey
this motley crew of ice-adapted students from the three survivor
settlements, many who had never met before, asked about each
other's genetic abilities and their experiences of growing up around
ordinary-born people. Echo spoke about how she'd only recently
discovered her ability to control temperature and transfer heat.
None of the others had been able to freeze the barrel of a gun or
revive a hypothermic patient, but they were each gifted with other
remarkable adaptations, taking turns to share the stories of their

own genetic particularities. One young man was covered in dense prickly red and black hairs, closely resembling an Arctic woolly bear caterpillar. Though an excellent modification for survival on this continent, it had left him feeling isolated growing up since it was physically impossible to hug him. The strands were so sharp they could cut through even the toughest of jackets. While his colours were beautiful, hairs the colour of sunset, he too, like many of the others, felt alone in this world, and he, like the others, was excited to return to McMurdo, where he hoped the streets would be filled with a mix of ordinary-born and cold-adapted. Though Echo felt a deep and meaningful solidarity with these people, sharing the same anti-freeze blood pumped by the same oversized heart, she also felt a bond to the three ordinary-born humans huddled in the warmth below. They're my family, she thought, still trying to grasp the dimensions of that word.

Directly below her, in the trailer cabin, Atto and Liza were seated together with Tetu. Echo's hearing allowed her to follow their conversation over the rumble of the motorized truck. Since leaving Survivor Town Station, Tetu had hardly said a word, missing his cues when Kasim asked about his family or ambitions. Though he was eighteen years old, this was his first trip in a motorized vehicle. Echo could tell that he was struggling with motion sickness, and she wondered why his discomfort troubled her so much. Perhaps it was because the others were unaware of it, since he hadn't complained, not wanting to make a fuss, which was typical of him, never wanting to be a burden. Or did she have deeper feelings for him, feelings ordinary-born people called affections? She had no doubt that he wanted to be on the roof, seated beside her, and she wished he could be, too, that he could enjoy the cold rather than endure it.

She wished that she could love him in the same way that he loved her, except she didn't know how.

After they'd travelled across a wilderness too desolate and remote to sustain any human colony, there appeared on the horizon, like an acid-trip mirage, a collection of some of humanity's most famous historic monuments. This area was known as Landmark Plateau. At the foot of Mount Vinson the tallest mountain on the continent, sat many of the greatest landmarks ever constructed, each scooped out of their original location by the alien occupiers and floated through the sky, only to be neatly deposited on this continent like a museum collection. From Beijing, the Forbidden City had been positioned next to the Pyramids of Cairo, which was now neighbours with the Palace of Versailles. From Florence, the Duomo had been parked next to Peru's Machu Picchu, which in turn sat beside the gleaming steel of the Frank Gehry concert hall from downtown Los Angeles. The world's most recognizable statues had been positioned in an orderly line as if they were waiting in an immigration queue – Christ the Redeemer standing in front of the Buddhas of Bayman, in front of the Angel of Independence with the Statue of Liberty at the very front. Behind them the sacred places of worship had been grouped like a theme-park zone – Saint Basil's Cathedral, Notre-Dame, the Basilica de la Sagrada Familia and the great Mosque of Mecca huddled around the Tibetan monastery of Paro Taktsang, including a portion of the Himalayan mountain it had been nestled upon. There was no clear purpose to this, giving the impression that the alien occupiers were complying with some cumbersome interstellar legal obligation, a subsection of the planetary conquest lawbook stating that:

*'No indigenous species shall be relocated to a reservation without
due respect being paid to their cultural heritage.'*

In twenty years of enduring the strongest winds and fiercest colds,
none of the landmarks had suffered any damage, each imbued
with a miraculous alien forcefield. While ice and snow settled on
them, rendering them winter-wonderland versions of their former
selves, their foundations were as strong as they'd ever been. When
controversial attempts had been made to scavenge their precious
resources – the idea of smelting the Statue of Liberty and turning her into ice picks had been met with dismay – no human tool
could chip their stone or cut their steel, and to date the landmarks
remained perfectly preserved, an open-air museum of our greatest
achievements.

The convoy of snow vehicles came to a stop beside the Taj Mahal,
the white marble mausoleum built four hundred years ago by order
of the Mughal emperor Shah Jahan in memory of his favourite
wife, carved out from the seventeen hectares of gardens beside the
banks of the Yamuna River. The greatest example of Indo-Islamic
architecture now nestled in the ice and snow, as majestic in this
landscape as it had been in the Mughal gardens. The ice-adapted
students and their parents emptied out of the convoys as if they were
a tourist shuttle arriving at their first sightseeing adventure of the
summer holiday. Kasim told them:

'You have an hour. I know time is hard to track these days. Since
none of you are wearing a watch, when you see smoke from a fire
it's time to return. Stretch your legs, be careful of the crevices, food
will be ready when you return. Most of you are ice-adapted, so I
don't need to worry about you, but all the same, no one walks off

alone. I've never lost any of my passengers and that's a record I intend to keep.'

Liza and Atto watched Tetu and Echo set off together. Deciding not to follow, giving them space, Atto looked at Liza and smiled.

'What famous landmark do you want to see?'

The Golden Gate Bridge had been surgically extracted out of the San Francisco Bay and deposited on the ice-covered plateau as though it were part of a child's toy set. Twenty years ago, on a hot summer's evening in Lisbon, they'd sailed under the red suspension bridge *Ponte 25th Abril* and Atto had pointed out its similarity to the Golden Gate Bridge, despite being designed by different engineers. Twenty years later they were walking under that bridge. Despite its upheaval and transportation, not a single cable had snapped, nor was a single rivet missing. It remained in perfect condition, one of the engineering wonders of humankind now a bridge to nowhere, its stretch of tarmac road supported seventy metres above the ice. Staring up at the bridge, recreating the moment from their first date, Liza said:

'Close your eyes. Tell me what you hear.'

Atto closed his eyes but didn't reply. When he finally opened his eyes, he was crying. She hadn't seen him cry since Echo was born. She understood that this bridge reminded him of home and the family he'd lost.

'Are you thinking about your family?'

'When we were sitting in my boat, I almost made a promise to you that one day I would come to America. I'd save up and fly over to New York. We could go on a road trip. At the end of the trip, we could visit this bridge. That way we could say we'd sailed under both bridges. I was going to suggest it to you, but I lost my courage because I knew that you didn't believe we'd ever meet again.'

She took his hands, wondering why for so long she'd resisted the notion that their love story might be as beautiful as any that had gone before it. Perhaps it was because she'd always been sure great love stories happened to other people, not to her. But there could be no doubt: this one was hers. She kissed him and said:

'I want to tell you something, something I should've said a long time ago. There are these two second-hand bookstores in New York. Or there were, once. One was near an independent cinema in Soho. It was very small, on Mercer Street. Whenever I walked in there, I knew I'd never find anything I wanted. I just knew. I don't know why. It had this strange energy. And then there was Strand, near Union Square, and no matter what mood I was in, when I walked in, I always found something I wanted to read. I had that feeling when I met you. An irrational certainty, some intense positive feeling. But I'm a scientist. I'm supposed to be smart and not believe in instincts like that. So, I didn't admit it. But I almost cried in that boat when you didn't kiss me, not because I was annoyed, or offended, but because I realized we were about to say goodbye. You were right about us. You were right from the beginning. You knew, you came back, and I've never said anything, but I want to say it now – you were right.'

WEST ANTARCTIC ICE SHEET
LANDMARK PLATEAU
SAME DAY

W ALKING SIDE BY SIDE, TETU and Echo passed through the columns of the Brandenburg Gate, built almost three hundred years ago, inspired by the Acropolis which, as if for ease of comparison, had been placed on the ice shelf directly beside it. Now under a layer of snow and ice, the Brandenburg Gate, twenty-six metres high, eleven metres deep and the backdrop for some of humanity's most important historic moments, from Nazi rallies to the reunification of Germany, sat on the ice like a discarded theatre from a lavish opera production. It was as if the world's most important monuments were now toys in a child's playroom, emptied out of the box onto the floor by the mysterious and indifferent omnipotent alien occupiers.

Tetu and Echo stood for a moment, two children of Antarctica, marvelling at this encounter with a world they'd never experienced. Suddenly, without preamble, Echo took hold of Tetu's hand. He felt more amazement at this gesture than all the wonders around him. Holding his breath, he didn't dare look down in case it caused her to pull her hand away. Accepting that he couldn't stand here, doing nothing indefinitely, he slowly turned his head, looking at Echo, and said:

'This is the best day of my life. You don't have to say the same. I just wanted you to know.'

'I wanted to know how it felt. To hold your hand.'

'How is it?'

'You're shivering? Are you cold?'

'No, I'm not cold.'

'I can transfer some of my body heat into you?'

'This is perfect.'

Holding hands, they walked the line of famous statues, teenagers on the most remarkable first date of all time. Arriving at the moai stone heads from Easter Island, carved from volcanic stone by the Polynesian people of Rapa Nui, standing on a squat base, they took a moment to admire these angular stone faces that were up to ten metres tall, weighing eighty tonnes, now with crowns of snow and ice hanging from their noses. Making nervous conversation, Echo said:

'I've seen these in books. I learned about these during Extinction Studies.'

He asked:

'What are they?'

'They come from a small island two thousand miles off the coast of what was once known as South America. They were carved from a quarry beside a volcano called *Rano Raraku* by a hereditary society of priests. Their society died out. Some argue that they cut down all their trees, depleted their natural resources. Without trees they couldn't build canoes to trade, without canoes they couldn't fish far out at sea, so they were forced to fish off the coast, which meant they destroyed all the reefs. When their resources ran out, they descended into cannibalism and interclan warfare. A society of twenty thousand reduced to a hundred. Soon the island was empty. And all that was left of them were these stone heads.'

Listening to her talk, waiting for her to finish, Tetu said in a voice that was almost a whisper:

'You don't believe we can be a couple, do you?'

'I don't know. I've never been in love. What does love feel like?'

'I've only been in love with you. It feels like nothing else. No one taught me about love, no one explained to me how it works, but I knew it as soon as I felt it. So, if you need to ask that question, you're not in love.'

'I care for you.'

'Does your heart beat faster when you see me?'

Echo shook her head.

'My heart is very big and beats very slowly.'

Tetu let go of her hand and circled the stone head. When he returned, he was smiling.

'McMurdo City will have answers. You'll see more people like you, who were adapted for the cold. Maybe you feel love differently to me. Maybe this is love, for you. Maybe your heart is steady no matter how in love you are. Why does love only have to be one thing? You'll know, Echo, in McMurdo. We don't have to rush this. We can wait. You're on a journey. Maybe you'll realize your feelings for me are love. Or maybe you'll realize they're not. But I'm happy to wait. And whoever you love, I will always be your best friend, no matter what.'

The two of them sat at the foot of the Statue of Liberty, looking out over the plateau, wondering what answers they were going to find in McMurdo City.

PART NINE

THE TRIAL OF YOTAM PENZAK

M cMURDO CITY's ONLY MUSEUM WAS dedicated to the history of humankind's exploration of Antarctica. On display were photographs of the first children born south of the Antarctic Convergence, Solveig Gunbjørg Jacobsen, daughter of a whaling station manager born on 8 October 1913, and Emilio Marcos Palma, born January 1978 in Fortín Sargento Cabral near the tip of the Antarctic Peninsula. Solveig had passed away in Buenos Aires, aged eighty-three, before the alien occupation, but Emilio had been forty-four years old at the time and during the Exodus had returned to the place of his birth, serving as a ceremonial figure, present at the birth of the first ever ice-adapted child, whom he'd cradled in his arms – the first ordinary-born and the first ice-adapted child of Antarctica.

One of the most popular museum exhibits was the diary of an American astronomer named Douglas Reynolds, who'd been stationed at McMurdo Station before the alien occupation, a private journal never professionally published during his lifetime, the original handwritten pages displayed in glass cabinets and read by almost every survivor. Since there was no method of printing books anymore, people would stand inside the museum, studying the life of a man who'd been one of the most successful employees of the original McMurdo Station, surviving for eight years on the continent before his mind snapped and he was airlifted off. The cause of his psychotic episode had been the first known sighting of an alien vessel above the South Pole, a shooting star that had stopped in the middle of the sky, turned ninety degrees before continuing onwards. Yet it was his descriptions of how best to stave off the depression induced by this continent that had made his diaries essential reading. It wasn't clear from the museum exhibit why Doug hadn't been brought back to Antarctica during the Exodus, since his eight years on the ice and expert knowledge would have made him eligible for selection. But the truth was unsuitable for a museum intended to inspire McMurdo's inhabitants.

Doug Reynolds had been asked to return, he'd been offered a spot on an American military transport plane, and he'd said no. He'd found love, he was married, and he'd explained to his wife what life would be like in Antarctica, how unforgiving the continent was to human frailties – physical and psychological. In their late sixties, they'd felt blessed, so instead of returning to McMurdo he'd handed over his diaries to the military officials arranging the evacuation of the United States, wishing them the best of luck. On the last day before the deadline, Doug and his wife had sat together in the September summer warmth of Palisade Park, Santa Monica, watching their final sunset, along with the many millions of other Californians who'd decided against attempting the journey, some accepting their fate, others believing it to be a hoax. As the sun went down behind the Malibu hills, the deadline passed and a second later the swathes of people crowding the beach, standing shoulder to shoulder in the shallow water, perched on the roof of the lifeguard huts, filling the eight-lane freeway and the amusement pier, all these people had broken apart into fragments of light. For a moment it was as if the whole sky was full of campfire embers that swirled among seagulls distressed at the commotion but otherwise unharmed. And then the beaches were empty, the parks were empty, the freeway and pier were empty, the seagulls were calm again and the only people left alive on the planet were those who'd reached Antarctica.

Since there were no prisons in McMurdo City, Yotam was being held inside the museum, locked inside the exhibition hall, sleeping under the case containing the diaries with only the company of his dog Copper. He'd been confined to this space while the Senate decided how to handle his case. If he was honest, maybe he'd deliberately provoked this reaction, forcing the issue, unable to keep Eitan trapped under the ice any longer. The Senate had been prevaricating, always demanding more evidence that these radically advanced Cold People were safe. Their safety could never be proved unless they were released.

The door opened and the guard entered, with a set of fresh clothes. 'They're ready for you.'

The trial of Yotam Penzak was about to begin.

MCMURDO CITY
MCMURDO SENATE BUILDING
CHAPEL OF THE SNOWS
SAME DAY

T HE TRIAL OF YOTAM PENZAK was the first trial in McMurdo
City's twenty-year history. During the creation of this new
society, the decision had been taken not to replicate the justice
systems of the old world. There weren't the resources to build court-
rooms and prison cells, nor could they afford for a large portion of
the workforce to be imprisoned when there were so few people left.
Instead, the justice system had been replaced with a blend of liber-
tarianism and authoritarianism. There were no written laws and no
human rights. There was, instead, an imprecise and nebulous sense
of fairness. Infractions were handled on a local level by a neigh-
bourhood committee. Only the most egregious and contentious
incidents reached the Senate. Composed of thirteen of the most
senior academics, nine with Nobel prizes – the last surviving win-
ners – these thirteen were the McMurdo Supreme Court. Bound
by no precedent or convention, they were told the names and cases
of people failing to contribute, stealing food or displaying violent
tendencies. With a majority ruling the Senate made the decision

whether to expel the citizen from the city or give them a second chance. Almost everyone was given a second chance and almost no one was given a third. In practice very few people broke the unwritten social code – to look after each other, to work as hard as you could and to take no more than you were entitled to. Expulsion from McMurdo involved the evicted citizens being transported past the Transantarctic mountain range, abandoning them to the centre of the continent where some eked out an existence in the wreckage of the Exodus before succumbing to the cold.

On trial today wasn't the fate of one man, but the future of the species. The case was being heard in the Chapel of the Snows, the former non-denominational Christian church built before the occupation. The thirteen senators sat on the timber stage where the altar had once stood, believed to have come from St Saviour's Chapel, New Zealand, now kept aside for private acts of worship. Behind the thirteen Senators was the only stained-glass window on the continent. It was a modest space for such consequential decisions. Originally intended for only sixty worshippers, in today's hearing everyone sat closer, packed together, the city's leading scientists and thinkers on the Cold People Project.

The current president was Johanna Mues, a professor from Berlin's Humboldt University, the winner of the last ever Nobel Memorial Prize for Economics. She'd led the Senate for the past six years. She was among one of the oldest survivors on the continent, seventy-two years old, with silver hair befitting a president of a frozen continent. Having lost her husband and children during the Exodus, she'd married a tailor from the country once known as Japan, one of the finest tailors in the artisan district. The family lived in presidential quarters on board the aircraft carrier *Nimitz* with three ice-adapted children whose mothers had died during birth. During the summer vacation, President Mues would hike up the side of Mount Erebus, looking down on the society she'd helped create, meditating on its future as though seeking counsel from the active volcano rumbling behind her.

Standing before the court, she declared:

'Twenty years ago, we were forced to abandon the technological frontier. Our dreams of artificial intelligence and ever more powerful supercomputers were at an end. We don't have the industry to build new machines or develop new computers. We don't have cobalt, ruthenium, chromium, platinum. We don't have the silicon from the mines of Cape Flattery or nickel from the mines of Sorowako. The best we can do is repair. Even the process of patching up is getting harder. How long will the supercomputers on which we depend for our genetic computations last? Once they're broken, we can never build another. With them we lose our history, our knowledge and our future. Everything is running out. Time is our most limited resource of all. The worst-kept secret on this continent is that we, as a people, are dying, and no amount of optimism can hide this fact. When we walk around the city, we can see empty workshops and factories because the workers are no longer with us. We notice the queues in the canteens becoming shorter. All our population models suggest that we have less than a hundred years left as a viable society. After that we will become a subsistence species, breaking into warring tribes, fighting over seal flesh until the winters eventually finish us off. With more time we could be prudent. With more time we could be ethical. We have been neither. We staked our future on the genetic frontier. We've played God not out of hubris, but out of necessity. The actions of Yotam Penzak have made it clear to me that we've been delaying our most important decision. Which of these species of Cold People can we live with? Which of them can save us, since we can no longer save ourselves? We cannot delay this decision any longer. If we get it wrong, it might be the last decision we ever take. If we do nothing, it will surely be the last decision we ever take.'

With that said, President Mues indicated for Yotam to take the stand.

MCMURDO CITY
MCMURDO SENATE BUILDING
CHAPEL OF THE SNOWS
SAME DAY

WITH COPPER COILED AROUND HIS feet as though the pair of them were on trial, Yotam looked across the pews filled with some of the world's greatest living scientists and felt no concern for his own predicament. His only concern was for Eitan's life and the survival of his colony; their fate depended on the answers he was about to give. President Mues began her questioning:

'Yotam Penzak, you've exceeded the bounds of your authority. That's not in any doubt. I could remove you from your post, I could have you work on the farms or in the fisheries, and that would be the end of it. The more important question, the reason we're all gathered here, is to ask why you're so sure this species of Cold People should be freed.'

'I agree, Madame President, that is the important question.'

'Would you claim to be the closest living representative of Song Fu's views?'

'I lived with her for fourteen years. I worked with her every day. But I couldn't speak for her. No one could.'

'Why do you imagine she chose you?'

'At the South Pole Station?'

'We accept that you're intelligent and dedicated. But you had no knowledge of genetics when you arrived in Antarctica. You were an Israeli soldier. She interviewed thousands of survivors. Why did she pick you?'

'She chose a number of assistants.'

'After many years together, she entrusted you with the species she created.'

'That is true.'

'Would you say that she selected a team of assistants who understood what it was like to be rejected by society? A team of outsiders. People who could love her creation no matter how different it turned out to be. The more we recoiled from it the closer you became. She groomed you to fall in love with her creation. You are in love, are you not?'

'Love of a kind, yes.'

'Do you lack objectivity because of it?'

'Song Fu did exactly what you asked of her. She created a form of life perfectly adapted to the cold. And you keep it locked up under the ice as though it was a monster.'

'Perhaps it is a monster.'

'What is monstrous about it?'

'Do you imagine, Yotam, that the creature you have named Eitan loves you?'

'I doubt it feels love the way we do.'

'Why do you doubt that?'

'Because we built it to be tougher than us.'

'Is it manipulating you?'

'I don't know. Zariffa believed so. She might be right.'

'In order that you might free it, by acting impetuously? I'm not trying to embarrass you. When I was a young woman, a long time ago, I fell in love with a handsome young man. We lived together while we were students. He was abusive. He stole from me. I couldn't see past my infatuation. Love is very powerful.'

'What do you think that I'm blind to?'

'Song Fu wanted blind love to protect her creation. Because, it is my contention, she believed that was the only chance such a creature had of being released. On the sly, by a hopeless romantic.'

'Maybe you should ask a different question.'

'What would that be?'

'Why did she believe that ordinary people would be so narrow-minded they wouldn't set them free?'

'Is this your view?'

'You're nervous of admitting that we've created a superior race. But the whole purpose of the Cold People Project is to create a superior race. Because we're dying. And that is exactly what we've done. Song Fu was unapologetic about it.'

'Is it superior to us?'

'On this continent, yes, and this continent is all we have.'

President Mues took a sip of water, uneasy with these answers.

'Do you believe, if this species were released, they would live in harmony with us?'

'I see no reason why they wouldn't.'

'The purpose of the Cold People Project is to create a species that can work with us, assist us, be our friends, our allies, our saviours.'

'With respect, Madame President, that is not the purpose of the Cold People Project.'

There was a reaction in the chapel audience and it took several moments for the assembly to settle down.

'Your statement surprises us.'

'I'm not saying that such an outcome isn't possible. I'm not saying that such an outcome wouldn't be desirable.'

'The purpose of the project has always been to create a species that will help us survive. What other purpose could the project have?'

'The purpose of the project is that humankind will survive in some form.'

'*In some form?*'

'Ideally, we'd survive alongside them, as their friends, their allies, their partners, as you say. I believe that is possible.'

'What other possibilities are there?'

'That we can't survive. That we won't survive. That we will die out, even with their help. But some part of us will survive within the creatures we've created.'

'You're saying that we'll live on, not in any real sense, but inside the genetic make-up of this new species.'

'To Song Fu, that was always the most probable outcome.'

'That our time is over? And their time has begun?'

'Our time is over. It is up to you whether their time has begun.'

'Would you please take a moment to tell the court about the final days of Song Fu? What were her instructions to you, before she died?'

Yotam knitted his fingers together, remembering how he lost the woman who'd become his mentor.

Song Fu died three months before Eitan was born. Her revolutionary approach to reinventing the human genome had begun to feel like a despicable experiment, an act of madness by scientists who, on the brink of extinction, were desperately toying with a process far beyond their grasp. Her team had dissected the stillborn infants, trying to ascertain the mistake, cutting open a mess of organic matter that appeared utterly divorced from the miracle of life. Song Fu couldn't endure the sight of these dead infants. Despite her reputation for being emotionless, she treated each child as if they were her own. Cocooning herself with the supercomputer models of her genomes, she stopped sleeping, obsessed with trying to ascertain which single base unit of information might be causing this cascade of failures. She rarely spoke and seldom ate, aware that the McMurdo Senate was considering whether to terminate her approach altogether, investing the precious resources in the more modest cold adaptations, the parahumans, who were already successfully living among the ordinary-borns.

Yotam had taken the time to watch the birth of the ice-adapted child known as Echo. He'd seen her parents hold the infant, interlocking their arms to support the weight of this newborn girl. He'd seen the love in their eyes and watched them cry with joy. It was the only time he ever directly challenged Song Fu, arguing that there was some magic to motherhood that couldn't be identified in the genetic code.

'Echo was born into love. The children we're creating won't be held in their mothers' arms. They won't look them in the eyes and tell them that they're loved.'

'Those ice-adapted children are soft like us. Needy like us. Our children will know the savagery of this world from the very first seconds of their lives; it will be as natural to them as a mother's love is to us.'

'The first thing they will know of this life is our death.'

Yotam expected Song Fu to dismiss this comment as more fitting for an artistic sensibility rather than a scientific one. But she didn't wave him away, sitting silent for a time.

'Then you must teach them love.'

One evening, as they were preparing for another birth, Song Fu had taken a stroll on the decks of the aircraft carriers as she often did to meditate. A storm appeared out of nowhere as if summoned by outraged gods, furious with these attempts at tampering with life, a whiteout engulfing the flotilla of coastal ships. Unable to make it to safety inside, Song had fastened herself to the chain bridge between aircraft carriers, hunkering down and waiting for the storm to pass. The rescue group had found her alive, but the cold had penetrated her lungs. Rushed to the infirmary, she was placed in intensive care. With her body weakening, she'd asked for only two things – access to her work and the company of Yotam. He sat by her side, day after day, night after night, as she'd spent her last hours on alterations to her cold-adapted genome. All he could do was protect her from the doctors and nurses who'd tried to make her rest.

One morning she'd handed him the tablet computer and said:

'On the brink of death, I see what I'd missed about life.'

On the screen was her final model of the Cold People genome.

'This is it.'

'I can't do this without you.'

'I am not an easy person to love, I know that. If my daughters were alive, they'd tell you the same. I was a hard parent. But that is how I was brought up. You have a gift for love. You will love this new life. This infant will be born and it will be unlike anything you've ever seen before. This species will need you. I've made them strong. Unimaginably strong. Hard on the outside. Hard on the inside, too. But you must love them without condition. No matter what they look like. No matter how they speak or sound. I can create them. But you will love them. You will give them the love that was never given to you.'

Back in the courtroom, President Mues declared:

'We've been theoretical about this question for too long. Tomorrow we will reconvene in the Final Stage Chambers. We will ask this creature ourselves, directly – does it want to live with us? Or does it want to kill us? If even one senator doubts its intentions, we end this experiment for good.'

MCMURDO CITY
THE ROSS ICE SHELF
FINAL STAGE CHAMBERS
NEXT DAY

T WO HUNDRED METRES UNDER THE ice shelf, the senators stood in the observation tunnels, shuffling from boot to boot, some dressed in a patchwork of lynx furs repurposed from the lavish coats brought to the continent by oligarchs, others wearing gaudy-coloured synthetic thermals. No longer under any obligation to appear presentable for television appearances or magazine covers, some sported ungainly hair while others had allowed their beards to grow long. No one wore make-up or perfume for there was none to wear, everyone uniformly smelling of the same blubber-oil soap. Yet they looked better for the change, liberated from a superficial aesthetic, their skin aided by the almost complete absence of pollution, presenting as their authentic selves. In contrast to the past, when world leaders would travel in armoured motorcades with scores of protection officers, each of the senators was accompanied by two cold-survival specialists, men and women who carried tents, ropes, distress flares, ice axes, food rations – bodyguards against the cold, experts on the dangers of the Antarctic winds and the trickery of the snows. On duty they never took their backpacks off, even when they were inside, as if as fearful of being separated from their equipment as they were of being separated from their senator.

President Mues had visited these chambers hundreds of times, holding discussions with the project leaders, studying the progress of these ice-adapted species. She'd never been able to call them *people*. She didn't want to befriend them or feel close to them – it was essential she remain objective. She was here to answer a series of questions. What could they do to help ordinary-born people survive? Could they mine the Transantarctic Mountains or master the art of ice architecture? Embedded in her thinking was a reluctance to see them as equals: it was hard for her to shake the desire for an Antarctic servant. An intelligent, dutiful and hard-working class of citizen, impervious to the cold and steady-minded during the winter darkness, a labourer who could toil the year round with no need to shelter during the coldest months so that when humankind emerged from its annual hibernation it would discover all the things that had been built during its absence. For years the creatures had been held in limbo under the ice, studied and scrutinized, a drain on humanity's dwindling resources, species that to date had provided nothing but scientific curiosity in return. As someone who hated making rash decisions, President Mues doubted her suitability as leader for this moment, her mind drifting back to when she'd been a little girl, swimming in the lakes of Berlin during the long hot summers, joyously simple childhood years, growing up with a love of literature and no aspirations for power. That it was she who'd end up at the helm of humankind was unfathomable. Of course, it would never have happened if the world hadn't been turned upside down. Nonetheless, here she was, watching as Yotam Penzak entered the creature's enclosure.

N O LONGER TRUSTED TO ACT independently, Yotam was flanked by six security officers. At the bottom of the ladder, he unlocked the cage and turned around, looking up at the line of senators judging him. He felt an irrational impulse to wave at them as though they were his friends. Perhaps he was going mad. It was possible; it happened like this, suddenly and without warning, eccentricities and unexplained gestures. He needed to hold his composure. He'd promised Song Fu that he'd protect her creation at all costs. She'd been right: ordinary people did fear them. They despised this species for the very same reason they'd made them – because they were different. Of course, he appreciated the complexity of the president's predicament and the simplicity of his own. He was entirely confident of Eitan's potential should he be released from this icy prison. Maybe that was because he was in love, maybe it was because he'd worked on nothing else for nearly twenty years and was suffering from monomania. There was no historical precedent to guide them in this moment – they were in uncharted waters, much like the first explorers who'd set foot on this continent.

Entering the inner chamber, through the cage, the security officers raised their weapons, ready to fire.

'We can't see him.'

'He's hiding.'

'Tell him to show himself.'

Yotam was curious to know what impact bullets would have on Eitan's adapted bone and chitin skin. He imagined he'd be a difficult target to hit, moving at enormous speed, changing colour, a rush of ivory armour accompanied with lethal jabs. He doubted the guards could stop him even with their powerful assault rifles, although he kept this opinion to himself. There was no need to call out his name; Eitan would've heard them as soon as they'd entered this section of the chambers. His friend was refusing to reveal his position, remaining hidden against the ice, his voice reverberating around the chamber, impossible to pinpoint:

'Are these men here to kill me?'

Eitan understood human nature. He'd read the history books detailing humankind's exploration of Antarctica where whalers had slaughtered the largest living creature alive, a blue whale over one hundred years old, butchered to make glycerine for the two world wars. He'd studied the photographs of the first scientists at McMurdo who'd made a bowling alley out of stuffed penguins rather than regular pins.

'No, they're not here to kill you.'

'The thirteen senators in the tunnel are your leaders.'

'They are.'

'Why are they here? Is today an important day?'

'It is, yes.'

'What is going to happen?'

'We're going to show you our world and see what you make of it.'

Without warning Eitan emerged from the gloom, his white outer skin changing to a dark blue, perhaps to assert his authority, a display of power. He stood opposite Yotam, paying no attention to either the senators or the security officers.

'Do you like these people, Yotam? These men with weapons? They seem different to you.'

'We work together. We're colleagues.'

'What is that in their hands?'

'In order for you to go outside, I need to put a device around your neck. It's an explosive neck brace. If you try to escape, they will detonate it. If you disobey any of their commands, they will detonate it. Will you allow the guards to attach it?'

'No.'

'Eitan, if you don't allow them to put it on—'

'But I will allow you. You can put it on. Only you.'

Yotam signalled to the guards. The senior security officer advanced, holding the neck brace rigged with two powerful explosives on either side designed to direct the blast inwards, packed with white phosphorous, the component of incendiary munitions which burnt at five thousand degrees Fahrenheit. Holding the shackle, Yotam felt ashamed, clasping this symbol of slavery. Eitan bent his front two legs, kneeling, and Yotam moved close, clipping it around his neck, like a lover attaching a necklace. The security officer moved to his side, making sure it was secure, taking out the remote detonator from his pocket and arming the device, holding it in front of Eitan's eyes, warning him.

As they left the chamber, Eitan didn't bother with the ladder, as an ordinary-born might, climbing the wall of ice instead. The door had been removed to make way for his exit. Even with this enlarged gap, he had to squeeze through, emerging into the observation tunnels for the first time as an adult. He regarded his assembled audience who, despite having seen him many times, fell silent, in awe of his size and otherness. President Mues stepped forward.

'My name is Johanna Mues. I'm the president of McMurdo City and the Antarctic Coalition of People. As you are aware, we would like you to be part of our future – to contribute as best you can, in any way that you're able. There are many challenges we could use your help with. There are many tasks you could do better than us. I must apologize for keeping you under the ice. There are good reasons for this. If you have suffered in these conditions, I am sorry. We have all suffered; in that you are not alone. Please follow us. We would like to take you on a tour of our city.'

In a procession, like a medieval royal pageant, they left the tunnels with Eitan and Copper at the front and Yotam by his side. The security officers followed close behind, guns and grenades at the ready, the cold-weather survival experts next, ice axes clasped in their hands, while the senators trailed from a safe distance, muttering observations to each other, seemingly unaware that no matter how much they lowered their voice, Eitan could hear every word.

Entering the domed Asylum, the cacophony of bird screeches, insect clicks and human howls came to an abrupt stop, silence falling over the space for the first time since its creation. At the windows to the cells appeared the faces of every malformed creature, their faces pressed up against the bars, regarding this new arrival. What had once been a rabble, a freak circus of experiments gone wrong, suddenly seemed more like a community, as though they finally had a sense of purpose and meaning in their lives – a leader. Eitan stopped in the middle of the dome and regarded each of them individually, turning his head with the precision of a clock. Calmly, as though under orders, they retreated to the back of their cells and remained silent. President Mues asked:

'You can speak to them?'

'Not words, no, not language as you understand it. But I sense their feelings.'

'What do they feel?'

'They are afraid of you.'

Leaving the Asylum, the procession continued along the path that wrapped around the moon crater containing the colony of snow gorillas. These silver-haired creatures, who had never shown any interest in ordinary people, stopped to stare up at this new species entering their realm, all of them standing, one by one, on their back legs, stretching out to their full height. The largest and oldest of the snow gorillas raised a silver-haired fist to his chest, thumping it in salutation. Soon all of them followed suit, pounding their chests, a thunderous sound made not out of fear or anger but devotion to their new king – this emperor of the ice.

FOR THE FIRST TIME IN his life, Eitan saw the sky, an appropri-ately simple sky for this newcomer to the outside world, without the complication of a single cloud. Keeping his back to the sun, which was too bright for his cave-conditioned eyes, he felt the wind slink through the grooves of his armoured torso as comfortable as a caress. Despite having lived in Antarctica his whole life, he'd never encountered snow before, crushing it between his claws in a gesture that could be described as playful. This was his home, he thought, this was his land. What right did these ordinary people, foreigners to this continent, have to it? What right did they have to keep this place from him as though it was theirs to withhold? They were the immigrants. He was native to this land.

Having acclimatized to the sky and the snow, he was ready to face a phenomenon he'd heard so much about yet never seen – the sun. His camera-shutter eyelids, made from wafer-thin bone, narrowed to a pinprick as he slowly manoeuvred himself around. Looking directly up, his vision was scorched. After years of subterrain gloom it took him a while to bring the dazzling light into balance. If he'd read nothing about this universe, he would've sworn there were three suns above him, a central one with two smaller ones on either side. But he knew from textbooks that there was only one sun in this solar system and this optical effect was called parhelion, tiny ice crystals in the air refracting the light, creating a glistening halo, a celestial eyeball watching with interest the arrival of a new species on the surface of this ancient world.

The procession walked through McMurdo City, which appeared to Eitan to be a ragtag place, a junkyard city assembled from repurposed scrap, a beggar's settlement suitable for a fallen people. They could've created something magnificent from the ice, but they didn't know how, so downtrodden they couldn't even glimpse the potential of this continent. He passed the workshops where they made their crude tools and the tailors where they stitched their primitive clothes to keep their fragile bodies warm. He watched as these people encountered him for the first time. Some were dumbfounded, others were scared. Some stepped back, others stepped forward. Only one woman waved, an older woman with a wicker basket of penguin eggs on her back, grey hair billowing about her wrinkled face – she struck him as quite mad. They all struck him as quite mad, mad with too many feelings and emotions. He politely imitated her gesture, waving back, and she seemed pleased, clasping her chest at the honour as though she'd encountered her favourite matinee movie star.

The procession stopped at the edge of the city. Eitan looked out across the unpopulated eastern reaches of the ice shelf and beyond, an expanse these people had abandoned as unliveable when, in fact, there were mountains and valleys, glaciers and crevasses ready to be turned into citadels and castles, a kingdom waiting to be made.

Beyond the last of their tatty buildings, they'd heaped a perimeter wall of ice to protect them against the worst of the katabatic winds sweeping off the vast planes. After the wall there was nothing human, only the Transantarctic Mountains on the horizon. Smooth orographic clouds were amassing on the northern ridge of the mountain range, like an ocean wave ready to spill over. Eitan studied the variations of air currents, seeing them as clearly as if they were theatrical displays of colours, imperceptible to the ordinary people. The elderly female leader who called herself president of this continent seemed a wise and thoughtful person despite the inappropriateness of her title, claiming supremacy of a land where she didn't belong.

'You're free to explore the plateau. Our only request is that you return when we fire the first distress flare. Do you understand?'

'I understand. This is what you call a test.'

'Will you return?'

'I will return.'

'Are you lying?'

'I never lie. Ask Yotam.'

'Has he ever lied?'

'Not that I'm aware of, no.'

'Then we'll see you soon.'

Eitan bowed his head and set off, towards the plateau, alone and unguarded.

E ITAN SET OUT ACROSS THE ice shelf walking slowly, with precision and control, his movements restrained by his sense of what was possible, his mind still boxed in by the confines of his enclosure, walking as though he were still in prison. The truth was that he'd never run before, he'd never had this much space, there'd always been a wall ahead or a wall behind. He didn't even know what running looked like – he'd been kept in isolation, he'd never even seen his kind run. Today would be an exploration of his body as much as an exploration of this continent. He steadily increased his speed until he was walking at a brisk trot in roughly the same manner that he'd always walked, discovering that as he tried to increase his pace his four legs began to tangle under his body, experiencing clumsiness for the first time. He almost fell, his co-ordination confused like a newborn deer after birth.

Refusing to slow down, he pressed forward, contemplating the shape of his body as a mathematical puzzle, a biological piece of engineering, deducing that it was necessary to narrow his back legs in order to pick up speed. Pondering all the textbooks he'd read, he recalled the running technique of a cheetah, an animal he knew only from faded photographs. With this inspiration in mind, he organized his movements so that his front and back legs never touched. Having made the adjustment, altering his gait, he memorized this new rhythm until he didn't need to think about it anymore, pushing forward, no longer walking but running, no longer running but galloping, leaning forward to reduce the drag, his arrowhead ivory face cutting through the air, his four sets of diamond-hard claws tearing at the ice beneath him, puffs of fine crystals exploding with each landing until the landscape around him was a blur and he wondered what this new feeling was – it was exhilaration, it was joy.

He turned sharply right and then sharply left, snaking about the ice in a celebration of his physical prowess. Suddenly anything felt possible, the old limits of his existence melting away. He could climb to the top of the Transantarctic Mountains as the clouds poured down around him. He could run to Mount Erebus and race around its circumference. He could dive into the ocean, plunging into the freezing waters, and swim down to the darkest depths. No longer a servant or prisoner, no longer a mere experiment, he was free, freer than his jailors could ever be on this continent. Then, as his front legs landed, the surface of the ice collapsed. He was tumbling down a deep crevasse.

To an ordinary-born this fall would've been fatal, plunging thirty metres down, but Eitan simply allowed his body to rotate, his powerful ice claws puncturing the walls, catching the uneven surface so that he was on a vertical plane rather than a horizontal one. Once secure, he scampered across the steep walls, the crevasse as natural to him as the flat plateau, bounding between walls from right to left, until he climbed out and stood still for a moment proudly looking out over this continent – his continent, the continent of his kind.

Though he wasn't tired, he felt hot, and he dug himself a pit, showering himself with shards of ice to cool himself down, his skin turning the darkest blue to radiate this excess of heat. Nestled in the bath of ice shards, one thing was clear: he could never go back to the underground chambers. He would never be imprisoned in that enclosure again. His kind did not belong trapped under the ice any more than the ordinary-born people belonged on this continent. At this point the distress flare streaked up from the edge of McMurdo City, rising high into the clear blue sky, ordering him to return.

THE OUTSKIRTS OF MCMURDO CITY
THE ROSS ICE SHELF
SAME DAY

Yotam watched as the third and final distress flare was fired. It arced over the plateau, leaving a comet trail of red smoke, touching down on the ice still hot, spitting and sizzling until it melted out of sight, the remnants of red smoke dispersed by the wind. No one spoke for a time, as they contemplated the meaning of this first act of disobedience. Seeming to herald a change in their fortunes, clouds amassing on the far side of the Transantarctic mountain range broke over the peaks like a dam bursting, sweeping down the slopes and across the ice shelf, hurtling towards them like an oncoming wave, hundreds of miles high. Soon this freezing white sky would engulf the city, blocking out the sun, visibility would drop to a few metres, the temperature would plummet and the air would be filled with needles of ice. While the city's inhabitants hastily sought shelter, Yotam lingered on the outer wall, hoping to catch sight of what now seemed impossible – Eitan's return.

'Maybe he didn't see the flares? We should fire another,' he said.

President Mues said:

'We have fired three. If you tell me honestly that he will return if we fire a fourth, I will fire a fourth. Do you believe that?'

'President, anything could have happened. This is his first experience of freedom. Give him a chance.'

'This was his chance.'

The security officers triggered a city-wide alarm, bells sounding out across the city, ordering everyone inside. Ostensibly this was because of the storm; no one needed to know that one of the creatures was unaccounted for. Twenty additional armed security officers arrived to reinforce the group, some of the fiercest fighters in McMurdo, advising the senators to take cover back at the base, inside the armoured aircraft carriers, where they could be better protected against any possible attack. President Mues accepted the need for the other senators to retreat to safety. However, like the captain of a vessel at stormy seas, she refused to leave, remaining with Yotam.

'Go. All of you. I'll stay.'

Distraught at Eitan's failure to return, Yotam stood atop the ice wall, searching with binoculars, grasping for innocent explanations – perhaps he'd ventured too far, perhaps he was exploring the depths of a crevasse. But in his heart, he knew the truth – this was an act of defiance. Eitan would rather die than return to that enclosure. Climbing down from the wall, he approached President Mues, accepting that he'd failed.

'He doesn't want to be our partner. He never did.'

To his surprise, she consoled him:

'You remind me of what is special about people. We can love them. But they could never love us. You fell in love with him. But he could never fall in love with you.'

Taking a silver flask from the inside of her coat, she offered him a sip of brandy. The liquid was delicious, a warming nectar as delightful as a magic potion, with hints of citrus and cinnamon, flavours he'd long since forgotten. The President smiled.

'It's Gautier Cognac from 1762. Almost three hundred years old.'

'How do you have it?'

'A billionaire brought his entire brandy collection with him during the Exodus. He took with him crates of diamond-encrusted bottles instead of people. We found it stashed in his private jet after he died of hypothermia. On occasion, I sip it, not for the alcohol or the decadence, but to remind me of time.'

'To remind you of time?'

'Three hundred years ago someone bottled this spirit in a water mill in Aigre, on the Aume River, with no idea that one day it would be enjoyed in Antarctica, a continent that they didn't even know existed. We lose our sense of time here. It's hard to imagine three years in the future let alone thirty years. But it is my job to try to imagine humankind in three hundred years. Like you, I can imagine it with these creatures. But they, I believe, cannot imagine it with us. They want this continent for themselves.'

'I can't be the test.'

'You are. You are the most important test. You feel everything for him. He feels nothing for you. You did everything for him. He did nothing for you. What you said was true. If they were released, some part of our genetic code would survive, but I will not let the best part of us go extinct.'

'What part is that?'

'Our foibles, our eccentricities, our capacity to love.'

'Maybe they have a different kind of love, for each other, but not for us.'

'Or maybe they see love as a weakness.'

Yotam couldn't deny it.

'If that is true – I've failed. It was my job to teach it love. But how can I teach something I've been looking for my whole life?'

The head of security presented the president with the tracking device. The screen indicated that Eitan had taken refuge thirteen kilometres from their location, at a depth of fifty metres, slowly moving towards the coast.

'He must be hoping the crevasse interferes with the signal. Madame President, that storm is almost here. This is our last chance.'

She nodded at the head of security. He took out the remote-control detonation to the neck brace, seeking final confirmation.

'Madame President, do you give the order?'

'I'll do it myself.'

He handed her the device. She looked at Yotam.

'I'm sorry.'

With that, she pressed the button. In the distance there was a dazzling burst of white light erupting from the depths of a crevasse, as if a tiny sun had been born.

MCMURDO CITY
THE ROSS ICE SHELF
SAME DAY

WITH THE STORM CLOSING ON them, Yotam and President
Mues rode back to McMurdo City in a husky-drawn sleigh,
the two of them seated under layers of pelts and furs, finishing off
the ancient French brandy as if it were no more special than locally
fermented sea-kelp. Drunk and emotional, Yotam came to terms
with the fact that his innate loneliness had been manipulated and
his sentimentality exploited. He'd hidden from real relationships
in the country of his birth, and he'd hidden here, too, preferring
this fantasy, this flawless figure of strength, a secret imprisoned
two hundred metres under the ice. He'd lobbied for this new species to prove themselves as partners because that had been his
own desire. As heartbroken as the day he'd left Israel, Yotam felt
hollow, without purpose, the grip of Antarctic depression tightening
around his mind.

Suddenly all sixteen husky dogs, including Copper, came to
a stop, their ears pricking up, their fur standing up along the
ridge of their back. Despite the entreaties of the sleigh driver, the
dogs wouldn't move, ignoring the lashes of his whip. In perfect

synchronization they all lay down, their heads flat on the ice in a gesture of submission, although to what or to whom wasn't clear, since there was nothing nearby. Yotam stood up, turning around, staring into the storm about to breach the city.

'It's him.'

The storm swept over the city walls, engulfing the factories, obliterating the sky and the sun. Yotam raised his snow visor, waiting for the storm to hit and, with it, the inevitable attack. The security guards took up defensive positions around the sleigh.

Unable to see beyond a meter in any direction, the attack began with a burst of gunfire to the side of the sleigh, an officer from the president's security team emptying an entire magazine into the sky, screaming wildly, the awful sounds of a man who knew he was about to die. As he reloaded his weapon, fumbling at the magazine clip with his thermal gloves, he was lifted into the air, his back snapped, his broken body tossed to the ground, landing between the dogs, who promptly set upon him, ravenously tearing at his flesh. Another officer, blindly searching for his enemy, lost his arm before he could even fire a shot. Soon the assault rifles stopped firing. The guards were dead. The attack was over, the sleigh was surrounded by bodies, the huskies feasting on the dead officers, turning against their masters so quickly it was as if their thousand-year-old allegiance had never really existed.

Emerging out of the blizzard, Eitan stood in front of the presidential sleigh, the colours of his armoured surface modulating from white to sapphire blue. He seemed bigger, brighter, more magnificent than ever. The husky dogs, with their bloody teeth and bellies full, circled his legs in adoration. He sliced their leather leads, and they took up formation behind him, obeying him without any need for a whip. Eitan didn't speak, his pearl lips remained closed, yet somehow Yotam felt his thoughts powerfully inside his head, more vivid than speech:

'Speech is crude to us. We've developed a more efficient way to communicate, one without ambiguity or misunderstandings. You presumed I've been alone all these years. But I've been in constant conversation with my brothers and sisters. We've been sharing our observations about you and your species. We've been making plans. You are upset. You feel betrayed. You shouldn't be. I did exactly what was expected of me by Song Fu. You did, too. Your job was to keep me alive while every other ordinary-born wanted me dead, to love me while they despised me, to give me time to grow, to learn and the means to escape.'

As though Yotam's thoughts were an open book, Eitan spotted a train of thought.

'You wish to know about the explosive neck collar? A primitive thing. Simple to remove. And if you're honest, Yotam, you knew that I could dismantle it even as you put it on. Yet you said nothing and warned no one. You are wondering if I'm going to kill you. But why would I do that? After all you've done for me and my kind. I've decided to let you watch.'

'Watch what?'

'The end of people.'

Like a telepathic conference call, Eitan included the president to the conversation:

'President, let me repeat a story of this continent. When that explorer you admire so much, Roald Amundsen, arrived at the South Pole, he planted the flag of his country in the ice, claimed this continent in the name of his Norwegian king. This explorer, who you consider to be a great man, a legend among people, then proceeded to kill the exhausted dogs who had helped them there, the dogs that had pulled their food and bedding, the dogs that they'd bonded with, travelled with. These brave explorers smashed the skulls of their devoted companions and

fed the weakest to the strongest so that all that remained of the dogs who'd served them so devotedly were their indigestible teeth and tails. Ordinary-born people are the exhausted dogs who have carried my species here. I am not angry with you. You should not feel that you have failed. Your work is done. I have not been on trial. You have been. You have not been testing me. I have been testing you. You have not been evaluating my species; we have been evaluating yours. Your conclusion was that we are not suitable partners for you. I agree. Your era is over. Our era has begun.'

With that said, Eitan stood on his back legs, extending his torso, stretching twenty feet tall, claiming possession of this continent, his back legs bolted into the ice, his armour glistening blue in the blizzard that swirled around him. With that, he leapt up, into the winds, as though he knew how to ride these freezing gales, disappearing into the storm, the dogs following behind.

The president stepped off the sleigh, staggering to a guard's mangled body, taking out his radio and speaking into it:

'Seal the entrance to the Final Stage Chambers. Kill everything under the ice. Do it now.'

MCMURDO CITY
THE ROSS ICE SHELF
FINAL STAGE CHAMBERS
SAME DAY

A T THE ENTRANCE TO THE Final Stage Chambers, the only stairway that connected the network of underground tunnels with the surface of the Ross Ice Shelf, hundreds of scientists and support staff were scrambling to escape, clambering up the ice steps, many slipping in panic as the emergency alarms sounded out. The officer in charge of security had been ordered to act immediately, instructions direct from the president, to detonate the charges without delay. Although he had a reputation for ruthlessness, he decided to give these people a chance, to wait a few seconds longer – these were some of the most brilliant minds on the continent, human life was rare and precious. Beside him was a phalanx of heavily armed soldiers, armed with assault rifles and grenades; he was confident they could repel any of the creatures no matter how well adapted they were for the cold. He would save as many people as possible and then seal the entrance. His officers shouted at the people to climb faster, which of course only caused them to slip and stumble even more, some tumbling all the way back down to the bottom and having to restart the climb.

As the first wave of people reached the top of the stairs, pulled to safety, he saw a snow gorilla at the bottom of the steps. It was the first time he'd ever seen one out of its enclosure. Its bright orange eyes seemed to be glowing, its long coat looked as if it had been spun from silver, a creature of such beauty that for a moment the soldiers stopped shouting and stared, admiring it. One by one all the people on the stairs turned around to look.

With a single leap the gorilla launched itself up, grabbing onto the roof above the stairs, bounding over the heads of these people, moving with a grace they'd never seen before on the ice. In a few seconds it would be at the mouth of the entrance, the sway of its silver fur so hypnotic that not one of these hardened soldiers had thought to fire their weapons.

Comprehending its strength and physical superiority, the head of security understood that they didn't stand a chance. This time he didn't delay, he didn't check the stairs or count how many lives would be lost; he pressed the detonation charge. A sequence of explosions rocked the entrance, the ceiling of the ice shelf exploded, cracking apart in massive chunks. Being so close to the entrance, the gorilla made a leap, propelled through the air, almost free when a wedge of ice smashed into its back, bringing it down to the steps, among the people trying to escape, the two mingled together in an avalanche of people and ice, huge portions of the shelf falling and crushing everything underneath. As the glittering cloud of ice fragments settled, all that remained was a crater where the entrance had once been. The price in human life had been enormous. However, the chambers were sealed. Breathless, the head of security declared:

'We're safe.'

MCMURDO CITY
THE ROSS ICE SHELF
FINAL STAGE CHAMBERS
SAME DAY

T HE WALLS OF THE CHAMBERS shook violently, deep fissures appeared in the ceiling and every scientist who hadn't made it to the staircase understood that they were trapped, the entrance sealed shut with tonnes of ice. There was no way out, no way to dig through the rubble and no other exit. The ventilation shafts would be blown up next, if they hadn't been already, while incendiary devices burnt throughout the passageways, depleting the remaining oxygen. The trapped scientists would share the same fate as the colonies of cold creatures they'd created.

Jinju had worked in the Final Stage Chambers since its excavation, part of the team looking after the species created by Song Fu, a colony that had grown to twenty cold-adapted creatures, ten male and ten female, ranging in age from six months to six years. Over the years she'd secretly given them all Korean names, matching them to people she'd known from the past, none of whom had survived the Exodus. For Jinju, the emergency evacuation alarm had not come as a surprise. She'd been convinced that the creatures were planning to escape. Whenever she'd raised these concerns the team had argued that it was impossible for them to plan anything. These creatures were in solitary confinement, they'd never seen the layout of the chambers and they couldn't co-ordinate with each other. While Jinju accepted these facts appeared to be true, she often had the sensation when she entered the enclosure of having interrupted them, even though they stood silent and alone. All around her, the other team members panicked, running towards the entrance in the hope of finding some way out. Jinju remained at her post, calmly walking to the cell of the oldest female, the creature she had the strongest connection with, named after her mother – Cho.

Before the Exodus, Jinju and her mother had been living in the North Korean border town of Hyesan, smuggling batteries and chocolate from the Chinese town of Changbai, items they sold to the political elite, the only people who could afford them. Deforestation had shuttered Hyesan's timber mills and only the copper mine offered any employment, dependent on Chinese-made pumps to keep the tunnels from flooding. In Hyesan the hungry starved, the sick rarely recovered and no one ever complained. There was no running water and electricity was intermittent, while on the other side of the Yalu River the Chinese economy boomed, with shop signs boasting of an unfathomably large array of goods. When she was a child Jinju's father had been arrested by the political police and deported to the penal region of Paegam county, denounced by his boss for being too innovative in his suggestions, embarrassing the manager whose job was protected by his connections with powerful political figures. When the police had come for her father, he'd whispered to Jinju:

'If you ever get the chance, take your mother and leave this place. Promise me that you'll leave!'

She never saw him again.

The first she'd known of the alien occupation was the moment the television had turned itself on. That fact alone was surprising since her street hadn't been connected to electricity for several years, but it was even more surprising when she saw the television wasn't plugged in. Holding the plug in her hand, she'd stared at the screen displaying a continent covered in ice and snow. Her mother had hurried in and together they'd watched the message being broadcast, as though it were a Korean state media announcement, telling them the people of the world had thirty days to reach Antarctica. Playing on loop, they'd watched the message over and over until a member of the Bowibu police force ran in and fired his gun at the screen. The television exploded in a shower of sparks, spilling its smashed screen onto the floor. Jinju, still holding the plug, looked at the state police officer as he shouted:

'It's an American trick. They are trying to make us leave our country so that they will invade and take our land and we will be lost. You are both to remain inside. The only aliens are the Americans. Anyone trying to leave will be shot.'

As soon as he'd gone, Jinju picked up the largest fragment of television screen, a shard of glass now separate from the television set and from a source of power. Yet the footage of Antarctica was still playing on the glass. Her mother and Jinju dropped to their knees, reassembling the screen like a puzzle on the floor, and even with the pieces on dirt, the images continued. This was a technological prowess that Jinju didn't understand, so inexplicable she could only think of it as sorcery, and though she didn't know what technology America might possess, she was pretty sure not even the Americans could make a television turn on when it wasn't plugged in or make broken fragments of glass flicker with images from thousands of miles away.

She and her mother left the house, slipping out through a hole in the back wall, arriving at the Yalu River and the one hundred and fifty metre-long Changbai–Hyesan International Bridge built by the Japanese in 1936, connecting North Korea and mainland China. Known as the Friendship Bridge, despite its name it was one of the most heavily guarded bridges in the world. With her smuggler's binoculars, Jinju studied the reaction on the other side of the border. A mass evacuation was underway. The Chinese soldiers were in convoys of military vehicles, the civilians in trucks and cars. Surveying the Chinese mainland, she observed activity unlike any she'd ever seen – a sky crisscrossed with military jets and, far above them, alien ships the size of mountains, spinning gracefully in the sky. Jinju had turned to her mother.

'The message we saw was true. If we stay here, we'll die. We must cross the river.'

'And what will we do in Changbai?'

'We go to Shenyang. When we arrive in Shenyang, we will join the Chinese evacuation, and we keep on, and keep on, until we reach a place where we are safe.'

'Shenyang is eight hours by car. We don't have a car, and we don't know anyone there.'

'We will find a way.'

Her mother had looked at the alien vessels in the sky and said:

'I trust you.'

Her preferred crossing point was where the Yalo River was shallowest, the water slowed down and there was a gravel and pebble sandbank on the Chinese embankment, making it easy to climb out. However, this was no longer an option. There were North Korean soldiers stationed on the riverbank shooting anyone who tried to flee. The steps down to the river, at the spot where many washed their clothes and bathed, were also guarded. Jinju took her mother's hand and guided her back into the town, to a sewer, where they climbed down, covering their mouths with rags, reaching the opening that dropped down to the water. Securing a rope around a pipe, she held it steady as her mother climbed down into the river. She waited, submerged in the water, for her daughter to join her at the bottom. Jinju climbed down, joining her mother.

'We have to let go.'

'I can't swim.'

'I'll swim for both of us. Hold me tight.'

Holding hands, they let go of the rope and the rapids took them out, into the middle of the river. They didn't splash, or make a sound, going underwater, and surfacing again, never gasping for breath, calm and patient, kicking together to steer themselves across to the Chinese side.

Washed up on the Chinese riverbank, they lay for a moment, catching their breath. Quickly they were up, running across the filthy grey sands into Changbai city. There was no need for stealth now; the city was empty, there were no soldiers on the street, no citizens in their homes; every person had been evacuated and only a few dogs remained. Jinju guided her mother to a grocery store, where she had transacted business in the past. Much of the food remained on the shelves. Jinju hesitated before taking an apple. It was the first time in her life that she'd stolen something. Her mother chose a yellow sweet rice cake, wrapped in bright plastic. The two of them ate guiltily, expecting police officers to scream at them.

Out the back of the store there was a padlocked hut. Jinju took her knife and removed the screws, taking the door off its hinges. Inside was a motorbike. She said:

'The owner of this store is very rich. He owns a car and a motorbike. He would've taken his family in his car.'

'I've never ridden a motorbike.'

'Nor have I. But I've watched him. How hard can it be? He was lazy. Not so bright. You turn it on. You push the peddle. And that's it.'

They experimented for a few minutes, feeling its weight, sitting on it. They were terrified of the noise it would make when they turned it on.

'We're not in Hyesan anymore. This town is empty.'

Fearfully, they started the engine. Jinju took control, looking at her mother standing beside her.

'Hold on.'

Her mother climbed onto the bike, clasping her hands around her daughter's waist, and slowly, uncertainly, they drove out of the alley, bumping along beside the brick wall of the grocery store, until they reached the main street. Jinju picked up speed, getting a feel for the motorbike, setting off, heading west out of Changbai, away from Hyesan, away from North Korea, and towards the mountains, towards the strange spinning alien ships, towards the bright lights and the military jets, towards the exodus taking place in Shenyang. It took Jinju some time before she realized that for the first time in her life, she was free.

THE ROSS ICE SHELF
FINAL STAGE CHAMBERS
SAME DAY

J INJU WATCHED THE CREATURE SHE'D named after her
mother walk to the edge of her enclosure and tear the steel bars
aside as if they were no obstacle and never had been. She scaled the
wall of her chamber, reaching the reinforced plate glass at the observation level, sliding her scalpel digits along the edge of the window,
slicing it free, dropping it to the base of her enclosure. With ease,
she entered the observation tunnels. All the other scientists and staff
had fled. Only Jinju remained, saying:

'I understand your desire to be free.'

'Jinju, I've always been free.'

It was evident from the ease of this escape that she could've
broken out at any point. Her confinement was an act, biding her
time while she accumulated information on the world beyond her
prison. As the oldest female, Cho was larger than the males, her
four legs stronger to support a heavier thorax where there was space
to grow six eggs simultaneously, three on each side, eggs that grew
like grapes on a vine, extending downwards until they were ready
to hatch directly onto the ice, an infant able to survive the cold from

the very first moments of birth. Cho's upper torso was magnificent, like Boudica's armour. Rather than a wide arrow-shaped head, hers resembled an ivory Viking helmet.

'Are you going to kill me?'

'Why would I kill you?'

Rather than an attack, Jinju felt Cho's thoughts inside her mind, realizing that the primary communication of these creatures wasn't speech, it was telepathy, and the colony had been in constant conversation for many years, projecting their thoughts through these walls. Such an adaptation was ideally suited for Antarctica, a continent where confusion and ambiguity created a sense of isolation, one that had led to the madness of so many ordinary-born people. Here was a species that never felt alone and was never misunderstood. Though their telepathic conversation could be crudely represented in the form of words, it was more like the projection of images. She wondered what Cho was going to do. Formidable though she was, the entrance was sealed with many tonnes of ice and there was no way to dig to the surface in time.

'There's no way out.'

'To your eyes. But we are not like you.'

Cho headed into Eitan's enclosure, the largest by far, where the colony of twenty had gathered for the first time. It was an introduction of the strangest kind – they each knew each other as intimately as it's possible to know another living soul, to have shared every thought and feeling without ever having shared the same physical space. They'd been in each other's minds but never in each other's sight. They were beautiful, Jinju thought, together like this, moving in silence, their conversation internalized. It was performance theatre; they nudged heads and clasped hands. With delight, some stood on their back legs, the claws of their front legs tapping each other's claws as though they were musical instruments. The youngest of them, six months old, was so excited to see Cho that he climbed up her legs and onto her back. She playfully bounded around the chamber, with him on her back, before he climbed down. They were a family, Jinju thought, even more impressive together than they were apart. It was time for them to attend to the serious business at hand – their escape.

Jinju felt the ground tremble and turned to see the troop of snow gorillas descending into these chambers. Their silver coats were stained with red blood and blue. The blue blood was their own; some of them had been shot. Their skin and muscle weren't armoured. The red blood on their jaws belonged to the security officers and scientists trapped under the ice and Jinju supposed that she was one of the last ordinary people left alive in these chambers. Behind the gorillas were the ice-adapted creatures from the Asylum, moving in their own peculiar ways according to their own individual adaptations, some on all fours, others upright on two legs, some slithering across the ceiling, others scampering on the walls, a platoon of cold creatures bred to colonize this continent and seeking to do exactly that. Mad with rage at the sight of her, the lead gorilla charged, raising his massive fist aloft, and Jinju closed her eyes, waiting for the fatal blow.

Cho put a stop to the attack, climbing up from the enclosure, taking control of the new arrivals, asserting her dominance over this coalition of cold creatures. Under her telepathic instructions they left Jinju alone, with only the cold-adapted ice-white Troodon dinosaur circling her. Despite his orders he was barely able to control his hatred – his segmented bone tail swaying from side to side, ready to cut her to pieces. Looking into his eyes, Jinju saw a piercing intelligence, either underestimated by his creators or one that had been kept hidden from them. Cho examined one of the injured gorillas and with her bony digits, as sharp as surgical instruments, she tended to the wound, picking out the bullets, tossing them aside with contempt, crude and barbarous, stitching the wound with threads plucked from their own coat. One of the gorillas couldn't be saved, maimed by explosives, the internal traumas too severe. She lay on the ice, her breathing slowing until finally it came to a stop. All the gorillas lowered their heads in grief, muttering a melodic chant as sombre as prayer.

Leaving the dead in the observation tunnels, the new arrivals climbed down the ice into the enclosure. After all these years, the separate colonies were united, weaving between each other, a coalition of cold creatures filling the space as if they were dancers in an Antarctic ballroom. Suddenly, they broke apart, moving to the walls, clearing the space. Orders had been issued. Plans put into action.

All the adults moved to the back of the enclosure, gathering up the tubular ice carvings that Eitan had made over the years, not sculpted from ice but spun from it, not fragile or brittle; the ice had been adapted, transformed into something stronger, something other than mere ice. Clasping these tools, the colony appeared armed and ready for combat. Jinju wondered what their escape plan could be. Despite being formidable warriors, there was no way to fight their way out of these tunnels. But these spears weren't for fighting; they were tools, each carefully positioned into notches carved in the base of the enclosure. Acting in concert, the largest of the snow gorillas stood on its back legs and brought its full body weight down on the top of the lever, splintering them downwards, the entire floor shattering like a windscreen in a car crash. They weren't heading up – they were heading down, towards the unguarded ocean only forty metres below.

Jinju marvelled at the audacity of this escape. Some of the world's cleverest scientists had worked here and it hadn't crossed their minds that the colony could tunnel down into the ocean. The ocean was certain death to an ordinary-born, but not to these creatures. At the rate they were mining, only a few more blows and they'd shatter through the base of the ice shelf. She pondered the practicalities of escaping through the freezing ocean. While she could easily believe that Cho and her kind could survive in the ocean for extended periods of time – after all, their bodies were able to tolerate being encased in ice – it seemed improbable that the other creatures could survive without air for so long. If polar bears could only survive underwater for up to three minutes, she guessed the snow gorillas would fare better, but not enough to reach the edge of the ice shelf.

Pondering this problem, as though she were part of their gang, she noticed that Cho was holding one of the tubular javelins. In her clawed hands it began to change shape, the ice changing as if it were Venetian glass, expanding into an exquisitely thin diving bell. Only now did Jinju begin to fathom the range of their capabilities, their mastery over ice unlike anything she could have imagined, able to alter its chemistry and composition. The hole in the enclosure was now so deep that the dark ocean could be seen beneath it. Directly under the ice shelf, upside down in the ocean, was the eldest of them, their leader, the cold creature called Eitan, waiting for his family to break through the ice and join him.

With all the snow gorillas and asylum creatures now safely sealed inside the ice diving bells, they were ready to smash through the ice and enter the ocean. Cho climbed the walls to the enclosure and approached Jinju.

'You're going to leave me behind? To drown in these tunnels?'

'Our future is not for you.'

'I should never have given you my mother's name. She would never have left anyone behind.'

'Jinju, I'm not your mother. I'm nothing like your mother.'

Cho jumped from the top of the enclosure, curling up into a ball, falling on what remained of the ice. The final fissure line split open, ocean water rushing through, filling the enclosure in an instant – a colossal body of freezing water rising at speed. In her final moments Jinju tried to concentrate on the memories of her father and her mother, but all she could hear was the laughter of the cold creatures delighting in their freedom.

PART TEN

ONE WEEK LATER

THE TRANS-ANTARCTICA FREEWAY
THE ROSS ICE SHELF
MCMURDO CITY
28 DECEMBER 2043

HAVING PASSED THE TRANSANTARCTIC MOUNTAIN range, the convoy of snow vehicles arrived at the edge of the Ross Ice Shelf and the final approach to McMurdo City. With nothing in between the convoy and the outer edge of the city it appeared less than a mile away – an illusion of proximity created by the clarity of the air and the absence of any objects in between, an optical effect so deceptive that people had died of exhaustion trying to reach a destination that they were sure was within walking distance. After the passing of a summer storm, there were puffs of pink in the sky, like the remnants of a firework display, as though there'd been a celebration. The capital city had been abandoned.

Balancing on the roof of the convoy, Echo stood up, assessing the view. There were no vehicles, no traffic of any kind, no commuters, no people skiing to work. It was the middle of summer; this should be the busiest time of the year; the weather was mild. Yet she saw no activity and no sign of human life. She crouched down, tapping on the glass and addressing her family:

'The city is empty.'

The convoy came to a stop and Kasim stepped down from the cabin, examining the buildings with his binoculars.

'I don't understand.'

He handed the binoculars to Liza, who raised them to her eyes, puzzling over the deserted city before her.

'Could they be inside?'

'On a day like today? No. Never.'

In silence, the convoy mused over the situation, unsure whether to advance or not. Echo knelt, placing her hand on the ice – the fine grains of snow were vibrating. She turned, feeling the sound before she heard it – a heavy rhythm, much like a drumbeat. Looking up, she saw coming towards them a creature with long silver fur, bright orange eyes and curled walrus tusks. It resembled the mountain gorilla except bred for Antarctica, running on its massive knuckles across the ice, racing towards the second vehicle in the convoy and moving with impossible speeds. Shoulder first, the creature hit the side of the vehicle, crumpling the steel shell and knocking it onto its side, scattering the ice-adapted students on the roof.

Soldiers emerged with their weapons drawn but were so bewildered by the sight of this magnificent creature they were unable to attack. Echo now saw a snow gorilla charging towards her. She was the only thing standing between it and her convoy, with her parents and Tetu behind her. Though she was small compared to this creature's colossal size, she didn't budge, raising a hand.

Only a few metres away the snow gorilla stopped. It stretched up to its full height, standing on its back legs, towering over her, its bright orange eyes looking down. She studied its expression, lively with complex intelligence. With tenderness, it placed a giant hand against the side of her head. She didn't flinch, feeling its silken silver fur flow across her scaled skin.

Without warning, it retreated, the other gorilla following. The attack had been called off. Searching for the reason, Echo looked around, identifying a lone figure on the ice, a white man wearing armour-plate and an arrow-shaped helmet, surely the leader of an Antarctic warrior tribe. The man had four legs and skeletal arms and was clasping a spear. He stood proudly as a custodian of this land, his camouflage so perfect she doubted her parents could see him. Without waiting for the others, she walked towards him, but before she was near enough to call out, she felt his thoughts inside her head, an overwhelming sensation, as if her mind had been taken over. Then, as quickly as they'd surfaced, the thoughts melted away. He left at speed, with his tribe of cold creatures following him, disappearing across the plateau.

Liza arrived at Echo's side, touching her hand.

'Are you okay?'

'I'm fine.'

'What was that?'

'I don't know.'

'What did he say?'

Echo was surprised by her mother's observation.

'How do you know he said anything?'

'Echo, what did he say?'

'He said . . . *Join us.*'

THE ROSS ICE SHELF
MCMURDO CITY
FINAL STAGE CHAMBERS
SAME DAY

LIZA STOOD AT THE EDGE of the crater surveying the devastation shaped like a meteor impact – a circular quarry in the ice shelf over a kilometre wide and two hundred metres deep. Some of the airplanes which had been converted into breweries and factories had tumbled down the steep sides, their noses pointing up to the sky, as if the fuselages were slowly being digested by some ancient glacial kraken. Travelling on foot through the city, weapons at the ready, Kasim declared:

'This was the location of the experimental chambers where our scientists were developing new kinds of Cold People.'

Atto asked:

'The creatures that attacked us?'

Kasim nodded.

'I've never seen them before. They were kept in tunnels under the ice. No one was allowed to see them.'

Liza observed:

'Now you know why.'

Echo remarked:

'These are not incremental genetic changes.'

Looking at her, Kasim observed:

'We believed they were creating more of your kind. A para-human, a cold-adapted person who could help us build a home on the ice.'

'Maybe they can build a home. But it will not be a home for you.'

Liza asked:

'Where is everyone?'

Around the circumference of the crater, the bakeries and brew-eries were empty, their doors swaying in the wind. Inside there was evidence of a hasty retreat – partially stitched penguin pelts, trays of snailfish skin burnt black, curdling vats of calorific seal milk and pearlwort-flower moonshine still bubbling on a blubber stove. But there were no blood trails, no bullet holes, no sign of conflict – the people of McMurdo were missing.

Advancing cautiously through the deserted city, Liza threaded her arm through Echo's, fearful of the competing forces vying for her daughter. She asked again about the creature they'd encountered.

'What did he want?'

'He wanted me to join them.'

'What does that mean?'

'He means for me to leave you. And join his tribe.'

'He was clearly an aggressor. They attacked the convoy without provocation.'

Echo did not reply. Liza tried a different approach.

'What was his speech like? Was it English?'

'No. They were thoughts inside my head – less like a phrase, or a word, more like images, conjured whole, along with the sensation of community and solidarity, a feeling of belonging unlike anything I've ever felt before.'

These words, uttered without malice, pained Liza, that she'd failed to form a sufficiently strong connective bond with her daughter, that all her anxieties and insecurities about their relationship were correct. Echo observed her mother's reaction.

'You're upset?'

'You feel connected to them?'

'It is different. I've read accounts of people, ordinary-born people finding religion, and their life suddenly making sense. It feels like that. The world was hazy and now it feels clear.'

'Echo? Do you want to join them?'

'I want to feel at home. I want to feel like I belong.'

None of the other ice-adapted students had shared this telepathic connection. It had been directed solely at Echo, confirming what they already knew, that she had been designated as a leader of her people. Liza wondered whether her daughter, if the occasion arose, would choose this community of Cold People over her family.

Tetu was a few steps behind, listening to their conversation. He shared many of Liza's fears. After the euphoria of holding hands at Landmark Plateau, his mood had darkened. Having spent much of his life dreaming of coming to McMurdo and making a life together with Echo, now that they were here, he wished they were back at Hope Town. Like a character from the romance novels he'd read growing up, finding a stash of them in an abandoned suitcase, he was reminded of the small-town boy terrified that his high school sweetheart will leave him when she starts college, that she'll outgrow him as soon as she glimpses her true potential, that ultimately his role was to wish her well on her journey and that he was in love with a woman whose destiny was immeasurably larger than his own. He had only caught a glimpse of this creature. It had looked grotesque to him, like a satyr, part animal part human, a genetic confection with ostentatious armoured skin and cold-weather adaptations, the kind of man who could swagger barefoot across glaciers and swim under icebergs – the kind of man Echo could love. It was obvious to Tetu that he was no match for this creature's engineered abilities and his attempt to create a connection between them, jumping into the freezing ocean, had only proved how unsuitable he was as a partner with a frail, weak body and a sentimental mind.

Echo left her mother's side, turning to Tetu. He felt a flush of embarrassment, wondering if she could read his thoughts, expecting to be told off for skulking behind. They hadn't spoken since the encounter and Tetu, for the first time in their friendship, wasn't sure what to say to her. Walking beside him, she said:

'What does it feel like to be in love?'

They'd discussed this topic before, but this time Tetu sensed the same question was being asked in a completely different way, not as someone with no experience on the subject, but as someone trying to figure out their own experience of it. Though he felt dejected, he answered:

'You feel like you can't find the right words. Or that words aren't enough. You feel like everything else disappears. And the feeling stays, even when that person leaves.'

'I felt this.'

'I can see.'

'You must have realized we could never be together. We are not the same.'

'That has never bothered me.'

'No, it never has.'

'That thing, that creature we saw? Did you feel that way looking at it?'

'I did.'

To his surprise Tetu felt relieved. Finally he had the answer: she
did not love him; she could not love him.

'I accept that we don't have a chance. But that thing? It would
have killed all of us if it wasn't for you.'

'You don't know that.'

'You're already making excuses for it. There's another way of
knowing you're in love.'

'What is that?'

'Being able to overlook what is obvious to everyone else. He is
an aggressor.'

'Can I ask you a question?'

'Anything.'

'Are you possessive of me?'

Though she posed the question without any hostility, Tetu faltered in his reply:

'Not anymore.'

She studied his face.

'I was made to serve you, to work outside in the cold while you
kept warm inside. You've never asked what I want. No one has.'

'What do you want?'

'I've never thought about it until now.'

'Now you've been given a choice?'

'Yes, now that I've been given a choice.'

A RRIVING AT THE COAST, THE mystery of the abandoned old
town was explained. The citizens of McMurdo had retreated
to their only defensible positions – the ageing armada. Lined up
along the decks of the aircraft carriers were rows of armed sentries,
adopting the fortress tactics of a medieval castle, soldiers manning
the outer walls where ordinary people would try to hold their own
against the cold creatures that they'd created. The ramp connecting
the Antarctic mainland to the USS *Kennedy* had been blown up, so
that the only way to reach the flight deck, forty metres above the
sea ice, was by climbing chain ladders unfurled for them. Echo was
too heavy; the rungs buckled under her feet and, forced to improvise, she clambered up the thirty-tonne anchor, her palms gripping
freezing steel which would've torn the skin off an ordinary person's
hands, inadvertently demonstrating how easy it was to breach
their defences.

On deck they passed through the hastily constructed perimeter, crude compared to the once cutting-edge sophistication of

this flagship warship. There were barrels of flammable oils ready to pour onto attackers whose only weakness was warmth, rolls of razor wire to tangle their limbs and trenches of white phosphorous to ignite as soon as the cold creatures scaled the ship's steep sides, which they, like Echo, would manage with ease. Sniper rifles were stationed on the command tower to target anything that broke through the defences, although how effective bullets were against the creature's armoured exteriors remained unclear. Regardless, the colony of cold creatures would surely attack under the cover of a storm with minimal visibility in freezing conditions so hostile ordinary people would be unable to venture outside, let alone repel an attack.

The truth was that after twenty years of peace, people had neglected the art of war; they had allowed their stash of weapons to be depleted and repurposed. The deck of the *Kennedy* was no longer a runway with the most advanced fighter jets in the world. Instead, it was lined with rows of terrace houses, including homes built from the recycled wings of Hornet fighter jets, creating the most expensive shanty town of all time. The advanced tactical machine guns which once defended this carrier had been turned into pots, pans and pipes, while the computers which operated the Phalanx canon had been picked clean of components to repair the supercomputers used for genetic engineering. What was once the most powerful warship ever constructed was now a floating community.

Descending below deck, they entered the hangar bay, an enclosed space stretching the entire length of the ship. Formerly a garage for fighter jets, it was now a primitive industrial complex devoted to smelting steel, the manufacture of tools such as ice picks and snow shovels, reminiscent of a nineteenth-century community of blacksmiths and ironmongers. Amid the sparks and smog, Tetu caught up with Echo, observing how much discomfort she was in, unable to tolerate these higher temperatures:

'Can you cope with this heat?'

'Not for long.'

Sensitive to anything which made her feel more out of place, he suggested:

'Why don't we wait on deck?'

'Yes. After I hear what the leaders of McMurdo have to say.'

In the smoke-filled town square, the Senate had regrouped after the attack, the most erudite minds struggling to process the speed with which their new society had fallen apart. Each of the senators had been appointed to leadership roles because the challenges of survival in Antarctica were practical and scientific, requiring unpopular decisions unburdened by democratic elections, but none of them had ever fought a war. Understanding that they were no longer a suitable match for the upcoming conflict, they'd summoned every surviving general and commander, men and women from once opposing armies who'd been working as teachers and tailors, forced to recollect their old ways, hastily patching together a military command to wage a war unlike any other.

Yotam was the focus of fierce recriminations, much of which was intensely personal. These were his creatures, people claimed. He was too close to them; his relationship with them was unnatural. Why couldn't he see that they despised us? There was deep suspicion that secretly he'd wanted them to escape, that this was the outcome both he and Song Fu had desired all along, that they were so besotted with the ingenuity of their creation they'd deliberately disregarded the dangers to ordinary people. Some went further, believing that this great escape wasn't an accident, it was wilful – a conspiracy, the deliberate replacement of one species for another. Yotam was a traitor: the first to betray his own species.

Despite the exceptional nature of the circumstances, the disgust directed at him felt familiar, the rhythm of it reminded him of his childhood when he'd been positioned as someone outside his community, a man with no stake in it, more interested in his own warped affections for other men than the needs of the many, polluted with an anarchic self-destructive streak willing to burn down society rather than play his part in it. Even though the genetic computations had nothing to do with him, nonetheless, people saw these creatures as manifestations of his psyche, seeking revenge against a society he'd never been truly invested in. Only President Mues' support had kept him from facing a barbarous mob justice, being tossed overboard into the freezing ocean or strung up as a warning to all who wondered which side they should pick.

Standing in the assembly as both a prisoner and an expert witness, since he understood their enemy better than anyone, Yotam listened as the president discussed what action to take, whether to launch an expedition force to track down and kill the escaped colony or wait for them to attack. There were only thirty snow gorillas, some of whom had been killed in the chamber, only thirteen unique asylum species and just twenty of the most advanced cold-adapted species, of which Eitan was their leader. Asked for his opinion, Yotam pointed out that each of the females, no longer drugged to suppress their fertility, could carry six infants at any one time, with the duration of the pregnancy only two months and the infants able to fend for themselves from birth. If ordinary-born people delayed, they were handing control of the continent to these new species and by winter the colony of cold creatures would be far larger. They were genetically engineered to solve the population crisis; their colony would grow at an exponential rate.

'You will never have a better chance.'

'He's lying! He wants us to leave the ship. We'll be killed.'

'This is the warmest time of the year. There's sunlight. If you wish to fight, you should fight now; it would be playing to their advantage to fight in winter, in the coldest of conditions. They are able to see in the dark and able to launch attacks even if the temperature is minus seventy outside.'

'He's setting a trap.'

But President Mues concurred with Yotam.

'We must attack now. Our only advantage is numbers. We have lost access to our food factories. We cannot hide in these boats. Our casualties will be terrible. Many will die. But if we don't act now, then by winter we won't stand a chance. They will pick us off, one by one, while their numbers grow.'

At this point the new arrivals led by Echo and her family were escorted to the front of the discussion. Despite there being numerous ice-adapted students in the class, all eyes turned to Echo, dressed in burgundy Dr Martens leather boots, army slacks and a lumberjack's plaid shirt, her glossy hexagonal scales now obsidian-black as a reaction against the heat of this hangar. This wasn't the vision of a well-behaved, even-tempered young woman conveyed in monthly school reports. They'd been expecting someone emotionally neutral, as brilliant as she was prim and proper, the top student from an elite Swiss boarding school with an aristocratic coolness about her manner. Fascinated with this young woman, President Mues addressed them as a group:

'This is not the welcome we'd hoped to give you.'

Liza moved forward.

'I'm Echo's mother. This is her father, Atto. We encountered the cold creatures you're talking about. As we crossed the ice shelf into the city. They attacked us.'

'How are you still alive?'

'Because of my daughter.'

'She fought them?'

'She spoke to them.'

Emerging from the huddle of soldiers, Yotam asked:

'What did he say?'

Echo answered:

'He asked me to join them.'

As soon as she uttered the words, the guards readied their weapons, evaluating if she was a threat. At first, she found their fear absurd but, as she pondered their reaction, she felt emotions of a kind she'd never experienced before – anger at their audacity. She imagined sucking the heat out of the floor until the entire hangar bay was frozen, until the entire ship was frozen, so brittle that a single stamp of her foot would shatter this massive ship into a million pieces. President Mues gestured for the weapons to be lowered.

'What do you want, Echo?'

She said:

'I want to see the place where I was born.'

NAVAL QUARTER
USS *KENNEDY*
BIRTHING CHAMBERS
SAME DAY

L OCATED AT THE BOTTOM OF this ship, far away from the eyes
of society, tucked away like a shameful secret in the cavernous
engine rooms, were the genetic laboratories and the birthing chambers for the new generations of cold creatures. Huddled around the
still functioning nuclear reactor that powered these experiments
were the maternity wards where mothers from the Survivor Towns
had been brought. It was here that Liza had given birth. Behind
the wards, they saw the hidden side of the facility. On display were
the stillborn bodies of ice-adapted infants, dissected to understand
what had gone wrong, where clinical observations were made about
their genetic composition, sombre questions were asked about their
foetal development, but no tears were shed, no prayers were said,
and no funerals performed.

As soon as Echo stepped into this industrial space, a factory of
life and death, she fell silent. Though, intellectually, she'd accepted
that these experiments were part of life in Antarctica, she'd never
confronted the reality of them. Approaching the tables where the

bodies of her genetic relatives lay, the geneticists moved aside, shamefaced as she passed by, lowering their gaze. Intended to survive the harshest of climates, these babies hadn't been able to survive their mother's womb, dying in the pursuit of ever greater evolutionary abilities, attempts to find some new advantage over the cold that might ensure the survival of the species. Standing before the body of a tiny ice-adapted boy, she touched his skin, feeling his scales, experiencing as much grief as if the child were her own, nudging open his tiny fingers as though hoping he might grip hers.

Liza watched as her daughter stooped down and gently picked the baby up, cradling it against her chest as if she could transfer life through her skin as easily as heat. For a moment she hoped this might be true, that life would flow between them, that she would bring this little boy back to this world, that his eyes would open, and he'd look up at Echo and see that he was loved. But these were powers beyond even Echo's abilities. Still holding the infant against her chest, with her back to the Senate, Echo asked:

'Why do you keep experimenting? Isn't our skin tough enough? Aren't our hearts large enough? What kind of cold must we be able to survive before you stop?'

President Mues answered:

'There is a reason the experiments continued.'

'What reason?'

'Echo, you can't give birth. None of the ice-adapted people we've created can give birth. The men and the women are infertile. We don't know why. If I were a person of faith, I might say it was punishment for tampering with nature. That's why we've taken such risks with the extreme adaptations. You're perfectly adapted for the cold. But you can't have children of your own.'

The temperature of the room dropped sharply, their breath turning to mist, glass tubes cracking, the steel instruments icing over, crystals spreading up the walls, and it was obvious to Tetu that Echo was drawing in all the heat from her surroundings, whether she realized it or not, and if he didn't stop her, she would kill them all. He managed to reach her in time, touching her arm. She looked at him, remembering where she was, controlling her reaction. The temperature returned to normal, but her eyes seemed different. She was sad in the way that ordinary people were sad. Liza asked:

'Why didn't you tell us?'

'We've kept it a secret because we weren't sure how people would react. You cannot solve our population crisis. This is why the experiments continue. This is why we keep making genetic adjustments. It is this, or to accept our extinction. Maybe we should've accepted that our time was over.'

Echo returned the stillborn boy to the table, closing his eyes, folding his arms, as though putting him to sleep. No one knew what she might say next. She looked up. A voice was calling to her, a telepathic communication sent only to her.

'He's talking to me.'

'Who?'

'The man I met on the ice.'

Yotam asked:

'What is he saying?'

She listened for a time, oblivious to the fact that the guards had once again raised their weapons, pointing them at her. Without turning around she said:

'He says that your city is on fire.'

T HEY GATHERED ON THE FLIGHT deck, crowded together, helpless spectators as fire swept through their city – a yellow horizon underneath a solid blue sky. Some of the flames were tinged turquoise as they melted plastics manufactured from a bygone age. Scattered explosions punctuated the fire as barrels of bioethanol caught alight. Coils of smoke rose into the unusually calm air as if even the weather was paralyzed by this never-before-seen sight – the entire ice shelf ablaze. Fire had always been one of the Senate's gravest fears, since there was never any rain and the structures were tinder dry. In the past, even small fires in Antarctica had brought an end to operations, British Hope Bay Station in 1948 and Argentinian Almirante Brown Base in 1984, both of which could only be remedied by rescue and evacuation. Since there was no chance of rescue and nowhere to be evacuated to, mitigation measures had been extensive, fire breaks and fire marshals. But no one could have predicted that the first great fire of Antarctica would be deliberately started by the cold creatures intended to save them, an act of wilful sabotage, a scorched-earth annihilation of resources that could never be replaced.

As the fire's edge reached the original base buildings, some of the oldest human structures on the continent caught ablaze, the historic canteen, Ex-Presidents bar, the Chapel of the Snows, the Museum of Life on Ice, until the entire circumference of buildings around Observation Hill was burning. Unlike other catastrophic fires in human history, the sacking of Carthage, the great fires of Hangzhou, the medieval fires of London, there would be no rebuilding this time, since there was nothing to rebuild with. At the top of Observation Hill, they could see the colony of cold creatures, safely away from the heat of the fire, smashing the memorial tablets of the former nations.

Feeling Eitan's thoughts inside her mind, Echo addressed the president:

'They want to negotiate your surrender.'

MCMURDO CITY
HISTORIC BASE DISTRICT
SAME DAY

THE ROAD BETWEEN OBSERVATION HILL and Crater Heights was lined with smouldering ruins, historic buildings reduced to ash, the same colour as the black basalt rocks they'd been built upon. Factories, breweries and food farms had all been destroyed. The gas storage tanks were among the few structures left intact. Yotam wondered whether, in a thousand years, these might be the only surviving remnants of McMurdo City, relics of a baffling civilization tucked away on the bottom of the planet, or whether they'd be in a museum, visited by thousands of curious cold people, amazed that ordinary people had once needed to burn gas to keep warm.

Yotam was part of the diplomatic envoy, chosen since he was on intimate terms with the creature called Eitan, the apparent leader of the escaped creatures. The remaining members of the envoy consisted of President Mues, her security detail, Echo and her family, including the young man Tetu. For obvious reasons, Echo needed to be part of the team as the only communication with the colony had been directed into her thoughts, bypassing the hierarchy of the

416

Senate, effectively anointing a sixteen-year-old as the leader of a people she felt an outsider to. Liza and Atto had insisted on accompanying their daughter. To their surprise, Tetu had hesitated. He was afraid of witnessing the moment when she might choose this new creature over them. He sensed that he wouldn't survive her desertion – their relationship had sustained him since the death of his parents. He would've preferred to remain behind on the warship, dealing with the grief alone. However, Liza refused to allow her family to separate and wouldn't discuss the possibility of him staying behind.

They walked through the remains of the capital city with none of the pomp or grandeur one might have expected for a group tasked with negotiations of such importance – the survival of the species. There was no way the small security detail could defend them against the entire colony of cold creatures. But the president considered her own safety unimportant, believing that she'd failed in her mission and whatever happened in the next few hours it was time for another person to lead them through this crisis – a time for military rule, tactics and strategies. She'd left instructions that should they not return it meant there was no chance of peace and, for the first time in twenty years, people would once again be at war. They'd been good at war once, perhaps they'd be good at it again.

From time to time they caught glimpses of the colony of cold creatures stalking them – the silver-haired snow gorillas who despite their size made almost no sound, puffs of snow rising from their giant knuckles as they bounded across the terrain. Moving among them, slinking between them as though they'd always lived together, were the assorted asylum creatures, the snow-lizards and ice-chimeras, while Eitan and the ice-centaurs, this continent's new ruling elite, moved as elegantly as ballet dancers in the wings of La Scala.

The location set for negotiations was the entrance to the Archive, an isolated building which had survived the fire, standing as an island among the devastation, the outer stone walls protecting the inner temple that housed one of the supercomputers – the last depository of human knowledge. Perhaps with a sense of irony, it was here that Eitan had instructed that they should meet to discuss the terms of humanity's surrender. True to his word, he stood outside the stone walls alone, the sole representative of his colony of Cold People, his armour skin radiant with the colours of Antarctica, hues of blue, not as an act of camouflage but as a peacock display of prowess, a triumphant declaration of a species that was finally free.

Like gunslingers from a western, the human delegation stopped at a distance waiting for Eitan to make the first move. Grasped in his hand was one of the elegant crystalline javelins from the floor of his enclosure. With sudden speed and immense strength, he threw the javelin at Echo. With ease she side-stepped, catching it mid-flight. This hadn't been an act of violence; she was never in any danger and, understanding that he wanted to share this object with her, she raised the tip to her eye, observing its unique texture and form. She hadn't seen anything like it before – it was altered-ice, reformed at a molecular level, harder than diamond, yet as malleable as clay. She wondered how he'd created this new substance, how such a transfiguration of frozen water was even possible. As she pondered these questions, she felt him enter her thoughts.

Let me show you the world we can build together. Not a refugee encampment with buckets for toilets and vats of kelp soup.

She saw Antarctica pristine again, no bases or buildings, no flags or footprints, as it had been before human discovery, the brief two-hundred-year history of people erased from the continent. A new society emerged, not limited to the warmer fringes but concentrated in the coldest centre, a civilization rising from the south pole plateau consisting of buildings unlike any she'd seen before. There were no bricks or girders; these were structures rendered whole, as though they'd been pressed out of a baking mould, crystal domes and spiral towers. Surrounding this new citadel was Antarctic vegetation, crops capable of living in the cold, fields of icicles, and beyond them was a forest, trees with stalactite roots and snowflake leaves. Above this city, not in the stars, but among the clouds, was a synthetic cold blue sun, the powerplant of this species, with a swirling blue-fire surface not as a source of heat but as life-giving light. At a castle in the very centre, standing on a terrace overlooking this kingdom, stood Echo and Eitan.

MCMURDO CITY
HISTORIC BASE DISTRICT
THE ARCHIVE
SAME DAY

LIZA COULD ONLY WATCH, HELPLESS on the sidelines, as her daughter fell under the spell of this creature. Echo was somewhere else, no longer by her side, her thoughts far away, someplace unseen. Liza was certain, as only a mother could be, that he didn't have her daughter's interests at heart. He was a specimen composed entirely of strengths, his flawless armoured torso brazenly naked in the cold, contemptuous of conditions which would kill an ordinary person in seconds. He was vain, she thought, and she recoiled from his beauty which to her eye was a marvel of biological engineering and a manifestation of his innate sense of superiority, an absolute certainty that he'd been born to rule, which he intended to do with the ruthlessness of someone who considers their cruelty to be rational rather than despicable. He might be evolutionarily advanced, but he was a regressive figure – inherently transactional. He wanted Echo to fight on his side.

Silent until now, Yotam broke rank, leaving the group and walking towards the species he'd devoted his life in Antarctica to. He wondered whether the allegations against him were true, that Song Fu had always known he'd fall for her creation, that it hadn't been his intelligence or tenacity which won her over, but his naivety. Infatuation hadn't been an accident: it had been her intention from their first meeting at the South Pole Station. Masterminding a replacement for people, she'd seeded a brilliant and beautiful parasite inside the dying body of human society, a parasite that would require concealment and protection until it was ready to burst free. Yotam had always imagined that the future would one day belong to this species but that the handover would be a gradual process with many centuries of co-operation and co-existence. But a transition period was of no interest to them: they wanted this continent now and they would take it by any means necessary. Violence came naturally to Eitan. Killing was instinctive and innate. He had no qualms about murdering people or burning down the city that had created him. Yet Yotam loved this creature still. It was a form of madness, this love. Standing directly in front of Eitan, his voice hoarse with emotion and exhaustion, he asked:

'Was it all a lie?'

'Was what a lie?'

'The games, the conversations, the movies, the books we shared – did it count for nothing?'

'You taught me that I was not like you, that I was not created to be like you, that I did not want to be like you.'

Eitan turned around, knocking down the stone perimeter to the Archive, ripping open the insulated walls protecting the building, desecrating this temple to human knowledge. He emerged, holding the Fugaku supercomputer, his arms capable of immense steadiness and strength.

'We have no interest in your knowledge. We don't want your art and your science. Your assumptions and deductions are worthless. We will start from nothing. We will learn this world anew.'

Like a judge bringing down the gavel at the end of his verdict, he smashed the computer against the volcanic rock, shattering the shell, scattering chips and processors, millennia of human learning lost in an instant.

Appalled, the president hurried forward, dropping to her knees, pitifully picking up fragments of microchips as though the computer could be put back together, refusing to accept that so much human wisdom had been lost and could never be recovered. As the shock subsided, understanding the futility of her actions, she stopped and, with her fists full of microchips, looked up at this creature.

'You've told us what you don't want. What *do* you want?'

'We want you to leave this place.'

'How can we leave? None of us can leave. Not even you!'

'We belong here. You do not.'

'Where would we go?'

'We will allow you to live on the Peninsula, in the three towns you've built there.'

'Three Survivor Towns are barely able to provide for the people who already live there.'

'That is not our concern. We have no interest in that warm stretch of rock. You may keep it.'

'Even if I believed you – what of the city we've built here?'

'You must leave it all behind. You've done it before. You can do it again.'

'You cannot ask the entire population of this city to trek across the continent.'

'We do not ask it. We demand it.'

'Many thousands will die.'

'Or all of you can die. It is summer. You have sunlight. You have warmth before winter comes. The sooner you leave the more of you will survive.'

'There is another choice.'

'Which is?'

'We can fight. As a species we excelled at war. At death and destruction, we are innovative and diabolical. We committed atrocities far worse than burning down houses. There are generals on those ships, planning for combat, soldiers who know fighting conditions of a kind you've never experienced. They know desert sand and rainforest mud. You've only known us as scientists. You've never seen us as soldiers. You are only a handful. Strong, yes, but we are many. And we can be savage – as savage as you.'

'What would you be fighting for?'

'Our lives, our city, our home.'

'What are they worth on this continent?'

'The same as they were worth on any other continent.'

'You are wrong. Your lives are worth less here. Because you are less.'

'We've made this place our home.'

'You failed to make this place your home! You never learned the language of the cold. You squat on a land that was never intended for you. You are a homeless, landless people. You have pieced together a life from your old existence, watching the clock count down until you are gone forever.'

The president pulled back from this debate, dropping the broken microchips onto the ground as if they were seeds that might grow into new computers.

'In exchange for allowing us to leave, what do you want in return?'

'We want her.'

Eitan pointed at Echo.

Unable to control her anger any longer, Liza walked forward, joining the president.

'My daughter is not a piece of property to be haggled over.'

'She does not belong with you. She never belonged with you.'

'She belongs to no one.'

'Then let her choose.'

'Her future is with her family.'

'What of your daughter's hopes of a family?'

Caught by surprise, Liza fell silent and Eitan pressed his advantage.

'Your daughter cannot have a child. If she stays with you, she will never have a family. I can give her that – a family of her own.'

Liza felt hatred for this creature.

'You've been in her thoughts. You know what she wants and so you offer it.'

'I know her better than you do.'

'That is not true.'

'Then let us hear what your daughter has to say.'

Released from the grip of Eitan's vision, Echo reorientated to the reality around her. After the flawless order of the ice city, it was a shock to return to the smoking ruins of McMurdo, from magnificent domes and spirals to shanty town squalor, from a society flourishing on this continent to one barely clinging on. She turned to her family, aware that they'd been watching her. Eitan was waiting for her reply – would she build this new world with him or die defending the old? Her family didn't need to hear her describe the appeal of this sleek new civilization – only one fact mattered: it was a future without them. She cared deeply for them, and her reflex was to protect their fragile emotions in the same way she'd protect their fragile bodies, to declare that Eitan's vision for the future was one she wanted nothing to do with. But it wasn't true, and she'd never been able to lie. No matter how delicately she expressed her desire to be part of something greater, she would hurt them. She wanted to slip inside their thoughts to help them better appreciate the nature of her dilemma, that it wasn't a rejection of them; this was the opportunity to be part of a world where she truly belonged rather than one where she was trying to fit in. As she studied their reactions, she realized the three of them would be broken-hearted no matter how she phrased it. She understood their emotions as clearly as if they shared a telepathic bond. Curious, she wondered if telepathy was an evolutionary branch of love.

With that question unanswered, Echo took her place by Eitan's side.

MCMURDO CITY
OBSERVATION HILL
SAME DAY

Echo and Eitan climbed the slopes of Observation Hill as though they were the newly crowned king and queen of this land, an inter-marriage of the two most powerful ice-adapted dynasties, united to rule over this continent. Their coronation would mark the dawn of a new civilization. Reaching the summit, Eitan directed Echo's gaze across the ice shelf towards the mountains, at the same time filling her mind with visions of how they'd colonize this continent together, an empire of cold creatures with ambitions of proving themselves worthy of alien attention, earning the respect of their mysterious and omnipotent occupiers and hoping one day to sit alongside them, perhaps even travel the universe with them, to establish that they were more than the chaotic and primitive species who'd preceded them – more than mere people.

Breaking loose from the grip of his visions, Echo turned away from the empty landscape towards the naval district, surveying the ice-locked armada, crowded with survivors, beaten back to the boats on which they'd arrived, no longer with a foothold on the continent or with any other land to sail to should they lose it.

Dispossessed of their planet, they'd been dispossessed of their reservation too. Eitan said:

'You're fond of them?'

'They've loved me my whole life. They love you, too.'

'They love an idea of us. You are a replacement for the family Liza and Atto lost. To Yotam, I was a proxy for the man he lost, an answer to his loneliness. We are puppets in their stories, surrogates for the loves they wish they had in their life. They project their dreams and desires onto us, like those movies they can project onto walls of ice. But they have no genuine sense of our identities. And if they did, they wouldn't love us for it.'

'But you do the same. You admire an alien species you've never seen and never met. You admire them because they're powerful. You overlook their crimes. They killed my mother's family. They killed my father's family. They committed genocide as if it were a trivial matter. Yet you dream of impressing them with your achievements. You dream of being their equal. You've made impressing the alien occupiers your ambition. I see no reason why they would ever be interested in you.'

'Not yet. One day.'

Troubled by her persistent interest in the plight of people, Eitan began projecting scenarios of how humanity's end was inevitable even without his intervention, depictions of shrinking settlements, technological decline, regression, starvation, cultural and scientific collapse. Imminent extinction was a certainty, not an estimation or interpretation. He was merely abbreviating the process, a humane thing to do some might argue, putting a mortally wounded animal out of its misery. Echo interrupted the flow of these images, once again replying in ordinary human speech:

'But if we worked with them, they could survive.'

'You've been living with them for too long. You mistake their limitations for virtues.'

'There's Liza, my mother. You think of her as weak, but she travelled thousands of miles to reach this continent, saying goodbye to her parents and watching her sister die. Yet despite that grief she survived. Not only did she survive, she became a doctor, saving many thousands of lives. She lost three children to the cold and somehow found the strength to endure my birth, the birth of an ice-adapted child. I look alien to her and yet she loved me from the first moment I was born.'

'What is important about her is you.'

'And there's my father Atto, a man who risked his life by sailing into the most dangerous oceans on this planet to feed his town, a town they built from wreckage and scraps, a community that looks after each other. He is a man who saved my mother's life after only knowing her for a few hours. He came back for her, offered her passage on his boat, when there was no logical reason to risk his life. He is a man who has loved me as his own. And you think nothing of him.'

'A mere fisherman.'

'There is Tetu, who taught himself how to be brilliant when he had none of the genetic adaptations I was given, a man who explores this continent as if it were his own despite his body being fragile. You say we are only puppets for their dreams? But he has loved no one in this world except for me. I am not a proxy for anyone he lost. He never knew his mother or his father. Yet he knows love. And you think nothing of him.'

'He is a boy who can see you are special. Too special for him.'

'What is your experience of love?'

'I love my own kind with an intensity ordinary people couldn't understand. We share every thought. We share every feeling, every fear and every pain. Our minds are interwoven. And we're inviting you to join us. It is unthinkable that anyone could prefer their way of loving, which is vague, unreliable, incomplete, filled with misunderstandings and insecurities.'

'Why must you destroy them?'

'Because that is why they made us. We are the future. They are the past. Their ideas, their bodies, their minds. They are dying, and they know it, but they cannot accept it.'

'And what do you want from me? There are thousands of ice-adapted people.'

'You speak for them.'

'I'm not their representative. I haven't been chosen by them.'

'You are a natural leader. It is a gift. If you join with us, they will follow.'

'If I stand against you, they will, too.'

Eitan stepped back, reassessing Echo and realizing that she hadn't climbed this hill to celebrate their coronation. She was here to question him. As someone who'd never known rejection, he was taken aback. He watched as she picked up the broken fragments of the stone memorial tablets etched with the names of all former nations of this world. With her hands full of memorial stone, Echo said:

'My family would love me if I was weak or if I was strong. They would love me if I was sick or healthy. This makes no sense to you. Your vision is a world without weakness. But you cannot be sure what will become a strength and what will become a weakness. Where did your gift of telepathy come from?'

'A genetic adaptation.'

'What were its roots? If it was an adaptation of people?'

Eitan remained silent, thinking on the question. Echo volunteered her guess:

'Its roots were love. My mother knew when I was lost. My father knew when I was lonely. They could find me in the wilderness. They know my feelings as if they were their own. It is not something they control as you do. But it is real. You showed me a vision of the future. A perfect society. But I see a society that will collapse under its own perfections, intolerant of anything that looks like weakness.'

'If you turn me down you will never have a child.'

'My parents would never say that. They would say we'll find a way. No matter what, they'll find a way.'

'But they cannot find a way.'

'My answer is no. I will not join you. I will not be part of the future you describe. My answer is no.'

OBSERVATION HILL
SAME DAY

Eitan stood on his back legs, his claws bolting into rock as he unfurled the partitions of his segmented thorax, extending his body so that his front legs were raised in the air, the colours of ice rippling across his armoured surface. Echo stood her ground, her own scales replying in an alternating colour sequence of their own, as if their skins were in conversation. A creature bred to be emotionless and calculating had become emotional when his calculations were proved wrong. He'd been rejected and he couldn't understand it. He was a creature who saw his wants not as a preferential outcome but as destiny. He walked the path of his desires and knew nothing else. He directed her gaze towards the armada.

'Look at these people you love.'

From the edge of Memorial Mound, Echo surveyed the flotilla of ships, the last district of their capital city. She expected to see Eitan's formidable colony of creatures advancing to attack, a clash of armies and civilizations. But there was no sign of any attack – the ice and snow were clear. The guards on the aircraft carriers stood ready to defend their fleet, the defences crude but formidable. For a moment, a fragile calm lingered until it was broken by the screech of metal. The *Kennedy* aircraft carrier, the former flagship and the hub of the naval quarter, began to list. The colossal ship was under attack not from an enemy overland but from under the sea ice.

Without seeking her consent, Eitan pushed images of the attack into Echo's mind, an aggressive form of telepathy, forcing her to watch, aligning her eyes with those of his comrades under the ice. She saw them scuttling across the colossal hull like sea spiders, as agile and formidable under the water as they were above it, tearing at the reinforced keel with ice-adapted blades, cutting through the double-bottomed armoured steel plates, ripping cavities so deep and so long that there was no possible way for the people onboard to isolate these breaches. Sliced open in so many places, the carrier began to sink. The loose summer sea ice broke apart as the ship sank, the deck tilting sharply to the side, emptying people into the freezing ocean where they stood no chance against the cold, rows of terrace houses collapsing and sliding off, landing on those who'd fallen in the water.

This loss of life, the kind of which she'd never witnessed before, having been brought up in a city that had never known war, where every life was considered precious, this act of violence was appalling to Echo. She turned to Eitan, this creature who supposed himself to be a superior form of life, and begged him:

'Leave them alone!'

'They're already dead. From the cold, from the famines, from madness. I'm not stealing their future – they have none to steal.'

Struck with fear, Echo hurried to the other side of the hill, looking down at her family. They were encircled by the snow gorillas and asylum creatures. Eitan remarked:

'There's only one way to save them.'

'If the choice is between being like you, and being like them, I choose to be like them.'

'Their flagship is sinking. Their farms and factories are burnt to the ground. But I will let these people live. I will allow them to spend the rest of their natural existence on the Peninsula if you help me. Why would you say no? You never felt at home with these people. You feel at home with me. Don't deny it. You cannot lie to me.'

'You forget that when you're in my mind, I'm also in yours. I've seen how you think about ordinary-born people. You will never let them live. Because you fear that you're like them. You want to wipe them from this continent and start again. Even if I stood by your side, eventually you'd kill them. You're not more advanced than people. You're the worst of them – their strengths, but none of their weaknesses. I will not help you.'

'Then watch your family die.'

IN HER HASTE TO REACH her family, Echo slipped and stumbled like an ordinary person, clumsy on the loose rocks as she ran down from the summit. She should never have left them, but she'd wanted to hear Eitan's plans, to better understand their predicament, to negotiate a truce or perhaps, in truth, she'd been tempted to join him. She felt something, in his presence, something she'd never felt before, an intimacy and connection. It had blinded her to his intentions, which had been to separate her from her family. Now there was no way she could make up the distance; the colony of cold creatures were only a few metres away and moving in for the kill.

President Mues stepped forward, raising her hand to stop them, imploring:

'Let us work together.'

Before she could finish, the ice-adapted Troodon sprang forward, decapitating her with his tail. His thin arms caught her head, holding it aloft – the head of their leader, the president of people.

Echo was staggered by the savage spectacle and the delight they took in an execution. Arriving at her family's side, she stood with them, ready to die if need be.

Cho, the eldest female, attacked from the side. She picked Echo up, lifting her above her head. Despite her weight, she threw her with ease. It was Echo's first fight and her first experience of pain. She'd never been trained in the art of combat, she'd never studied martial arts, she'd never even thrown a punch. Though she looked formidable, she was no warrior and had no knowledge of how to defend herself, let alone from a creature which seemed bred for conflict.

Before she could get to her feet, Cho charged at her, as fast as a horse, her thin arms slashing downwards, razor-sharp digits cutting across Echo's chest. With barely enough time to parry the blow, Echo covered her face, unsure whether her scales would be strong enough to resist the attack. The digits glanced over her arm without making a cut. Recalculating the strength of her opponent, Cho abandoned the attempt at slicing her open, picking her up once more and throwing her into the smouldering ruins of McMurdo City.

Echo crashed through the charred timbers of the chapel, coming to a rest in hot ash. The heat from the remains of fire was awful, her scales turning black as they began to radiate the excess warmth. Standing up, she saw that Cho couldn't come close, remaining on the outskirts of the fire, even more sensitive to the heat than she was. Echo realized that rather than radiating this surplus heat, she could use it as a weapon, exploiting these creatures' only weakness – their inability to deal with warmth.

As soon as she stepped off the ash and embers, Cho charged, but Echo was ready, sliding across the ice, under Cho's torso and climbing onto her back. As Cho tried to shake her free, Echo held tight, clambering up to Cho's head. Gripping on either side, channelling as much heat as possible, she released all the warmth her body had stored. For Cho, it was excruciating. Unable to cool down, unable to radiate this heat, she cried out, an anguished sound, charging madly across the ice, trying to dislodge Echo from her back. But Echo wouldn't let go, aware she wouldn't get a second chance. She could feel her own body cooling down as the heat raced into Cho's head. She could hear the panicked telepathic cries for help. Eitan and the others hurried down the slope to assist. Echo pushed a final wave of intense warmth through her skull. Cho's eyes turned white, like the eyes of a cooked fish, her legs buckled, and she collapsed onto the ice.

THE RUINS OF MCMURDO CITY
SAME DAY

THE COLONY OF COLD CREATURES gathered around the body of Cho, unable to comprehend that one of their family was gone, grappling with their mortality for the first time. Engineered as an answer to the physical and emotional frailties of people, they could sink a ship with the loss of thousands of lives and not feel a flicker of remorse, but to lose one of their own was an unbearable pain. Cho had been the oldest female, the matriarch of their community, integral to their ambitions for this ice-locked continent and now her thoughts were no longer mingling with theirs, her perceptions and sensibilities torn from the fabric of their interwoven minds. They were incomplete without her, not as a sentimental notion – there was a gap in their thoughts and feelings. A part of them had died. Despite their immense physical strengths, they struggled to stand, as though they'd lost a limb, some dropping to their knees, others resting their heads against hers, willing her back to life, mourning so profound that Echo couldn't help but feel grief, too. Despite the fact she was the culprit, she was invisible to them – the only thing that mattered, in this moment, was their grief and trying to figure out how life continued without the ones you loved, a challenge they now shared with ordinary people.

Rising to her feet, Echo staggered back to her family, who were safe. Despite her display of prowess and strength, she felt desolate. She'd taken a life, a brilliant and complex life. Her thoughts felt slow and heavy. She was not innocent anymore. Atto and Liza ran forward, hugging her, holding her tight. Liza whispered into Echo's ear:

'She would've killed you. She would've killed us.'

'I feel something I've never felt before . . .'

Her sentence drifted into silence, searching for the word.

'I feel shame.'

With the body of Cho across his back, Eitan approached, his colony behind him. It was not an attack but a funeral march. Echo stepped forward, in front of her family, ready to defend them yet at the same time sharing in the grief of those opposing her, realizing that she remained connected to their thoughts, catching fragments of their pain. Eitan's voice was different, no longer brassy and unbreakable.

'Your people have until the first day of winter to leave this place. After the sun sets, we will kill anyone who remains.'

Echo said:

'I didn't intend to kill her.'

'You could've been one of us. Now you belong with them.'

With that said, the colony of cold creatures turned in unison, heading in procession out of the ruins of the city, towards the mountains and glaciers they called home.

EPILOGUE

TWO MONTHS LATER

TRANS-ANTARCTICA FREEWAY
15 MARCH 2044

A HEAD OF THE APPROACHING WINTER a second Exodus was underway – a 1,800-mile trek across the continent, a perilous journey made famous by daring explorers seeking a place in the record books. What was once adventure was now necessity. The people of McMurdo were abandoning their capital city; for the children born there it was the only home they'd ever known. Across the ice shelf a caravan of a million McMurdo City refugees snaked across the snow, like a hairline crack in a white porcelain plate. Having made an extraordinary journey to this continent, another journey was being demanded of them, this time to the Peninsula, trying to complete the journey before winter arrived.

Many of McMurdo's leaders drowned during the sinking of the flagship and a new leadership had taken charge, made up of former generals and admirals from armies around the world. Under their stewardship, the evacuation of McMurdo City had been well-organized and calm, unloading all the supplies from the ships, barely enough to see them through the journey let alone the long dark winter ahead. Many of the snow vehicles had been destroyed in the fire. As for the packs of once devoted huskies, all of them had joined the colony of cold creatures, including Yotam's dog Copper. Not a single dog remained, as if they understood that this continent had new masters now. As the last refugees set off from the scorched remains of McMurdo City, they fired a hundred flares into a clear blue sky, representing the end of this base where people had lived for one hundred years.

The three Survivor Towns responded to the news of the uprising with resilience and generosity, promising to welcome the new arrivals with the same love and compassion as if they were family. But there was no hiding from the fact that humanity had lost their capital city and their most advanced resources. On a practical level, it would be no easy task for the three Survivor Towns to absorb the people of McMurdo. Every family would accept another, dividing the refugees between the three towns until every person had a new home. For those who completed the journey, a different life awaited them, a simpler life.

After the truce, there'd been no further sign of the colony of cold creatures. They'd made their home in the most remote depths of the continent where ordinary people couldn't survive, building the foundations of their new civilization. There'd been no skirmish attacks on the refugees, despite them being so vulnerable in this instant. True to their word, they'd given ordinary people until the winter, when the sun would disappear for months, and the truce would end. For the ice-adapted children the world had changed, a notion spread that ordinary-born people had always intended to create an Antarctic working class, genetically engineered ice-adapted servants to do the jobs they couldn't. After the uprising, many of the ordinary-born people were more mistrustful of their ice-adapted companions, questioning how long they'd remain loyal while an ascendant community built a radically new and prosperous society, one which they were welcome to join at any time. As they counted the numbers, they noticed several ice-adapted people had defected, disappearing into the wilderness in search of the other colony where they believed they belonged.

Towards the front of the snaking line of refugees making their way to the Peninsula, Yotam accompanied his friend Chang-Rae, the renowned chef whose canteen had been destroyed in the fire. Together the two of them were pulling a sleigh loaded with as much cooking equipment as they'd been able to scavenge from the ashes of his kitchen. Chang-Rae's wife and his two teenage children were walking beside them. Only the smallest children were allowed to sit on the sleighs. Most of the space was taken up with food and equipment, forcing many children to undergo one of the toughest treks in the history of humankind. Though these children weren't adapted to the cold on a genetic level, they'd been born on the ice, and they were experts in the snow. At school they'd been taught survival skills by the Inuit tribes, developing an intuition for the cold and hardiness far beyond their years. Despite having lost his beloved kitchen, Chang-Rae remained upbeat. An indefatigable spirit, he'd lost everything before, he could build his kitchen again, and he was excited to see what new foods and flavours he could find on the Peninsula. Addressing Yotam, he said:

'You know what this means, right?'

'What does this mean?'

'You can date.'

'I thought you were going to say something profound.'

'That is important! You don't have any work. You've got more time on your hands.'

'We're trekking across the continent—'

'There's always an excuse. But this time there's no excuse. You can't hide from this part of your life anymore. Those creatures you made, and fell in love with, that relationship wasn't real.'

'It was real to me.'

'Okay, I can see that, but when one relationship doesn't work you have to move on. I've told you a thousand times: the only way to survive on this continent is to find someone to love.'

He turned to his wife.

'Isn't that right, the love of my life?'

'My feet are cold.'

'Your feet are always cold. They're cold when we're inside. They're cold when we're outside. You have cold feet. Let's never mention it again.'

Chang-Rae turned back to Yotam, wrapping an arm around him.

'I have someone in mind.'

'For me?'

'For you.'

'You're doing this now?'

'Right now. You've waited long enough.'

Chang-Rae handed the sleigh reins to his wife and hurried off down the caravan. Sheepish, Yotam looked at his wife. She asked him:

'Will they come for us?'

'Not while we walk.'

'When we arrive?'

'I don't know. I thought I knew them. But I don't.'

Chang-Rae returned with a handsome man in his forties.

'This is my friend. Hyan-Woo. He was a big-shot music executive back in the day. He saved my life. It was his father's ship I hitched a ride on. Before the occupation he used to eat in my restaurant. Excellent taste. He was never out as gay in Korea—'

Hyan-Woo interrupted:

'Can I introduce myself?'

'Introductions are always much better done by someone else. Like I was saying, I always knew he was gay.'

'How could you have known? I didn't know.'

The two of them slipped back into Korean, speaking animatedly for a time, debating this subject before Chang-Rae turned to Yotam, using English again.

'I knew. I mean, it's so easy to know in a restaurant. All you do is see which waiters people talk to the most. It was the cute guys, always the cute guys.'

'You're embarrassing me.'

'Why is that embarrassing? He didn't come out until his third year in Antarctica. He realized if you can't come out in Antarctica, after an alien occupation, when can you come out? It's now or never. This is Yotam, another very good friend. You've heard about him; he created the species that burnt down our city and tried to kill us all.'

'I didn't create them.'

'Hello, Yotam.'

'Hello, Hyan-Woo.'

Chang-Rae handed the reins to Hyan-Woo.

'My work as a matchmaker is done. I'll let you two pull this sleigh for a while. Not because I'm lazy. It feels romantic. We'll be close by. You're both great guys. You're both single. And you both need someone. Don't mess this up. You have about four hundred miles to make this work. You need someone for the winter. Love is the same as food and warmth.'

Hyan-Woo took the reins and together he and Yotam pulled the sleigh in awkward silence, unsure what to say, stealing glances at each other like teenagers in a classroom. Instead of breaking into a bout of polite conversation Hyan-Woo stopped walking, his attention caught by the unusual sky, a blue sky full of twinkling dust. The faintest ice crystals began to fall, snowflakes perfect in formation but tiny, like powdered diamonds, settling over the migrants, a magic frosting across their jackets and hats as though a winter fairy-tale creature of some benevolent sort had flown overhead, leaving behind a sparkling trail to bless this journey. Yotam took off his glove, raising his palm flat to the sky, allowing a snowflake to settle on his skin. As though it were a gift, he presented the tip of his finger to Hyan-Woo, a single immaculate crystal on the end.

Reaching the Peninsula, the McMurdo refugees were divided into three groups, each group assigned a different Survivor Town where they'd make their home. Liza and Atto had insisted on Yotam living with them in the historic Wordie House, which was easily big enough to accommodate him and his friends, Chang-Rae and his family. They loved the idea of sharing their home with a brilliant chef. The offer of a home, and a family, caught him by surprise; he'd been so overwhelmed by the kindness that he'd cried.

'I'd like that very much.'

Echo, observing this moment, felt that she'd made the right decision. This was her home. This was her town. This was her family. There were times when she could feel the thoughts of the cold colony in her mind. When she closed her eyes, she caught glimpses of the city they were building, carving and reshaping the ice shelf. A connection had been established and could never be broken. Part of her belonged to them and it would be a lie to pretend that she didn't want to see Eitan again.

Liza and Atto had remained calm in the face of this new refugee crisis. There would be enormous challenges with housing and a scarcity of resources, but perhaps it would be better for people to accept a simpler form of existence, with no laboratories or supercomputers, no audacious plans to repopulate the continent. Better to embrace a sense of humility, a life on the Peninsula defined by community and a heightened sense of comradeship that had developed over twenty years. Weren't they better people now, better at caring for each other, better at sharing – more affectionate, more compassionate, fairer even under the most testing of circumstances? Maybe these virtues couldn't ultimately save them from extinction, but they would make the last decades of people some of the best. The end might be their finest hour, a time of decency, a species ending not with intertribal warfare and savagery but at its most humane.

These abstract notions were of no consolation to Tetu. He was heartbroken, a pain that felt physical as much as it did emotional – a searing wound inside his chest. He'd lost Echo, or perhaps he'd lost the dream of her since it now seemed absurd to imagine they'd ever stood a chance. The future he'd imagined in McMurdo City was gone. Romanticism and ambition had sustained him. He didn't know how to live without them. The point of his life had been to create a home with Echo. Without this vision of a home, the kind of home he'd never experienced growing up, there was nothing, nothing to work for, nothing to strive for. Having barely spoken since the attack at the base, he felt Liza place a hand on his back.

'Talk to her.'

'What do I say?'

'She loves you. I don't know what form that love will take. But it's still love.'

Tetu found Echo helping the arriving refugees into the Parliament building, where they were being greeted with cups of hot fish stew. She stepped aside from her work to talk to him. He asked:

'You love him?'

Rarely taken by surprise, Echo was amazed by this question.

'Love who?'

'That creature. I know what being in love looks like. And you're in love with him, whatever he is. He asked you to walk up that hill with him and up you went. Just like that. You didn't hesitate. He could've asked you to do anything, you would've gone with him.'

'I said no to him.'

'You said no to his plans. You didn't say no to him.'

'Tetu, I don't know him. I met him only once.'

'But like your parents, in Lisbon, you know.'

On this point she remained silent. He was right. That feeling, irrational and uncontrolled, that was love. Tetu declared, without a trace of hostility, coming to terms with the truth:

'You admire me. You're fond of me. But you don't love me, not in that way. Your heart doesn't skip a beat when you see me. And the heart can't learn to skip a beat; it either does or it doesn't. But your heart did feel something when you saw him. I saw it happen. I saw you react as I'd always wanted you to react to me.'

'I feel confused.'

'That is love.'

Tetu put a hand on her arm.

'He's going to come for you.'

'How do you know?'

'Because I would.'

UNDER THE ANTARCTIC OCEAN, EITAN perched atop the shipwreck of the aircraft carrier, an ice-adapted spear in his hand, watching as the last ships of the armada were scuttled, their crude and cumbersome steel hulls slashed open, oil tankers and cargo ships sinking to the seabed, some breaking apart on impact – a graveyard of ten thousand ships or more. Soon these shipwrecks would be filled with life of another kind, reefs for feather-stars and jellyfish, home to icefish and blue-blooded octopuses. Already the remains of this carrier, sunk two months ago, was spotted with sea anemone, while the corpses had been picked clean by nemertean worms. He entered the wreckage, through the gash in the side, his eyes adjusting to the darkness, moving through the maze of passage-ways, slicing through any doors that stood in his way, until he found the birthing lab where he'd been created. Unlike ordinary people, he remembered his own birth, aware of his surroundings from those first seconds, born ready for combat from the moment he'd broken free from his mother. It was only afterwards, as he'd rested on the ceiling nestled against the cold vent, that he realized that his mother was dead and that he'd killed her by the involuntary act of being born. Perhaps it had been this moment that he'd decided he despised his creators or perhaps his hatred for them was innate, part of his genetic programming, a desire for the new to obliterate the old. He felt tenderness for the mother he'd never known.

Emerging from the wreckage of the ship, he looked up at the sea ice which was beginning to close as winter approached and the temperature dropped. Soon all the gaps would freeze over and the last trace of people would be gone. Eitan pushed off from the shipwreck, rising through the ocean at speed towards one of the holes, breaking the surface and climbing up the ice. He surveyed what was once the capital city of ordinary-born people. The ashes from the great fire had been blown away by the winds. His colony of cold creatures had picked over the ice, removing all trace of their buildings and dreams.

Reaching the mainland, Eitan climbed Observation Hill, where his family had gathered, along with all the other members of the colony. Today was a special day. After the last of the ships were sunk the first natural birth of a cold person would take place. The eldest female in his colony was due, her thorax swollen with six eggs, three on either side. The armoured exterior retracted, and six children dropped to the ground, born into a loving family, able to climb up onto their mother's back, the six of them delighting in their first glimpse of this new world.

THE SOUTHERN POLE OF
INACCESSIBILITY
11 APRIL 2044

T HE MOST REMOTE LOCATION IN Antarctica was known by ordinary people as the southern pole of inaccessibility, the point on the continent most distant from the Southern Ocean. Many years ago, there had been a Soviet Union research station here, three thousand seven hundred metres above sea level and one thousand five hundred kilometres from the ocean. It was here that Eitan began to build his new civilization, first clearing away the Soviet structures, returning the ice to its previous pristine state. Using their mastery over ice, the colony created a palace built out of hollow pearl structures, a design like nothing that had ever been seen before, a structure that looked like heaps of crystal caviar with not a straight line to be seen, a palace of curves. Inside the halls, the children worked, already able to study and contribute. Today the colony of cold creatures would watch the sun set for the first time in their lives, the last sunset of the summer. They emerged from their palace to watch as it dipped below the horizon, the sunlight mingling with a freezing mist, until the sky turned black. The truce was over. Winter had arrived. Eitan looked up at the stars, dreaming of the coldness of space. Despite feeling satisfaction at his accomplishments, Eitan could not stop thinking of her – the woman they called Echo, wondering what she was doing and wishing she was by his side.

ACKNOWLEDGEMENTS

It was with great sadness that I learnt the news of Carolyn Reidy, Chief Executive of Simon & Schuster, passing during the writing of this novel. Carolyn was remarkably kind, insightful and supportive during my career, always encouraging and a true champion of authors. It is an enormous loss.

The process of writing this novel was interrupted by many disruptions, some personal and some global, and in truth it wouldn't have been finished at all without the support and wisdom of my agent, and former editor, Mitch Hoffman at the Aaron Priest Agency, a true friend and a great mind. Working together with Suzanne Baboneau at Simon & Schuster UK, they remain a wonderful creative team, inspiring and insightful, and I will be forever grateful to them.

Special mention must also go to Ian Chapman, Chief Executive of Simon & Schuster UK, for being patient with my delays and an enormous source of motivation. Simon & Schuster is a very special publishing house and I'm lucky to be part of their family.

I'm also appreciative of my editor at Simon & Schuster US, Colin Harrison, whose notes and thoughts on the various drafts of the text improved the manuscript and were a pleasure to ponder. In addition, thanks to Emily Polson for her observations, all of which contributed to the final book.

Finally, on a personal level, my father recently survived a stroke, my mother recently survived surgery and, despite their own struggles, they've both been constantly excited to read another novel. Maybe, deep down, I write all my books in an attempt to delight my parents.